A Royal FATHER

A Royal
Father

The Lion and the Butterfly

BOOK THREE

LINDA FERGERSON

Carpenter's Son Publishing

A Royal Family

©2019 by Linda Fergerson

Scripture quotations are from The Passion Translation®. Copyright © 2017, 2018 by Passion & Fire Ministries, Inc. Used by permission. All rights reserved. ThePassionTranslation.com.

Published by Carpenter's Son Publishing, Franklin, Tennessee.

Published in association with Larry Carpenter of Christian Book Services, LLC. www.christianbookservices.com

Cover illustrated by Rachelle Williams

Edited by Tammy Kling

Book production by Adept Content Solutions

Printed in the United States of America

978-1-946889-86-7

Dedication

I dedicate this book to all the fathers in my life.

Father YHWH:
Father of the fatherless
The one and only true God
I remember walking with you in darkness
I will never fear the dark again.
I love you!

Wallace B. Pedigo, my father:
I remember the many times you took me to "cowboy" country
Climbed the railroad bridge
Ate cinnamon rolls at the diner on Sunday morning
Drank root beer in frosty mugs
Licked ice cream cones from Fairmont
And cuddled on your lap
I love you, Daddy!

Steve C. Fergerson, father to my three sons:
I remember the times you rode go carts with our sons
Fished in Coldwater Lake
Hunted and cleaned pheasants
Put Legos together
Made a dinosaur out of turkey bones
Danced the happy dance
Golfed in tournaments
Sang to the horses
Prayed and read the Bible
And mostly just being Dad
For all those times and many more, I love you!

Dedication (cont.)

Patrick Holloran, my spiritual Father:
I remember when I first cried out teary-eyed, "Father, help me," in my hotel room
Then felt compelled to attend your I Will Never Leave You as Orphans class
You touched my heart with a father's love unlike any I had ever known.
You saw gifts and callings and talents I did not see in myself
You loved me where I was and never made me feel less
You inspired me to write and never give up
You said I'd do greater works than you
You left and entered His kingdom
I will remember forever
Your expression of the
Father's heart!

Contents

Acknowledgments *xi*

Prologue *xv*

Chapter 1   1

Chapter 2   7

Chapter 3   17

Chapter 4   27

Chapter 5   35

Chapter 6   41

Chapter 7   47

Chapter 8   53

Chapter 9   59

Chapter 10   65

Chapter 11   71

Chapter 12   79

Chapter 13   87

Chapter 14   95

Chapter 15   101

Chapter 16   109

Chapter 17   117

Chapter 18   125

Chapter 19   135

Chapter 20   143

Chapter 21   151

Chapter 22   159

Chapter 23   167

Chapter 24   173

Chapter 25   179

Chapter 26   185

Chapter 27   193

Chapter 28   201

Chapter 29   209

Chapter 30   215

Chapter 31   221

Chapter 32   229

Chapter 33   237

Chapter 34   245

Chapter 35   253

Chapter 36   261

Chapter 37   267

Chapter 38   277

Chapter 39   281

Epilogue   289

To My Royal Father   295

Letter to Reader   297

A Taste of Israel   299

About the Author   301

Acknowledgments

I want to acknowledge Pat Holloran and his book. Without his expression of the Father's heart in my life, I would still think and act like an orphan!

I Will Not Leave You as Orphans: Overcoming the Orphan Spirit
by
Pat Holloran

I want to acknowledge the intercessors who prayed this book into existence. Each one came through at different times as Holy Ghost led. It took each and every one for Father YHWH to accomplish His will in this book.

Thank You!

Sharyl Kells
Judy Ackerman
Janet Schuler
JoAnn Ripley
Janet Williams
Linda Bewley
Robin Pelton
Marlene Underwood

Thursday morning prayer group:

Peggy Burdick
Geni Stanley
Annette Aldape
Sherrie Fischer
Cheryll Mann
Tammy West
Barb Housman,
Jamie Stucky
Athena Gerber
Ann Warner

Now listen, daughter, pay attention and forget about your past.
Put behind you every attachment to the familiar,
even those who once were close to you!
. . . Your many sons will one day be Kings, just like their Father.
They will sit on royal thrones all around the world.

—Psalms 45:10,16 TPT

Prologue

"Faa theer Yahh wehh? Her cry echoed in the garden. The vibrations rippled into the heavens like pulsating light bursts. Thousands of dark creatures who watched and listened crept back in the shadows and snarled.

"His butterfly's at it again." Their guttural rumblings grew louder as her sobs exploded into the air. "The Lion of Judah will come," they grumbled. "His Father will send him. We must stop her. Immerse her thoughts in darkness."

She stood and reached up to the heavens. "Come—deliver my sons—they need to know you as Father."

A shofar sounded in the distance. They covered their ears.

"Do you believe my word?" the Lion of Judah roared at the woman.

Even though his words shimmered in the darkness over her head, evil creatures laughed and started to creep forward again. "She can't hear him." They mocked and descended upon the garden.

She wiped her tears away, rose and twirled around with arms lifted high.

"I love you, my Father."

"What a fool." A dark hooded demon crept closer.

She smiled and twirled again.

"I love you, Yeshua, my King, the mighty Lion of Judah."

"Ha! She worships in vain. She still can't hear him!" The other dark hooded minions cackled and pointed.

She twirled around one more time. "I love you, Holy Spirit, my helper who leads me into all truth."

At that moment another shofar blasted, and they watched His words that hung over her head consume the darkness that clouded her mind and slip into her thoughts. Within seconds a mighty force shook their dark kingdom.

"Do you believe my word?" The King's word shimmered.

"Yes. Yes. I believe your word." She laughed and twirled.

"Do you believe my word?" He asked again with even greater power. The dark creatures cringed.

Yes, yes, I believe your word." Another twirl and she bowed her head in humble submission and waited.

"All your children will be taught by me and great will be their peace."

"Thank you, Father. I believe." She wiped her tears away.

Now arise, take the authority I've given you. Decree what I have spoken over your sons and I will do it."

She rose, lifted her face to heaven, and declared, "It is written that all my children will be taught by the Lord and great will be their peace." Her words glimmered and sparkled and lit up the atmosphere around her in the garden. She twirled and shouted, "It is written, all my children shall be taught by the Lord and great will be their peace."

Darkness watched as she strolled through the garden and smiled. Suddenly, she stopped and bowed her head. "Father, I ask for a canopy of protection over my property from the north, the south, the east, and the west boundaries all the way to your throne, face down in the earth out to the boundaries, down to the core of the earth. For it is written, you give your people a peaceful habitation, a quiet resting place and secure dwellings. I ask that you set sight and sound barriers around my property that the enemy cannot see or hear what goes on here."

The darkness screamed in terror. "The warriors are here!"

Flashes of light struck and pressed them back as huge angels with swords hooked shields together around her property. As the evil hoards fled, a greater darkness engulfed them. They looked over their shoulders at her dwelling. The dark scribe peeked through the gaps to record her conversation with the King as shields locked into place.

"I can't see her," he yelled. "I can't hear her, either." They trembled.

Two red globes blinked in the blackness.

"Idiots! Stop her! Send the orphan spirit!"

Chapter 1
Spring, Sivan, AD 57

Jerusha shivered in the dark stairway and touched the damp, slimy walls. As she felt her way in the blackness her stomach churned into knots again. She thought she could not feel any more alone than when she served as a slave in this palace years ago. She stopped.

Closing her eyes, she sighed and tried to ignore the numb ache that visited more often of late. How she missed her husband. After ten years his image burned bright as ever in her memory—his crooked smile and that mischievous twinkle in his eyes.

Don't go there, Jerusha, she thought,; *it won't bring Timon back.*

She stubbed her toe on the next step and gasped as a critter ran across her foot. Ugh! A palace rat, no doubt. Why did Antonius insist she come this way? Why couldn't he have met her outside in the bushes at the bottom? Why make her climb this horrible stairway?

She took a deep breath and told herself to calm down. The air eased out of her chest as she remembered Antonius did not know about her time at Herod's palace—the abuse—the narrow escapes through this passageway to meet with Yeshua followers.

Anger burned in her bones as she remembered it. She clenched her fists at her sides and pursed her lips together. The corrupt priests still pretended righteousness in public and it made her stomach turn at what they did in private with helpless slave girls.

A sliver of light pierced the darkness as the heavy stone door scraped against the tiled floor above. She looked up. There at the top of the stairs she saw her. The one she came to rescue. The poor thing. Her face was swollen and bruised, her eyes, empty and and void of emotion.

Pools of tears threatened to overflow in Jerusha's eyes. Her own shame no longer held her captive. Just righteous anger at what these girls had to endure.

Antonius said the girl was ten. Her tiny bone structure gave the appearance of one much younger. The darkness under her eyes surrounded by long thick lashes spoke of nightmare happenings most grown women could not endure or even imagine.

As much as Jerusha wanted to run to the girl, she refrained. From past experience she knew better. It might not be Antonius who opened the door. She slipped back in the darkness and listened to the clank of a sword against armor. The light reflecting off something metal hit her eyes and blinded her momentarily.

She raised her hand above her eyes. "Antonius?" Her whisper was smothered by the door grinding open a little further. The lamplight in the room shone through the opening into the stairway. She blinked and let her eyes adjust to the brightness.

Antonius squatted beside the girl, his helmet beneath his arm. His golden hair, sweaty and unkempt, hung down around his face as he addressed the abused child.

"Do not be afraid." His voice was soft and comforting for a battle hardened Roman soldier who fought in the games to earn his citizenship. She released her breath in a slow sigh and watched him lift his eyes from the child and peer into the darkness.

"Jerusha? Are you there?" Her heart fluttered at the sound of his deep voice. She started to move out of the darkness. She trusted him. Felt safe with him. Most importantly, this little one felt safe with him.

Strange that someone who killed many for Rome would be trusted by a child. That mystery unnerved Jerusha.

A shadow passed over the opening, and she shrunk back again, aware that Antonius was not alone with the abused girl. When Jerusha glanced up, she saw the back of a smaller man, probably a head shorter than Antonius. Tzitizits dangled at the corners of his cloak. A Jew. Broad shoulders, too. Not as broad as Antonius but broad nonetheless.

"Shalom, my friend." He greeted Antonius with a kiss and stepped around the girl into the lighted room.

"Effah!" Jerusha clasped her hand over her mouth to quiet her gagging. She hadn't heard that voice since childhood. *What's—he— doing here?* The words formed silently through clenched teeth. And why call Antonius his friend? Her worst nightmare! She rolled her eyes and wiped her hands on her cloak. That pig will not stop me.

She raised up tall with shoulders back and chin lifted high, then grabbed her cloak above her sandaled feet and placed her foot on the step. As she rose to the next landing, her face was engulfed in a huge spider web. Several spiders ran down her neck, and she franticly swiped her shoulder with both arms and lost her balance.

Stumbling in the darkness, she fell forward into the opening and slapped her hands on the stone floor to catch her balance right at the men's feet. Her hair fell out of her radiyd. She stared at her long black curls that dangled over her eyes and quickly tucked them back inside her head covering.

"Shalom, Jerusha, I figured you'd be here." Effah's degrading chuckle tore open an old wound. "So like you to stumble in like this." He reached for her elbow.

"Don't touch me!" She jerked her arm away, managed to push herself up and sit on the top stair, then struggled to get her feet untangled from her cloak and tunic. Covering the black mole on her face, she glanced up at Antonius.

He scrunched his brow together. "Are you hurt?" With one quick swoop he wrapped his arm around her waist and lifted her from the cold stone floor. For one fleeting second their eyes met before he placed her sandaled feet down. She felt the blush rise up her neck and clutched her face between her hands. A slight tug on her cloak drew her attention away to brown eyes that looked up and blinked back tears.

"Are you taking me away from this place?" The girl wiped a lone tear off her cheek. The filth on her fingers almost made Jerusha gag. Clogged with dried mucus, the youngster's nostrils flared open, and she sneezed. A thick slime oozed into her hand as she cupped it over her nose. Jerusha felt the girl's embarrassment and clutched the child to her side and glanced around for a clean cloth.

Effah grabbed a piece of wool nearby and offered it to Jerusha. She hesitated. Such kindness in the past meant favors expected later. She shook her head and searched the room for another answer. Antonius stepped between her and Effah and pulled a red cloth from behind his breastplate and dangled it before her eyes.

"Take the cloth!" Jerusha's heart jumped at the old woman's words. From the other side of the room she glared through narrowed eyes and stirred something in a pot that hung over hot coals. Spear-shaped flames danced beneath it. It smelled like lentil stew. "The child's nose is disgusting. She's cursed." The humpbacked woman's guttural tone sent shivers up Jerusha's neck and made the hair on her arms stand up.

The girl snuggled closer. Jerusha bent down and stared eyeball to eyeball with her. "Yes, we are taking you from this place." She reached up, took the cloth from Antonius, and handed it to her. "What is your name?"

After a muffled snort, the youngster said, "Sarah."

Jerusha sucked in her breath. Another Sarah. She stood and leaned into Antonius. "I will not make the same mistake. This Sarah will live." She watched his head cock sideways and brows lift. His quizzical expression reminded Jerusha that he had no knowledge of her beloved Sarah who was ripped from her arms only to die in the streets of Jerusalem. Antonius dipped his chin, a blank look in his eyes. A shadow moved across her face, and she looked away from Antonius. Effah stood next to the girl and eyed Jerusha. She whipped around and faced Antonius, then pointed to Effah. "Why is he here?"

"He is the one who told me about this secret passageway."

She glared at Effah. He had not helped her escape when she stayed here. Why this girl? Why now? He seemed undisturbed by her perusal.

"Jerusha, you must hurry. The guards will be back soon for their evening meal." Effah's words sounded sincere. She scrunched her eyebrows and glared a few more seconds. Whatever his motive, she sensed an urgency to move. After wiping the girl's hand with the cloth, she handed it back to Antonius, took Sarah's other hand, and stepped down the first stair.

Sarah stiffened her legs and pulled back. "It's too dark."

Jerusha squatted before the trembling child and pulled out her treasured pendant from beneath her tunic. She had clung to this gift from Father while in captivity and hoped to give the same comfort to the girl. The firelight flickered off the purple butterfly jewel that rested on the wooden lion's nose and bounced sparkles across the youngster's face. "See this butterfly?" Jerusha pointed to the pendant. "It reminds me everyday that even in the darkness our King Yeshua is with us. He makes everything beautiful in its time. Trust me, I've been down these dark stairs many times. I know the way. At the end you will be free. A beautiful waterfall is at the bottom. Yeshua is with us." She glanced up at Effah, who shuffled from one foot to the other, then back at the girl. "Even when someone hurts you, Yeshua is with you." She took the pendant off and placed it around her neck. "Hold this in one hand and take my hand with the other. We can do this together." Jerusha smiled as she wrapped Sarah's tiny fingers around the wooden pendant, then patted her hand. "Ready to go?" She took the other hand and again pulled gently.

Sarah nodded and stepped down. Jerusha wrapped one arm around the girl, kept her other hand on the slimy moss covered wall for guidance in the dark, and looked behind one last time at the two men. Antonius's eyes glistened. He towered over the Jew. Effah turned and walked away as Antonius shoved against the door with his shoulder. The heavy stone scraped against the tile floor and shut with a thud. Total darkness enveloped them.

Chapter 2

"I'm scared." Sarah trembled and whimpered.

"Hold tight to the lion and butterfly pendant. Yeshua is with us. Count the steps. There are twenty-four to the bottom." Jerusha slid her sandaled-foot over the rounded ledge and eased down a step, being careful to hold Sarah's hand tight. Her other hand clung to the damp wall for balance. After her eyes adjusted to the darkness, she urged Sarah to move. "One step," she said and steadied the shaking girl. "There. You are a step closer to freedom." She let go of her hand and wrapped her arm around Sarah's shoulder. "Ready for step two?" She hugged Sarah closer.

"It's so dark in here." Sarah snuggled her head into Jerusha's chest.

"We will do it together. Slide your foot forward on the step." Sarah's leg moved slightly. "Now hold my hand, and we will slide down to the next step together. Say it with me. What step are we stepping on?"

"Two." Sarah's voice quivered.

"That's right. One step closer. Let's keep moving." Jerusha hoped the rats had fled, but as soon as it was dark and quiet again, they

7

would find their way out of hiding. *Please Father YHWH, keep the rats away and no more spider webs.* After her silent plea, a song came to mind. "I am the Lion of Judah." She sang and hoped the noise would keep the rats away. "Deep within my inner most being dwells the Holy God of all Israel. I am the Lion of Judah." She swung her hand to the beat.

"Three," Sarah counted and hopped down.

"I am the Lion of Judah. Deep within my innermost being dwells the Holy God of all Israel. I am the Lion of Judah." Jerusha stopped singing. "Keep counting."

"Four." Sarah hopped to the next step. "You are brave."

Jerusha chuckled. "If you could hear my heartbeat you would not say that. Keep counting." She held Sarah's elbow as they crept down another step.

"I am the Lion of Judah."

Sarah stopped and pulled on Jerusha's hand. "I have never heard that song."

"It came to me from heaven when I was a slave girl like you in the palace. On the back of the wooden lion you are holding are the words, "Arise, Lord. Let your enemies be scattered. Let all who hate you flee before you." Is that not like a lion?"

Sarah giggled and made a growling sound. "I am the Lion of Judah. Deep within my innermost being dwells the Holy God of all Israel."

Jerusha laughed. "You are a lion. I like that, Sarah. We will sing it that way the rest of the way. "I am the Lion of Judah. Deep within my innermost being dwells the Holy God of all Israel. I am the Lion of Judah. He does dwell with in us, if we believe Yeshua is the King. Do you believe, Sarah?"

"I don't know."

"Well, we will have to talk about that sometime." Jerusha continued singing, and Sarah kept counting as they wound down the spiral stairway.

"Twenty-three." Sarah stopped and joined Jerusha in song, "I am the Lion of Judah. Deep within my innermost being dwells the Holy God of all Israel. I am the Lion of Judah."

"Jerusha stopped singing and cupped her hand over her ear, then put her finger to her lips. "Shh. Can you hear the waterfall?"

"I can see light." Sarah pointed at the opening.

"Yeshua gave us a full moon." Jerusha cupped her hand again to her ear. "Listen. Can you hear the water splashing over the rocks?"

Sarah giggled. "We must be close."

Jerusha took her hand. "One more step." She saw a sparkle in Sarah's eyes as the moonlight peeked out from a cloud and hit their faces. "Last step. Ready?" They both crouched down. She swung their hands forward. "Twenty-four." She pulled, and they jumped together. Plop. Feet on solid ground. No rats. No spiders. Thank you, Father.

Jerusha released Sarah's sweaty hand, took a few steps, ducked under an arch, then twirled around and waved her hands. "Look. We are standing behind the waterfall."

Sarah came up beside her, her eyes fixed on the water. "I have never seen anything so beautiful."

"Beautiful. Just like you." Jerusha ruffled her hair.

"Not me." Sarah dropped her head and sniffed. "I'm cursed. Didn't you hear the old witch?"

"Come over here." Jerusha knelt beside the water's edge and dipped her cloak in the cool water and plopped down in the grass with her legs crossed. "Splash your face with the water."

Sarah knelt over the water and lifted several handfuls of water to her face. "I have never seen clean water like this." She let handfuls of it drop in her mouth and run down her chin. "They would not let me near the pools in the palace. Always kept me hidden. In the dark rooms below ground." She sat back and faced Jerusha.

"I am sorry." Jerusha wiped Sarah's face and hands with her wet cloak. "You are not cursed. That old witch doesn't know what she is talking about. You are free. No one will do that to you again."

Sarah started to cry and fell into Jerusha's arms. Jerusha kept silent and allowed the sobs to come. Only Yeshua and time could heal the hurt. After the sobs stopped, she wiped the wet hair from Sarah's face, lifted her chin, and stared into her eyes. "Never forget who you are. You are royalty. You are Father YHWH's daughter. He adores you. You are beautiful. Right now you may not believe that, but in time you will."

"I don't believe it." Sarah rubbed her nose with the sleeve of her cloak.

"Just because you do not believe it, does not mean it is not true. So wipe those tears from your eyes."

Sarah rubbed her eyes. "Jerusha, why did you come and get me? You don't even know me. And how did you know I was here?"

"I came because Father YHWH loves you, and he sent me, and . . . well, just know that I know how you feel." Jerusha felt uncomfortable sharing her past with this little one. Now was not the time or the place. "We must go." She rose to her feet and tugged on Sarah's arm, lifting her to her feet. "The guards will notice you're missing soon." She turned and walked along a narrow stone path lined with mossy grass and pomegranate bushes, some as large as a tree. Their red and orange blossoms filled the air with a fragrance similar to Jerusha's garden at home, a safe place.

At least it had been for most of her life. Lately, she sensed an unwelcome presence. Loneliness hounded her. A loneliness greater than she felt after Timon's death. Her father and three sons lived with her. So why this unnerving sense of loneliness?

"Where are we going?" Sarah caught up and took Jerusha's hand.

"To my villa in upper Jerusalem. My father is waiting for us there."

"Will the guards find me?"

"If they do, you will be safe with us." At least Jerusha thought they would be safe. With Effah's involvement she could not be sure. How did that snake become friends with Antonius, Father's closest friend? Her stomach started to knot up again. She could not think on that now. She closed her eyes and took a deep breath.

"Look!" Sarah pointed to the stars.

Jerusha smiled. "Do you know when I was your age I tried to count the stars. My father laughed, cut open a pomegranate, and said I had a greater chance of counting the pomegranate seeds than the stars. He always told me to remember Father YHWH has more thoughts toward us than there are stars.

"That's a lot of thoughts." Sarah arched her head back and stared at the stars.

"Look! Can you see that bright star?" Jerusha squatted and lined her arm and finger up where Sarah could eye the star if she followed where she pointed with her eyes.

"That star is Regulus. It represents our King, the one who crushed the serpent." Jerusha thought she heard something behind her and turned to see. A breeze rustled the bushes. She held her breath.

"What are you looking at?" Sarah drew closer. "You look scared." She nestled her head on Jerusha's chest and whimpered. "Is it the guards?"

"I don't know." Jerusha chided herself for not being more careful. "We have taken too much time talking about stars. This is not the place. Let us hurry. My home will be safe."

She lifted her cloak above her feet and walked at a quickened pace up a steep incline. "Can you keep up, Sarah? Am I going too fast for you?"

"I can keep up." Sarah's sandals clip clopped up the hill.

At the top Sarah gawked at the hippodrome as they passed. "Is that where they race chariots?"

"Sometimes." Jerusha ducked into the shadows behind a marble column, put her finger to her lips, then hugged Sarah to her chest and froze. Her heart pounded. A soldier's shadow passed over the mosaic landing of the portico where they hid. Jerusha put her hand over Sarah's mouth and held her own breath. The soldier's outline looked more like a temple guard than a Roman soldier. Jerusha closed her eyes. "Father YHWH do not let him see us."

In the distance the hob-nailed sound of Roman soldiers' feet pounded the stone street in unison. Their marching grew louder and kept time with her beating heart. Thump. Thump. Thump. Thump. The changing of guard told her it was the second watch. Why did she dawdle so long at the waterfall? Another shadow passed. Jerusha peeked around the column, then motioned Sarah to follow. She slipped behind the next column and grabbed Sarah just in time. His shadow moved across their feet. She pressed Sarah's face into her chest, held tight, and waited. When she heard his sandal thud down the steps, she peeked her head out from the column.

He stood by the fountain with his back to her and looked up and down the agora, then shook the locked gates of a few shops. Jerusha wondered why he hadn't checked behind the hippodrome columns where they hid. Maybe he wasn't looking for them. Maybe he was a watchman for the shops. Or maybe YHWH intervened. She thought the latter. He laid his hand on his sword's hilt and clomped downhill toward the temple.

"We must hurry before he comes back. It's not far, but it's a steep climb." She took Sarah's sweaty hand and rushed across the agora past the fountain. Sarah stumbled along behind. Jerusha stopped and looked back over her shoulder. As far as she could tell, no one followed. She turned uphill, and at the top of the incline, she stopped and caught her breath. A gentle breeze blew across her sweaty brow, and she leaned against an old olive tree, its twisted trunk a good place to rest.

Sarah crawled up on it and dangled her legs. "How much farther?" She leaned her head on Jerusha's shoulder.

"Not much. See those lights at the top of Mt. Zion. That is our front gate. We will be safe there."

***

Jerusha searched her girdle for the key and fumbled it to the ground. Olive oil burned in lamps on each side, which gave just enough light for her to find it. She turned and looked at Sarah, whose mouth had dropped open.

"Is this your house?" Sarah blinked and gulped. "It is almost as big as Herod's palace."

"It belonged to my grandfather. Now my father and I live here with my three sons . . . and a few others." She grinned. "This will be your new home."

"Why do you do this for me?"

"It's Father YHWH's desire for you to be free. You will not be a slave here. You will be a daughter of the King, one who serves others, not because she's forced to, but because she loves her father."

"I do not have a father. I for sure do not love him!" She stomped her foot. "He abandoned me." Her voice quivered. "And left me to be uh . . . uh . . . well, he left me! She turned her back to Jerusha. "And the men forced me to . . ." She spun around. "What father does that to his daughter!" She pounded her fist against the gate. Blood ran down her hand.

"Oh, Sarah, let me see that." Jerusha reached out.

"No! Don't touch me!

"I know you are angry." Jerusha squeaked the gate open. "When I was your age, I thought my father abandoned me. I was angry, too. Later, he found me. It is a long story. Tonight is not the time."

"I have been wondering where you were." Jerusha's father walked down the blue and white tiled path that led to the gate.

Sarah scrunched her hand underneath her sleeve.

"That is my father." Jerusha greeted him with a kiss, then turned to Sarah. "You can call him Jacob, or, in time, you might want to call him father."

Sarah glared. Jerusha held back her chuckle.

So much like me when I was her age. "I will share his love with you. He has enough to go around to all YHWH's sons and daughter. I do not know what I would do without him."

"And I do not know what I would do without you, my precious daughter. Who do we have here?" He bowed slightly toward Sarah.

"Father, this is Sarah." Jerusha admired her father's build and good looks. The graying hair and beard were signs of wisdom. And beneath the blue stripped cloak with titztzits tassels at the ends was a muscle-hardened soldier of many years. He had kept his physique taut since coming home from serving in Rome's army. His blue-rimmed green eyes, like hers and grandfather's, spoke of a mixed bloodline, a royal heritage from the tribe of Judah, no less.

"Another Sarah." He winked at Jerusha. "We shall take good care of her."

"Yes, we will." Jerusha caressed Sarah's head.

"I have her room ready, Father." A young woman walked up behind Jacob and smiled at Sarah. "You can call me Hannah. Jacob and Jerusha took me into their home ten years ago. I was about your age at the time. If you will follow me?" She swooped her arm out toward the path.

Sarah dawdled past and glanced over her shoulder at Jerusha. "Are you coming?"

In a while. I need to talk to Father." When the two girls had gone around the corner into the villa, Jacob led Jerusha to the wall outside the gate and looked out over the city.

"It is a beautiful night for the travelers who come for the feast. Their campfires speckle the mountainside like the stars of heaven. Another Pentecost. I wonder every day how much longer before Yeshua returns to judge this generation for not recognizing him as King."

"Do we have to celebrate with them in the temple?" Jerusha despised the priest's haughty display among the people. They could not fool her with their religious phylacteries tied to their foreheads. Every time she saw them, she wanted to rip that little black box off and stomp on it, even if it did have part of the Torah written inside. Pious pigs!

He looked down at his daughter. "You are so much like your mother. A little more fire in your gut, as you call it, than her." He chuckled. "She may still be alive if she'd had more of that characteristic. But she loved those without a family, just like you. And beautiful, too."

Jerusha covered the black mole on her cheek with her radiyd. She had pulled a single white hair from her thick black curls earlier that week. At age thirty-seven, she only hoped to be as beautiful as her mother, who died seven years earlier at age fifty. Jerusha remembered touching her ima's face and admiring her beauty, even in death. "I miss Mother, too. With her and Timon both gone into the kingdom, I do not know what I would do if something happened to you."

"Your faith is strong, Jerusha. Stronger than you know. But what is troubling you?"

"Someone followed us." Her words blended with the rustling olive leaves overhead. Crickets chirped and the full moon shone over the temple below. She picked a grape from the vine growing on the waist high wall and popped it into her mouth. It tasted so good. Being with Father took the knots away, and yet the gnawing fear threatened to resurface. Edgy, she glanced around. "I am not sure we will be safe here anymore. Effah knows what we are doing."

"How?"

"The pig befriended Antonius. He showed Antonius our secret passage in the palace. I do not trust him. I am not sure I trust Antonius."

"So, you still do not trust me," Antonius said as he walked up the steep incline.

"Antonius! Have you been there all the time we were talking?"

His grin broadened. "Maybe."

"Oh, you are impossible!" Jerusha stomped inside the gate.

Her father chuckled. "Come, my friend, stay the night with us. We have much to discuss. Jerusha, we will finish our conversation in the morning, no?"

Jerusha hurried up the path, past the fountain, and wound her way through the courtyard to her room. She slammed the door and leaned against it. Breathing heavily, she listened as the men passed her room.

"As beautiful as my daughter is, she can be difficult. Give her some more time. She will come around."

"I am not a little girl anymore, Father. You will not choose my husband for me this time." She waited till they passed, then turned. Sarah stood wide eyed in the doorway of the connecting room. "It looks like Hannah provided you with a new tunic and cloak."

Sarah nodded. "May I sleep with you tonight?"

Jerusha smiled. "Of course. Just for tonight."

Chapter 3

The next morning, while Sarah slept, Jerusha slipped from the mittah and dressed. She shivered in the crisp morning air before covering Sarah with the soft lambskin cover and reflected on her conversation with Father the night before. *What would happen to them now that Effah knew of their secret?* While eating, she intended to finish their conversation that Antonius so rudely interrupted. That man. She rounded the fountain, crossed the courtyard, and entered the dining hall.

"Father, . . . oh!" She stopped and stared at Antonius, who wore his white linen under-tunic and reclined on his elbow at the table. The morning sun's rays reflected through the shutters and glistened off his dark golden hair. "I forgot you were here. I expected to see Father."

"I am sorry to disappoint you." He dipped his head and popped a grape in his mouth, then started to rise.

"Do not bother to get up." She walked to the window, opened the latticed shutters, and let the breeze cool her blushed face as she admired the butterflies that rested on the pomegranate blossoms. Why let him get to her? It was her home. He was the intruder, even if he was her father's best friend. She started to turn around, then thought better and turned back and faced the window. "When Father gets here, tell him I need to talk with him in the garden—that is—after you have eaten. Or better—after you have left. We did not finish our conversation last night—thanks to your abrupt appearance." She had not intended to be so rude. She released a deep sigh, moved to the brazier to warm her hands, then looked up. "Antonius?" She crossed the room and walked out into the portico and looked both ways. *That man. He did it again. He appeared without warning last night. And disappeared the same way this morning.* She kept her head down and mumbled as she walked down the portico. "I was rather rude, but he deserved it. Hanging around here like he owned the place."

"I found your Father." Antonius startled her.

She gasped and looked up. "How do you do it? How do you sneak up and disappear without a sound? I think you find pleasure in tormenting me like that."

"Jerusha, I promise I do not find pleasure in tormenting you. I do find pleasure in"—a smile curved his lips—"well, let's just say in serving you. You will find your father in the garden." Then he bowed, turned his back, and walked away. Jerusha stared at his broad shoulders and listened to his slight chuckle.

That man. After ten years of being around him, you would think I'd be used to his ways. She wrapped her radiyd around her shoulders and headed for the garden. Her youngest son bumped her arm as he ran past.

"Sorry, Ima." He stopped, then backed away and called over his shoulder. "Antonius, don't leave. I need you to show me a new drill."

"Joshua!" Jerusha followed him, her steps quickening to keep up. "No ten-year-old needs to learn Roman fighting drills." She glanced at Antonius's stoic expression and scrunched her brows together. "Why don't you say something?"

Antonius's mouth tipped up at the corner, and he shrugged.

Joshua pulled a wooden sword from his belt. "Grandfather made this for me so I can practice."

Jerusha rolled her eyes. Even her father encouraged these activities.

Joshua lunged with the sword. "I want to be a Roman soldier like my father."

"Timon was not a Roman soldier." Jerusha watched with hands on her hips.

"Timon was not my father. I was just a baby when he died. Isn't that right, Antonius?" He stopped and let the sword hang at his side. "If he would have let Antonius fight in his place, he would be alive to tell me what to do." He stabbed the air with the wooden toy. "But he didn't, and he's dead."

Jerusha pursed her lips before responding. She understood his lack of connection with Timon. She had accepted Joshua from his wet nurse when he had been killed along with his wife for letting Peter escape from prison. Timon only held Joshua one time, the day before he died in the arena. "My son, I told you why Timon did not accept Antonius's offer. He knew Antonius would kill the poor man. And the gladiator would not have entered into Yeshua's kingdom."

Antonius knelt on one knee before Joshua and stopped his pretend sword fight. "I was not a follower of the way at that time. His dark blue eyes rested a while on Jerusha, his pain evident as he blinked back tears. Jerusha stood motionless. Joshua jabbed at him again. Antonius dodged it and grabbed his arm. "Your father was a brave man to give up his life for another."

Joshua replaced the sword in his belt. "Well—then—he cared more about that man than about being my father."

"Joshua!" Jerusha stomped her foot. "Do not talk like that. He would have given his life for you, too."

"But he didn't. My real father was a Roman soldier. I want to fight like him and Antonius. It's YHWH's fault my father's dead. The angel opened the prison doors and let Peter escape. My father was just the guard that day. He died for what YHWH did."

"Your "real" father, as you put it, was a Yeshua follower, too, even though he was a Roman soldier. He would not want you to be angry with YHWH. Neither would Timon, if he had lived." She stared at Antonius for a few seconds and added, "Nor does Antonius." She grabbed Joshua's shoulders. "I beg you to stop this nonsense of wanting to be a Roman soldier. It will only get you killed."

"Antonius did not die." Joshua put his hand on the wooden sword. "He can teach me how to fight the right way—so I will live, like him."

A whiff of frankincense hung in the air. Thank YHWH. Her father was near. She glanced over her shoulder.

"What is all this yelling?" Jacob strolled past Jerusha and stared down at Joshua. "I heard what you said. You will honor your mother. Do you understand? Maybe I should not have made you a sword. Your mother is right. It is not good you want to be a Roman soldier."

"You were a Roman soldier." Joshua blinked back tears. Jerusha saw the hurt in his eyes. His grandfather rarely admonished him. "Antonius is a Roman soldier." Joshua's voice quivered.

"Sometimes YHWH allows us to be in a position to show others the way to Yeshua. If you are not called by him to do it, it could get you killed, like your mother said."

I'm mad at YHWH. He could have kept my father alive, like he did for you."

Jerusha gently lifted his chin until he would look into her eyes. "Oh, Joshua, I understand being angry at YHWH. I, too, was angry at him when I was your age. It only hurts you. YHWH loves you and his ways are best, even if you do not understand them. Trust his love for you." The words came from her mind, not her heart. She felt like a hypocrite. The fountain gurgled in the distance and the song thrush twittered. Hypocrite. Hypocrite. Hypocrite.

"Jacob tapped his grandson's head.

"You know what the Torah says will happen if you honor your mother and father?"

Joshua nodded. "Things go well for you."

"Do you think an apology would be the right thing to do?" Jacob's words carried an authority that eluded Jerusha when she conversed with her sons. Maybe because he was not a hypocrite. The boys respected him, although she wondered why he encouraged them to spend so much time with Antonius.

"Yes, grandfather." Joshua rubbed his eyes with his fist, then turned to Jerusha. "I am sorry for arguing, Ima." He shuffled his feet and wrung his hands.

"I forgive you." She gripped his chin in her fingers. "I am so glad Miriam brought you to Timon and me. Her obedience to your dying parent's request was YHWH's provision. You needed parents, and we needed another son. You have been handpicked by him to be here."

Joshua hugged Jerusha. "I am glad you are my ima. But I want a father, too."

He arched his head back and grinned. "Maybe Antonius?" Jerusha rolled her eyes and shook her head.

***

That afternoon Jerusha sat on Father's cedar bench in the shade and held an uncut pomegranate. The sun's rays broke through and shone on the olive trees and pomegranate bushes that had flourished since the years when she was a little girl who played with butterflies, twirled in dance before her father, and watched him work at his carpenter's bench. She came here often after Timon died. It helped her grieve to be in the same place he had offered his betrothal. And yet, of late, nothing soothed her unsettled thoughts.

Antonius offered his hand in marriage a year after Timon's death. She refused. She would not desecrate Timon's love by giving her heart to another man. Yeshua's deep love carried her through those empty, hopeless days when the tears came—and they came often. His presence in this garden brought her out of a dark place and put a dance in her feet again. Now she slipped deeper and deeper into another dark place, an aloneness she'd never experienced, even in those days after Timon's death. She feared for her sons.

"Father YHWH, where are you?" She threw the pomegranate across the path. It hit green leaves and caused one lone bloom to fall to the ground She picked it up and twirled it in her fingers. "I feel so alone. My sons need you. I need you. You promised all my sons would be taught by you and great would be their peace." A familiar churning twisted her insides into knots. "I cannot go on like this." She crumpled to the ground, her face in her hands, the flower falling to the tile. Her whole body trembled as she sought to hold back the sobs. One tear dropped from her chin. Another one rolled down her cheek. And another and another until convulsing cries echoed through the garden. After several minutes, she searched her girdle for a clean cloth and wiped her eyes and nose. Frankincense, a familiar fragrance, permeated the air.

"Father?" She hiccupped and looked up.

"Yes, my daughter." He reached for her hands and lifted her. "Why are you so distraught?" He snuggled her to his side and walked her back to their bench. "You have not been yourself of late. What has captured your thoughts?"

"Father." She sniffed and wiped her nose again. "I don't know what to do with the boys. I carry their pain with me always. I cannot shake it. It eats at my gut."

"Gut?" Her father's eyes twinkled.

"Oh, Father, I know it's not proper to use such a word, but that describes best how it feels. My gut aches."

"Go on." Her father patted her hand.

"Well, each son has a different issue. I just irritate them when I try to help. I feel so alone. More alone than I did when Timon died." She stood and swung her arms out and let them fall to her side. "And now with Effah showing up at the palace with Antonius, I fear we all may be in danger. I think I was followed last night, but I cannot be sure."

A deep voice spoke from behind her. "You were followed."

"Uhh! Jerusha swirled on bare feet. Her cloak flopped around her legs. "Antonius! There you go again. Appearing out of nowhere."

"Do not be so hard on the man, Jerusha." Her father opened the gate.

Antonius came inside and stood before Jerusha, feet shoulder-width apart, hands on his hips. "Why did you go alone? I told you to bring Samuel." His intrusion irritated her.

"He would not come." She clenched her fists, not sure if she was angrier at Samuel or Antonius. "Not that I owe you an explanation." She glared. "Samuel left Jerusalem to visit the Essenes somewhere by the Dead Sea. Quaram, I think he said."

"Your son is twenty years old. He should know it's not safe for a woman alone on the streets at night, especially in these troublous times. I will speak to him about that."

"He did not know I would be going to the palace in the darkness," she countered. "If he knew, he would have been more than willing to come." She had her doubts. Samuel's preoccupation with the Essenes took him away more often than not but owning up to her doubts before Antonius, who stood before her like a pompous king, clawed at her gut. A gnawing ache gripped her stomach again, and she wrapped her arms around herself.

"Where was Stephen?" Antonius's question sounded like a command.

"You will not treat me like one of your soldiers." She lifted her dipping chin. "And I will not answer like one. It is not any of your concern what my son was doing. At fifteen, he is a grown man and answers only to his grandfather." She lifted her shoulders. "And me."

Antonius's mouth tipped up at the corner, and he raised his eyebrows. "A grown man answers to his ima?"

She swirled around toward her father. His half-grin infuriated her. Two against one.

"Aren't you going to say something?" She glared at Jacob.

He cleared his throat. "I believe the Torah says a man should leave his mother and father and cleave to his wife."

"Father, I do not mean any disrespect, but my sons have no wives to cleave to."

"Jerusha, I know it's been hard for you to raise three sons without a father, but Samuel and Stephen are grown men now." He came close and took her hand, placed it in the crook of his arm, and patted it. "It is time for them to lean on Father YHWH. He will teach them whom to listen to. I think Antonius would be a good choice." He spoke of the soldier with deep affection and respect. Jerusha had resisted for nine years to see Antonius through her father's eyes. No one could replace Timon. She glanced over at the man who, at the moment, infuriated her. Her Father's words drew her attention back to him. "And whom to marry. Or not to marry." His blue rimmed green eyes sparkled with life. "Trust your heart to love again the man who loves them." She lifted her eyes to the tall, battle-hardened soldier who stood next to her father. His soft, compassionate eyes rested on her. A warmth spread through her body. His smile broadened as if he knew what she felt. She covered her ugly black mole and looked away.

Her father bent over and kissed her forehead, then whispered in her ear. "He loves you Jerusha."

"Father!" She pulled away. "I think, I . . . I think . . ." She refused to look at Antonius. "I-I-I- . . ." She stuttered like Moses and walked toward the gate. She must escape before she made a bigger fool of herself than she already had.

Her father chuckled. "I am taking Stephen and Joshua to the carpenter's shop in the market. I need their help, and I need time to work on Miriam's pendant. Moses is afraid if she loses another baby she might not come back from the darkness that swallowed her heart after their last loss. We must pray." Jerusha stared at the ground for a moment, glad to get the topic off Antonius. She felt a fondness toward Moses, the orphan named after the prophet who led the Hebrews out of Egypt. "You have been a great help to Miriam in her time of barrenness." Her father's voice carried a tenderness that caused her to look up. He knew the pain she went through to become a mother. He understood well what she felt when old women stared and mumbled about being cursed because her belly never swelled with child. He caught her arm.

"Fear not Jerusha. Believe what YHWH has spoken. Your sons will be taught by Him and great will be their peace." He hugged her tight for a moment. "I will be back shortly. I leave you in capable hands." He pointed to Antonius, then left through the garden gate. A whiff of frankincense lingered as she watched him walk the tiled path to the fountain, his stripped robe with blue tzitzits on the corners blowing in the breeze.

She felt Antonius's presence behind her. "How is it you are still here?" Her voice trembled, and she remained motionless, unable to turn and face him. "So often you disappear at times like these." The breeze blew her radiyd, and it slipped to her shoulders.

"Jerusha." His nearness caused her heart to flutter. Why did he affect her in this way? She turned to leave, then felt his hand on her shoulder and stopped. "Please. Do not go." She felt his warm breath in her hair and closed her eyes.

She could not let herself fall for his ploys. She grasped her chest as if that would calm her racing heart. *This cannot be. I cannot be falling in love. Not after all this time.*

"I offer my apologies for treating you like my soldiers. That was not my intent."

"Excuse me." Hannah stood at the gate and looked uncomfortable that she had interrupted. "There is a man at the entrance." She stammered and looked down. "He says his name is Effah. He wants to talk to Jerusha. Should I let him in?"

"No!" Jerusha stepped away from Antonius, then turned back and glared. She had almost forgotten. "He is your friend . . . *you* see what he wants . . . outside the gate." She swirled around and faced Hannah. When she turned back, Antonius was gone.

Chapter 4

"Effah insists he talks with you and only you." Antonius wore his gold embossed tunic with his sword sheathed at his side and strode past the fountain toward Jerusha. She flipped her radiyd over her shoulder and waited under the marble archway that opened to the dining hall. Antonius carried himself with dignity, like a king. She admired that about him and often wondered if he had royal lineage in his Gallic bloodline. He never talked of his past. "He's waiting at the gate," said Antonius as he looked past her to Joshua, who was entertaining Sarah with his sword in the dining hall behind Jerusha. "For his age, your son is quite good with the sword," he remarked.

Jerusha would use any distraction possible to keep her from talking to Effah. She glanced behind her and said, "Never mind my son's fighting skills. Why haven't I noticed before today that you talk and act like royalty?"

His grin spread wide. "So, after all these years, you have finally taken notice of me." He chuckled a very infuriating chuckle and then bowed. When he rose up, his eyes caught hers, "Maybe, I do have royal ancestry." He drew closer. "I might be persuaded to share my humble beginnings with you . . . under the right circumstances."

Uncomfortable that her heart raced at his nearness, she looked away and changed the subject. "Maybe you should not be teaching my son to sword fight."

He stepped back and moved around her, his manly scent stirring feelings inside her that she had not felt even when Timon was alive. "I know you do not approve." His words sounded far away, but his scent lingered. Jerusha turned and was surprised by his nearness. "But every boy needs to know how to defend himself." His dark blue eyes locked with hers again.

"And every woman as well." Jerusha slipped around the marble column hoping to calm her pounding heart. A flirtatious woman she would not be.

"You protect too much." The corner of his mouth tipped up.

"A woman needs protection from the likes of you."

"I was talking about your son. Let the boy be a boy." He raised his brow. "And the woman a woman."

"Oh, you are so infuriating."

His laughter echoed in the dining hall, and the children stopped their play momentarily and stared. "Antonius!" Joshua ran toward the soldier and squatted in his best fighting position and jabbed with his sword.

"That's my man, Joshua. You did that quite well."

"Teach me some more drills."

"I am sorry. I will be accompanying your mother to the front gate." He tipped the corner of his mouth and looked at Jerusha. "That is if she will let me." He looked back at Joshua. "A visitor waits to talk with her. Then I will be going back to the barracks."

Jerusha rolled her eyes. She remembered well what went on in Antonia Fortress. Young slave girls used by soldiers, only to be cast out to starve in the streets. Over the years she wondered if Antonius was able to resist the temptation to partake of such debauchery. She bit her lip. Only minutes ago she acted the harlot with her racing heart and the tingling that ran up her spine at his nearness. She wondered what had become of her since Timon's death.

"The praetorian guard awaits my return." Antonius patted Joshua's head.

"Can I go with you to the barracks?" Joshua held on to Antonius's cloak and pulled.

"No. That would not be a good idea. It is enough that you are able to defend yourself. You should stay away from 'the likes of them,' as your mother would say." He winked at Jerusha.

A warmth rose in her neck.

"May I?" He offered the crook of his arm to Jerusha.

She swished past him. His laughter could be heard all the way around the corner where she stopped and looked through the olive trees at him.

Antonius waved his arms toward her. "I must see if I can make amends with your mother." His eyes met hers through the branches.

She pulled back and covered the blush that rose in her face. It happened so often these days. Timon had told her not to be afraid to love again and even gave her his blessing to marry again if YHWH willed. But Antonius? This Roman soldier? She wondered what good that would serve her or her sons. To have him gone and possibly die while fighting for Rome? Maybe even watching Yeshua's followers being killed? It was enough that she, while growing up had to endure seeing Father with enemy soldiers' cohort in obedience to YHWH. Her sons would not have their father doing the same. Not if she could help it.

She strolled through the garden pathway, in deep thought, confused. Her father had made his opinion clear when Antonius offered his betrothal. Her father had turned down Antonius only because she resisted. Rays from the setting sun flickered through the silver olive leaves and warmed her body. Flustered, she dropped her hands to her sides as she rounded the corner. Light reflected off a shiny object and cast sparkles that momentarily blinded her. She cupped her hand above her eyes.

Antonius stood in the pathway in full armor, his red-plumed helmet under his arm, his expression stoic, no broad grin or flirtatious gleam in his eyes. She stopped.

"Let me accompany you to the gate. It is quite obvious Effah disturbs you." He placed his helmet on his head. The sparkles bounced on her arm.

"I-I . . ." She stuttered and looked down.

"You owe me no explanation." He drew near. The old panic gripped her heart. If he knew what had transpired between her and Effah, would he still want her for his wife? He tipped her chin up and looked for a few seconds into her eyes. "Effah is an acquaintance, not a friend. I am not sure how he learned of Sarah's escape." He took her hand and placed it on his forearm.

"With your father gone to his carpenter's shop, I will see to it that he does not hurt you or Sarah. Or anyone under the protection of this household."

***

Jerusha saw Effah across the courtyard. She felt sick. After all this time, the same nauseating torment still twisted her stomach into knots. She thought she was healed. No nightmares in twenty years. Of course, she had not seen Effah since he married that beautiful woman or since her surrender to Yeshua and entrance to the kingdom. She swallowed and glanced up at Antonius, comforted by his presence. Her fingers dug into his arm. His brows furrowed, and he placed his hand over hers. Relaxing her grip, she wondered if he knew.

The childhood secret flashed before her eyes. Effah's weight on her naked body. The blood. The pain. The unwanted touches and when he said, "Don't tell anyone. My father will have you stoned."

Jerusha scrunched her face at the remembrance and kept her eyes down—for the first time in years, she felt shame. Maybe Father told Antonius. Maybe he was flirtatious because he knew she was a soiled woman? He hadn't offered marriage in nine years. Suddenly, the thought occurred to her. Maybe he would cast her off as the young girls in Herod's palace, after he had had his way with her in the marriage bed. Or worse, try to take his pleasure with her without marriage, then stone her as Effah threatened. She stood numbly before the two men. Why did it matter? Antonius meant nothing to her. The flutter in her chest when in his presence said differently. He did matter.

"Jerusha? Are you alright?" Antonius spoke, his tone soft, gentle, not his usual gruffness.

"Ye-yes." She straightened her cloak. "I am alright. Do I appear to be a helpless child?"

He grinned. "I believe I am seeing your father's little lioness arise. He told me of your ability to transform in an instant from a delicate butterfly to a roaring lioness."

"My father confides too much." She walked past him toward Effah. Her heart thumped in her chest, and she stopped a short distance away from the gate and stared. Then, she sighed, her breath getting caught up in her throat. She saw why she was so enchanted by Effah as a little girl. His broad shoulders, narrow waist, and high cheekbones had an appeal that any woman would admire, let alone a ten-year-old child, who hoped her father would choose him as her betrothed. The seriousness in his eyes troubled her.

"You are not coming inside this gate." Her hands trembled.

"Then listen. I don't have much time. You are in danger." His dark eyes darted back and forth. "They may have followed me."

"Huh! Danger!' I am not in any danger, except by the likes of you." She glared back at Antonius.

Effah glanced over his shoulder, then glanced back. "Your father is in danger, too. Everyone who lives here is in danger."

"Do not talk to me of your lies." Her heart raced even faster.

Jerusha felt Antonius's hand on her shoulder. "Effah, we have not known each other long, but know that I protect her and her family with my life."

For a change, Antonius's nearness and words calmed her down, giving her courage and confidence. She glared at Effah. "If we are in danger, it is because of you." She removed Antonius's hand from her shoulder. She could take care of herself.

"You must trust me, Jerusha." Effah's begging annoyed her.

"Trust you? You are the last person I will trust."

"Even after I helped save Sarah?"

"That means nothing. I would have got her out without"—she glanced at Antonius and back at Effah—"without the likes of you."

"Jerusha, they know you are helping the girls and hiding them in your villa. Their spies are everywhere in the city. They want to kill your father because then there will be no male heir in your bloodline. They will discredit your sons' bloodline. All they need is the scepter, and they will steal your villa. You will be out on the streets." The evening shadows formed an eerie design on his face. Or had that monster from her nightmare come back to haunt her? She shook her head and looked again. Only shadows.

"If it is true," she said as she advanced closer, "your father would be involved." She shook her finger. "So why would you betray him?"

"I don't have time to explain. "He glanced around. "They may be watching. Tell your father."

"Tell me what?" Jacob trudged up the incline. The sun dipped below the horizon behind him.

"Jacob! I implore you. Tell your daughter to listen." Effah hid behind the jujube tree in the darkening shadows. Jerusha almost laughed at his cowardice.

"First, I do not tell my daughter anything. She has a mind of her own." He winked at her. "Second, why should either of us listen to you?" Jacob stopped at the gate.

Effah stepped out from the shadows. "I have converted. I am a follower of the Way."

Jerusha burst into laughter.

"Why do you laugh? If that murdering Paul can convert, anyone can change his ways and repent."

"Anyone but you." Jerusha's boldness increased in her father's presence.

"Give us time to see the fruit of this change." Jacob motioned for Jerusha to unlock the gate.

"You do not have time. Your life is in danger. The priests and Sicarii plot to kill you and take your villa. I beg you, Jacob. Do not go to the temple on Pentecost."

"Effah, this pretense is nauseating." Jerusha fumbled with the key.

"Jerusha, I beg you." Effah grabbed the gate.

"Enough! Step away from my daughter." Jacob closed in on Effah and stared at him eye to eye. "As for this threat, it will not keep me from bringing my first fruits offering. Go and do not return unless invited."

Effah glanced both ways, then at Antonius. "Keep a close watch on Jacob, especially at Pentecost." The orange globe had gone down behind the temple. Lights flickered in the pilgrim's campsites on the mountainside. Jerusha watched Effah descend the terraced pathway.

Converted to the Way. What blasphemy! The knots tightened in her stomach. "Humph. I do not trust him."

"Did you see that?" She threw the gate wide and ran to the terraced steps. "Two men came out of the shadows. I couldn't tell if they followed him or joined him."

"I'm on the first watch at the fortress tonight." Antonius stepped to Jerusha's side. "I will ask around. I have friends in both camps. He turned toward Jacob, who had come up behind Jerusha, and clutched his forearm. Jacob nodded. Jerusha stood by her father and watched Antonius disappear in the darkness.

"I fear for his life. It is a dangerous thing to be a Roman soldier who follows the Way. He has hidden it well so far, and many soldiers have come into the kingdom because of it." Her father's eyes showed his admiration.

Jerusha shivered. "I would not want to watch another crucifixion like Grandfather's," she said, then smiled. "Or Yogli, as he wanted to be called."

"He was so close to death when we took him from the cross. It is a good thing no one knows he is alive." Her father patted her hand.

"Have you heard from him? I miss talking to that giant." She stared at the darkening sky.

"I have not heard in a while. The last word I received, said a place is readied for us in Pella. The time draws near."

"I long for him to be with us here." She searched for Regulus in the stars.

"When the time is right, he will return to get us. More troublous times are ahead before Yeshua's judgment comes to this generation."

"Father, do not talk about those things. It causes my stomach to knot up. I am concerned enough about my sons without hearing about the tribulations ahead." She rushed to the gate. "Hurry, Father! Get inside. We don't know who might jump out of the shadows." She came back and took his arm. "What are you staring at?"

"The moonlight reflecting off the temple is so beautiful. It's a peaceful but deceiving sight. Yeshua said one stone will not be left upon another."

She pulled on his arm. "Father, please let us go inside." Tears threatened to overflow.

"If Effah is telling the truth, we all are in danger."

Chapter 5

Jerusha rubbed Boaz's nose and snuggled her cheek against the horse's silky coat. The morning sunlight filtered through the window on her face. Being with the stable animals brought great comfort. The newborn lamb suckled at her mother's teat. The turtledoves nested in the rafters above her head.

"Yes, I know what you're saying, little friends. My father's quoted Yeshua's words numerous times." She stroked Boaz's coat with the brush. "Do not be anxious for your life . . . look at the birds of the air." She glanced up at the two lovebirds. "They do not sow, neither do they, reap, nor gather into barns, and yet your heavenly Father feeds them. Are you not worth more than they?" She fell back into the pile of hay and listened to the cooing doves.

"Father YHWH, I do not know what has happened to me. Darkness crowds my thoughts and steals my joy and peace. Most of the time my stomach's in knots. I cannot shake it. Even the dance in my feet is gone." Jerusha waited. Father YHWH seemed so distant. Had he abandoned her? She stood and continued brushing Boaz.

A little while later, she heard Sarah giggle in the herb garden. Jerusha patted Boaz's neck, dropped the brush in a bucket, and stepped to the door.

"Look, Sarah. Here's another one." Joshua had an uncanny way of finding the butterflies when they emerged from the chrysalis. It had been a long time since Jerusha had watched one struggle its way out of its dark home.

She smiled, pulled hay from her hair, and covered her head with her striped radiyd. Just what her troubled thoughts needed—a trip to the butterfly section in Hannah's herb garden.

"Ima, come and see. A butterfly is coming out." Joshua pointed to the tip of a purple wing that peeked out of the hardened chrysalis attached to the olive branch. It hung low over the garden where the two children could see it. Joshua's smile spread wide, his hand on Sarah's shoulder as the two watched, then he looked up over his shoulder at Jerusha. "Are you coming, Ima?" His grin could cheer any downtrodden heart.

"I'm coming, Smiley." She wound the path between herbs, flowers, and shrubs to the back part of the garden.

"Do not touch the butterfly. Or try to help it." Jerusha warned. "If it works its way out alone now, it grows strong enough to fly later." She repeated her father's words from childhood.

"It's alright, little butterfly. You will be strong soon. You are not alone." Sarah bent over and stared at the emerging butterfly.

"We are here." Joshua pointed toward the sky. "And YHWH is watching, too."

"That is right. YHWH is always watching, even when we feel alone." Jerusha laughed. She smiled at the purple butterfly that landed on her arm. Several more fluttered in the air around her head. "Thank you, little friends, for that lesson."

After a while, Sarah plopped crossed legged in the tall grass, a pout on her lips, her elbows on her knees and chin in her palms. Jerusha wondered what captured her thoughts.

"Joshua, will you feed the horses, then see if Hannah needs help?"

"Oh, Ima."

"Without argument."

"Alright." He trudged to the stable and searched for something in his girdle.

"Joshua. No slingshots in the stable. It scares the animals." Jerusha chuckled. "That boy. Sometimes I wonder how David's mother dealt with her son and his slingshot."

"Why such a sour face, Sarah?" Jerusha sat down next to Sarah and crossed her legs.

"I'm cursed, as the old witch said. I have no father and mother." Sarah sighed and plopped her hands in her lap.

Jerusha scooted closer and wrapped her arm around Sarah's shoulder. "You have me and my father. And Father YHWH and . . ."

"Will I have to go back?" Sarah sniffed and rubbed her nose on her sleeve.

"Ima," Stephen hollered from the villa. Jerusha smiled at how grown up her son looked. At fifteen he almost had a full beard. A dark cloud crowded her thoughts as a picture of him talking with the Egyptian in the marketplace came to mind. She had overheard the man, who claimed to be the messiah, urging Stephen to come with him into the desert and join his band of converts. Her talk with Stephen about it had gone nowhere. He interrupted her musings. "There is a man at the gate with temple guards. They are asking for Sarah."

"Oh." Sarah buried her face in Jerusha's chest. "They'll take me back to the palace." Her muffled words felt warm in Jerusha's tunic.

Jerusha's heart thumped in her chest. "Quick, get up!" In years past, she had held one Sarah in her arms and watched her die. Whoever this man was with the guards—father or not—he would not take this Sarah with him. "Follow me," she demanded.

She grabbed Sarah's hand and ran to the stable. Sarah stumbled to keep up. Jerusha pressed on the wall behind the stalls. It creaked open a little. "Help me pull." The two shoved on the door until it budged enough for them to get through. Sarah stared into the darkness. "I'm not going in there."

"It is a secret hiding place." Jerusha lit a lantern, ducked into the darkened room, and hooked it on an iron ring. Sarah stopped and peered inside the cold room.

Jerusha knelt in front of Sarah. "I must go back and talk to the men. I'll send Hannah and Joshua to keep you company." Sarah's eye widened, the fear that Jerusha saw reminded her of her time in Herod's palace as a child. She grabbed the sheep's rope and led it through the opening. The lamb cried and followed its mother. Sarah tagged along.

"Here." She handed Sarah the rope and plumped some linen-covered fleece in the corner. "Sit here."

"I am scared." Sarah wiped tears away and hesitantly plopped on the puffy pile. "Do not leave me by myself."

Jerusha slipped her arms beneath the lamb's loins and lifted and placed it in Sarah's lap. "That is why I moved this little fellow in here. He needs a friend, too. If he gets hungry, let him suckle at his mother's breast."

Sarah hugged the lamb's neck and snuggled her face into its soft coat. "I will call him Merea, my friend." She ran her fingers through its fleece and hummed the melody Jerusha had taught her.

"I am the lion of Judah," Jerusha whispered the song's words in Sarah's ear, then turned to leave. "I'm going to shut this door. If you hear it creak open, do not panic; it will be Hannah and Joshua."

"Deep within my innermost being dwells the holy God of all Israel," Sarah continued the song Jerusha started. The words echoed in the cave. Jerusha pointed into the darkness. "Back there is a secret passage that no one knows about, except my family. If we need to escape from the city, we will use it, but stay put until I return."

***

Jerusha rushed past Joshua, who had just stepped inside the stable, then stopped and turned back. "Find Hannah, and the two of you stay with Sarah." Jerusha's heart pounded. "She's hiding in the secret room. Keep her company. Do not come out until I come back."

"What is wrong, Ima?"

"I do not have time to explain. Just do as I say!" Her words sounded harsher than she intended. She hurried through the herb garden to the kitchen. The aroma of freshly baked bread and the herbs hanging from the rafters reminded Jerusha she had not eaten since getting dressed. Stephen poked at the hot coals beneath the oven and talked with the cook, who kneaded dough on a wood table. Jerusha motioned for him to follow her.

A cool breeze blew across her sweaty brow as she lifted her radiyd and tucked her dark curls inside. She sniffed the air. Ugh. The smell of body odor and hay convinced her to go to her room and freshen up.

"Stephen, tell the man at the gate I will be right there. Is Father here?"

"No. He is at the carpenter's shop."

Jerusha rolled her eyes. "Never here when I need him." She hoped Stephen had not heard her grumblings. "Well, it's up to you to converse with them until I come. I will hurry." She turned and quickened her steps under the columned archway, crossed the courtyard, and went up the stairs to her room. After shutting the door, she opened the shutters, removed her radiyd, and let the breeze blow through her hair while she stared at the garden below.

Red-blossomed pomegranate bushes lined the tiled path to her favorite fountain. She tried to quiet her pounding heart. If only Father or Timon were here to tell her what to say to the man. Even Antonius would be helpful, although she was not sure she should be around him. She shrugged her shoulders and sighed. *Well, I do not need them. I can take care of myself.*

She dropped her cloak and tunic at her feet, splashed water beneath her arms from the bowl on the small table, and dried with a towel that hung on a gold ring on the mosaic wall. Holding the towel next to her breasts, she recalled the time when Antonius caught her unexpectedly in the bathhouse in Caesarea before Timon had been killed. Thank YHWH she had covered herself with the towel before he stepped into the steam room. His explanation that he had thought the bathhouse was empty never rang true. She hugged the towel next to her face. However, his demeanor did change after he accepted Yeshua. He apologized. She heard the men's voices below. How could I be thinking about Antonius? Poor Sarah. She's waiting for me.

Guilt-ridden, Jerusha hurriedly hung the towel on the ring and reached for a fresh tunic from a peg on the opposite wall. Her hand slid across a rough tile on the wall, and she remembered the scepter. Of course, if need be, she could use the scepter. She ran her fingers along the edge of the blue tile until she felt a groove, then pushed with her fingers and wiggled the stone until it fell into her other hand. She stared at her hiding place, a deep hole where she had hidden the scepter many years ago. Until now, she'd had no reason to take it out. Her mouth dropped open and she blinked in the sunlight. "It's gone!"

Chapter 6

"Maybe father took the scepter," Jerusha mumbled and replaced the tile, then slipped the fresh tunic over her head. She had been so concerned about Sarah she had forgotten about the threat against him. She hurriedly tied her girdle around her waist, wrapped the radiyd around her head, and grabbed her cloak from the mittah; then she stood at its edge and rubbed her hand across the fleece cover. Timon had calmed her fears many nights while she snuggled next to him in this bed. What would he say now? "I know, Timon," she whispered. "Our lives are in YHWH's hands." A light rap at the door interrupted her thoughts.

"Jerusha? Are you in there?" Timon's mother seemed to know when she needed a mother's counsel.

"Yes, Chaya," Jerusha opened the door. "Shalom." She greeted the aging woman with a kiss. Ever since Jerusha's mother had passed into the kingdom, Jerusha depended on Chaya's wisdom, older woman to younger.

"There are men at the gate asking for you. Stephen asked me to tell you that your father is back, and he is talking to them now. But they insist on speaking to you." Chaya's countenance glowed. Her braided hair shined in the sunlight like a silver crown beneath the blue striped radiyd. She took Jerusha's hands. "Fear not, Jerusha. You are not alone."

"Your insight always surprises me. How did you know?"

"It's not hard to discern when you know someone as well as I know you. Remember, I birthed you and placed you in your mother's arms. A miraculous birth I will never forget." She hugged Jerusha.

"The scepter is missing. Danger hovers like a dark cloud. I am not sure if any of us is safe without it." Jerusha rested her cheek on the older woman's shoulder.

"If our Father in heaven sees when the sparrow falls to the ground and counts the hairs of our head, we can trust him to care for us." Chaya stroked Jerusha's head.

"So many of the followers of the Way suffer and are killed." Jerusha lifted her head and looked at the aged woman.

"Through many tribulations, we enter the kingdom." Chaya caressed Jerusha's cheek.

"How much longer, Chaya, before Yeshua comes?"

"It cannot take long. He said this generation shall not pass away until all these things come to pass." The elder woman grasped Jerusha's hand. "Come. I will go with you to the gate and pray."

***

"This man seems to think we are harboring his daughter in our villa." Her father took her hand and squeezed. "He said she disappeared from the palace a short while ago." He extended his arm and Chaya rested her hand on it. "Shalom." He greeted both women with a kiss.

"You stole my daughter." The man at the gate spoke through gritted teeth, his face red, eyes narrowed like a cat watching his prey. "I demand you give her back! He grabbed the gate and shook it. The birds fluttered from their resting place overhead. Jerusha glanced at a dove that landed in one of the pomegranate bushes lining the path.

Jerusha smiled as she remembered, "YHWH's with us." For a brief second, she felt as if she'd entered another world.

"These guards are here to see that you do." The man's gruff voice broke her peaceful bliss. He rattled the gate again, and she stared at him, then at the soldiers behind him.

Accustomed to Antonius and the other Roman soldiers he brought with him to their gatherings, she took note that these men lacked the same stature or hardened build. Not intimidating at all. A calm peace came again and spread through her body. Briefly, she glanced at Chaya. Her mouth moved in silent words and being thankful for the older women's prayers, Jerusha grinned, then grew somber as she addressed the man at the gate. A sudden flurry of questions poured into her thoughts. She lifted her chin and stood a little taller.

"Tell me, sir, what does your daughter look like? Can you describe her for me? Is she tall? Short? What color is her hair or eyes? How old is she?"

"Uh, uh, she's about this tall." He held his hand at shoulder height. Dark brown hair. Brown eyes. Uh, uh, she's about twelve years old."

"You do not know exactly how old your daughter is?" She saw YHWH's wisdom in giving her such questions. A knowing, a deep feeling grew inside her that this man was not Sarah's father.

"It has been a long time since I have seen her."

"Do you not know the year she was born?"

"Stop stalling with the questions. Open the gate."

"We do not have anyone in our home that fits that description." She unlocked the gate, "But you may search for yourselves."

The guards shoved Jerusha aside. Her father caught her elbow and steadied her. The shorter guard stopped and looked back. "One day the priests will own this villa."

The tallest one glared. "You will not be able to stop it."

Jerusha looked first at her father and then at Chaya. They both smiled. Peace radiated from their faces: The same peace she experienced after Timon's death. The same peace that carried her through the last nine years raising sons without a father. The same peace that evaded her these last months, until now. It must be Chaya's prayers.

"I am not concerned with your threats. Make your search and get out." Jerusha sounded more confident than she felt. She lifted her chin and walked in front of the taller guard. Her Father and Chaya followed. Stephen watched from a distance. She stopped at the fountain and listened to the rustling leaves in the garden as the guards thrashed through the bushes.

"I hope Joshua and Hannah got the door closed tight in the stable. They are with Sarah in the secret passage," she whispered to her father.

He nodded.

"Fear not. Father YHWH will protect them." Chaya's countenance showed she believed what he said. She wanted to believe. She closed her eyes.

"Father YHWH will help." She felt her father's hand on her shoulder.

"It will be all right Jerusha. He has never failed us yet."

At the moment, her father's words sounded empty and unbelievable. Father YHWH let her husband die, and her sons had lost their way without him. What good could there be in their future without a father to guide them? She felt so helpless. She glanced up at her father and half smiled. "The scepter is missing. Did you take it?"

Her father raised his brow and backed away as the guards tromped past the fountain and headed toward the stable. He leaned into Jerusha and whispered in her ear.

"Fear not. Father YHWH has a plan."

Jerusha's breath caught in her throat. He must not know where it is either, or he would not have answered that way. *Where could it be? Only Father and her sons knew of the secret hiding place in her room. Had Father told Antonius? Did he take it? Surely Samuel wouldn't have taken it? Or Stephen?*

She glanced at Stephen, who stood next to her father. He shook his head indicating it wasn't him. Joshua? Surely not. Even as young as he was, he understood its importance, the power, and authority behind the one who owned it, which was that it would give that person ownership to their land. If Father died, what would she do if pressed by the priests to give up the land? Effah said his life was in danger. She took her father's hand and squeezed. He had been her rock and strength since Timon died.

A door slammed upstairs. She jumped and grabbed Stephen's arm with her other hand. Her father wrapped his arm around her waist and pulled her close. She glanced at Chaya—such peace! Anger arose in Jerusha's chest as she listened to pottery being shattered against the tile floor and wooden table and chairs being thrown over. There was no need for them to destroy her home.

She looked at her father. *Why isn't he doing something? It is his home they are desecrating.* She remembered when once he reprimanded a Roman soldier for treating their belongings with disrespect. It seemed to not matter to him anymore. Why? He stood erect, obviously unafraid and peculiarly undisturbed by their actions. *What did he know that she didn't?*

"She has to be here!" the man who claimed to be Sarah's father screamed over the banister of the veranda. "Check the stables."

Jerusha rushed beneath the portico toward the kitchen. The cook screamed as the soldiers crashed open the kitchen door. "Which way to the stables?" one of the soldiers yelled. The trembling cook looked at Jerusha as if asking permission, then pointed toward the exit that led to the herb garden.

Jerusha hugged the young girl. "It's all right. You did the right thing."

The horses whinnied in the stable. Jerusha held her breath, closed her eyes, and gripped the cook tighter. She hoped the secret door had been closed tightly. "Oh, please, YHWH, do not let them find Sarah." She let go of the cook and hurried to the stable. Before she reached the entry, she heard one guard holler.

"What is this?"

Had they found the secret passage? As she stepped under the lentil, she stopped and held her breath, then noticed the soldier held a scroll Samuel had copied from the Torah for her father. She smiled and relaxed. He had not found the secret passage but stood in front of the hidden opening in the wall. She must move him away from it before Joshua and Sarah got restless and tried to open it. She snuggled her head against Boaz's nose.

"Help me, Father YHWH."

The man who claimed to be Sarah's father grabbed the parchment from the guard. "It's in Hebrew. Maybe a secret message to Sarah's new family. I have heard how you find new homes outside Jerusalem for orphans, especially girls. Making a profit, no doubt." The taller guard sneered and drew near Jerusha. Her heart pounded in her chest. Surely he could hear it. A shadow passed over her face.

"Get away from my daughter." Jacob stood in the entry, his face red and jaw twitching. "You have searched our home. Now get out!" He stepped back and pointed to the pathway. "All of you." He glared at the two guards." "And take the back gate. Stephen, show them the way."

Chapter 7

That night, Jerusha stood hand in hand with Sarah beside the
back gate and waited for her father to walk them to Paul's sister's
house. After careful thought for Sarah's safety, she had decided to
go. She supposed it would be all right. So much excitement over the
apostle's return to Jerusalem. Many gathered to hear his testimonials
of believers in Yeshua's Way who lived in distant lands, especially the
Gentiles and how they fared.

Maybe Paul, a childhood friend of her father's, would take time
to talk with her about the questions she held in her heart concerning
Effah and Antonius, her sons' troubling behavior, and this loneliness
that unnerved her day and night.

That is the only reason she risked taking Sarah outside the villa.
Under no circumstances would she let this Sarah go with anyone else,
anywhere. She'd learned her lesson well with the last Sarah that came
into her life. Nothing would happen to this Sarah, not if Jerusha had
anything to say about it.

She looked up at the sky. Regulus or Little Prince, the brightest star in the lion constellation, was a comforting reminder of the king's sovereign rule over all the earth. In these troublous times when peace eluded her, it helped to keep her eyes above where Stephen, her beloved guardian who had been stoned, had seen Yeshua standing at the right hand of Father YHWH on his throne. Her heart quieted at the thought of her mother, Stephen, Timon, and little Sarah, who had called her Ima, walking together in heaven's kingdom, their suffering over. No wonder Yeshua taught his disciples to pray, "Your kingdom come on earth as it is in heaven." Was that even possible? Weary and tired of the battle, Jerusha's faith had wavered in these last months.

The stars twinkled against the black sky like sparkling diamonds, so beautiful. She breathed in the cool, dry air and released it from deep in her lungs, an exercise she used often lately to relieve stress in her shoulders. Yeshua had told his disciples that if they had seen him, they had seen the Father.

How she longed for her sons to see Yeshua's Father. They had never seen the love in Yeshua's eyes when he walked on earth or laughed with him as he played with the children like she had the privilege of doing as a young girl.

And Sarah. How could she explain a father's love to a girl who had only known a father's abuse and hate? She released Sarah's hand and wrapped her arm around her shoulder and pulled her close as she thought, *Yeshua, you said you are the way to the Father. Show Sarah and my sons the Father.* The breeze blew across her cheek. Mother had always said it was the touch of angel wings. No doubt, Mother walked and talked with angels in Yeshua's kingdom now. She closed her eyes.

Jerusha. It was Yeshua's voice. She knew it well. She stopped breathing for a second and waited. *I have not left them orphans. Neither have I left you an orphan.*

"Orphan. Orphan. Orphan." A different voice. An eerie voice echoed in her thoughts. Tears threatened to overflow. *He has forsaken you,* the voice went on. Jerusha tended to agree with this voice. She felt forsaken. Abandoned. Left to work out things in her own power. Even when she cried out to Father YHWH, He seemed distant, unconcerned. She had a hard time believing what John, Yeshua's beloved apostle, said about being one with the Father and how he said,

*I will come to your sons, as I have come to you . . . that where I am, they
will be also.*

She sighed. At one time, her spirit had been drawn away to
his throne—one moment in her marriage bed on earth. The next
moment sitting on Father YHWH's lap. The light in his face was so
glorious she could not look upon him. She heard the sound of his
voice like thunder, and yet it landed so gently on her ears. He'd said,
"Do not be afraid to receive Timon as your husband. He is my gift to
you." The experience pierced the wall around her heart with YHWH's
love and enabled her to surrender to YHWH's perfect plan in her
marriage bed.

Another time, she had watched Yeshua play with her as a child
in a meadow of colorful flowers and butterflies and call her his
little butterfly. After Timon's death, the veil between earth and his
kingdom was torn back so she had seen Timon and Sarah in the same
colorful meadow where Timon mouthed the word, "Later," like he had
done so many times while on earth. Afterward, she found herself alone
in the garden with a knowing peace that all was well.

That was years ago. This was now. She had experienced no such
encounters for a long time, only a deep-seated sense of loneliness and
abandonment.

"Look, Jerusha. I see Regulus. Can you see it?" Sarah's words jarred
Jerusha from her musings. She looked at Sarah, who pointed to the
sky and giggled in joyful glee. "I found it." The young girl's dimpled
smile shown in the moonlight and was even more of a glorious sight to
Jerusha than the shining star. If only Sarah understood how beautiful
she looked to Father YHWH.

Jacob came out of the shadows and knelt beside Sarah. "I see
Jerusha has taught you about Regulus." Jerusha grinned at his
tenderness with the girl as he continued to discuss the constellation,
then added, "When Jerusha was little, she tried so hard to count the
stars. It's impossible." He tapped Sarah on the nose. "That, my little
stargazer, is how many thoughts Father YHWH has toward you—too
many to count. He even sings love songs over you while you sleep."

"Sarah giggled. "I would like to hear those songs sometime." She
got serious. "But did he see me at Herod's palace when all those bad
things happened to me? Did he sing over me then?" She stopped and

looked down in silence for a moment, then raised her head. "I think he forgot about me."

Jacob swooped her up in his arms and hugged her tight against his chest. "Father YHWH did not forget you. Why do you think Jerusha found you and took you out of that horrible palace?"

Sarah lifted her head. "I do not know." She squirmed in his arms. "Put me down." He placed her sandaled feet on the ground, and she ran to Jerusha and looked up. "Why did you come for me?"

"Because a loving Father above has been watching you and he sent me to help."

"I do not understand why he loves me."

"He has always loved you. He created you and has plans for your life."

"I do not love him.

"That does not change his love for you."

"I will have to think about that." Sarah crossed her arms and pouted beneath the jujube tree. Jerusha looked at her father and grimaced. How could she show her the Father, if Sarah had never seen Yeshua in the flesh like she had when she was a child? Many of the other young girls Jerusha rescued had found the faith to receive Yeshua as YHWH's son and enter his kingdom—a miracle for sure. It was quite a mystery to her why anyone would come to believe in an invisible Father with an invisible kingdom.

"I hope Antonius will be there tonight." Joshua came running up the path waving his sword, then stopped and stared at Sarah who stood under the jujube tree. "Sarah, stop pouting. This is the day the Lord has made. Rejoice and be glad in it."

Jerusha chuckled. Maybe her teachings had made more of an impact on her sons than she had thought. Almost every day upon arising, she had spoken that psalm to them. At least Joshua remembered. Chaya followed close behind him along with Hannah and Stephen.

"We must split up into smaller groups so as not to bring attention to ourselves as we walk the streets." Jacob's authoritative demeanor made everyone somber. "Stephen and Joshua, you walk with Hannah and Chaya. Sarah, you go with me and Jerusha. Moses and Miriam will meet us there."

"Father, I want to walk with Sarah. Antonius has taught me well how to defend myself, and I have my sword with me. She might need my help."

"And I want to walk with Hannah by myself," Stephen protested. "Can't Chaya and Joshua go with you and Mother?"

Jacob lifted his right brow and looked at Jerusha. She shrugged. Since when did Joshua get so enamored with Sarah? And Stephen with Hannah?

"I have made my decision. You go with those I have put you with. Stephen and Joshua, it is not proper for a boy and girl to be left alone together."

Joshua blushed. "I-I-I did not mean . . ."

"I know, Joshua. You care about those who need protection and want to be Yeshua's warrior."

Jerusha shook her head in disapproval, then out of the corner of her eye, she noticed Stephen drop his head and shuffle his feet. Hannah, who stood next to him, looked at her toes. Maybe she should talk to Stephen about their relationship. They are old enough to marry. Or maybe it would be better if Father did that. At times like this, Jerusha missed her husband. She had no idea how to talk to a boy about manly things and marriage.

"Where is Samuel?" She glanced around at each face in the group. Everyone avoided her eyes. "Has he not come back from visiting with the Essenes?"

"He came in through the back entrance, grabbed the scroll he'd copied that was in the stable and left again." Stephen hardly looked at Jerusha as he spoke. "He left with a man dressed in a white robe." Stephen continued, his head down. "I think it was the man he argued with in the synagogue, the Essene," He then lifted his chin and said, "Do not worry, Ima. The Essenes will not persuade Samuel to follow their teaching."

"I am not as sure as you, Stephen."

"I know you are worried, but Antonius has been talking to him as well."

Jerusha rolled her eyes. Everyone, including her father, admired Antonius, seemed to think he had the answers to everything.

"Did I hear my name?" Antonius climbed the terraced steps beneath the olive trees and emerged out of the shadows into the lamplight and grasped her father's forearm in greeting. His nearness to Jerusha took her breath away. The fragrance on his cloak permeated the air, mixed with the burning olive oil from the lamps, and overpowered her father's frankincense. His deep blue eyes lingered momentarily on Jerusha before greeting Stephen and Chaya with a holy kiss on their cheeks. The wind blew his shoulder-length hair, and Jerusha noticed for the first time a scar on his forehead. He wore a regal embroidered cloak over a gold embossed purple tunic, not his usual Roman toga and breastplate. She eyed the embroidered symbols. They meant nothing to her. She lifted her eyes from the cloak and felt a familiar, yet uncanny blush rising up her neck as his eyes fell again on her. He leaned in to give the kiss of greeting, and the brush of his lips on each cheek sent a tingle up her spine.

"Shalom." She spoke the expected peace greeting even though a stormed raged inside. She looked away. What was Antonius thinking? She hoped he had not interpreted her behavior as a harlot's lust. If he knew about her past, he might be so inclined. Like the sun creeping over the horizon and lighting the new day, an unsettling knowing arose in Jerusha's thoughts that she loved Antonius.

"Antonius, you look like a king," Joshua spoke the words everyone else must have been thinking, including Jerusha. "Why are you dressed like that?"

"The colors and symbols on this cloak belong to my tribe. I am leaving tonight for my homeland."

Jerusha's heart skipped a beat. *How could Antonius be leaving?* Somehow, she thought he would always be there, protecting, teasing, and loving her. Yes. She knew he loved her. *Why had she waited so long to respond? Now it may be too late.*

"Antonius you cannot leave now." She pointed to Jacob. "My father is in danger. We all are in danger." She swooped her arms out in a circle and dropped them at her side. "You promised to protect us." Jerusha's eyes blurred with tears. Her voice trembled.

"No!" Joshua ran and clung to Antonious. "I need you. Who will teach me to defend myself?" He struggled to control his voice and sound like a grown man. He looked up at Antonius. "Why?"

Antonious looked behind him and motioned to someone, who stood in the shadows. A beautiful young girl about Samuel's age— maybe twenty years old, stepped into the light. Her beauty took Jerusha's breath away.

Chapter 8

Jerusha stared at the woman. Golden threads interwoven into the reddish-blond braid that hung over the girl's shoulder glistened in the moonlight. Wispy curls lay over a silver headband around her forehead. She recognized the emblems embossed on the headband to be the same ones embroidered on Antonius's cloak. They also ran along the edges of the girl's royal blue hooded cloak tied around her shoulders with a silver cord that covered a shimmering silk tunic. The hood's folds fell around an oval face with light-colored blemish-free skin that accentuated deep blue eyes. The most beautiful creature Jerusha had ever seen! Almost more beautiful than her mother, who she admired and wanted to look like all her life.

Jerusha looked down at her own worn cloak and yellowed tunic. During these past years since Timon had died, she had not taken care of herself. It's a wonder Antonius wanted anything to do with her. Maybe what Father interpreted as love was only pity. This beautiful specimen standing before her put her to shame. She glanced at

Father, then Antonius, who locked eyes with her. An embarrassed blush arose again in her face. This time it was as much about how she looked. She desired to please him, run to him, beg him not to go. If only she had listened to her heart before this and given him a reason to stay, to not go away with this beautiful young girl. She stared for a moment. His eyes glistened with tears. They almost seemed tormented, confused.

"This is Brigid, my daughter. I thought she was killed by the Romans when I was captured." He took a step closer to Jerusha. She kept her eyes on him. No one else mattered. Not Father. Not the beautiful woman. Only him. He took her hands, kissed them and let his lips linger there, then looked up into her eyes. "Jerusha, I love you." He hesitated. "But she says my wife is alive. She awaits my return. Rome has released me to go to my homeland." His eyes never left Jerusha's. She froze. How could he do this to her—lead her to believe he loved her—when all along he had a wife? It took ten years, but she played right into his trap. It was all a game. And just when he knew he had her love, he leaves? She jerked her hands away. "I am sorry, Jerusha. I did not mean to hurt you. I thought they were dead."

The old protective wall began to harden around her heart again, like it did when she was an abused little girl, vowing no one would hurt her like that again. She struck at Antonius, like a viper, hoping the poison hit his heart.

"What makes you think you hurt me? I would never pledge my love to the likes of you, even in all your fancy clothes. Timon is the only man I will ever love." Her throat constricted. Her chin quivered. Every muscle in her body tensed. If she relaxed, even a little, she would crumple to the ground and turn into a crying mess.

"Jerusha," Antonius said as reached for her hand. She jerked it away and slapped his cheek. He touched his face and stared, his eyes never leaving hers.

"I deserved that." He spoke softly. A tear fell from his watery rim. Why would the sting of a woman's hand hurt this battle-hardened soldier? He cocked his head slightly and continued staring, his brows scrunched as to figure out what she desired. His puzzled expression tore at Jerusha. She needed strength to resist the urge to embrace

Antonius, tell him she loved him, that she was sorry she struck him. She moved closer to Father and grabbed his hand.

Antonius looked at Jacob.

"I am sorry. I never meant to hurt her."

Jacob looked puzzled. "Are you sure she lives? I saw what happened with my own eyes."

"I wondered, the same as you. It seems impossible. I do not know what else to do but return and see for myself."

He glanced back at Jerusha, then Stephen and Joshua, who had his sword drawn and glared at the soldier. Antonius knelt before him. "I am sorry, little man, that I have to leave. I know Yeshua will use you. You will be a great warrior." Joshua dropped his sword and fell against Antonius's shoulder. He swooped him up and stood before Jacob. "I want to thank you again for preventing me from taking my own life. When I pledged my protection to you and yours, I had no idea my family lived. I ask to be released from that vow, so I can go to my own family.

Jacob grasped Antonius's shoulders. "You are like a brother. Of course, I release you. Go with my blessings."

They clutched each other's forearms. "YHWH's blessings on you, Jacob. I put you in His hands. He is your greatest protection."

Jerusha squeezed her eyes shut and gritted her teeth. This cannot be happening.

Jacob released his grip. "Are you coming to the meeting tonight?"

"If you would allow me, this one last time, I would like to see you and Jerusha safely to the meeting and back home." He walked with her father to the path's edge. Another man climbed the terraced steps and greeted them, and Antonius introduced him. "This is Patrick. He accompanied Brigid on her journey here." Jacob nodded.

The man stood as tall as Antonius; his muscular arms and broad shoulders similar to his. His blond hair was wavy and long to his shoulders. He dressed simpler than Antonius. His hand rested on his sword sheathed in an ornate scabbard. The leather band tied around his forehead had the same symbols as Antonius's. A leather belt around his midsection held an axe and mallet.

"I owe you for saving Rory's life." Patrick bowed. "I am at your service."

"Rory?" Jacob's brows raised.

"My Gaelic name," Antonius said looking embarrassed. "I am a prince. This man is my bodyguard who'd vowed to protect my family."

Jerusha sucked in her breath. So he did have a royal bloodline. No wonder he commanded everyone around like a king. "It would be better, Patrick, if you called me by my Roman name here."

"As you wish," Patrick bowed again.

"Father, must we call you by Antonius?" You are king now. You need to take your rightful place. Our people need you," Brigid responded as she glared at Jerusha. "It does not matter that you love this woman."

Antonius looked at Jerusha and answered. "My name is Antonius, servant of Yeshua. He is my God and my king. His kingdom is unshakeable. I pledge my love to him." He stepped closer to Jerusha, his manly scent strong and fragrant, a pine smell new to Jerusha. Conflicting emotions swirled in her heart. Should she slap him again? Should she run away? Or, succumb to the strong urge to kiss him? She froze. He took her hands and held them tight. "And I pledge my love to those in his kingdom family." His eyes locked again with Jerusha's. He moved in closer and whispered in her ear. "I will return."

She wanted to pound his chest and scream, *I love you. Do not leave me.*

But how could she do that? His daughter stood beside him. He had a wife. Jerusha leaned her forehead into his chest and savored his nearness this one last time. Even if he returned, he would bring his wife with him. She had lost him forever as a husband. He belonged to another. He loved her as a brother in Yeshua's kingdom family.

A sudden burst of her tears poured into his fancy embroidered cloak. A wind gust blew her radiyd from her head. He laid his large hand on her head and stroked her hair. She felt the warmth of his arms tighten around her waist. Her cheek lay against the soft cloak. "Jerusha, Jerusha, my Jerusha." His words echoed above her sobs. "I am so sorry. May Father YHWH watch over his little butterfly, until I return." Jerusha wanted to linger in his arms, to never let go.

"Come, come, Jerusha, Come," Chaya pulled on her shoulder. Jerusha let go of Antonius and fell into her arms, the sobs erupting again. "Shalom, my child, shalom." She caressed her head.

"Jacob." Jerusha heard Antonius's voice, soft and gentle, yet firm. "Effah does not lie. I checked around with those I know at the fortress, and the priests do conspire to have you killed, with the intention of taking the villa. You must be careful."

"Of course, Antonius. I will be careful. You are a loyal friend. I welcome your companionship this one last night." Jacob looked at Joshua. "Since this is Antonius's last night, you may walk with us. Stephen, you accompany Chaya and Hannah."

Chapter 9

Jerusha walked in silence. The damp night air soaked into her threadbare cloak. She shivered. Why had she not taken better care of herself? These last ten years she poured all her energy and love into her sons and father, except when there was a troubled young girl that needed to be rescued. She hugged Sarah and stared at her father's back as he walked with Joshua ahead. Antonius guarded behind with Patrick. Brigid walked alongside Jerusha and Sarah, the women between the men.

"My father's torn between you and my mother," Brigid spoke with a lilt, something foreign to Jerusha. Her voice sounded somewhat like Antonius's. "I heard him speak to Patrick about it."

"I do not want to speak of this with you." Jerusha sounded more brusk than she intended. The entourage descended a steep hill and entered the narrow maze of paths in the lower city. Joshua slashed with his sword at wild dogs in a dark corner that approached with bared teeth. Jerusha smiled at her son's protective nature. Antonius taught him well. Joshua would miss his times with Antonius. She thought everyone would miss him. Why had she not seen, until now, the good he had done with her sons? They all loved and admired him.

An eerie sound echoed in the distance and disrupted her thoughts. Jerusha's hair raised on her arms, and a dark shadow passed over her face. She looked up. A thick cloud had drifted over the moon, blocking its light.

Without warning, Antonius rushed past, grabbed her father, and pulled him aside. At the same instant, Patrick yanked her into an alcove and then shoved a stranger face down on the dirt path. Sarah screamed and rushed to Jerusha's side and hid in the shadows with Brigid, their backs against the rough limestone. No lamplight in the window signaled that the owner was not at home.

Jerusha felt Sarah's trembling fingers against her arm and embraced her in a tight hug, With the young girl's cheek resting against her chest, she peered into the blackness and looked for Antonius and Father. Sarah pressed her face into Jerusha's cloak, then raised her head.

"They're after me."

Jerusha put her finger to her lips, and Sarah buried her head again, her breath warming Jerusha's cloak. A dark silhouette moved across the wall. A spindly figure. Neither father nor Antonius. She held her breath.

Within seconds the man swooshed out of the shadows and smacked Patrick with his fist and loosened Patrick's grip. The man he had pinned down wiggled free and took off running into the darkness. The other two intruders followed. Joshua, sword in hand, started to run after them. With two quick steps, Patrick caught him and jerked him around.

"Let them go, little warrior. Your grandfather and the others are safe."

"Father, are you all right? Jerusha spoke into the darkness, her racing heart thumping in her ears.

"Thanks to these two." He clasped Antonius by the shoulders. "If you had not been with us, I might be dead. My dear friend, I will miss you."

Her father's chuckle annoyed Jerusha. "How can you be so joyful at a time like this? What will happen to us when Antonius leaves?"

"We must trust Father YHWH," said Antonius.

"Of course," Jerusha spoke with sarcasm in her tone. Anger burned in her veins. "He took such good care of Timon and Sarah."

Hidden animosity surfaced. "And mother. Why did she have to die? I think YHWH does not care if we suffer. He seems to add one trial upon another."

"Jerusha!" Sarah's eyes widened. "You sound like me."

Jerusha squeezed her eyes shut and wiped a lone tear with her fist. "I am sorry, Sarah. In these past months, loneliness overwhelms me at times, and I feel hopeless. This is one of those times. I have not always been this way."

"You have me." Sarah hugged Jerusha's waist tight and buried her face in her robe, then looked up. "I will never leave you."

"I felt the same way. Alone, abandoned, angry," Brigid spoke, then hesitated and turned toward Antonius. "When I thought I lost my father. . ." Her voice trilled with that unusual lilt making it hard to understand. "I am grateful that the gods helped me find him."

"It was not the gods." Antonius stepped toward Brigid, then stopped. "It was the one and only true God, YHWH, who led you to us." Jerusha heard the pain in Antonius's voice. "I am sorry you felt abandoned. If I only had known you were alive, I would have searched for you." Brigid ran from the shadows into his arms.

Jacob drew Sarah and Jerusha close. How could she be angry that Brigid found her father? She remembered the longing she had for her father while in slavery at Herod's palace with her mother. She never gave up believing he was alive and would find her one day. Little did she know that her Hebrew father would turn out to be a Roman soldier and have to leave again at Yeshua's bidding and lead Gentile soldiers into His kingdom, Antonius being one of them.

"Should we be going before the scoundrels return?" Patrick's tone carried more than a respect for Antonius, his King. He loved him.

Everyone who knew him loved him. She knew that now. She loved him, too. Not as a brother. She loved him as a man she desired to marry. She dropped her arms at her sides. It was too late.

***

The music and laughter from Paul's sister's house drifted into the streets. Jerusha shook her head at the merriment. Many had suffered separation from family, endured beatings, and been thrown in prison, all because they loved Yeshua. These brethren had an endurance that Jerusha coveted.

In the last months, a heavy fog hung over her thoughts and crowded out the simple joy she walked in after Timon had died. She had rejoiced then, like James, Yeshua's brother, had been said to do. "Count it all joy when you meet various trials. The testing of your faith produces endurance."

Something happened between then and now, maybe too many disappointments with her sons. She felt disconnected from these joyful ones, who danced and celebrated, in spite of their losses. She felt disconnected from Father YHWH and his love. She took a deep breath and stepped over the threshold into a crowded lamp-lit courtyard shared by three households.

"Shalom," Paul's sister said as she greeted each visitor with a kiss. Women brought platters of roasted lamb and baked bread from their respective kitchens to a large table spread with platters of figs, grapes, and pomegranates. Jerusha avoided the joyful chatter, made her way to a dark corner, and slumped to the floor. Hot lentil stew bubbled in a cauldron that hung over burning donkey dung. After the recent drought, it was difficult to find firewood. Children danced the circle dance while others played timbrels and flutes.

Sarah gawked at the dancing girls and moseyed over to Jerusha and peered around the room. "Will I be safe here?"

Jerusha looked at Antonius and Patrick. "As long as they are with us, you are safe."

"Will you teach me that dance?" the little one begged with her eyes.

"Not tonight. Maybe another day. Ask Chaya." Jerusha grimaced when Sarah's chin dropped.

Jerusha kept her eyes on Antonius as her father introduced Paul. Quite a contrast in stature and looks. Paul, the smaller man with scraggly hair, large eyes, and eyebrows that met together over a long nose that appeared hideous and weak compared to Antonius's tall, muscular build with wavy shoulder-length blond hair, his blue eyes perfectly framed with thick brows—a handsome, strong specimen of a man. Somehow she ignored these traits, until now. A flush rose in Jerusha's face. Only a harlot admires the physical traits of a man whose wife awaits his return.

Brigid laughed and drew Jerusha's attention to Joshua's antics with Paul's sister's son. Both boys entertained with sword fights followed by victory chants. The young woman's dimpled smile radiated. Her blond braid shone in the lamplight.

Jerusha surmised that Antonius's wife must be beautiful. She did not think she could stand it if Antonius returned with her by his side. She would rather he did not come back at all. She would find a way to take care of herself and her family. She did not need the likes of him.

"Effah," Antonius called and broke away from his conversation with Paul and turned toward the entry. "Shalom, my friend. Come, I want you to meet someone." Antonius motioned him to join his conversation with Paul.

"What is he doing here?" Jerusha mumbled.

Effah reluctantly moved in Antonius's direction, his eyes searching the room.

"Paul, this is the man who helped with Sarah's escape."

Distracted and unimpressed with Paul, Effah paid no attention. He found Jerusha instead. "Excuse me, I must talk to Jerusha."

She glared at the stout muscular man, who captured her heart as an innocent eight-year-old, then destroyed her trust of all men, until Timon. With Antonius leaving, the last thing she wanted was to see or talk with Effah. Follower of the Way, or not, she would never trust him. He may have Antonius fooled. But not her.

She looked down at her sandaled feet and hoped Effah would get the message.

Since she forgot to dip her dusty toes in the wash basin before sitting, she pretended to be busy and wiped them with the sleeve of her cloak. She would never think of doing that if she wore Brigid's fancy cloak. For the first time since being an abused child, she felt less. She bent her knees up under the same cloak she had worn for ten years.

A man's sandaled feet stood at its edges. She glanced up. Effah offered a hand.

Flustered, she dropped her head and hugged her knees.

"Go away," she mumbled. "I will not talk to the likes of you."

"Jerusha, it is urgent."

"Humph. I do not believe you. I am not a child any longer who falls for your tricks." She would not look up. She smelled that unusual pine scent and saw the edge of Antonius's fancy robe. Not again. An unexpected intrusion out of nowhere. How does he do it?

"She does not want your company, Effah." Antonius's display of kingly protection perturbed her. He had no right. Just hours ago, he stomped on her love. The whole scene almost made her laugh. She kept her head down and hoped they would both go away. "I do not know what you have done," Antonius said hesitantly, "to earn such distrust from a woman as caring as Jerusha. I do not need to know. Step away from her. Or I will remove you from this meeting." Jerusha's emotions fluctuated between wanting to show her gratitude with a kiss and screaming her displeasure that Antonius thought she could not take care of herself.

"But Antonius, it is urgent that I speak to her. Sarah's life depends on it."

"What?" Her head jerked up and she tried to stand. Antonius lifted her to her feet. His eyes caught hers and lingered for a second. His brow crinkled, and he looked at Effah.

"We were attacked tonight." Antonius placed his hand on Jerusha's shoulder. "I thought the men were after Jacob. Maybe it was Sarah they wanted."

Jerusha looked up. "Sarah was afraid. Thought they might be after her."

Antonius's jaw tightened. "Nothing can happen to that girl."

"At least we agree on that." Jerusha scanned the room. "Where is she? I do not see her. Did Chaya arrive with Stephen? She was to teach Sarah the circle dance."

Jerusha bobbed back and forth between the gatherers, most taller than her until she broke through the crowd and stood beside her father, the children circled to the right in front of them—chanting crossover, dip, crossover, dip—arms on each other's shoulders. She grasped his arm, "Father, I cannot find Sarah or Chaya."

Chapter 10

Jerusha fumbled with the key in the shadows. "Father hold the lamp closer. I cannot see." She jiggled the lock and dropped the key. "Sarah has to be here." She wanted to think Sarah was all right. Her heart told her otherwise. "Chaya must have taken her home for some reason." She did not believe her own words, only hoped. She knelt and felt around in the dust. "It is not only because she has not told me what she is doing. She knows I worry."

"We will find her." Antonius dropped the lost key in her hand. "The others are praying. Effah is searching for them at Herod's palace."

"That man infuriates me with his pretentious conversion. His warning came a little late. How convenient for him." Her fingers shook. "If we do not find her, I will never forgive myself for taking her out tonight. It was so selfish of me. Why? Why? Why did I do such a foolish thing?" She mumbled and threw open the gate. "Chaya! Sarah! Are you here?" She rushed to the fountain and splashed its cool waters over her face. "Think, Jerusha, think." She snuggled her face in the linen cloth on the bench and dried her hands. "Where would she be?" She listened for footsteps. "Chaya! Sarah!" She yelled again. Their names echoed in the empty halls.

"This cannot be happening." She grasped her chest and wobbled back and forth. Black spots blurred her vision. "Not another Sarah," she said as her knees crumpled, down, down, down. She felt cold tiles on her cheek, then blackness.

Someone held her upper body close. The pine fragrance smelled so good. "Antonius?" She snuggled her nose in his cloak. "I love you." Her legs hung over his arm and flopped as he walked. Her head bounced against his chest as he bounded up the stairs. The door slammed against the wall.

"In here, Antonius."

She breathed a mixed odor of pine and frankincense. "Father?" The soft fleece cover felt so warm as his strong arms released her on the mittah. She rolled on her side. "Timon?"

"No, Jerusha, it is Antonius who carried you." Her father's voice sounded soft, soothing. "I love him." She moaned. "So sleepy." Her words slurred.

"She hit her head hard. But I think she will be all right. We must find Sarah before she wakes up." Father's words sounded so far away. So did the creaking door. She lifted heavy eyelids. Shadows flickered on the wall. Several tears rolled from her face and dropped onto the sheepskin. His last words floated into her consciousness. *Find Sarah.* Her eyes popped open. "Sarah!" She tried to sit up, then grabbed her head. "Ohhh, ooow," she moaned and eased back down. "What happened?" The door creaked again. She lifted her head and rose up on her elbows.

"Chaya, you're home. Where is Sarah?" Unable to hold herself up, she slid down on the soft fleece and watched Timon's mother carry a bowl of water with a towel over her arm.

"Shh, little butterfly. You fell and hurt your head. You must rest. Sarah will be all right." She sat the bowl on the table, shut the door, then dipped a cloth in the water and wrung it out. "The others are looking for her. You are in no condition to be up moving around." The wet cloth touching Jerusha's temple stung at first, then soothed.

Jerusha grabbed Chaya's hand. "Stop! Where is Sarah?"

"YHWH knows. We will trust him to take care of her."

"I am going after her." Jerusha tried to sit up, then fell back on the mittah. "I will never forgive myself if something happens to her. I was more concerned about getting answers from Paul about my problems than about her well-being. How is Joshua taking this?"

"He is missing."

"What?" She tried to sit up again to no avail. "And Stephen?"

"Gone. We think the boys went to look for Sarah, too."

"Has Samuel ever returned?"

"No one has seen him since he took the Torah and left with the Essene."

Jerusha gripped her head between both hands. "It hurts so much." Black spots whirled before her eyes. She fought to stay conscious. "I cannot . . . I must get . . . Sarah," she groaned, "Antonius, do not go." She rolled her head back and forth and moaned "Antonius . . . Sarah" over and over until she slipped into darkness.

***

Hours later Jerusha opened her eyes and listened to Chaya mumbling indistinct sounds to YHWH. The older woman sat next to her on the mittah, her silver braid shining in the lamplight. Jerusha's head throbbed. Curious, she touched the cloth that lay over the egg-sized bump above her temple and scrunched her brow.

"Oww." She rose up and stared around the room. Hot coals burned in the brazier. Her cloak had been removed and hung on a peg. She felt warm, and her hair was sweaty on her neck.

"Why are you in my room praying?"

"You do not remember what happened?"

"I am not sure."

"Maybe it is better you do not remember right now."

"What do you mean? What are you not telling me? Why do I have a horrible bump on my head? Are father and the boys alright?" Did they get hurt like me? What happened?" She stared at the orange coals while Chaya continued to pray. "Sarah. Is Sarah alright?"

"Are you beginning to remember?"

"Remember what?"

Chaya stopped praying and patted Jerusha's hand. "You have always been a woman of many questions. This time you have a good reason. You crumpled to the tiles and hit your head."

"Why?"

Chaya's eyes became serious. "You were so upset about Sarah that you fainted."

"I remember now. We could not find her. Or you. Where were you?" Jerusha sat up and leaned against the bunched up lambskin Chaya placed behind her back.

"I saw Joshua slip outside at Paul's sister's house." Chaya took a breath and continued. "I followed and found him and Sarah standing in the street counting stars. Before the children saw me, someone came from behind, covered my mouth, and dragged me away. Two others shoved Joshua aside and snatched Sarah. The last thing I saw before they pulled me around the corner was Joshua running after them, his sword drawn, waving in the wind. A neighbor heard the scuffle and found me outside his house gagged and tied lying in a dark alcove. By that time, you had left Paul's sister's house to find us. The gathering prayed for her safety. Stephen and Hannah walked me home. I am sorry, Jerusha."

"It is not your fault. I should not have taken her. And if I would have taught her the circle dance, she might not have gone outside with Joshua. Oh, Chaya, I lost one Sarah. Do I have to lose another one because of my own foolishness?"

The door flew open. Joshua threw his sword on the floor, knelt beside the mittah, and buried his face in the fleece cover. Jerusha had never seen him so upset. She stroked his head and listened to muffled cries. After a while, he rubbed red eyes with his fist and hiccupped.

"I followed them. They took Sarah back to Herod's palace." He hiccupped again.

Jerusha clasped her hand over her mouth.

"Then I came here for help. Stephen was the only man here, so I showed him where they took her. By the time we returned to the palace, the guards had the gate locked and would not let us in."

"That is true," Antonius spoke from the doorway. "Sarah is in Herod's palace. Your father and I could not get entrance either."

"It is my fault." Jerusha placed her hands on her lap.

"Could I help?" Brigid stood next to Antonius. "Would they let me in?"

"Why would they let? Jerusha stopped and stared again at her beauty. "Of course, they would let her in, a stranger dressed like royalty. The guards would think she had been summoned." Jerusha looked at Antonius. He scowled.

"It might work. I could give her a map of the palace and a note to give to my contact inside the palace." He spoke slowly, then stopped and waited in silence before continuing. "But I do not like putting my daughter in such danger."

"You would do this for us?" Jerusha cocked her head and looked at Brigid.

"Your father saved my father's life."

"Brigid will not need to do that," Effah spoke from behind Antonius. "I have found her." He maneuvered between Antonius and Brigid and stepped into the lighted room. "She is locked in Antonia Fortress."

"Antonia's Fortress? Is she all right?"

"She is pretty shaken but appears to be all right. You must get her out of the city tonight. If not, she will be sold tomorrow as a sex slave and leave with the trade caravan. The man who came here with the guards and searched your home is not her father. He works with the corrupt, greedy priests who are in bed with Rome."

"You should know about corrupt greedy priests." Jerusha glowered.

"I have a plan to get her out." Effah ignored her tart response.

"My daughter's sleeping room is not the appropriate place for this conversation."

"I am sorry, sir. I tried to stop them, especially him." Hannah stood with Stephen behind the others and pointed to Effah. "He insisted he had news of Sarah, so I let him in. He heard you talking and found his way." Hannah's eyes darted between Stephen and her father. Stephen placed his hand on her shoulder, a protective gesture for sure. His wide eyes shined.

"It was not Hannah's fault, Ima. I told her it would be all right." Stephen stared at Hannah, then back at Jerusha. He seemed enamored with the young girl.

Jacob motioned everyone out the door. "Let us go to the courtyard garden." He glanced over his shoulder. "Jerusha do you feel good enough to join us?"

"Yes, Father." She held the fleece cover over her chest and glared at Effah, "I would not let the likes of him decide what happens to Sarah, even if he did find her. I do not trust him." Antonius looked back and grinned as he shut the door.

"Your little lioness appears to have awakened, Jacob."

Chapter 11

J erusha stopped in father's garden before going to the courtyard. The gate clanged behind her, and she wound her way along the pomegranate-lined path to her father's bench, a safe place to think. Everything was happening too fast. Trusting Effah to rescue Sarah made no sense at all. There had to be a better way.

No one had lit the lamps. The moon, a tiny white sliver, gave little light to her path. She knew her way. She had twirled and danced these paths many days with her eyes closed. When she turned the corner, she gasped and backed up a step.

Antonius knelt at her father's bench wearing the Hebrew garment with tzitzits at its corners. Never had she seen him dressed in this fashion. She wanted to reach out and touch the tassels. She stared at the blue cord and remembered the Torah portion taught by Father. *It shall be a tassel for you to look at and remember all the commandments of the Lord to do them,* not to follow after your own heart and your own eyes, *which you are inclined to whore after.*

She came seeking answers about Effah. Maybe she was the problem. Had she followed after her own heart and her own eyes? Yeshua said to love your enemies, pray for those who persecute you, so that you may be sons of your Father in heaven. She surely did not love Effah. Nor did she have any intentions of praying for him. Humph. She crossed her arms over her chest.

Antonius raised his head and looked into the night sky. She was glad he had his back to her, and she looked up at the twinkling lights, too. YHWH seemed so far away.

"Father, I failed." Antonius's cry echoed her feelings. "I may never forgive myself if something happens to this little one."

His pain added to her own. She needed to escape before he saw her.

"And Jerusha." He spoke her name in a whisper.

She stopped. *Was he talking to her?* She glanced his way. His eyes still looked above.

"I hurt the only woman I have ever loved."

Her? Or was he speaking of his wife?

"If only I'd known my wife was alive. I would have searched for her and maybe not have fallen in love with Jerusha."

Jerusha covered her mouth. She needed to get away, but her feet felt like iron, too heavy to pick up.

"I believed you chose her for me." His voice cracked. "The most fascinating woman I have ever known, and I have to leave her at a most dangerous time; abandon the one I waited for ten years to be mine."

Tears streaked Jerusha's face. She wiped them away. *Antonius, my love.* Her words vibrated in her thoughts, like the love in her heart, silent, unspoken.

"Father YHWH, you knew all along I had a wife waiting. How could I have been so wrong? Give me a chance to redeem myself. Help me rescue Sarah. She does not deserve what they are planning. Then I will leave and go back to my arranged marriage."

Arranged marriage? Jerusha looked over her shoulder again. Antonius started to rise. He must not see her. Her mind swirled. *Arranged marriage? Is there love in an arranged marriage? Timon loved me, and it was an arranged marriage.* She raised her tunic above her ankles. *It does not matter. The woman is his wife.* She swished behind the nearest pomegranate bush, ducked down, and held her breath and waited.

Had he gone? She never knew about that man. He appeared and disappeared on a whim, like a ghost. A song thrush sung in the olive tree overhead, and a wind gust rustled its silver leaves. She listened for the clang of the gate and heard only the night sounds around her, the crickets keeping time with the song thrush and the howl of a wild dog in the distance. After several minutes, she saw two sandaled feet beneath the bush and looked up.

"This is not a good time to be looking for a chrysalis." Antonius towered above and grinned. Shadows flickered across his eyes.

"How long have you been standing there?"

"Long enough to enjoy the beauty of a butterfly hiding in the darkness. "Come, Jerusha, we have another little butterfly to rescue."

"I hope you are referring to Sarah." Jerusha rose up.

"Unless you need to be rescued? I'm at your service." He bowed.

"Oh, Antonius, you can be so infuriating," She stepped out from the bush.

"Infuriating like Effah?" He held her chin and looked deep in her eyes. "I have seen the fear. What has he done, Jerusha, to cause such distrust?"

She pulled away and dropped her chin. "It is none of your business."

He pulled her close and lifted her face. His eyes held hers for a long moment. Her heart pounded inside her chest. Ashamed of what happened with Effah, a warmth spread up her face.

"Tell me, Jerusha."

Flustered, she tried to move away. "Why would I tell you anything?"

He held her tight. "I cannot protect you if you do not tell me what happened."

"You cannot protect me because you are going away." She wrestled against his hold.

"Is what happened with Effah the reason you rescue these young girls? You understand how they feel because you have suffered the same in his hands?"

"Stop!" She crumpled in his arms and buried her face in his chest, the tears flowing in an unhindered whimper. After a while, she lifted her head.

"I-I thought I had forgiven him, she stuttered. I mean, he has a wife too." Anger rose up. "I-I was only a child. He forced me," She trembled. "He took what he wanted, then cast me off like a dirty rag and married the beautiful girl I'd seen him with at the palace." Jerusha reached for her mole.

"Do not cover your mole." He took her hand away. "I like it. It draws attention to your beautiful dimples." He tenderly held her hand between his." "You're shaking." He wrapped his arms around her and held her tight. "I am so sorry, Jerusha. You do not deserve this. Any of this." He stroked her hair. She closed her eyes and breathed in his fragrance. She never wanted to forget this moment. She might never see him again.

"Tell me what happened to the other Sarah."

It had been ten years since she felt safe in a man's arms. She snuggled her head into his chest and opened her heart. "Timon and I loved her as our own daughter. We thought her parents were dead. Then one day they came for her, and I let her go with them. She did not want to go. She only went because I asked her to." Jerusha lifted her head and looked up.

Antonius looked down, the grimace, in his face a sure sign of his concern.

"A short time later, she died in my arms. She gave up her life for her father when she stepped in front of a sword intended for him. If I had kept her with me, she would be alive today. Although it was because of her love for her father that he accepted Yeshua as King. She lives in heaven with him and Timon."

"Jerusha, Jerusha, you have had so much heartache." He lifted her face and bent close, his beard rubbing across her cheek. His lips met hers, and she relaxed in his embrace for a second, then shoved against his chest.

"You are a married man. I cannot do this."

He let her go. "You are right. I overstepped my own boundaries. Forgive me." Their eyes locked. Jerusha saw again his pain.

"There is nothing to forgive. I will only tell you this, this one time. I love you, Antonius." She lifted her cloak with both hands and moved swiftly up the path.

"Jerusha," he called, "please, do not go."

She stopped and glanced back.

"I've seen how Effah looks at you. If it wasn't for the fact we need him to get Sarah back, I would take the privilege of beating that smirk off his face, believer or nonbeliever."

Jerusha's eyes filled with tears. "Are you any different?" She sniffed, "Playing with my emotions, then leaving me for a wife you thought was dead?" She regretted her words immediately.

Antonius's eyes clouded. "Maybe you're right. I hope one day you can forgive me."

Jerusha's chest tightened. "I-I," She squished her eyes together. The tears came anyway. She resisted the urge to run back into his arms.

"Ima, grandfather's waiting on you." Her youngest son skidded to a stop at the gate, "Antonius, he's looking for you, too."

***

Jerusha hurried down the steep hill. Darkness swallowed her path. She had travelled this way numerous times over the years. Even in this moonless night, the temple glistened as she walked past. Breathless, she ducked into a darkened alcove and waited for temple guards to finish checking the gates. A dog growled at her feet, and she scampered to the next alcove unnoticed.

She questioned the wisdom of her decision to rescue Sarah alone. Her plan depended upon her ability to sneak past the Roman guards when they opened the gate for the women of the night. Her heart thudded in her chest. If necessary, she would pretend to be one of them. That is why she borrowed Brigid's cloak. Brigid promised not to tell Antonius or her own father about her plan.

Jerusha was sure the Roman guards would be too preoccupied gawking at the other women to notice her, even in Brigid's fancy cloak. Once inside, she knew her way to the dungeon where they probably held Sarah. She had gone there, one time, to visit Timon.

Maybe not a great plan, but one she hoped to pull off without help from Antonius or Effah. She failed to protect Sarah. The rescue responsibility fell on her shoulders. She did not need the likes of those two. Jerusha looked in the distance at the foreboding structure built on a rocky hill.

Antonia Fortress. She hated the fortress's name, after Marcus Antonius, Herod's friend. She preferred Antonius's name; it had nothing to do with the Roman garrison where they flogged and imprisoned Timon before taking him to fight in the games in Caesarea.

She stepped out into the street and arched her head back to view the top of the south wall that towered above the temple. Torches lit up the guard houses, a reminder that Roman soldiers watched the coming and going of visitors not only through its own gates but the temple as well. Thankful for the cover of the new moon, she started up the steep incline that led to the west wall built on a cliff overlooking the Tyropoeon Valley.

She edged along the wall that lined the pathway, heart thumping like a drum in her chest. The smell of some dead dog's rotting carcass wafted in the night air and almost made her gag. She assumed it was a dog and not a person. In these perilous times, one could not be sure. She stared at the city below as she gathered her cloak around her shivering body and tucked her dark curls inside the royal blue hood. Scattered lights twinkled in the lower city. Campfires of pilgrims coming for Shavuot spotted the blackness on the hillside outside the wall. Total darkness over the valley prevented the sight of the accumulated debris piled in the ditches. What had happened to the holy city? It becomes more corrupt and violent with each passing day. Grandfather had said he would come back when the time was right. No one knew he was alive, and it needed to remain that way for now, at least for his safety. She missed him and remembered well the day Timon removed his barely breathing body from the cross. The Romans and the priests thought he was dead. It tore at her heart when he left secretly to prepare a place in Perea. He always said YHWH's ways are not our ways. They are better. How can this be better? The time would come when her family would meet him in Perea. How much longer?

She sighed, lifted her cloak above her sandaled feet, and took a few more steps up the steep incline. A rock tumbled down the stone path behind and startled her. She wondered if her foot knocked it loose? Or if someone followed? Not used to this steep of a climb, she wanted to stop and catch her breath. She glanced back over her shoulder, saw nothing in the darkness, then urged herself to keep going.

The hair stood on her arms. An eerie chant echoed across the valley. In between indistinct syllables, Jerusha heard, "Orphan curse. Orphan curse. Orphan curse." A loud evil laugh cackled, and then silence ensued. A cool breeze whipped around Jerusha's face. She hoped it was the angels' wings mother had talked about before she died. She remembered the old woman at Herod's palace. The creepy witch said Sarah was cursed. Jerusha leaned over the wall and looked again into the blackness from where the eerie sounds had come.

At that moment, someone smothered her mouth with his hand and jerked her body in close range. Their cloak's tassels whipped in the wind against her leg. A Hebrew.

"Don't scream and I will let you go."

Effah?

Chapter 12

Jerusha nodded and Effah released her mouth. Old memories flooded her mind. She stomped on his foot and swung her elbow into his gut.

"That was not necessary." He groaned and released his grip.

She whirled around and kicked his shins, then started running up the hill. She glanced over her shoulder and saw his silhouette following at a methodical pace. She stopped at the top and hid beneath an old olive tree, its twisted branches casting ugly finger-like shadows at the torch-lit entrance. Jerusha heard women's laughter, and the gate creaked.

"You! Under the tree!" An old toothless soldier yelled and pointed at her. His straggly white hair and pot belly spoke of one whose fighting days had ended long ago. "Get in here!" He waved. His eyes roamed her body. "It would be a shame to lock you out. I saw you hurry away from Effah! He looked at the Hebrew, who had made the climb and now leaned against the stone tower. "Is she with you?"

Jerusha gasped.

Effah chuckled. "I don't think she'll have me," he said and placed his hands on his hips.

"Since when does that matter to you?" The soldier roared with laughter, his belly bouncing with every guffaw.

"She's with me." Antonius grabbed her arm. "Uhh!" Jerusha's eyes widened. He did it again. Came out of nowhere, this time dressed in a Roman toga with gold clasps on the shoulders.

"I will not go with the likes of him." Jerusha struggled against his grip to no avail. "Or him." She pointed to Effah.

"Little lady, you will go where ever the Centurion tells you. He's in charge of this watch."

Jerusha's mouth dropped open. "Centurion?"

Antonius lifted her up. Her legs dangled over his arm, and he squeezed her shoulder against his chest. "You're coming with me." After walking past the gawking soldier, he whispered in her ear. "Brigid told us of your foolish plan."

Jerusha had not seen this part of the fortress. Curious soldiers, who stood beneath a portico, stared and laughed. Marble columns lined the Roman styled cloisters that surrounded a well-manicured garden and a large courtyard.

"Cover your eyes. Never know when a naked soldier may step out of the steaming bath to your right. Maybe one day you'll stop thinking you have to do everything yourself." His jaw tightened. "I only hope you are not killed before you learn that lesson."

Jerusha yanked on her hood and kept her eyes down. "I wanted no part of Effah's plan. I do not trust him." She felt a gentle bounce against her cheek and took a quick glance.

Wide marble steps gleamed in the moonlight beneath Antonius's feet. A soldier, his red plume waving in the breeze, his shiny helmet glimmering in the moonlight, saluted Antonius and opened an elaborately carved cedar door embossed with a golden eagle.

"Do not bother us," Antonius commanded and carried her under the lintel into a large room furnished with a Roman bed and several couches around a marble table lavished with food delicacies, some unknown to Jerusha. Orange coals burned in the brazier, and steam rose above a red tiled bath in the corner.

She gawked around. "This is your quarters?"

"My temporary quarters." He placed her on the couch.

Beyond a marble archway on the far side of the room, steps descended into a colorful garden, its winding pathways lighted with lamps. The odor of burning olive oil blended with Antonius's pine fragrance, a reminder that Antonius had another home. "After we free Sarah, will you leave tonight?" Her eyes lingered on his.

"Your father and I discussed it. Sarah leaves with me and Brigid. We will take her to your grandfather in Perea where she will be safe."

"So the two of you decided this without asking me or Sarah what we wanted." Jerusha crossed her arms over her chest.

"Would you prefer she travel with the merchant caravan?" He chuckled. "I am sure the sex trader would be happy to accommodate you."

"Is Effah involved? He's almost as bad. Why was he at the gate? Was he with you? Does he know of this plan?"

"We need him. He knows the way through the deep underground passageway to the temple. It's our only way to get Sarah out safely"— he shook his head—"and you, now." He paced back and forth. "How did you think you would get out of here?" He stopped in front of her. "You could have . . . the soldiers could have . . . never mind. Our time is short. Turn your back."

"Why? So you can sneak out without me?" She stood up and faced him.

He grinned and reached for his scabbard and sword on the gold hook beside Jerusha, then began to unclasp his toga.

"What are you doing?"

"I told you to turn around." He dropped its folds and bared his upper torso, then began to belt the scabbard beneath the toga. Jerusha swooshed around, but not before she saw the numerous scars cut into his chest. She grimaced.

"Ruffle up your hair. Look like I have lain with you." A red blush rose up her face. "They must think you are a lady of the night."

"What lady meets men unattended outside marriage?" She kept her back to him.

"My sentiments exactly. You may turn around now. I am dressed."

Jerusha peeked between fingers as she turned, ready to hide her face.

"Do you have any idea how much danger you were in by coming here alone?" His gruffness startled her.

She swallowed the knot in her throat. "I think I know better than you," she acknowledged, then dropped her head and stood motionless. The old shame resurfaced. A lump of coal sparked in the brazier, the only sound in the room. His shadow passed over her feet.

"I am sorry, Jerusha. Hold your head up." He lifted her chin. "You are more than a lady of the night. You are a queen. Father YHWH revealed your destiny. More power, more authority, than you know. Reigning with him."

"You sound like grandfather."

"It would be my honor to meet him. Let's straighten your hair." He tucked her curls inside the hood, twisting a few around his fingers and letting them fall over her shoulder, then tied the silver cord in a perfect bow under her chin.

"Tonight I escort you, not as a lady of the night, but as royalty, the queen of my country." He wiped the lone tear on her cheek. "No one will dare question me. Besides, this cloak speaks of royalty."

"Shall we?" He extended his arm.

***

Jerusha clung to his arm as they wound down the narrow, dank passageway. He held a torch in his other hand. She held her cloak over her cold sandaled feet and stared into the darkness. A shiver ran up her spine. It reminded her of the stairway in Herod's palace. He placed the torch in a holder, reached into his toga, and drew out keys on a ring. She thought she heard a slight whimper.

"Sarah?" Jerusha cupped her eyes and looked between the bars. "Is that you?" She heard metal chains rattle. It was too dark to see.

"Jerusha?" Sarah sounded so weak.

Antonius fumbled with the keys, found the larger one, and started to unlock the cell, but it was not locked. He grabbed the torch, threw open the barred door, and Jerusha rushed inside. Even in the dark shadows, Sarah's face looked swollen and bruised. Her cloak was torn and hung over her shoulder. Antonius helped Jerusha raise her up and unlocked the chains on her legs and wrists.

"I fought them. They would not stop. One after the other, they came. One would hold me down. The others . . ." Sarah clung to Jerusha and sobbed. Antonius clutched them both with one arm. After a while, Sarah stumbled to the corner and felt in the dark. "I closed my eyes and sang our song, Jerusha—the lion song. I tried to be brave. I held onto this. She lifted Jerusha's lion and butterfly pendant that she'd given her in the stairway at Herod's palace. The jewel glittered on her face. "I do not know why they did not see it or try to take it." Sarah's voice grew stronger. "It was a miracle. When I thought I could not take any more, I mustered enough strength to cry out the words on the back as you taught me. You know the words: "Arise, Lord. Let your enemies be scattered. Let all who hate you flee before you." He came, Jerusha. He came. A light appeared. It shone so bright it scared them, and they fled." Sarah grasped Jerusha around the waist. "YHWH loves me. He really loves me. Just like you said." More sobs erupted and soaked Jerusha's cloak. She looked up at Antonius, his face wet with tears. Anger burned in his eyes.

"We must go. Effah waits outside."

"Effah?" Sarah perked up. "That is the man who came after they left and brought me a blanket and food. He said you were coming to get me."

"Are you sure his name was Effah?" Jerusha crinkled her brow.

"Yes, he was the man who helped us escape from Herod's palace."

***

Jerusha and Sarah followed Antonius, who lit the way with the torch. Some prisoners reached through bars and cried out for mercy as they passed. Others moaned in dark corners. She assumed many were followers of the Way. It made Jerusha sick at her stomach. Yeshua's parable rang in her ear: "'When did we see you . . . in prison and visit you?' And the king answered them, 'when you cared for the least of these my little ones, you demonstrate love for me.'" After she got Sarah to safety, she would return with her father to visit these ones.

Sarah whimpered and repeated the words on the pendant. "Arise, Lord. Let your enemies be scattered. Let all who hate you flee before you." Jerusha stopped.

"Do you hear that? Someone is singing a psalm." She sucked in a deep breath. Her racing heart quieted as she listened to the melody. She remembered again what James had taught. "Count it all joy when you meet various trials." Their joy infused her with the strength to keep going. How strange. The prisoner, blessing the free one. Maybe she was not as free as she thought.

"Jerusha, we must hurry." Antonius urged, "Sarah is not safe until we get to your father's villa where he is preparing for our departure. Sarah and I must leave Jerusalem before the sun rises."

"Antonius, Jerusha, this way." Effah's torch lit up the passageway at the end. Antonius let Jerusha and Sarah pass before him. When they reached the end, they followed Effah around the corner and down a spiral stairway.

"Keep your hand on the wall," Effah warned. "Some of the stone steps are crumbling at the edges. It's a long fall to the bottom." A rock broke off by his foot and tumbled down. He moved closer to the wall. "Stay behind me. Antonius will light the path before you."

Jerusha hoped he led them to safety, not into a trap. She had no other choice but to trust him. "Sarah, you walk in front. I'll be right behind you."

"Arise, Lord. Let your enemies be scattered. Let all who hate you flee before you." Sarah's words echoed, a new calmness in her tone that surprised Jerusha.

At the bottom, Effah placed the torch in a holder on the wall and shoved on the wall. A secret door opened slightly. Antonius helped push against it with his shoulder, keeping the torch in his hand. He stepped back and let Sarah and Jerusha slip through. She looked up at Antonius.

"I hope this is not a trap," she whispered softly, not wanting Sarah to hear, then followed the young girl and joined her voice in the declaration, "Arise, Lord. Let your enemies be scattered. Let all who hate you, flee before you."

She squeezed through the opening and stood in a well-lit room, oil lamps burning on all four walls in ornate golden holders, a marble floor beneath her feet. After shoving the door, a little more, Antonius followed, still holding the torch. Effah stood at the far end, a priest beside him.

Jerusha gasped and leaned into Antonius. "I knew this was a trap." Her heart pounded in her chest. She came up behind Sarah, bent near her ear. "Stay close to me and Antonius," she whispered and glared at Effah.

"I know what you're thinking, Jerusha. He's a Yeshua follower, too. We must hurry before the other priests awaken. He knows a secret way out." Effah tried to assure her.

The priest ducked under a low archway and disappeared. Effah motioned for them to follow. Jerusha looked up at Antonius. He nodded, eyes stern, brow furrowed. His obvious concern disturbed Jerusha.

Effah led the way, then Jerusha ducked under with Sarah. Antonius went last. They entered a shadowy tunnel with a high arched ceiling. Antonius stayed close to Jerusha and Sarah, his hand on the hidden sword. Sarah became quiet and kept looking back at Jerusha.

The damp air smelled of cassia, myrrh, and sweet cinnamon, ingredients in the holy anointing oil. If caught in this holy place by the other priests, they would, at the least, be banned from the temple, most likely cast out of the city, and possibly stoned.

"I know that man," Sarah said as she pointed to the priest.

Jerusha stopped and pulled her aside. Effah motioned for the priest to stop. Antonius guarded, his eyes alert.

"How do you know him?"

"Sometimes, he brought me food when I stayed in Herod's palace. He talked of Yeshua's love for me. I should have listened. After today, I know he is right."

"You trust him?"

"He loves Yeshua, Jerusha."

Jerusha looked at the man next to Effah. His eyes. She saw Yeshua in his eyes. How did Effah know such a man?

"We must go," Effah urged.

Jerusha nodded, took Sarah's hand, and followed. Antonius, still alert, stayed close and checked behind as they wound through the tunnel. At last, they stopped at a large cedar door. The priest unlocked the bolt, opened, and glanced around outside.

"It is safe. Hurry. There is little time before daylight." He swung the door wide.

Jerusha and Sarah followed Effah outside. She glanced back.

Antonius stopped by the priest. "May your kindness be rewarded."

"I do it unto the least of these," the priest answered as he patted Antonius's shoulder. "As Yeshua would do."

Antonius grasped his arms. "Stay safe," then turned and caught up with Jerusha, who waited.

"This is where we part." Effah stood before Antonius whose toga flapped in the breeze, he in his Hebrew cloak, the tzitzits dangling at his ankles. Quite a contrasting sight. "Until we meet again, my friend." He looked at Jerusha. "Tell your father to be careful."

Chapter 13

"Your Father waits in the stable." Chaya opened the gate. "Everything is ready for Antonius and Sarah's departure." She hugged Jerusha and took Sarah's hand, leading her up the tiled path. Antonius came from behind and placed his hands on Jerusha's shoulders. The crickets sang their nighttime song.

"I am afraid for father," she whispered and flopped the radiyd over her shoulder. "What will I do? Who will protect us?"

"Trust YHWH."

"Sounds so simple."

"Let go, Jerusha. You cannot fix everything. Not for Sarah. Not for your sons. Not for your father. Not even for yourself."

A foreboding presence settled in her thoughts. She gripped her forehead. "It is no use. Hope only brings disappointment. For ten years I hoped for a father for my sons."

"They have your father."

"For how long? Effah says his life is in danger."

She turned and lay against his chest. "I am afraid, Antonius. Afraid for me, my father, and my sons." Tears coursed down her cheeks. She pushed away from him and ran up the path.

"Go, Antonius." She opened the garden gate, then let it clang behind her. She needed time at Father's bench. She fell to her knees at the pomegranate-engraved wooden seat. "Why, YHWH, why cannot I trust you?" She placed her hands in her lap. "Everything seems so hopeless." Her chest heaved with uncontrollable sobs. When she stopped, she smelled Antonius's pine scent and glanced over her shoulder. The tip of his toga swooshed around the bush at the path's corner. He had been there, watching and listening. Now he was gone.

Jerusha arose. YHWH had not answered. No words in her thoughts. No visions. No songs in her heart. No dance in her feet. She felt only darkness. Even the twinkling stars above brought little comfort. She felt so alone, abandoned even by YHWH. She raised her hands.

"What have I done, that you do not answer?"

She waited, her eyes closed and breathed deeply of the night air. A slight breeze rustled the leaves in the twisted olive branch that hung overhead.

I am in the darkness, too.

"Where?" She turned and looked around. "Where are you?" She walked the garden's familiar path to the vine-covered wall in the back and looked out at the city. "Where are you?" Her words bounced off the rock cliff below. Where are you? are you? are you? "I cannot see you." She shouted. The cliff responded, see you, see you, see you. She turned and slumped to the ground and clutched her knees, her head down.

After a while Yeshua's gentle words broke through. *Blessed are those who have not seen me, and yet believe.* It felt as if he stood right there.

She lifted her head and remembered the story told by her father when she was a child while sitting on the very bench where she had knelt. His animated expression floated into her memory, the flash of joy in his eyes, his upturned smile. She had sat upon his lap and stared intently while he spoke. He said, "A man desperate for help brought his son before Yeshua. '*If you can believe,*' Yeshua had said, '*all things are possible.*'" Her father had lifted her chin. "Jerusha, it only takes enough faith like the size of a mustard seed. In hard times, if your faith wavers, respond like this, and hold on to the small amount of faith that you have and cry out, 'I believe. Help my unbelief.' Yeshua will answer."

She raised her head and looked up "I cannot see you in this darkness, but I come, as my father taught me." She extended her arms. "I lay my family and myself before you. Deliver us, Father YHWH." She swallowed. "I believe." She screamed into the darkness. "Help my unbelief."

She squeezed her eyes shut and waited in the stillness, not moving, barely breathing, a tingling in her hands. The shofar blasted the beginning of the fourth watch and awakened her senses to the battle she faced for Sarah's safety.

She struggled to her feet. She must hurry. Only a short time before the new day started. Telling Sarah goodbye would not be easy. She rushed through the gate and listened to it clang shut as she passed the fountain. She ran through the kitchen, grabbing a fresh loaf of bread for Sarah, then slowed a little and wound through the herb garden maze.

She stopped and took a deep breath. Her eyes fell on a chrysalis hanging on an olive branch. *I am in the darkness, too.* She stared and remembered the once ugly, furry caterpillar emerging out of its dark home, a beautiful, purple butterfly. *A miracle.* She wiped the sweat from her brow and kept moving. Early morning darkness still hovered as she stepped inside the stable and smelled fresh hay and burning olive oil.

She hugged her father briefly, then nuzzled her face against Boaz, who stood in the next stall and whinnied.

"I am glad to see you, too, my old friend, but this bread is not for you." She patted the horse's nose and glanced at Father. He scowled.

"What were you thinking? Going alone to find Sarah."

"I did not trust Effah or his plan." She hated it when her father got upset.

"You are fortunate Brigid told us where you went. You and Sarah could've both been sold." His voice softened a bit.

"I cannot talk of this now, father." She approached Sarah, who fiddled with her fingers and stared at Joshua. "Look what I found." She waved the bread.

Delighted, Sarah took it, tore a piece, and popped it in her mouth. "Mmmm. Bread from heaven."

"I am sorry to interrupt." Chaya held a blue striped garment over her arm. "Sarah needs to change cloaks."

"That is your cloak." Sarah's eyes widened. She tore and popped another piece of bread in her mouth.

"Give me that old thing." Chaya removed Sarah's old outer cloak, slipped the new one over her soiled tunic, then stepped back and eyed her. "Just what I thought. It looks better on you."

Jerusha smiled. Along with a new cloak, a new life awaited Sarah, a life with Grandfather, or Yogli, as he wanted to be called when in Jerusalem. A giant of a man, in stature and heart, the perfect guardian. Jerusha longed to go with Sarah to tell Grandfather everything. Seek his wisdom. If she travelled with them, she would have more time with Antonius, too, the man who captured her love.

He leaned against the stable doorway, his eyes fixed on her. If only he did not have a wife. He had packed away his toga and donned the Hebrew cloak with tzitzits, no doubt to fit in with the travelling pilgrims coming to Jerusalem for the Feast of Shavuot. Brigid stood next to her father and tried to hide her golden hair beneath a radiyd. Even in a simple Hebrew tunic and cloak, she radiated beauty for all to see.

Jerusha covered her mole. Antonius furrowed his brow, and she removed her hand. His reaction was so much like Timon when he was alive. She had grown accustomed to having Antonius around. The same empty ache she felt when Timon died griped her stomach.

She looked away and watched Stephen show Hannah the newborn foal that nursed in the stall next to Boaz. Its mother died giving birth, and Stephen milked the mare after her death and fed the newborn with its mother's milk every thirty minutes, day and night until Antonius brought another mare from the fortress.

Stephen and Hannah helped the foal to stand on wobbly legs, and Antonius moved to the stall, knelt on one knee, and massaged the foal's leg. "This little guy is fortunate to have you, Stephen. You will make a good father one day. I hope to return to see it." He glanced up at Hannah. She covered her blushing cheeks with her hands.

"I will miss you." Stephen's deep voice quivered. "You have taught me well."

Jerusha felt ashamed. Ten years had passed, and she had never taken notice how much Antonius cared for her sons. How self-centered and fearful she had been, her eyes only on wrong choices they made, like Stephen's companionship with the Egyptian, who stirred up trouble and claimed to be a messiah.

She had feared for Stephen's life and was thankful he had not gone with the imposter the day the Romans slaughtered nearly 4,000 of his followers in the desert. Stephen stayed safe only because Antonius had kept him busy that day in the stable. She wondered, *What would happen after he left?*

"I mean no disrespect, sir, but shouldn't we be leaving?" Patrick finished packing the donkey with supplies and led Antonius' stallion and Brigid's mare toward the stable door.

"Hold on, Patrick." Father moved toward the back wall and pushed on the stone that opened the secret passage, then shoved against it with his shoulder. "We have a less conspicuous way than going through the city gates."

Patrick looked at Antonius, who nodded and took his horse's reigns. Brigid hugged Jerusha, then took her reigns, and followed Patrick, who led the donkey and his own horse. At the entrance of the cave, Brigid stopped and looked back. "We will take good care of Sarah."

Sarah heard and ran to Jerusha. "I do not want to go."

"I don't want her to go, either," Joshua shouted.

"She will be safe with Grandfather." Jerusha needed to stay strong for Joshua's sake. She wanted to scream the same thing; instead, she spoke what she knew to be true. "We can trust Antonius to take care of her." She rubbed Joshua's hair and looked at the only man to win her heart, other than Timon. Tears threatened in both their eyes. She blinked. One rolled out the corner. She wiped it away with her sleeve.

Antonius released the reigns and squatted before Joshua. "Little warrior, be strong and courageous. YHWH goes with you wherever you go. Take care of your mother. She will need a good warrior like you. And remember your real fight is not against flesh and blood, but against principalities and powers in heavenly places."

"I remember, Antonius. I'll put on my armor every day." He patted his head: "Helmet of salvation," hit his chest: "breastplate of righteousness," grasped his waist: "the belt of truth," stomped his foot: "the shoes of peace," held up his arm: "shield of faith," and pulled out his sword: "fight with the word of YHWH."

She never knew how much Antonius taught him about spiritual things.

He stood and put his hands on her shoulders. Their eyes locked for a second.

"Shalom, little butterfly," He kissed her cheek, his lips lingering. "If YHWH wills, I will return." She closed her eyes and savored his touch. Then took a deep breath, and stared into his blue eyes.

"You are bound to another. I cannot wait for you." She spoke softly, so no one but him could hear.

She felt a tug on her cloak and looked away, glad for the interruption. She must stay strong. No tearful outbursts. The lion and butterfly pendant hung around Sarah's neck. Jerusha slipped her hand beneath it and pictured the hardened chrysalis that she had seen on the olive branch in the herb garden.

"No matter how scared you might get, Sarah, remember Father YHWH is working in the darkness, too; just as he does with the butterfly in its chrysalis."

"I want to stay with you." Sarah buried her face in Jerusha's chest.

"I know. I would like that, too." She took a deep breath. "But you will be safer with Grandfather and Antonius."

"Father, we must go. Daylight approaches," Brigid called from the cave's entrance, her horse stomping its hooves.

"Take my hand, and I will walk with you through the dark cave." Jerusha slipped the pendant beneath Sarah's cloak.

Her father lifted the lamp from the hook and showed the travelers the way. After entering and crossing the larger room, Brigid filed into the dark narrow passageway that wound for half a mile to the outside. Antonius followed with his stallion, then Patrick with the donkey.

Sarah whimpered and sniffed, then ducked under the archway with Jerusha and turned into the darkness, Joshua caught up and took her hand.

"Do not be afraid." His words echoed off the stone walls. "Antonius will take care of you."

Jerusha heard Chaya behind, singing the Tehillim. "Lord, even when your path takes me through the valley of deep darkness, fear will never conquer me. You remain close to me and lead me through it all the way. The comfort of your love takes away my fear . . ."

The tunnel lit up a little more. Jerusha figured Stephen and Hannah had ducked under the archway with another lamp. The horses whinnied and snorted, their hoofs clicking on the stone floor.

"Hold the harnesses tight," Father instructed. "Keep them under control, or we will all be trampled.

The limestone seal ground open at the tunnel's end. The horses clomped their displeasure, then quieted. Since the shadowy figures ahead disappeared into the blackness Jerusha surmised Father had rolled it open and stepped outside with the lamp, but why did he leave the others in the dark?

"Father, I cannot see." Brigid sounded calm. "What do I do?"

"Let me get my stallion outside, then I'll help you with the mare." Antonius sounded anxious. "Patrick, hold that donkey steady. Stephen, can you bring your lamp?"

"I can help," Joshua offered.

"You stay with Sarah and the women."

Jerusha heard footsteps and looked back over her shoulder. A light became larger and brighter as it moved toward her.

"Effah! Jerusha gasped. "What? How?"

"It's a trap." Effah bumped against Jerusha and hurried around the women, who stood motionless and gawked, as if they saw a ghost. "Where's Jacob?" His torch came alarmingly close to Sarah's head.

"Outside." Jerusha pointed to the darkness.

"Antonius. Get to Jacob. Quick. Before it's too late." He slid past the back end of Brigid's horse. "Jerusha do not bring Sarah out until we tell you it is safe." His voice thundered against the whinnies.

Chapter 14

Jerusha had no intention of taking orders from Effah. How did he know about the tunnel anyway? And how did he get in their villa?

"Joshua, stay with Sarah and Chaya. Stephen, give me that lamp. You and Hannah stay here." Jerusha's heart raced. She had not heard her father's voice since Brigid complained about the darkness. It was unlike him not to be more considerate of others as to leave the lantern for them inside the cave.

She closed the gap between them in a hurry. Patrick and Brigid parted and gave her room to pass. She ducked under the four-foot opening and stepped outside the cave. Effah knelt over a man's form laying in the tall grass.

"Father?"

"Effah nodded.

"Nooo." She rushed to his side and placed the lamp on the ground. Blood oozed between Effah's fingers where he placed pressure on a wound in her father's gut. She looked around. "Where's Antonius?"

"He's chasing the man who did this."

She glared at Effah. "Get your hands off my father." She slapped at his arm.

"Jerusha. He's dying. Talk to him." When Effah removed his hand, more blood oozed out and covered the ground. "He's been stabbed."

She lifted his head. "Father," she said and stared at his ashen face and pressed her hand on the wound.

He groaned and opened his eyes. "Jerusha, my lioness." He grimaced. "Never forget who you belong to."

"Father, stop talking. We need to get you inside." She longed for Antonius to come back. The clouded sky left a black covering over the landscape. She searched the darkness for his silhouette on horseback and listened for the thud of hooves on the dry ground, then leaned over her father and protected until a dust swirl passed. He tried to sit up and talk. She brought her ear near to his mouth.

"You are wife to Yeshua, Father YHWH's daughter. Promise me." He gasped for breath, placed his hand over hers, and squeezed weakly. "Promise me, Jerusha, that you'll never forget it."

"I promise, Father."

His head dropped to the side. "Nooo!" She hugged his head to her chest. "You cannot be dead. No. No. No." She rocked back and forth, then patted his face. "Wake up. Aba, wake up." She looked to the sky. "YHWH, I believe." She screamed. "I believe. Help my unbelief." She held him and rocked back and forth, the tears pouring onto his face. "I believe. Do not take my Aba."

A shadow moved across her face. She smelled the pine scent and looked up at Antonius.

"Why? Why?" she screamed.

He knelt beside her and placed his cheek next to her father's nose and waited a while. Then felt his neck and put his ear to his chest.

"There is a slight breath and heartbeat. He is still alive." He took her father's girdle and tied it tightly around the wound, then lifted and carried his body back inside the cave.

She turned and faced Effah. "This is your fault. You did this. You and your corrupt father. He hated my father all his life. First he tried to take my mother and me. That failed. Now he tried to take his life. You will never get this villa. Do you hear me? Whether he lives or dies,

I will never allow your father to get this villa. It is my inheritance, and I will find a way to keep it." She stomped away, then turned back. "My sons may not have a natural tribe of Judah bloodline, but they belong to Yeshua. His blood is enough. My father is right. We are royalty. Children of Father YHWH through Yeshua his son. I will never forget it. And you better not either. Follower of the Way. Humph! How could you let this happen?"

"I tried to warn you." Effah lifted his shoulders and hands palms up.

"Yes, just like you warned about Sarah, after it was too late. How convenient. Your warning is never on time. You act like a concerned Yeshua follower, when all the while you conspire against us."

She picked up the lantern and marched to the cave opening and almost laughed. If she had not been so angry at Effah and worried about father, she would have. Five faces peeked out the opening, one on top of the other, then disappeared.

***

The sun peeked over the horizon outside her father's window and left a soft orange glow in the morning clouds. The brazier warmed the room, and Chaya tore clean linen rags to replace the old bloodied ones and stacked them on the table.

Jerusha wiped the beads of sweat from her father's forehead, then grasped his clammy hand between hers. "His fingers are so cold, his face so pale." She tucked his hands beneath the sheepskin cover. "Is he still breathing?" She looked up at Antonius, who stood behind her.

He leaned over, touched his neck, and placed his cheek before his nostril. "Yes."

"Is he going to die?" she grabbed Antonius's hand. "You have knowledge of these things with wounded soldiers." She begged with her eyes.

Antonius pinched his lips together and took a deep breath letting his shoulders drop. "I don't know," Jerusha. "Perhaps you should send Stephen for Paul. He was going to the temple today. I know he would come, if he knew his old friend lingered near death."

"I will go. That way Stephen can stay with father, in case the intruder comes back to finish what he started." She looked at Sarah asleep on a mat. "She is not safe either, especially now that they are aware of the tunnel." She stood and paced back and forth, then stopped at the window. A cool breeze caressed her cheeks. "It is now more important than ever that you get Sarah out of the city." She turned around. "You must leave at once."

"I'm not leaving you."

"We will be all right. I have Stephen and Samuel. I'll send Joshua for Moses and Miriam. They can stay here for a while. Paul and the others will help." She looked at dozing Sarah. "Please. I never thought I could part with her. But I trust you. Take her and go. Your supplies are still in the cave. Have Grandfather send his word when she is safe with him."

"Chaya, will you leave us?" He nodded toward the door.

"No! Do not leave this room." Jerusha clutched her shaking hands.

"Then I will say what I have to say in front of her." Antonius moved around the mittah toward the window. Jerusha scooted along the wall. He caught her arm, then shook her by the shoulders.

"You cannot do everything yourself. Do you hear me? Your life may be in danger, too. Not just your father. Go nowhere without one of your sons with you. Do you understand?" He stared into her eyes for the longest moment. "I can't lose you." He brushed a kiss across her cheek, then released her. "Chaya, bring Sarah to the cave. We leave immediately."

Jerusha watched him cross the room, stop at her father's bed for a second, then look back, his eyes begging. "Promise me. Do not go anywhere without one of your sons with you." A brazier coal popped. Jerusha blinked back tears.

"I promise." She nodded and Antonius walked out, his pine scent lingering.

"Sarah, wake up." Chaya jiggled the young girl's shoulders. "You are leaving."

"Huh?" Sarah sat up and rubbed her eyes. "What about him?" she pointed to Jacob.

"Leave him to Jerusha. Come along." She pulled on her arm. "Be up with ya. Jerusha is leaving for the temple to find Paul."

Sarah ran to Jerusha and held her tight. "I do not want to go."

"Be brave, Sarah. I cannot be worrying about you and Father." She unwrapped the girl's thin arms, bent over, and looked face to face. "I promise someday we will be together again. Antonius and Grandfather will take good care of you."

"Mother," Samuel said as he stood in the doorway, "what happened to Grandfather?"

"If you had been here, instead of communing with the Essenes, you would know." Jerusha regretted being so sharp with him. "Your grandfather was stabbed." She stroked Sarah's hair.

"What? Why?"

"I do not have time to explain. Stay here with him. Do not leave his side. And, pray, I am taking Stephen with me to the temple to find Paul. Antonius is taking Sarah to Perea to be with Grandfather, then he leaves for his homeland with his daughter."

He scrunched his brows together. "But I thought Antonius's daughter was dead."

"We all thought that. She is most certainly alive, and so is her mother."

"He has a wife?"

"Who's waiting for him to come home?" Jerusha's voice choked.

"Then the beautiful woman in the garden is his daughter. I wondered who she was. Too bad she cannot stay, so I can get acquainted."

"I do not have time for this. Stay here with your grandfather and guard him with your life." She led Sarah by the hand out the door, the young girl's tears pulling on her emotions. *Stay strong, Jerusha.* Chaya followed and coaxed Sarah along. Her lips moved in silence. Jerusha was thankful she prayed. They all needed prayer, and at that moment she had no unction for it.

"Crying will not help. Be brave." Jerusha counseled herself as much as Sarah.

Stephen, Hannah, and Antonius waited at the fountain. Antonius picked up Sarah, who hugged his neck, her sobs ringing throughout the garden. Jerusha restrained herself from hugging them both. If she did, she might change her mind and beg Antonius to stay.

"It will be all right Sarah. We will see you again." Hannah patted her back. "We love you."

"Yes, Sarah, we love you more than you can possible understand right now." Jerusha gulped and waved Antonius to go. She kept her

100 A Royal Family

eyes on his back. "We love you both." He stopped, looked over his shoulder, and locked eyes. His eyes glistened, and his mouth turned up at the corner with his lips forming the silent words, I love you, too.

Jerusha nodded. Her chest tightened and she gave a slight wave. As he walked away, she noticed Joshua coming toward her.

"Do not worry, Mother." He stopped and saluted Antonius with a fist against his chest, then strutted past him and stood at attention before her. "I will guard Grandfather." His eyes filled with tears. "I have a real sword now." He patted his side. "Antonius made it especially for me. He said I am ready."

Jerusha stared at Joshua. His build had thickened, shoulders wider, with muscular forearms. How is it she had not noticed these changes? Antonius had groomed him into a strong young man both spiritually and physically. She looked at Stephen, three years older, a head taller with his full beard, thick chest, and narrowing waistline. Her sons had become men under Antonius's influence. Her heart filled with gratitude.

"Yes, Joshua, I know you would keep him safe, but I need you to find Moses and Miriam and bring them to the villa." Chaya touched her arm. Jerusha looked at her and Hannah. "Do not let anyone into this villa, until I return," then she grabbed Stephen's arm and motioned, "Come with me." To Joshua, she said, "You come, too."

She stopped and looked one last time over her shoulder past the fountain. Antonius and Sarah were gone.

Chapter 15

Jerusha stopped at the gate and looked at the bikkkurim. The basket, interwoven with gold and silver cords, overflowed with her father's first fruit offering of grapes, pomegranates, olives, and barley bread. If he had not been stabbed, she and her three sons would have accompanied him to the temple and offered it to the priest. She clenched her fists and listened to the joyful songs drifting in the air from the families coming to celebrate Shavuot, the feast of ingathering, or Pentecost, as the Greeks called it. Tears threatened. Only fifty days earlier, she had rejoiced with Father and her sons at Passover.

She pitied those coming into the city. Most followed the priest's teachings and had not recognized Yeshua as the Messiah. Father stayed in Jerusalem, hoping to sway them and warn of the coming judgment for rejecting their King. She sighed. He may have stayed too long.

She appreciated and admired her father's love for his people—her people, too. Yet hatred for Yeshua and the followers of the Way grew more intense every day.

Her main reason for staying was to save as many young girls as possible from the perversion heaped upon them by the corrupt priests and the cruel Roman soldiers, or else she would have left a long time ago and gone to live with Grandfather in Perea.

She wiped the tears running down her cheeks with her fist. If Father died, she might lose the villa, the only safe place in Jerusalem for the girls and her family. But he would not die, she encouraged herself.

Jerusha swallowed the lump in her throat, walked outside with her two sons and locked the gate, then shook it to make sure.

"At least Sarah will be safe." She must get to Paul before her father died. He carried a healing anointing, unlike anyone she knew.

As she left her villa and descended from Mt. Zion, she saw the pilgrims flowing into the city from the Mount of Olives, their wagons of bikkurim pulled by oxen with garlands of flowers in a grand procession. So much dust in the air.

Out of breath, she licked her lower lip and decided to turn into the garden where she spent a lot of time with Father and Grandfather in the past years and wound the path among flowering pomegranate bushes and olive trees, the pomegranate's larger red blossoms a striking contrast against the olive tree's smaller white flower.

Jerusha hurried to a rock ledge and cupped her fingers beneath the cool waters flowing from it and sipped. It soothed her dry throat. She breathed in the fresh air and tried to calm her racing heart, then turned toward her two sons and gripped her shaking fingers. They both looked so grown up. Standing side by side, Stephen stood a foot taller.

"Moses and Miriam will be at Father's carpenter's shop." She tried to address her youngest son as a man. She needed him to be, now that Antonius was gone and Father lingered near death. "We were to meet them there before ascending the holy mount to present our offering at the temple." She tried to not talk down to him. After all, he was close to the age of Yeshua when he astounded the teachers in the temple with his wisdom. "Tell them what happened to your grandfather and ask them to come to our villa. But most importantly, ask them to spread the word to the other followers of the Way and ask them to pray." She watched him place his hand on the sword's scabbard and crinkle his brow. He looked quite solemn as he studied the streets below. "What's wrong, Joshua?"

"Nothing, Mother. Just remembering Antonius's instructions— 'love your enemy.'"

"Be anxious for nothing. Pray without ceasing." Stephen's voice, rich and deep, boomed over the noisy crowd below. "Antonius and I spent many nights in prayer in the stable with the horses." He knelt, the tzitzits at the corner of his cloak whipping in the wind. "Should we not pray, Mother?" He looked up with glistening tears.

Jerusha felt overwhelmed by her sons' wisdom and tenderness. "Yes, Stephen, you are right. I should have thought of it myself. Come, Joshua, let us pray so we can love our enemies as Antonius taught you." She felt an urgency to get to Paul. Father was dying. But she knelt beside Stephen, beneath the flowering olive tree.

"And we will pray for Grandfather, too." Joshua knelt beside her.

"And for Antonius and Sarah's safety as well" she added.

As Jerusha listened to her sons pour out their hearts before Father YHWH, she held her face in her hands and sobbed. The breeze rustled the olive leaves above, and a lone, white blossom fell in her lap. She picked it up and stared at the tiny flower that lay in her palm. "Father, I love you." The wind carried her whisper unnoticed by her sons and the clamoring crowd in the marketplace below. Her sons helped her rise, one on each side, a hand beneath each elbow. Stephen gave her a piece of cloth for her nose, then the three embraced for a minute and listened to the melodious crowd entering the city.

She looked below at Roman soldiers interspersed among the people. "Be careful, Joshua. The zealots may cause a disturbance today."

"Do not worry, Mother. Antonius taught me well what to look for." He grasped his sword's scabbard and wound his way out of the garden. The sun's rays broke through the olive branches and warmed her face. When he turned onto the path, she saw him bounce down the hill, then look back and wave. His maturity shined in his demeanor and warmed her heart.

***

Stephen protected Jerusha against the jostling crowd. Ahead of them, families stood in line on the altar steps and watched the priest wave loaves of bread as each family recited the required portion from the Torah, "A wandering Aramean was my father. And he went down into Egypt and sojourned there, few in number, and there became a nation, great . . . And he brought us into this place and gave us this land . . . And behold, now I bring the first of the fruit of the ground, which you O LORD, have given me." Blood covered the steps as the priests sacrificed the lambs and goats and waved them as an offering. The burnt offering odor filled the air. It all made Jerusha sick in her stomach. She saw little or no purpose for these sacrifices since Yeshua made the ultimate sacrifice—his shed blood and bruised body.

Paul, her father's good friend, had tried to persuade them, to no avail, and then YWWH sent him to the Gentiles. Oh, how she longed to go with him, anywhere out of this city! She wondered why he came back to Jerusalem anyway, except maybe to see her father. She had heard he had a meeting with James. Others said YHWH sent him to Jerusalem.

"Stephen, let's get up higher so we can see. Unless YHWH helps, we will not find Paul in this crowd." Jerusha allowed him to guide her up the wide steps until they came to the next landing.

"Israel, help!" Asian Jews who stood next to the temple gate cried out and pointed to Paul. "This is the man who is teaching everyone everywhere against the people and the law and this place. Moreover, he even brought Greeks into the temple and defiles this holy place."

The people roared against Paul and ran toward him.

"Nooo! He is a godly man." Her plea, engulfed by their angry outbursts, fell powerless and unheard.

"Watch out, Mother. You'll be trampled." Stephen pulled her against the marble wall and shielded her against the frenzied men who rushed down the stairs toward Paul. When she was able to look, she saw Paul dragged outside the temple area and beaten. Bloodied and bruised, he fell to the ground. She covered her eyes and listened to thud after thud against his body. The temple gate slammed shut. Her heart sank. They hated him as much as Father. Anger rose in her bosom. She gritted her teeth.

"How dare they do this to him? If anyone knows and obeys the law, it is Paul. What has become of YHWH's people?" She unclenched her fists. "They will not be content until every follower of the Way is dead. It is pure hatred. How do you fight against such thinking?"

"Love them, Mother." She felt Stephen's arm around her shoulder. He and Joshua understood more than any in her family how to love and forgive those who persecuted you. Many days they had been mocked in the synagogue and asked to leave because they were Gentiles, even by some of the followers of the Way. Father and Antonius had talked to them about Yeshua's teachings—turning the other cheek, and praying for their persecutors. She had not understood, until now, how much Stephen had absorbed their teachings. He towered above, a giant of a man. His big dark eyes illuminated a softness and gentleness that could only come from Yeshua's spirit. It calmed her rage.

"Come, Mother, I know another way out of the temple." He took her hand and led her around a marble column and down a stairway into a hallway. Their sandaled steps echoed as they crossed the empty room. He opened a large cedar door and glanced outside. "I think it is safe," he said and held the door as she stepped into the street.

Roman soldiers shoved with their shields through the murmuring crowd that surrounded Jerusha and Stephen. Stephen guided her to an alcove.

"Arrest him," the tribune shouted.

"What has he done?"

Some in the crowd shouted one thing; some another.

"Paul must still be alive." She grasped Stephen's cloak. "Look! There is Effah. How is it that he is always around when something evil occurs? I do not trust him. I suppose he warned Paul right before he was attacked as he did to Father and Sarah."

"Bind him with two chains and take him to the barracks," the tribune commanded.

"What is the tribune afraid of?" Jerusha spoke in anger, "Paul is a small man in stature, beaten and weak; if only Antonius were here. He would not treat him that way." She clenched her fists.

"Away with him! Away with him!" The crowd shouted and followed as the soldiers dragged Paul past Jerusha and Stephen and up the hill to Antonia Fortress. The mob shoved so hard against Paul that the soldiers had to carry him up the steps. At the entrance to the barracks, Paul conversed with the tribune; then the tribune motioned with his hand. A great hush fell on the people, and Paul spoke in Hebrew.

"Brothers and fathers, hear the defense that I now make before you." When they heard their native language, they became even quieter. Jerusha watched, encouraged the crowd had calmed.

"Help him, YHWH," she prayed and clutched Stephen's arm; "Maybe Paul will be released." A flicker of hope ignited. Maybe he could help Father, yet.

"I am a Jew." Paul's voice sounded stronger than his battered body looked. "I was brought up in this city. I persecuted this Way to the death. I journeyed to Damascus to bring them in bonds to Jerusalem to be punished. On my way, a great light suddenly shone around me. I fell to the ground and heard a voice, saying to me, 'Saul, Saul, why are you persecuting me?' and I answered and said, 'Who are you, Lord?' and He said to me, 'I am Yeshua of Nazareth whom you are persecuting. The Lord said to me, 'Rise, and go into Damascus and there you will be told all that is appointed for you to do.' I could not see because of the brightness of the light; I was led by the hand by those who were with me and came into Damascus. Ananias, well-spoken of by all Jews who lived there, said to me, 'Brother Saul, receive your sight,' and that very hour I received my sight. Rise and be baptized and wash away your sins, calling upon his name."

Jerusha gripped her cloak and held her breath, her head down. So far the crowd had listened. "Please, YHWH, please. Father needs Paul," she begged.

"When I returned to Jerusalem and was praying in the temple," Paul continued, "I fell into a trance and saw him saying to me, 'Make haste and get out of Jerusalem . . . Go, for I will send you far away to the Gentiles.'"

The crowd threw off their cloaks and flung dust in the air. "Away with such a fellow from the earth. For he should not be allowed to live."

"Take him to the barracks," the tribune ordered, "Examine him by flogging to find out why they are shouting against him like this."

Jerusha felt numb. "Take me back to the villa."

Chapter 16

The sun dipped below the horizon casting a pink glow across the mountaintop. Jerusha trudged up Mt. Zion, her feet weighted with every step. She had heard laughter and song and caught whiffs of roasted lamb as she wound through the maze of lower Jerusalem. She had little hope Father would live. She missed Antonius.

She wondered why Father YHWH had not rescued Paul. He knew how much her father needed him. How much she needed her father. She heard her grandfather's wisdom echoing in her thoughts: *Jerusha, Father YHWH's ways are not our ways. They are higher.* She had questioned YHWH's ways when Timon died only to have Father tell her his ways were better. She had accepted that truth and raised her sons without a father. Here she was again questioning not only his ways but her faith, too.

At the last incline, Stephen took her arm.

"Mother, are you alright? You seem especially tired." His strength helped her take the last few steps.

Samuel ran out to greet her.

"Shalom," he kissed her cheek, "Let me help." She collapsed in his arms and began to weep.

"It all seems so hopeless." She spoke between cries, then allowed him to walk her inside the gate and waited while Stephen locked it.

"When it seems as though you are facing nothing but difficulties, see it as an invaluable opportunity to experience the greatest joy that you can." Samuel words surprised and yet strengthened Jerusha.

"For you know that when your faith is tested, it stirs up power within you to endure all things." Stephen continued the encouragement.

"And then as your endurance grows even stronger it will release perfection into every part of your being until nothing is missing and nothing lacking." Samuel grasped Stephen's shoulders, grinned, and then turned toward Jerusha. "Mother, count it all joy."

One part of her wanted to reprimand them for having such joy in these troublous times. It did not seem appropriate. Another part of her admired their strength and wisdom. She shook her head.

"When did my sons become such spiritual giants?"

"Antonius taught us." They spoke in unison, and then they chuckled.

"What he heard from James." Samuel wrapped his arm around her shoulder.

"Is your grandfather alive?" Jerusha's voice shook.

"He is still breathing but not awake. I have been watching this gate. Joshua and Moses are at the other entrances keeping guard. Miriam, Chaya, and Hannah are with Grandfather. We heard the noise in the city. What happened?"

"They arrested Paul." Jerusha walked with her sons, one on each side. "He is in the barracks at the Antonia Fortress. As soon as I see Father, I am going to visit him." She felt weary but determined. She could not give up.

"You will not go without me," Samuel spoke sternly.

"Or me," Stephen chimed in, then stopped and grabbed her arm. "Mother, I know how independent you can be. It would be foolish and dangerous to go alone."

Toughen up, Jerusha, she spoke inwardly.

"You will be needed here to guard the villa." She spoke to them with more energy than she felt and then took a deep breath. "Yeshua says visit those in prison, and visit I will. Your grandfather needs Paul's prayers." She turned and forced herself to rush up the path.

"Not without one of us. You promised Antonius." Samuel's voice echoed. Darkness had descended. Shadows bounced on the tiled path from the lighted lamps.

She stopped by the fountain and listened as it gurgled. "Well, he is gone. I make my own decisions now," she then raised her cloak above her sandaled feet and rushed up the steps.

"What about Grandfather? Don't you want to stay with him? What if he dies while you are gone?" Samuel never gave up on an argument.

His words stopped Jerusha. She looked over the railing to the garden below, Father's garden where she danced and listened to his stories as a child. "I-I will count it all joy, just as you said." She squeezed her eyes shut, breathed deep, and waited, then lifted her chin.

"If that happens, he will be rejoicing with Yeshua in his kingdom. I will rejoice with him." She walked a bit slower along the colonnade. She wasn't sure she believed her own words.

"What if he wakes up? Won't you want to talk to him before he dies? Tell him goodbye?" Samuel knew how to argue where it hurt.

Jerusha stopped with her hand on the latch and waited a second before opening the door. Telling her father goodbye and watching him die had not entered her mind. The only option she cared to contemplate was getting Paul to pray for him. She had seen others healed. Father would be healed, too, she hoped.

When she opened the door, she watched Chaya close the latticed shutters and turn to face her. "We have been waiting for you." She went to Father's mittah and stood at his head. "Your father passed into Yeshua's kingdom this morning."

"No. It cannot be true. Samuel said he still breathed."

"We did not tell anyone while we awaited your return. His body must be prepared for burial soon. We will leave you alone with him." Chaya motioned to Miriam and Hannah. Miriam wiped tears and hugged Jerusha. Hannah stopped at his body.

"I will miss you." She sniffed and nodded to Jerusha. "I have grown to love your father as my own." She rushed from the room. Miriam and Chaya followed, closing the door quietly.

Jerusha caressed her father's lifeless face and touched his cold hands, even colder than before she left. She knelt on the floor beside the mittah and lay her head on the soft fleece cover. How could YHWH take her father? She needed him now more than ever with Antonius gone.

"Is this how you answer my cry? Help my unbelief." Her tears soaked the cover. The words "Your ways for sure are not my ways" came to her.

She rose and sat on the mittah, then lay her head on father's chest and savored the frankincense on his cloak. "What will I do without you?" she whispered in the darkened room, the only light coming from the brazier coals, and then she remembered Yeshua's words, "*I am in the darkness, too.*"

She listened to the crackle of the coals; then the sobs erupted from deep in her chest. She never thought she would stop crying. After several minutes, she hiccupped and wiped her nose on a piece of cloth from her girdle. In the quiet darkness, her father's words sounded so loud in her thoughts. He could have been standing next to her, alive.

"*Jerusha, in hard times, believe.*" She lay her head back on his chest.

"I believe," she whispered.

Warmth spread over her body like a cover.

"I believe." She spoke in her exhaustion, her eyelids becoming heavy.

"Help my unbelief," She blinked a couple of times, then relaxed and drifted off the words "I believe" still on her lips.

A beautiful light shimmered in the darkness.

"I believe." She heard her voice in the distance.

It moved even closer, brighter.

"I believe."

The brilliance grew before her eyes.

"*I am the resurrection and the life.*"

***

"I believe," Jerusha mumbled in her sleepy stupor. Her eyes popped open. Sunshine. "It's morning." She sat up and stretched, then rubbed her neck. "I must get Chaya to prepare Father's body."

She opened the shutters and let the room become filled with the smell of the fragrant blossoms in the garden below. She felt light as she walked—a new day. She would rejoice and be glad in it. That is what Father would want. She could hear his voice in her thoughts.

Dance, Jerusha, dance.

She sat on Father's mittah and took his hand. "For you, Father, I will turn my mourning into dancing." His hand felt warmer than before. She must have lain on it in the night. She kissed it and held it to her face. "I will miss you." She felt a slight movement against her cheek, and it crinkled her brow. "Uhh!" She threw his hand on the mittah and jumped up.

"Dead bodies do not move." She backed away.

"Jerusha." Her heart jumped. She thought she heard her name called, ever so quietly.

"Dead bodies do not talk." She tried to convince herself.

"Jerusha." The sound came again from the mittah.

She crept closer. "Father?" Her ears roared. Thu-thud, thu-thud, thu-thud. "Calm down," she said to herself. Of course, she talked to herself. There was no one else in the room—only a dead body. "It is your imagination." She lifted her chin and dropped it. "Father is dead," she instructed herself and took a deep breath, then bent over his body.

"Jerusha," His lips moved slightly.

She raised herself and stared. He looked dead to her. His eyes were closed.

"Dead bodies do not talk," she argued again.

"Jerusha." He lifted his finger. "I am in pain." He groaned.

"Father, you are alive," She threw herself on his chest in joyful glee.

"Oh," he groaned.

"I am sorry, Father," She looked at the fresh blood leaking through his bandage and jumped up.

"I thirst," He licked his lips. She ran to the table and poured water in a goblet, then lifted his head and let him sip. "I thought you were dead."

"No, my daughter. As you can see, I am very much alive. Yeshua sent me back." He sipped. "The way I feel right now, it would be better to be with Him." He sipped again.

Jerusha scrunched her brow and sat the goblet on the tile floor.

"I am sorry." His eyes spoke of his love. "It's not that I am not glad to be with you again; it's just that once you have been to the other side, you do not want to come back." He lay his head back down. "It is only for a little while that I am here."

"No, Father. You will be healed. I will get Paul, that is if he gets out of prison. He will pray, and you will be healed."

"Paul is in prison?"

"Yes, they arrested him, yesterday."

"My dear friend fights the good fight."

"You must fight the good fight, too, Father."

"Soon it will be my time to cross over and be with your mother in the kingdom."

"No, Father, you cannot leave us. I need you."

"It is time for you to put your whole trust in Father YHWH. He will never leave you or forsake you. He has honored your faith."

"What faith? I had no faith."

"It only takes faith," he began and smiled.

"The size of a mustard seed," she interrupted. "I remember."

"Jerusha, my little lioness." He took her hand. "Bring me my grandsons that I might bless them."

"Stop talking like you will not live."

"There is a thin veil between here and the kingdom. It is a wonderful place."

"Father, please. I need you here. Do not give up."

"Bring my grandsons."

She arose and stared. He talked and looked so different.

"Go, Jerusha. Get them. I will still be here when you return."

She backed out the door, then turned and yelled over the bronze banister. "Samuel, Stephen, Joshua!"

Chaya came up the steps. "I told them their grandfather had died. Samuel went to prepare the tomb and fetch the burial ointments."

"He is alive," Jerusha said as she grabbed Chaya's shoulders. "He is alive."

Chaya's eyes widened. "Your father is alive?"

"Yes. I do not have time to explain. I must get Samuel." Jerusha ran down the steps and met Stephen coming up.

"Come with me." She pulled on his arm as she descended. "We must find Samuel. Your grandfather is alive and wants to see his grandsons.

"But-but-." Stephen looked bewildered.

"I know," Jerusha interrupted, "you thought he was dead." She stopped and waited at the fountain. "He was dead, but now he lives."

Chapter 17

"You search the shops in the upper city. I will search the shops in the lower city," Jerusha commanded Stephen as she stood atop Mt. Zion outside her villa. "We can meet back at gate beautiful in the temple.

"No, Mother, I will stay with you. You are not safe." He crossed his arms over his chest.

"Since when did you stop taking orders from your ima?" She put her hands on her hips.

"Since when I promised Antonius to protect you."

"Well, a promise is a promise. I guess we go together." She started down the terraced steps to the lower city. "We will check the carpenter's shop first."

Jerusha walked past many families saying their goodbyes to friends as they prepared to depart for their homes. Children laughed. Some cried and followed donkeys laden with supplies for their journey. Oh, how Jerusha longed to pack her family and leave with them! She sensed it would not be long. She waited for a camel that blocked the entrance to the maze of dwellings in the lower city. Stephen helped the young boy pulling on its rope. One tug from him and the animal rose up from its haunches and trotted forward. The boy smiled back at her and Stephen.

She laughed and walked under the arched entrance to the lower city, a bounce in her step. Father lived. She would rejoice and be glad, even if an underlying fear gripped her inner being.

"Shalom," she waved at neighbors she knew.

Stephen stopped and talked to a friend, then hurried to catch up.

"He said he saw Samuel earlier this morning with a donkey heading down the hill to the market. He thought he turned at the next bend."

"Well, then we turn at the next bend, too." Jerusha walked a little faster and began singing Tehillim 56, one of her favorite psalms memorized as a child.

"Lord show me your kindness and mercy, for these men oppose and oppress me all day long . . . in the day that I'm afraid." She bounced to the beat. "I lay all my fears before you and trust in you with all my heart."

She remembered how much this psalm meant when she was a slave in Herod's palace. Jerusha threw her arms out and twirled around. Stephen watched with a grin. "What harm could a man bring to me?" She pointed to herself, crouched down and faced Stephen, then threw out her arms. "With God on my side I will not be afraid of what comes, the roaring praises of God fill my heart, and I will always triumph as I trust his promises."

She remembered the lonely and fearful days as a child, and how difficult it was to trust YHWH. Yet, in that dark time, he heard her angry cry and delivered her, in spite of her feisty protests, fears, and doubts. The times seemed even darker now than before. When alone, something gripped her inner being, a haunting fear, a sense of impending doom. She had tried to cast it off. Nothing helped. But today she rejoiced in Father's recovery.

Stephen grabbed her hand and pulled her closer while staring at a man who had his eyes on her as he walked past them. When the man looked away, Stephen continued singing the psalm.

"Day after day cruel critics distort my words; constantly they plot my collapse," he bellowed in deep full tones that filled the air. "Lurking in the dark, waiting, spying on my movements in secret to take me by surprise, ready to take my life." King David's words from the psalm described Jerusha's fears about Effah. Even as charming as he had tried to be, she did not trust him.

She clutched Stephen's arm. "They don't deserve to get away with this," she joined in. "Look at their wickedness, their injustice, Lord. In your fierce anger cast them down to defeat." Thoughts of Effah swirled in her thoughts. His smile, and his laughter. Did she genuinely want his defeat? Or did she want him to know and understand Yeshua's love? She shook her head. Wise up, Jerusha, she chided herself; it is just your childhood infatuation coming up again. YHWH, help, she cried silently and kept singing.

"You've kept track of all my wandering and my weeping. You've stored my tears in your bottle; not one will be lost. For they are all recorded in your book of remembrance." She grinned at Stephen and enjoyed his dimpled smile. "The very moment I call to you for a father's help, the tide of battle turns, and my enemies flee." She let go and twirled once and continued walking a little behind Stephen. He turned and waited. "This one thing I know: with God on my side, I will not be afraid of what comes."

She stopped. The hair stood on her arms. Stephen stared and drew close.

"Why did you stop?" he asked.

"There is an evil presence here. Can you feel it?" She rubbed her arms. "Who lives in that home?" She pointed to a limestone structure with a lone window, the cedar shutter covering it, one lone eye carved on it that matched the eye carved on the lintel. "I do not remember seeing it in all the time I have lived in Jerusalem."

"The woman who lives there was a slave in Herod's palace and somehow managed to get free." Stephen stepped closer to Jerusha.

"The witch in the kitchen. I remember her from when I got Sarah out of there." Jerusha scrunched her brow.

"That's right, Mother. She is a soothsayer who works witchcraft and casts spells. Many around here revere her. Another girl, much younger, lives with her." Stephen's deep voice resounded against the noisy crowds that passed.

"What an abomination before Father YHWH." Jerusha shivered. "Antonius was correct to have Joshua protect himself from the fiery darts of the evil one with the armor of YHWH. Our war is not against flesh and blood. Remember that, Stephen." She tapped his chest. "That is why Yeshua commands to love our enemies. Our battle is against principalities and powers in high places, although"—she hesitated and glared at the door—"they may be used by ungodly people. We must watch out for her."

"Did you hear that?" Stephen's eyes opened wider. "It sounded like a screeching animal, followed by a chant."

"Do not fear," Jerusha comforted. "Isaiah says no weapon formed against us will prosper, and every tongue that rises against us we can refute." She spoke the words with a calmer tone, more than her racing heart felt.

"As it says in the chronicles of the kings about Jehoshaphat's fight," Stephen moved farther away from the witch's door and motioned to his mother. He continued, "After he sought YHWH, Jahaziel the Levite told him, 'Fear not, the battle is not yours, but God's. You shall not need to fight in this battle: set yourselves, stand still and see the salvation of Jehovah with you.'" After pausing to catch his breath, he added, "Then Jehoshaphat sent out the Levites and those called to sing first before the army, and the enemy was ambushed."

"I continue to be astounded how much Father and Antonius have taught you." Jerusha laughed and moved close to him. "Such wisdom for one so young; much more than I had at your age." She took his arm and began to sing,

"My heart overflows with praise to God and for his promises. I will always trust in him." Some in the crowd gawked as they passed. Jerusha chuckled inwardly. She did not care what they thought. Today Father lived. They would sing, too, if their father had been dead and now lived.

Stephen joined in and kept a constant eye on those around them. "I'm thanking you with all my heart, with gratitude for all you've done."

Jerusha let go and twirled around, then caught up with Stephen, who glowered.

"Stay close," he said as he grabbed her arm. "The zealot who stabbed Grandfather may be in the crowd."

Jerusha's stomach knotted, then she lifted her chin and pulled free from his grasp. She glanced over her shoulder at him and saw Effah standing in front of the witch's door. He pulled his shawl over his head and covered most of his face, then looked left and right before walking fast between the people and crept closer and closer to them.

"I will not walk in fear today." She began to sing again. "I will do everything I've promised you, Lord." She stopped singing. "Look who is behind us," she leaned in and whispered.

Stephen stood almost a head taller than those in the crowd. He cranked his head around and stared. "I see him, Mother. Keep moving and singing."

"For you have saved my soul from stumbling so that I can walk before the Lord bathed in his life-giving light." This was one time she was glad Stephen disobeyed and demanded he come with her. His presence gave her courage. She relaxed and rejoiced in YHWH's love and protection. Father was alive. That was all that mattered.

***

Jerusha waited while Stephen rolled up the tent's front tarp at Father's carpenter's shop. It had been a while since she had been there. After Timon died, she stayed away. It hurt too much. Little by little, it became easier. As she stepped inside, her eyes fell on the workbench. Some of Father's moving stories about Paul and Father making tents from black goat's hair when they were boys in Tarsus darted through her mind. Her father loved Paul.

She stepped to the back wall and fingered the bow-drill that hung there and stared at the worktable below it. Many days she sat at his feet amidst the sawdust and listened to story after story from the Torah and dreamed of dancing before Yeshua in his kingdom.

Father's face, pale and in pain, flashed into her thoughts. Tears filled her eyes. He said a thin veil separated earth and the kingdom where Mother, Timon, and Sarah waited. Jerusha sighed and looked around. Timon. Ten years had passed since YHWH gave her a glimpse of him in the kingdom right after he died, and she'd seen the twinkle in his eyes, the crooked upturned grin.

She bent down and grasped a handful of fresh sawdust and put it to her nose and picked up the half-finished goblet.

"Samuel's work," Stephen said as he held a matching goblet that he sat on the bench.

"I remember you and Samuel playing in the sawdust and stacking wooden blocks with Timon. He loved you so much."

"I am grateful to him for training us in the ways of carpentry and leaving this shop as our inheritance. The people well respected him. Because of him and Grandfather, the people come."

Jerusha scanned the crowds and watched the families, families she had known all her life. She grieved that so many still did not acknowledge Yeshua as the Messiah or know that his kingdom was not of this world. She loved Jerusalem and her people. In some ways, it would be difficult to leave.

"We'd better hurry, Mother," Stephen spoke tenderly. "Grandfather is waiting." He guided her outside and closed the flap. She raised her cloak over her sandaled feet and watched her step as she crossed the path and began the ascent up the temple mount. Camel, donkey, and horse manure spotted the road, and she zigzagged her way up higher and stopped to catch her breath beneath an olive tree. Stephen pulled a goatskin bottle from his shoulder and offered her a drink.

She sipped and watched the sun glisten off the temple in the distance.

"Look, there is Samuel." Stephen pointed up the hill. "Stay here, Mother; I will get him. Samuel! Samuel!" Stephen hollered and waved.

Samuel stopped and looked, then turned his donkey.

The crowd moved against him, and Roman legionaries galloped past toward the temple, shoving men and women out of the way. The crowd railed against a man bound with chains who was jerked along behind the horses, then fell. Jerusha feared for her sons as both helped the bound man to his feet and Stephen gave him a sip of water and conversed. Her heart jumped when she saw the man's face. It was Paul.

She forgot her tiredness and ran up the hill, darting between travelers leaving the city. Before she reached her sons, the foot soldier guarding Paul shoved them away with his shield and pushed Paul along, the crowd yelling and spitting on him.

Tears rolled down her cheeks. The thought that her father's good friend, once loved and admired by all, was now hated and treated like a criminal by those same friends tore at her being. So much had changed in the city she loved.

She stumbled along in a daze, not caring what happened to her, only wanting to get to her sons. Someone grabbed her arm, and she looked up. Stephen. She buried her face in his chest and sobbed.

"They are bringing Paul before the high priest and the council," a man yelled as he ran past them.

Chapter 18

Jerusha wiped her tears away and fumbled in her girdle and pulled out a piece of cloth for her nose. She wondered at the number of people that had changed directions. Instead of leaving the city, they followed Paul as the soldier dragged him uphill.

"What has Paul done?" one man asked his fellow traveler and bumped against her shoulder; oblivious, he hit her as they passed.

A young boy ran up to Samuel. "Did you see Paul? He stands trial in the temple."

Samuel nodded and straightened the leather bags of linen and tightened the jugs of burial ointment. The donkey brayed and looked back.

"I have everything ready at the tomb, Mother."

"He is alive." Jerusha could not contain her joy, in spite of her sorrow over Paul's arrest. "Samuel, your grandfather is alive." She raised her voice.

"Yes, I know he is alive in the kingdom of God with grandmother." He kept fiddling with the burial supplies.

Jerusha looked across the back of the donkey at Stephen. He grinned and shrugged. She pulled on Samuel's shoulder and made him turn and face her.

"He has been resurrected." She held her hands on his shoulders and stared into his eyes.

Samuel scrunched his brow. "You-you mean Grandfather is alive, back from the dead?"

"That is indeed what I meant. Isn't it wonderful? He wants to see all his grandsons. That's why we came to find you."

The crowd shoved against Jerusha and moved uphill. Samuel wrapped his arm around her shoulder and pulled her close against the donkey's side.

"Look at them, Mother. Lost sheep without a shepherd." Samuel's eyes brimmed with tears. "Here, let me help you up on the donkey, a safer place. I would not want my mother to be trampled." He lifted and sat her on a woolen blanket across the beast's back. She dangled both legs on one side of the donkey, straightened her cloak, and glanced down the hill at the multitude of people, most heading up Mt. Zion toward the temple. Her eyes caught the cloaked figure she had no desire to see: Effah.

Samuel yanked on the donkey's rope. Jerusha held tight to its mane as the donkey trotted a short distance, then slowed. She wondered why Effah followed but then cast the thought off. Father's alive. Nothing else mattered. Pauls' arrest was in YHWH's hands. Effah's lurking was in YHWH's hands, too. She hugged her waist. A gnawing ache in her gut troubled her, though.

The noise grew louder as they got closer to the temple. The pious Pharisees in their colorful robes with wide fringed borders strutted back and forth and mumbled among themselves, their phylacteries tied to their arm or forehead. Samuel stopped the donkey and waited while one Pharisee, who stood at the temple corner, bent over and recited his prayer. The people distanced themselves and waited while he finished. Whispers among the crowd spread until the Pharisees heard their mumblings about Paul.

"Let us pass," one Pharisee shouted. The mass parted before them. The Pharisees hurried up the steps and entered the chamber hall where the council met with Paul. His words echoed outside.

"Brothers, I have lived my life before God in all good conscience up to this day. I am a Pharisee, the son of Pharisees. It is with respect to the hope and resurrection of the dead that I am on trial."

Jerusha looked at Samuel and Stephen. "Let us go. Your grandfather awaits your return. Only YHWH can deliver Paul." Her stomach churned.

"We find nothing wrong with this man. What if a spirit or an angel spoke to him?" a man inside the chamber yelled, and uproar could be heard between the Sadducees and the Pharisees.

Jerusha looked at the tribune at the top of the step, who watched over the temple courts.

"Get him out of there, before they tear him apart and we answer to Rome for a citizen's death." He motioned to several legionnaires, who dismounted and entered the chamber. Other soldiers tromped past Jerusha.

"Move out of the way." They shoved with their shields.

The donkey brayed and stomped.

"Hold tight, Mother," Samuel instructed. Stephen grasped her around the waist until the donkey calmed.

Most people in the crowd mocked Paul as the soldiers dragged him past. Others turned away. Some, who Jerusha knew to be Yeshua followers, prayed and cried. Jerusha looked past the soldier's shield and locked eyes with Paul. He looked so peaceful. The crowd jeered and followed the soldiers toward the fortress. Samuel turned their donkey toward home.

***

The late afternoon sun dipped behind the mount and cast shadows across the path that Jerusha climbed. The donkey trailed behind with Samuel and Stephen. Her feet ached, and weariness clung to her body in every muscle and joint. The day had drained her strength.

She contemplated why Effah had followed them and why the whole city seemed to turn on Paul, a man of honor and dignity, a man they took counsel from in the past. She saw Chaya at the gate, her long silver braid hanging over her shoulder; what a blessing to have her around. YHWH knew she needed a woman to understand her way of thinking and to console her when she was misunderstood by her father and sons, and even Antonius, too. She wondered if he found Grandfather. She hoped he and Sarah were safe.

Jerusha closed her eyes and envisioned his face near hers, his fragrant pine smell. Her eyes popped open. "He has a wife," she chided and stomped on up the hill.

"Jerusha, I have been worried. Come in." Chaya opened the gate. "Let me wash your feet. I have water prepared in the courtyard."

Jerusha glanced back at her sons. "After the donkey is in the stable, clean up and meet me in Father's room." She followed Chaya to the bench beneath the olive tree in the courtyard and sat down.

The warm water poured over her achy feet felt wonderful. She leaned back against the tree and enjoyed Chaya's gentle foot massage with fragrant oil that Samuel had brought back from the Dead Sea area. She felt guilty enjoying a few moments of pleasure with all the chaos swirling around her.

"I know what you are thinking, Jerusha." Chaya looked up. "You feel guilty for not running immediately to your father's room."

"Is Father still breathing?" Jerusha sat up and slipped on one clean sandal that Chaya had readied, then the other.

"He is very weak, but breathing." Chaya poured the water beneath the bushes.

"You must take care of yourself, love yourself as Yeshua taught before you can love others." Chaya took her hand, "Father YHWH's wisdom awaits you. You only have to come to him with faith the size of a mustard seed."

"Sometimes I think I do not even have that much faith."

"Do not give up, Jerusha. He meets you where you are," Chaya wrapped her arm around her shoulder and hugged her tight, then chuckled. "Your Father's little lioness has more wisdom than she knows. It just needs to be released. Watch out, world, when it does."

***

Jerusha hurried up the steps past two marble columns and waited outside Father's door. The setting sun spread a fuchsia glow across the horizon. She could not help but think of Antonius and the many times she stood on this balcony and viewed the sunset, and talked—that is, whenever she gave him a chance. *Why? Why? Why, Father YHWH? You knew he had a wife. Why did you let me fall in love with a married man?* She missed him more than she thought possible. She missed his laughter, his banter, his passionate engagement with her sons.

"It is beautiful." Samuel came up the stairs. "Antonius often talked of the setting sun's message—a new day begins tomorrow, he'd say."

"I had no idea," Jerusha grasped the banister afraid to speak further. Her love for a married man could not show. *Forgive me, Yeshua.*

"He taught me many things. If it had not been for him, I would be living with the Essenes. That would not have served me well since they do not believe in the resurrection and Grandfather experienced it." He opened the door and waited for her to go in first.

She took one last glance at the sunset before stepping under the lintel into Father's room.

"Jerusha, my little lioness, come," her father said and patted the fleece cover. "Sit here." His voice sounded stronger than before. He sat with his back propped up with silk pillows. Stephen and Joshua stood on each side at his head.

"Samuel, you sit here." He patted the other side of the mittah.

Jerusha sat beside her father and held his hand against her cheek. It felt warm and alive.

"I love you, Father." She kissed it and laid it in his lap. "It looks like you are feeling better."

Joshua came around and sat on the end of the bed and faced his grandfather.

"What did it feel like to be dead?" he asked, with his hand on his sword. "Was it scary?"

"Joshua!" Samuel glared.

Joshua cowered. "Well, I was just wondering. I do not know anyone who died and came back. Do you, Samuel?" His eyes perked up.

Jacob put his hand up. "It is alright, Samuel. He asks many questions, like his mother always did. You cannot blame him for his curiosity. It will serve him well one day," He smiled at Joshua. "I felt more alive than ever. Great peace. Surrounded by love and beauty beyond words and people I knew who had died before me."

"Like Grandmother? You saw Grandmother?"

Jacob stared for a minute in silence. "She was so beautiful," he whispered.

"Did you see Yeshua?"

"Yes," Jacob squinted, "He sent me back."

"Why?"

Father looked at Jerusha and grinned. "Your mother pulled on him with her faith. I am here for a short while until I accomplish all He has for me."

"How long, Grandfather?" Stephen spoke. He had moved around and stood behind Joshua.

"I do not know. I only know one thing, and that is I want to release a blessing. That is why I summoned you here now. First, I must talk to my daughter alone."

"Yes, Grandfather, we will be outside when you are ready to give us your blessings." Samuel took the lead. He kissed Jerusha's cheek and left the room.

"Do not worry about Mother, Grandfather; we will take care of her." Jerusha looked up at Stephen, her gentle giant, who had tears in his eyes. He kissed her cheek as well, then left so quietly for a man of huge stature.

Joshua hugged Jerusha. "I am sorry about what has happened to Grandfather, Mother. I never had a father. At least yours is alive. Antonius was my only father besides Grandfather. He is gone, and I miss him." His voice cracked, and he stopped, unable to speak, then threw himself on his grandfather's chest, his cries muffled against her father's cloak. "I love you, Grandfather. Do not leave me, too." He hiccupped between cries.

Jerusha leaned over Joshua's back and covered him with a mother's hug. She ached inside for his pain. He acted so grown, whereas on the inside, he was a little boy who longed for a father.

Jacob stroked his head. "My time on this earth is limited."

"Do not say that," Jerusha cried, "We need you here forever." She felt like a little girl begging, hoping for the impossible.

"When I am gone, you will not be left orphans. Father YHWH is with you, and where He is, you may be there, also, one with the Father through Yeshua's blood. Look to Him. He will never forsake you or leave you. He is your Royal Father." He patted Joshua's head. "Now I need to talk with my little lioness alone."

Joshua wiped his tears. "Just as Stephen had said, we will take care of Mother." He kissed her cheek, rose, and left the room.

When the door was closed, her father took her hand.

"Do not be ashamed of your love for Antonius. He has been a father to your sons these last ten years. I have seen his love for you. He often spoke of it to me. He had no idea his wife lived, or he would have looked for her. Do not hold it against him. Besides, I question whether she is alive. Remember, I was there—unless, of course, YHWH resurrected her." He squeezed her hand. "But she did not have one with faith cry out for her as I did." He smiled. "I have also seen your love for him grow, even though you denied it, until recently. You have done no wrong. You allowed him, even coerced him, to leave and go to his wife. Keep your heart pure. It is only normal to miss him, now that he is gone. I do not know why YHWH allowed this to happen. I only know that YHWH is a good Father. He is working for you and Antonius' good. Trust Him, Jerusha, especially when I am gone."

She lay her cheek on his chest. The sobs grew inside. She swallowed the knot in her throat—*no more tears*, she commanded silently and enjoyed his soothing caress.

"You are stronger than you know my little lioness. "I am leaving you an inheritance. A time will come when you will leave Jerusalem. You will know when it is time. Listen to Father YHWH. Yeshua said we should flee when we see the armies surrounding Jerusalem. You will know the time. When it comes, do not worry about leaving the villa. Father YHWH's kingdom is greater than any earthly possession. Your grandfather has prepared a place in Perea, but your earthly inheritance is in Father YHWH's hands. Never forget who you belong to. You are royalty. The nations are your inheritance, mother of nations."

"Father, I do not know where the scepter is. Do you know?"

"It is safe. When you need it, you will find it. Its power is temporary. The true power is in Yeshua's scepter of righteousness."

"I do not understand."

He smiled. "You will. Now bring my grandsons."

She rose and opened the large wooden door that had pomegranates carved around its edges, Father's handiwork, a reminder of the box he made for her pendant. Her three sons each hugged her.

"Are you alright?" Samuel asked.

"Yes," she sniffed. "Thank you for asking."

Father sat up straighter, reached beneath the pillow, and pulled out a vial with oil. "Samuel, Stephen, and Joshua, line up behind

Jerusha," She took her place beside Father and bent over. He poured oil on her head. "I bless you with the blessings of Abraham, Isaac, and Jacob." Drops from her head fell to his chest. She knelt beside him. Her heart swelled as he anointed each son. Tears coursed down her cheeks as each one knelt around the mittah in honor of their grandfather. The aroma of frankincense permeated the room. When he finished, he raised both hands and extended them over their heads.

"You are royalty, the seed of Abraham by the blood of Jesus Christ." He looked at each grandson, then smiled at Jerusha,

"You are the beginning of grace and elegance, the mark of purity in Christ, and the excellence of dignity and the excellence of power. I bless you now!

"YHWH before whom I have walked and served, the God who has fed me all my life, You have protected and guided me. The Son of God, Yeshua Christos, who has redeemed me from evil. The Holy Ghost, who has empowered me and resides in me, and the angel of YHWH who walks with me and protects me, bless you now!

"You are they whom many shall praise for the glory of God in Yeshua Christos! YHWH's hand shall be on the necks of your enemies, and their children shall worship and bow down to the God of Abraham, Isaac, and Jacob through Yeshua Christos. The rod that buds forth will be in your family to a thousand generations. All that you put your hands to shall prosper, and it will be nourishing bread to many. They, too, shall become rich by the Lord and they will bless many.

"May you be a great speaker who does not flatter but speaks the truth that is received. May you be a fruitful bough by a clean and pure well, and may your branches run over the wall.

"I bless you with forgiveness for people, mercy to be in your heart, and passion for the Lamb of God and YHWH Almighty. May you have intimacy with the Father in heaven and that this will lead to knowing His heart in all matters. May grace flow into your family line from the favor of God.

"May your bow of battle remain in strength, and may your arms be made strong by the Mighty God of Abraham, Isaac, and Jacob, in the name of Yeshua Christos.

"May you hear the voice of the Holy Ghost clearly and obey it at all times. May you know Yeshua Christos as Lord and Savior with love built on our heavenly Father's precepts.

"May the marketplace open up to you as you take ownership in this realm, and may you treat those who come into your hands as Yeshua Christos would do.

"When you marry, I speak forth that your marriage will be as strong as Christos in His love for His bride. May you seek your helpmate's best at any cost in love and all living.

"May God, the One True God of our fathers, help you, and may the Almighty bless you with the blessings of heaven above and the blessings of the deep beneath.

"The blessings that I have as a father have exceeded the blessing of my ancestors in lands, hills, deeds, and successes. They shall be on your head and in your hand and so much greater. May the crown of the Lord, from the ancient paths of Jeremiah 6:16, be on your head, and may you have wisdom as your sister, and understanding as your intimate friend.

"May you seek that which is above, where Yeshua Christos is seated. You will be the head and not the tail, the lender and not the borrower, with your steps ordered of God.

"May you dwell in secure camps, peaceful habitations, and quiet resting places. And may the Captain of the Hosts be with your seed.

"I seal this in the Holy Ghost in you, in the name of Yeshua Christos! Amen!"

Jacob dropped his hands and closed his eyes.

"Father," Jerusha grasped his shoulders and shook him. "Father!" Her tears dropped on his cheek.

Samuel felt his neck. "He is gone, Mother."

Jerusha laid her head on his chest, hoping to hear a heartbeat and then looked up at Samuel, who shook his head.

"I am sorry, Mother. He is gone."

"No, Father I need you." She tried to hug him. His body felt limp, lifeless.

"He went to see Grandmother." Joshua's eyes filled with tears.

"He is with Yeshua and the others in the kingdom." Stephen grasped Jacob's hand. "I will miss you, Grandfather." He wiped one lone tear from his face.

Jerusha clung to her father's body. Her sobs echoed in the room. After a few minutes, she looked up, her eyes burning and swollen. Samuel knelt beside Stephen and Joshua, head bowed and prayed. She arose from her father's bed and went to them. All three looked up.

"We will be all right, Mother." Samuel spoke with a new authority and stood. "Yeshua is with us, and His Father will take care of us."

"We have the blessing," Stephen added and rose up.

"The Lord of Hosts will fight for us." Joshua stood and patted his sword.

"Group hug." Jerusha extended her arms. As they huddled together, her thoughts went to the promise she had clung to for years. *The Lord shall teach all your children, and great shall be their peace.*

"Bring the burial spices, ointment, and linens. Tell Chaya, Hannah, and Miriam that I will need their help. When we have the body ready, we will let you know."

Chapter 19

J erusha stood barefoot in the early morning darkness beneath the jujube tree outside the gate. Her father's body lay on the bier, ready to be carried to the tomb. She removed the veil over her mouth and reached down and kissed him.

"Shalom, Father. Until we meet in the kingdom." She replaced her veil, reached beneath her cloak, and tore her tunic to show the rending of her heart. She nodded to Samuel, Stephen, Joshua, and Moses, who lifted the bier and carried it down the terraced steps. She took a handful of dust from under the jujube tree, where she had spent many hours with Father discussing the condition of the city, and threw it on her head, then followed the bier. Chaya, Hannah, and Miriam lamented and cried out a qinah of old.

"And all the people bewailed with great lamentation . . . And said: How is the mighty man fallen, that saved the people of Israel." The three women wailed in honor of Jacob, their feet and heads bare and lips veiled. Chaya's silver hair glistened beneath the morning sun, a striking contrast to Hannah's shiny black locks.

As they made their descent through the streets, the sun peeked over the Mount of Olives and cast orange ribbons through white clouds that streaked across the mountaintop. One lone butterfly fluttered before Jerusha and then landed on the bier. Her Father's words from years past echoed in her thoughts. *"Jerusha, never forget who you are. You are royalty from the tribe of Judah. You will dance before the king."* She remembered dancing in the garden and chasing butterflies, carefree and childlike in faith. *"My little lioness, He makes all things beautiful in its time."* Tears rolled down her cheeks. What would happen to her and her family now that Father was gone? The other side of the veil in YHWH's kingdom was so close, and yet, it seemed so far away. How would she find her way without his counsel? How would Father YHWH make all things beautiful?

She watched the winged creature flitter down the hill in front of the bier and land on a pomegranate's red blossom. *"My little butterfly, you do not look like you know where you are going, but you always get where YWWH wants you to go."*

The sun shone brightly on the limestone dwellings in the lower city and many—man, woman, and child—followed their procession. Her heart swelled with love for them, the same love Father had. He gave his life that they would know Yeshua. If she had to, she would do the same. Her heart beat with Yeshua's love—the same love that beat within Father. No better way to honor him. She could do no less. It was in her blood, Yeshua's blood.

She smiled at a young girl, a stranger. The little one cried, her tears making clean streams down a dirty face. The youngster scurried to catch up.

"Your father loved me and made me a pendant." The girl smudged her face as she wiped the tears and walked beside Jerusha, and then reached beneath her tunic and pulled out a wooden image that hung on a leather cord. "I will never forget him. He told me about Yeshua, and that I was royalty, and . . . and, how much he loved you." The little girl stumbled and fell face down on the dusty path. "I want to be like you." She looked up at Jerusha. Why would this girl want to be like her?

Jerusha yelled at Samuel to stop. She raised the little one to her feet and hugged her tight. "You will do greater things than me," she whispered in her ear, then brushed her cloak and noticed the girl's hand still clutching the pendant.

"May I see?" Jerusha touched her fist.

The girl's small, slender fingers slowly opened and unveiled a lion's face carved into the wooden pendant, a butterfly image on its nose. Tears formed in Jerusha's eyes.

"I had one like this." She picked it up. "I gave it to someone." She turned it over, and just as she thought, the same words were carved on the back, "*Arise, Lord. Let your enemies be scattered. Let all who hate you flee before you.*"

Her thoughts turned to Sarah, the one with Grandfather, who had her pendant and the one in Yeshua's kingdom with Father. She smiled at the thought that the latter danced with him and Timon in a meadow of butterflies. *Maybe Yeshua had many daughters he called "his little butterfly."*

"Where is your mother?" Jerusha looked around at the hundreds that gathered to honor her father.

"There. She is waving. See?" The little girl waved and darted between the people to get to the woman, then looked back and yelled, "We will pray for you and your family."

Jerusha turned away. Father's life had touched so many. She scanned the crowd. She recognized many widows Father had helped. They cried and threw dust on their heads. What would happen to them?

One came and threw herself at Jerusha's feet. The old woman's tears dripped on her feet.

"I would have died during the drought had it not been for your father." She threw dust on her head. "He never tired of me showing up at his gate." She kept her head down. "I never left empty handed." The fragile woman looked up and wiped the tears away.

Jerusha raised her to her feet. "You are welcome at our gate anytime," she said, then motioned for Samuel to continue. She never knew the full extent of her father's love for the people until now. His influence in the city humbled her.

As the brier moved under the arch into the marketplace, a Roman legionnaire cleared their path. When her father's body passed, he saluted him with a fist against his chest. Even Rome had been touched, and so many others, too, in faraway lands like Antonius, who came to know Yeshua, only because her father chose to obey YHWH and serve in Rome's army. A Hebrew in Rome's army seemed an impossible feat. Somehow, YHWH kept him safe.

Jerusha had feared he would die by Roman hands or while fighting with Romans in Gentile nations. The opposite happened. According to Antonius, a Jew brought the death blow. Antonius never caught him, but the man was dressed in Hebrew garments with tzitzits on his cloak's corners.

As Father's bier passed beneath the eastern gate, another Roman soldier, who stood atop, saluted. Jerusha wondered if these who saluted had secretly converted to the Way. Her father cared that men of all nations enter Yeshua's kingdom, even Romans.

How she longed for Antonius's presence, his strength, and wisdom—without Father's guidance, she felt so alone, almost abandoned.

"Never forget who you belong to," Father's dying words reverberated softly.

Her mind went back to a little girl in the garden, sitting on Father's lap.

Who am I, Father? She had stared into his eyes, the same color as hers, and green with a blue rim, most unusual for a Hebrew.

"You are royalty, from the tribe of Judah." He laughed and smiled at her, the butterflies fluttering around his head, then the picture changed. She saw in her mind's eyes, his head in her hands, face pale, almost lifeless, his eyes glazing over in death. Jerusha's eyes overflowed with tears. She sniffed and wiped at her eyes.

"You are Yeshua's wife, Father YHWH's daughter. Promise me you will never forget it. Promise me, Jerusha," he begged.

"I promise, Father. I promise never to forget." She felt tired and thankful it was only a little further up Kidron valley to their family tomb in Shaveh valley—the valley of kings.

Jerusha remembered sitting with Father at her mother's burial site while he reiterated the story of Melchizedek, king of Salem, the priest of the Most High. He said he brought bread and wine and blessed Abram after YHWH delivered him from his enemies. Afterward,

Abram gave him a tithe, keeping nothing for himself of the spoils of war. She must remember to give her tithe to Yeshua, who reigned as High Priest and King. No wonder so many priests hated him. They could not humble themselves and become as little children and enter a kingdom they could not see.

She glanced up high on the Mount of Olives where many priests gathered and watched from a distance, not wanting to dirty themselves by getting too near a dead body. Inwardly, she laughed. Yeshua called them whitewashed sepulchers, full of dead men's bones. A little lower on the hill and scattered among another crowd that watched from afar, the Pharisees, Father's former teachers, and friends sneered and mocked.

The sun shone high above. Samuel, Stephen, Joshua, and Moses placed her father's body inside the limestone tomb. She stood outside and looked at all those who mourned. She had heard Paul admonish in the synagogue to weep with those who weep and to rejoice with those who rejoiced. So many heeded his words, and for that, she was grateful. It made her not feel so lonely.

Joshua stepped outside the tomb first, his eyes red and swollen.

"I will miss him." His voice quivered.

Stephen, her gentle giant, came out behind him and put his hand on his shoulder. "We all will miss him." His deep voice echoed in the valley.

"Because of his prayers, I am healed of my stuttering," Moses said as he stepped out of the tomb.

"Mother," Samuel shouted from inside, "Come in here!"

Jerusha hurried to the tomb and ducked under. Her father's body lay on a limestone slab. The damp, cool air felt good against her sweaty body. Sunrays shone through the opening and lit the cave. The aroma of frankincense filled the air. She smiled.

"He leaves his fragrance everywhere he goes, even in death." She touched her father's body and stared at his face. He looked peaceful. "What has you so troubled, Samuel?" She looked up.

"I thought I heard something when we laid Grandfather's body on the slab. I waited for Stephen and Joshua to leave before looking." Samuel rubbed his hand on the tomb wall. "I think this crack in the wall opened when we placed Grandfather on the slab. "Look," he said as he pulled with both hands. "It is another room." He ducked low and stuck his head inside the three-foot opening. "It is too dark to see what is in there without a lamp."

"Probably another burial room," Jerusha said as she peeked inside and saw only darkness.

"Can we bring a torch and look inside?" Samuel's question reminded her of Joshua's curiosity. Father said that it might serve him well someday. Maybe this new adventure would help them all through this dark time.

"When we come in to apply the final ointments, we will bring a torch or lamp."

"What could be in there?" His excitement was contagious.

"Probably nothing too exciting, but it will give you something to think about for three days while we grieve and wait."

Jerusha ducked outside and stepped into the bright sunlight. She squinted against the sun. A figure stood next to Stephen. She could not make out who it was. He was not as tall as Stephen. He had a fringed robe with tzitzits at the corners. She shielded her eyes.

"Effah? What are you doing here?"

"I heard about your father." He stepped near.

"Of course you heard. The whole town wailed and lamented." She exaggerated some but made her point and then stepped away and watched the stream of mourners make their way through the valley away from the tomb. Chaya, Hannah, and Miriam stared at Effah. Chaya's lips moved—silent prayer, no doubt. Jerusha turned and faced Effah.

"You followed me. Why?" She placed her hands on her hips.

"You are in danger." His scrunched brow seemed sincere, but she did not trust him.

"There you go again. Pretending you care." She spread her arms out in a circle.

"I do care. I promised Antonius I would take care of you."

"That I do not believe." She crossed her arms and turned her back. "Go. This is not the time for such talk."

"I have a soft place for you to rest." Joshua squatted beneath a makeshift tent, a tarp thrown over the limbs of a scraggly brush. "We have enough water for three days."

"You are not staying at the tomb for three days?" Effah's eyes widened.

"It is our custom."

"Someone must stay. Not you."

"But why not me?" Jerusha cocked her head.

"I told you. You are in danger." He straightened his small stature and moved toward her, his finger pointed in her direction.

"But just how would you know that? Did you stop off at the soothsayer to get that information?"

"I have my sources." He glanced at the backs of the priest who walked under the city gate.

"On second thought, maybe I should believe you. You have your sources because you are one of them. Is that what happened to your wife? You had her killed? Or did you accuse her of adultery? Have her put away, or stoned? You do not care about me. You only care about yourself."

"My wife died of natural causes." He stared at Joshua and turned to her sons. "You must not let her be alone. Stay alert at all times."

"I believe my Mother told you earlier to go." He pulled his sword from the scabbard. "I believe you should take heed and get out of here."

Jerusha almost laughed. Antonius and Father would be proud. She watched Effah walk away. He carried himself like a soldier, maybe because of Antonius's influence. His behavior was a mystery. An unnerving fear spread over her body. *Maybe he was right.* She tried to shake off the thought and made herself comfortable beneath the tent. Chaya and the other women sat beneath another tent with burial ointment for later use.

She heard the grinding sound of limestone as Samuel closed the tomb. The sun glistened against the city's white limestone walls. Jerusha shaded her eyes against the blinding light and watched the Sadducees cross the bridge over Kidron Valley and walk into the temple. In the past, while with Father, she watched as the priest led the scapegoat across the bridge into the wilderness.

"*We no longer need a scapegoat,*" Father had instructed. "*Yeshua carried our sins away.*"

"I will miss you, Father." She removed her cloak, rolled it and placed it beneath her head, and then stretched out in the shade and closed her eyes. Exhausted, she relaxed her body. Not so easy with her mind. It swirled with one thought after another. Father. Antonius. Effah.

The sun's warmth cooled as it dipped behind the Mount of Olives. She removed her cloak from under her head, and used it as a cover against the evening chill and lay her head on the folded tarp that had been over her head.

Chaya, Hannah, and Miriam sat with Samuel, Stephen, and Moses around a campfire. Chaya's lips, as usual, moved in silent prayer. Joshua stood guard on a rock ledge above. Jerusha's eyes became heavy. She let go and closed them. After she breathed in deeply, she let the air escape slowly and tried to relax. She opened her eyes and looked one more time at her surroundings.

"Joshua," she called, "are you up there?"

"Yes, Mother."

Everyone appeared to be safe. She closed her eyes. Darkness came. *"I am in the darkness, too."*

Chapter 20

Jerusha awoke to the jackal's eerie howl in the distance. She sat up. The fire had gone out. The women slept beside orange coals that popped and crackled. Stephen leaned against a rock protrusion next to the women's camp, his cloak wrapped tight around his shoulders, his head down. Samuel sat against a tree, his head bobbing several times before his chin hit his chest.

After Jerusha stood, she lifted her shoulders and turned her head back and forth, then locked her hands and stretched them above her head and let them drop to the ground while arching her back. It felt good to stretch her achy muscles. She grabbed her cloak and walked up the steep incline and looked for Joshua, who had been stationed on a rock formation above her head. It was too dark to see.

In the distance another jackal screeched and howled. She shivered and looked for the moon and found a tiny sliver. The stars twinkled against a black cloudless sky. The sparse shrubs and trees stood like dark cloaked figures with spindly fingers. Her feet slipped on the rocky soil, and she fell to her knees. She saw no sign of Joshua. Her heart beat increased and drummed in her ears. She pushed against the ground with her hands, stood, and leaned into her steep climb.

At the rock cliff, where Joshua sat earlier, she saw no sign of him. She lifted her cloak above her sandals and continued her climb, dodging thorny shrubs and meandering between fig and almond trees. Where could he be?

She came to a flat, cleared opening and found a small goat with its throat cut, its blood poured upon the stone altar in the middle of a circle of stones, his body cut down the middle and laid open. She stopped and gazed at the eyes and the remnant of white fur that had surely been soft and shiny yet was now caked in red, some kind of blood sacrifice to a false god. In the distance, cries, like the ones coming from the witch's dwelling, disrupted the nighttime quiet. Scanning the darkness, she shivered at the abomination she saw before her.

A tiny light in the distance flickered.

Why would Joshua make camp that high up? she wondered. She hoped it was him and wondered if it really was as she wound her way between a grove of tamarisk trees and kept her eye on the campfire. It grew brighter the higher she climbed. Hair stood up on her arms the closer she got, and it finally dawned on her. This could not be Joshua's camp.

A rock tumbled down the hill behind her, and she turned. Was it a gazelle? Or did someone follow? High above, a loud cry broke the silence.

"Satan, satan, your kingdom come. Your will be done on earth as it is in hell." The chant repeated again and again, increasing in volume.

She raised her cloak above her sandals and started to run back down the hill. Her heart raced. She scampered as fast as she could, and the chant stopped. She stopped to catch her breath and waited in the dark, her heart thumping wildly. Where could Joshua be? Panic gripped her thoughts. *He's dead. He's dead. He's dead.*

No. She squeezed her temples between her hands, trying to train herself not to think the worst. *No.*

All you touch die. Your father's dead.

A stream of toxic thought swirled in her mind.

Her head felt like it would explode, as if Father's carpenter tool had gripped it like the boards he held in place while he sawed. The wind picked up and carried a new chant. New words reverberated across the valley, chasing her.

"Orphan. Orphan. Orphan."

Jerusha felt dizzy and stumbled to the nearby tamarisk tree. Its scant pink blossoms scattered in the wind, and she held tight to its trunk.

The crunch of footsteps in the dry rocky soil startled her, and she held her breath. Is that what it was? The smell of danger filled her with fear. The footsteps seemed louder, but she couldn't be certain. The wind and chants made it impossible to be sure. She turned, and looked downhill into the blackness, at a shadowy figure making its way up. It was too tall to be Joshua, so she ducked behind the tree and watched.

The wind whipped her radyid off her head, and she quickly grabbed it before it blew away and clutched it to her chest. The dark apparition stepped into the cleared opening below and kept moving. Whoever it was walked with purpose, like they knew their way. As the dark figure approached, Jerusha scrunched farther behind the tree and crouched down.

The figure wound his way through the tamarisks, turned away from Jerusha, and continued a steady upward climb toward the fire above. *Who is that man? What is he doing here? What does he have to do with Joshua's disappearance?* She choked back tears. *Is Joshua alright? Did that man kill him?*

"I cannot take another death," she whispered to YHWH. "Let them take me." Tears formed. "Not my sons."

After several minutes, when she knew she would not be seen, she came out from the tree. She wrapped the radiyd over her head and held it tightly against the wind, then started her descent. She must find Joshua. The chants stopped, and the wind calmed. Rocks tumbled down below.

She stared in the darkness, frustrated that she could not see. She squinted, as if that would help. She crept behind another tamarisk and waited for whoever it was to get closer or go away. Or maybe it was Joshua. She hoped it was Joshua. *Please be Joshua.*

Two figures climbed steady, like the other man, but they seemed not sure where to go. The larger figure stopped at the cleared opening a short way below.

"Mother?" Stephen's deep voice echoed across the valley. "Joshua?" Samuel called.

Relieved, Jerusha came out from hiding. "Oh, I am so glad it is you. I could not tell in the dark who was coming, so I hid. Did you hear those eerie chants uphill?" She made her way down to where they waited.

"I see someone has sacrificed to a false god," Samuel said, touching the bloody stone. "It is fresh. It has not been long since someone has been here."

"Do you suppose this has anything to do with the witch in the city?" Stephen asked.

"I am sure it does. Did you hear what they chanted? Jerusha tugged on her radiyd.

"No, I could not make it out. Samuel grabbed the loose end and handed it to her. "Here, Mother, let me help."

"The wind muffled their words and carried them another direction," Stephen said and offered his arm.

"Well, I will not repeat the abominable curses. What really worries me is where Joshua is. Have you seen him?" She grabbed Stephen's arm and steadied herself.

"No. When I awoke and found you and Joshua missing," Stephen said as he took small steps, "I woke up Samuel and we came looking for you. We left the other women with Moses."

Samuel came to her other side and offered his arm, "We must get back. No doubt the others are awake and wondering where we are." He took her elbow.

Jerusha felt sick. Fear—that old enemy from her past—knotted her stomach. Her hands shook and her knees felt week. She had to hang onto Stephen and Samuel all the way down. She collapsed on the folded tarp. Chaya, Miriam, and Hannah gathered around while Moses conversed with Stephen.

"Is Joshua here?" She knew the answer, but hoped she was wrong. She grasped her shaking hands.

"No. We have not seen him. We assumed he was with you." The peace in Chaya's voice calmed Jerusha's inner quaking. Moses placed the extra burial ointment inside the tomb.

"Let's go back to the villa," Samuel said as he took charge. "If Joshua is not there, Stephen and I will go look for him. It would be better if you stayed behind locked gates at the villa. We cannot be sure about Effah's warning. I will not take a chance with your life, especially after what we saw and heard up there." He gathered the tarp. "We will take a different way back—across the Kidron Bridge that goes into the temple. Surely no harm will come as we make our way through the temple court."

"I would not be so sure of that after what happened to Paul." Jerusha felt she could trust no one in the religious community. She even wondered if spies harbored among those who followed the Way. How else did the Sanhedrin know who to arrest?

"I am not that cynical, yet," Samuel answered.

Jerusha shrugged.

"Show us the way. We'll follow you."

Samuel and Stephen went first, then the women. Moses guarded from the back. They climbed a narrow path up the Mount of Olives that led to the bridge. At the bridge, Jerusha glanced at the city. Only a few lights speckled the darkness. Even with little moonlight, the temple's beauty stood out against the maze of dwellings in the lower city. As they crossed the bridge and came nearer to the temple, the shofar blasted the changing of watches. She hoped before this watch ended she would find Joshua.

For some reason, Chaya seemed especially occupied with Miriam. She held her hand and stopped periodically to whisper in her ear. Hannah, too, seemed concerned. Jerusha hoped it was not trouble with her pregnancy. Weeks ago, Father had said Moses felt Miriam might not come back emotionally from another miscarriage. Jerusha shook her head. She remembered well the pain of miscarriage after miscarriage.

"Father YHWH, do not allow another little one to be taken from her womb," she whispered into the darkness. "And do not allow my son, my precious son, to be taken." She pictured Joshua's face. "Smiley, I hope you are safe."

***

The sun peeked over the horizon by the time they reached the gate. The roosters crowed, a sign of a new watch. Stephen jiggled the key in the lock and opened the gate. Chaya led Miriam inside.

"Jerusha, will it be alright if Miriam and Moses stay with us?" The tension in Chaya's voice answered Jerusha's question about the miscarriage.

"Of course," she answered.

"I will prepare the room." Hannah ran up the path.

Moses rushed past Jerusha and caught up with Miriam.

"Joshua!" Jerusha hollered. "Joshua!" She hurried through the garden gate. Doves cooed in the olive trees as she wound the pomegranate lined paths. "Joshua!" she yelled again.

In the courtyard Stephen yelled for him, too. When she came out the gate, she saw Stephen take three large strides up the stairs to the marble colonnade. He ran its length yelling Joshua's name.

"I will check the stable," Jerusha said and ran through the courtyard and kitchen. Once outside, she hustled along the herb garden paths. She wrinkled her nose at the smell of fresh manure added to the plants the day before. She pulled with both arms and slid open the stable's heavy cedar door. The horses whinnied and stomped.

Joshua," she yelled, "Joshua, are you in here?"

A goat nudged her leg as she rubbed Boaz's nose and glanced around. She ran to the back wall and pressed hard with her shoulder against the secret door. It budged a little. She shoved a little harder and it opened enough for her to go inside.

"Joshua! Joshua!" she hollered as she looked into the darkened cave. His name echoed back.

She grasped her head and slumped against the stone wall to the cold floor. Where could he be?

The secret door opened further, and Samuel stepped inside.

"He is not here." Her voice quivered. "Where could he be? It is not like him to leave, shirk his responsibility to protect."

"He has been known to wander off. Maybe something got his curiosity up. I will search for him in the city and ask around."

"I will go with you. Two will be better than one."

"No, Mother, promise me you will stay here. Besides, I think Chaya will need help with Miriam. Stephen and I will find him." He helped her to her feet.

"If you find him, you three come straight back her, so I know he is alright." She straightened her radiyd and brushed her cloak.

Samuel smiled. "What else would we do?"

"Who knows what two boys . . ."

"Men, mother."

"Barely men. Would find to do." She stepped through the secret door. He followed and pushed it shut. "Go! Hurry! I just hope you can find him and he's not-not-," she hesitated and continued, "hurt or, or worse."

Chapter 21

"Miriam?" Jerusha tapped lightly and listened. "Miriam? Are you alright?" Chaya peeked out, then opened the door wider.

"She is spotting. So far, not much. When she has done this before, it turned into a full miscarriage. She is afraid it will happen again," Chaya whispered.

Jerusha looked at Miriam, who lay on the mittah, her eyes closed, her belly protruding. Jerusha's own pregnancy never lasted long enough to have a protruding belly. She sat down beside her and laid her hand on her belly. The movement beneath her hand meant life, a beating heart, a baby growing. Miriam opened her eyes.

"What is wrong with me, Jerusha? Am I cursed that I cannot give Moses a son or daughter? What have I done wrong that I do not have the blessing of a fruitful womb?"

A little bulge puffed up beneath Jerusha's hand.

"Your baby knows your voice." She smiled at Miriam. "I have never felt a baby's movement in a mother's womb. No wonder Chaya loves being a midwife. Every birth a miracle. Some more than others."

Jerusha stared at Miriam's belly and remembered what Chaya had told her about her birth. "*You should have died. Your father paced the garden with Yeshua. Yeshua told him that YHWH makes all things beautiful in its time, then handed him a round wooden piece with a butterfly carved on it.*" His little butterfly.

"I can only tell you that you have a Creator and Father who loves you. His ways are not our ways. They are better. There was a time when I did not believe that and felt cursed. In time, I came to accept him as a good Father. Jerusha thought of Joshua. Would she be able to say that if he turned up dead? "Sometimes, even now, when things do not go the way I want, I have to remind myself of that truth." She closed her eyes. "Help me Holy Ghost."

"I am afraid," Miriam whimpered. "I cannot be as strong as you."

The baby pushed against Jerusha's hand again. "He knows your voice. Speak to your baby, Miriam. Tell him he will not die, but live and declare the works of the Lord."

"I can't Jerusha. I can't. I have no faith."

Jerusha smiled and thought of Father.

"You only need enough faith the size of a mustard seed. Speak, Miriam, speak to your baby. I will do it with you. We will do it together."

"Baby, you will not die—say it, Miriam," Jerusha encouraged.

"Baby, you will not die." Miriam's words were weak and soft.

"But live and declare the works of the Lord," Jerusha spoke with authority.

"But live and declare the works of the Lord." Miriam smiled. "Baby, you will not die, but live and declare the works of the Lord." Her voice sounded stronger. She placed her hand on the bulge in her side. "I think he is dancing." She laughed, then became serious. "Oh, no, she groaned, "I felt more blood ooze out."

Chaya checked beneath the cover. "It is only a little. If you can wait for a few more weeks, this baby will be big enough to live."

"I am so afraid, Chaya," Miriam started to weep.

Jerusha continued confidently. "This baby will not die, but live and declare the works of the Lord," Jerusha spoke with a stronger faith than she had ever felt. "I speak life to this baby. You will not die, but live and declare the works of the Lord."

"Baby, you will not die, but live and declare the works of the Lord," Miriam repeated.

Jerusha smiled at Chaya who added her voice to the decree.

"Baby," she bent down, her face inches from Miriam's belly. "You will not die, but live and declare the works of the Lord."

Jerusha sat beside Miriam and wiped the tears from her cheeks.

"You keep making your declaration, Miriam. YHWY's word will not return void. This baby will be born." She stood and walked to the door. "I will be in the garden praying, if you need me."

**

The sun shone through the olive tree branches. A soft breeze rustled the silver leaves. Jerusha opened the garden gate and walked the pomegranate tree-lined path. The fragrant red blossoms against dark green foliage cheered her thoughts. Her radiyd had dropped to her shoulders, and her hair hung free. She stopped and picked a blossom and twirled it in her fingers. She walked around the corner to Father's bench. Oh, how she missed him, his wisdom and strength. When he was around, she felt wise and strong. How ever would she make it without him?

She thought about what she had seen and heard in Kidron valley. It made her angry. How dare them turn Yeshua's prayer against him and send an orphan curse. They should know his power is greater. She began to pace back and forth. "It is written, no weapon formed against you will prosper, and every tongue that rises against you, you can refute. I take authority against every word spoken against Yeshua and his people and put them under his feet and render them powerless."

She stopped pacing and knelt at Father's bench, her head down, eyes closed, and listened to the thrushes welcome the morning with song. A soft breeze blew through her hair.

"Our Father." She raised her head and looked up. "Who art in heaven. Hallowed be your name. Your kingdom come." She paused and contemplated Father's words. *"There is a thin veil between here and the kingdom."* "Your kingdom come, your will be done, on earth as it is in heaven." Remembering what she had heard on the mountain, she repeated. *Your kingdom come. Your will be done on earth as it is in heaven.* Give us this day our daily bread. And forgive us our debts, as we forgive our debtors."

She stopped. *Had she forgiven Effah? She had chosen to forgive, but had she really forgiven him? Help me, Holy Ghost, to forgive him fully.* Lead us not into temptation, but deliver us from evil." She stopped again. *So much evil in the city—corrupt priests, witches, false teachers, zealots.* "Sing songs of deliverance over my family, Father YHWH," she whispered. "For yours is the kingdom and the power and the glory forever." Restless, she stood and paced. "Your kingdom come, your will be done, on earth as it is in heaven." She repeated the words, "Your kingdom come, your will be done, on earth as it is in heaven."

She heard the gate open, stopped, and spun around.

"Joshua!" She ran straight at him and hugged with all her might. "I am so happy you are not dead."

"I am happy I am not dead, too." He laughed. "I kinda like it here."

"Where have you been? I have been so worried." She grasped his cloak front and shook him.

"Let's sit on Grandfather's bench." He freed his cloak. "We need to talk."

"Yes. We do need to talk." She sat down and pulled on his arm until he sat beside her.

He looked into her eyes. "While you were sleeping at the tomb, I heard something and decided to find out what it was, so I circled around the sound." He motioned with his finger. "It was a man spying on you."

Jerusha's eyes widened. "He had not seen me and did not know I was watching. About that time, you woke up and went looking for me."

"Oh, Joshua, if I had known what you were doing." She dropped her hands in her lap.

"Mother, you are interrupting."

"Oh, I am sorry. Be quick to listen, Jerusha, slow to speak," she chided. Joshua put his finger to his mouth. She frowned.

"He followed you, and I followed him." He continued, "It was so dark he could not see you hiding behind the tamarisk, so he passed you and headed toward the fire uphill. After Samuel and Stephen found you and I knew you were safe, I found that man and watched him. He conversed with the witch, then I followed him into town where he entered Herod's palace."

"Herod's palace?" Jerusha hated that place. "More evil goes on there than anyone knows."

Joshua stood and slapped his sword. "Mother, I think Effah is telling the truth. Someone wants to hurt you. You need to be careful."

Jerusha sighed.

"Well, after what I saw last night, you may be right. I just do not understand why Effah knows all this, if he is not involved somehow. There are things in our past that makes it difficult to trust him."

"Antonius trusted him. He told me. He asked Effah to look out for you. He asked all of us to look out for you."

"What am I? Some kind of child that everyone thinks I need looked after?" She stood and paced again.

"What business is it of Antonius anyway? He left—to be with his wife. I can take care of myself."

"If you say so, Mother." Joshua walked toward the gate. "I need to find Stephen and Samuel. We are going back to the tomb and see what is in that hole."

"Not without me," Jerusha put her hands on her hips.

Joshua raised his eyebrows.

"Did you hear anything I said?" She shook her finger.

"Excuse me, Jerusha, there is someone at the villa entrance asking for you." Hannah stood at the garden gate.

Jerusha looked at Hannah. "I will be right there," then she leaned into Joshua. "We will discuss this later."

"You are not going, Mother. It is not safe." Joshua continued his plea and followed her to the front gate.

"Effah! Can I not get rid of you? You seemed to be stuck to me like a bad dream." She talked through the iron gate.

He chuckled.

"Jerusha, Jerusha, my friend. When will you understand that I have your well-being in mind?" He bowed and smiled. For the first time, since she was a girl, she saw a twinkle in his eye that was much more attractive than what she saw in his eyes as a child. It reminded her of Yeshua. She shook her head. Not a chance.

"Do not 'my friend' me," she countered.

"As much as I would enjoy this banter, I came for a much more serious matter. I heard talk in the palace that more than forty men have bound themselves by an oath neither to eat nor drink till they have killed Paul. They came to the chief priests and elders and told them of their oath and asked them to give notice to the tribune to bring him down to them, as though they were going to determine his case more exactly. And they will kill him before he comes near."

"Why do you care what happens to Paul?" Jerusha felt Joshua standing behind her.

He interrupted the conversation by whispering in her ear.

"Ima, I have seen Effah in the synagogues listening to Paul's teachings. He seemed genuinely interested."

"Send Joshua to Paul's sister." Effah continued, "Tell her to send her son to the fortress to warn Paul. I will arrange it with the centurion to let him in the barracks. She will not believe me, but if the warning comes from this family, she will act on it."

Jerusha stared at Effah and contemplated in silence. Could he be trusted? If she dismissed his warning and Paul was killed, she would never forgive herself. But what would Effah have to gain by telling such a story? she reasoned. If what he says is true, wouldn't he be in danger for telling them about it? Why put himself in such danger? His warning about her danger seemed to be true. Maybe, he can be trusted. Maybe he *is* a Yeshua follower.

"Jerusha, please," Effah begged, "there is not much time."

"Go, Joshua, give Paul's sister the message," Jerusha kept her eyes on Effah, "If anything happens to Paul's sister, her son, or Joshua, I will never trust you or your word again. You will answer to Father YHWH. It is a fearful thing to fall into his hand." She looked at Joshua, who was unlocking the gate. "Joshua, come back here immediately. Do not go with her son to the barracks. Promise me."

Joshua shut and locked the gate, then hurried down the steps, his sword at his side, then looked back. "I cannot promise. Tell Samuel and Stephen to wait on me before they go back to the tomb." He patted his sword.

"Joshua!" Jerusha yelled.

Dust swirls covered his head as he ran down the hill. Jerusha shook her head. Most would consider him a man. Not her. He was her youngest. Her baby.

"Father YHWH be with you," she whispered.

"He will be." Effah drew near the gate. "And I will protect him as well."

A well of emotions whirled inside Jerusha. She trusted Antonius with her sons, not Effah. But Antonius was gone. Father was gone. Would Father YHWH use Effah? Not a chance.

"Joshua is in your hands, Father YHWH." She glanced at Effah, who had turned and ran toward the fortress. "And Effah, too."

Chapter 22

Jerusha sat on the ground in the courtyard and stared at bare feet, hers and all those mourners who gathered and wailed her father's death. Not all followed the Way. But all loved her father. Lamps flickered in the dark and cast shadows against her toes.

Their sing-song moans irritated her. It may be custom, but father would not want this kind of display. What about what James said: "Count it all joy when you have various trials"? How could she speak this truth in love? Turn mourning into dancing?

She did not feel like dancing, but experience had taught her that every time she chose to dance to her King, especially when she did not feel like it, it brought tremendous freedom and victory. Should she ask them to dance? She thought of one of Father's favorite Tehillim quotes: "Weeping may endure for a night, but joy comes in the morning."

"Let them mourn," she whispered, then stood and walked to the front gate. The purple and blue mosaic tiles felt cool against her toes.

"Joshua, where are you?" She wanted to go find him but had strict orders from Samuel and Stephen to go nowhere without them. She sighed, looked back at the mourners, and took a path around the inside edge of the wall that surrounded the villa. It avoided going through the main courtyard.

Miriam may need her. It would, at least get her mind off Joshua for a while. As she approached the back of the villa and was ready to turn onto the path to Miriam's room, the back gate rattled. Her heart jumped. She replaced her radiyd and wrapped it around her shoulders, tucking her hair inside, and tried to adjust her eyes to the darkness.

Without lamps lit on this part of the path, she found it difficult to see more than one step ahead at a time. *I am with you in the darkness, too.* She glanced up at the stars and saw Regulus, its brightness even more powerful and bright against the black night.

"Lion of Judah, I know You are with me, One with me, ruling and reigning." Overwhelming peace flooded her entire being like a warm blanket. She tightened her radiyd and walked toward the gate. It was a short distance ahead, through the herb garden, just before she got to the stable.

She had forgotten the lamps had not been lit and chided herself for not having Moses light them. She was able to see the narrow dirt path between the herbs that lead to the stable. Her toes squished in the muddy path, and she stopped beneath the olive tree where Joshua and Sarah watched the butterfly emerge from its dark chrysalis.

"Father YHWH, I do not feel like I know where I am going, but I trust you to get me—get my family—where you want us to go." She encouraged her own spirit. She sensed someone followed and watched. She looked around and saw no one. An eerie presence permeated the atmosphere. Hair stood up on her arms.

"Even though we walk through the valley of the shadow of death, you are with us." She sang the Tehillim to disperse the darkness that threatened to disrupt her peace. The gate rattled, louder this time.

"Mother, open the gate. We forgot our key," Samuel yelled.

Jerusha slopped through the mud and continued singing the Tehillim. "Your rod and your staff they comfort us." She turned up her nose at the manure smell and was careful not to step in it.

"Where have you been? Joshua returned a long time ago and has left again." She fumbled in her girdle for the key, then unlocked the gate. "That boy—I mean man. He exasperates me."

"We know why he is so late," Stephen interrupted and walked inside the gate.

"We talked to him at Paul's sister house." Samuel took the key from her and locked the gate. "We were there when he told her about the conspiracy against Paul." He handed back the key.

"That would have been in the afternoon. Why are you so late getting back here?" She tucked the key in her girdle.

"Stop interrupting, and we will tell you."

"I am sorry. I will try to let you finish before I ask another question."

"When Paul's nephew left, we took Joshua and went back to the tomb to see what was in that hole."

Jerusha opened her mouth to voice her opinion of their decision, then shut it and kept quiet as she had promised. Her sons were grown, and she needed to give them room to be men and make their own decisions. So hard to do. If Father YHWH taught them, then he would guide their steps, too.

"You will not believe what we found there." Stephen offered his arm.

"What? What did you find?" Jerusha could not help herself.

Both sons spontaneously broke into belly laughs.

She stared, annoyed at their amusement.

"We knew you could not do it Mother," Samuel spit out between cackles, "keep quiet, that is." He burst out laughing again.

A little chuckle escaped her mouth, then a deep laugh exploded that lasted so long it made her sides hurt.

"You know me well." She breathed deeply and rubbed her sides. "It felt good to laugh like that again. It has been awhile. Do I dare ask the question again?"

"The scepter! We found the scepter in that hole. The weight of Grandfather's body on the slab opened the secret door."

Jerusha gasped.

"Did you bring it with you?

"No. We left it. Grandfather made a good hiding place for it. When you and the other women go back in a couple of days to apply the final burial ointment, you can see for yourself. But we will go with you, especially now that it has been proven that you are in danger."

"I am tired of all this talk of my danger, but I agree that your grandfather wisely hid it so when we needed it, we would find it. He knew after his death we would need it most. It is only a temporary solution, though. He said in Yeshua's kingdom the scepter of righteousness gave greater power to rule." She scrunched her brow and looked into the darkness.

"Where is Joshua?"

"On our way here, he slipped away." Samuel chewed on his nail, a nervous habit.

"How could he just slip away without you knowing it?" she reprimanded.

"Well, he did. I guess we were not paying enough attention. We think he may have gone to the barracks. He wanted to go with Paul's nephew, but we talked him into going with us."

"Then let us go find him," she said as she lifted her cloak and hustled up the path into the kitchen. She sat on a bench and dipped her feet into the foot washing bowl, rubbing the mud off between her toes, then redipped to get the mud off the bottom. "Do not try to talk me out of this. I am going to the barracks—with or without you. You choose."

"Well, you don't give us much of a choice. Stay and protect the villa. Or go and protect our mother, who insists on going into danger." Stephen's normally gentle voice sounded irritated and annoyed.

"I am going." Samuel shook his head.

"Me, too." Stephen towered above Jerusha. "Antonius said you did not always listen to reason."

"He did, did he?" Jerusha looked up. "Well, if he returns, like he said he would, I will have to talk to him about that, even if he has his wife with him." She stood. "Let's go."

"What about Miriam?" Samuel still tried to persuade.

"She is in good hands. Let's go through the back gate so the mourners do not see us leave."

"Put your sandals on, Mother. It would be better they did not know we were in mourning," Stephen encouraged.

Jerusha leaned under the bench and grabbed a pair of old ones she used to walk in the herb garden. After she slipped them on, she lifted her radiyd over her head, and dropped the ends over her shoulders and raised it over her mouth.

"I am ready." She smiled, first at Samuel, then Stephen, and then headed for the back gate, turned, and waited. "Are you coming?"

Both sons shook their heads.

"Not because we think this is a good idea," Stephen said.

***

Torches on each side of the southern tower of Antonia Fortress cast eerie shadows at the entrance.

"Stop! Who goes there?" the guard called from the corner watch tower. She froze.

"We come looking for a young man who may have visited Paul today," Samuel said, standing in front of her. Stephen stood behind her. Horses whinnied inside the fortress.

"Tribune Lysias," the guard called and waved to a man below. The thick thud of hobnailed sandals climbing the guard tower distressed Jerusha.

"Can we see Paul?" Stephen's voice boomed loud enough to be heard over the ruckus inside, the sounds of soldiers marching, shields and armor being slapped in place.

The tribune stopped at the top and looked down.

"Centurion, that is not enough spearmen. I said two hundred."

"Lysias, it is only one man we escort," the centurion responded.

"Do you question my authority?"

"No, sir."

"I said two hundred spearmen, seventy horsemen, and two hundred foot soldiers. Get them ready. Mount the prisoner in the middle of the horsemen. This man is a Roman citizen. I found no charge against him that deserved death or imprisonment. Do as I command. He is under Rome's protection."

"The prisoner must be Paul," Samuel whispered over his shoulder.

"No one is allowed to see Paul." He turned away, ready to dismiss them, then hesitated and turned back. "Why do you seek him?" he yelled, then whispered to the guard, who hurried down the tower steps. "Who is this boy you seek?" The tribune clutched the tower edge and stared.

"He is our brother," Stephen said and stepped in closer to Jerusha.

The guard and one other soldier opened the cedar door in front of them and began to raise the iron gate.

"Mother, stay close to us. This is not the time to get independent and foolish," Stephen whispered.

The gate creaked and lifted at a slow pace. She peeked around Samuel and saw through the crisscrossed bars a group of mounted soldiers with protective armor on their shins. In the corner of the courtyard, the centurion handed out spears from an armory. Several hundred red-plumed infantry marched, their shield readied, to the front. The war horses whinnied and tried to rear. The well-trained haustati kept their stallions under control and let the spearmen fall in rank behind he infantry. She scrunched her brow. All those to protect one man?

When the gate was high enough for a man to walk under, a contubernium surrounded Jerusha and her sons. She knew that Latin term for eight soldiers because Antonius taught it to Joshua.

"You are under arrest for conspiracy against a Roman citizen," the tribune yelled. "We know of your plot to kill Paul."

"No! You are mistaken. We are Paul's friend," Stephen pleaded.

"Bind them. Take them to the prison below," the tribune commanded.

Jerusha looked at Samuel and Stephen, tears filling her eyes. "I am sorry. I should have listened to you." The chain's weight almost brought her to her knees. The soldiers grabbed Samuel and Stephen, bound their hands behind their backs, and spit in their faces, then laughed after tripping and smashing their faces into the hardened path. It was her fault.

"Stop that," she screamed. "They have done nothing to deserve this." Tears rolled down her cheeks. With hands bound behind, she could not wipe the tears away or comfort her sons, whose swollen lips oozed blood.

"Enough. Take them away," the tribune ordered.

She looked up at Paul as he rode past, his hands tied in front. His peaceful eyes melted her fears momentarily. He had endured many floggings as a prisoner, and if he could do it, she could, with Yeshua's help.

"Tribune, these are my friends." Paul yelled.

"Shut up! Caesars's friend, Brutus, killed him. I trust no one. On with the floggings."

Chapter 23

Jerusha's eyes fell on the whipping posts in the courtyard. She stopped and stared. Could it be the same post where Yeshua had been flogged?

"Get going." A soldier shoved her forward through puddles of fresh blood. She looked behind at the bloodied footprints she left. It made her sick. Not the amount of blood. She had seen blood inches deep from blood sacrifices on the altar. It was the pain and suffering her sons would face from a flogging. Why did not she listen to their counsel? She trembled and glanced behind at Samuel and Stephen.

"Forgive me," she said after she stumbled, lost her footing, and fell to her knees.

"Get up." A soldier jerked her arm and dragged her to her feet, then shoved her back. "Do not talk," he commanded.

"Do not treat my Mother like that. Honor your elders," Samuel yelled.

"Shut up, you dog!" The soldier smacked his jaw.

Jerusha turned and looked. Blood trickled from the corner of his mouth.

Stephen looked somber and stern, his jaw set, eyes straight ahead, then he glanced at her. His large dark eyes softened. He half smiled, as if to say, it would be alright. Her gentle giant stood taller than ever.

"Take a good look." The soldier yanked her arm. "The next time you see your sons, you won't recognize them." He stopped. "Take them to the whipping posts."

"No! Why are you doing this? They have done nothing wrong." Jerusha trembled.

"It is the tribune's order." He cackled. "One I enjoy."

Four soldiers, one on each side of her sons, dragged and chained them to the posts. Jerusha stood helpless and watched, her stomach in knots. Two soldiers drew back their whips and struck Samuel and Stephen at the same time. The shards on the ends cut deep into their back. She heard their moans and cringed. The soldiers drew back the whips in unison. Jerusha closed her eyes. She would not watch her sons' backs be flayed.

"Stop!" A familiar voice commanded.

Antonius? Jerusha's eyes flew open.

He grabbed the whips and threw them to the ground.

"This family is under Rome's protection. Their patriarch is a Roman citizen given the cognomen, Regulus. Release them from the posts and take them to their cells with their mother."

Jerusha gawked, wide-eyed and stared at Antonius. Her feet dragged the rough limestone and smeared a trail of blood as two soldiers, one on each side, dragged her across the courtyard to the stairs. She twisted her head to look at Antonius. He stood, emotionless, hands on hips, his blue eyes stern, and watched that his orders were carried out.

"You will answer to the tribune," The soldiers glared as chains hit the ground, and Samuel fell to the floor, then Stephen.

"Let me worry about that. You will obey these orders, until further notice."

"But Centurion Antonius, you risk"—The soldier stopped.

Jerusha looked one last time over her shoulder. Antonius had his hand up. The soldier honored his request to be quiet and followed the soldiers who held Samuel and Stephen under their arms and dragged them towards the stairs.

Jerusha looked down the dark winding stairway. Her heart pumped wildly. Antonius was back. Why? She reflected on her walk down this same dark stairway to rescue Sarah. She had been foolish to go there that night alone. Antonius and Effah would have gotten Sarah out. She should have trusted them. She did not understand. Why must she do everything herself?

Darkness enveloped her. The smell of feces, urine, and vomit made her feel like adding to it. Her stomach lurched. She gagged and choked it back down. She heard the moans as she passed cell after cell. The soldier who followed maneuvered past her sons and their guards and unlocked the cell, his keys jangling on a ring, then swung the barred door wide.

Her two guards yanked her arms and threw her head first into the cell. She stumbled over a bucket and the contents splashed on her feet and cloak. She gagged at the smell, which was worse than urine and feces mixed together. She could not imagine what else had been in it. Her head hit the wall with a thud.

"Ow!" She grabbed her forehead. A sticky warm liquid dripped into her palm and ran through her fingers. Samuel and Stephen bounced off the back wall and slid down in a heap.

Samuel groaned.

Stephen managed to get to his feet.

When Jerusha's eyes adjusted to the dark, she walked the floor in steps and estimated a six by six cell, no window, one barred door, locked. Stephen, her gentle giant, could not stand up or stretch out without his feet hitting the other wall. She had never sat in such darkness and stench.

She thirsted. The only water available was in another bucket. She put her hand into the water, lifted some in her palm and sipped.

She threw it down and wiped her hand on her cloak. The taste was foul.

It was so dark she could not see her sons' faces, but she continued talking to them and slipped down in the corner and drew up her legs. Her whole body shivered. She wrapped her radiyd around her shoulders and held it tight, then tucked her hands underneath her arm pits. Samuel lay on his side curled up in a ball, and Stephen curled up on the other side.

"What will become of us now?" she asked, clutching her knees. "What is Antonius doing back here? I wonder if he got Sarah to

Grandfather's? Do you suppose Joshua is in one of these cells, too?" She rattled on, question after question, then stopped and listened. Both sons snored. How could they sleep at a time like this? She guessed it was the peace of God. Or, they were passed out from pain.

She bowed her head. A melody floated into her thoughts, and she tried to remember the words that went with it. She waited for them to come, like they did when Father taught her the Tehillium in song. Slowly they came to her conscious thought.

"Thank you Holy Ghost.

"O God, hear my prayer. Listen to my heart's cry. For no matter where I am, even when I am far from home, I will cry out to you for a Father's help. When I am feeble and overwhelmed by life, guide me into your glory, where I am safe and sheltered. Lord, you are a paradise of protection to me. You lift me high above the fray. None of my foes can touch me when I am held firmly in your wrap-around presence."

A light glowed before her eyes and spread throughout the room. She stopped shivering in its warmth and rose up.

"Keep me in this glory. Let me live continually under your splendor-shadow, hiding my life in you forever." She twirled and swayed in dance before her king. "You have heard my sweet resolutions to love and serve you, for I am your beloved. And you have given me an inheritance of rich treasures, which you give to all your lovers." She ascended into a realm unknown; whether in her body or out of her body, she did not know. "You treat me like a king, giving me a full and abundant life, years and years of reigning, like many generations rolled into one. I will live enthroned with you forever!" A sense of oneness with Father YHWH in his throne room opened a portal. She heard herself singing and Father YHWH smiled. The beautiful voices of the angels around him meant little. He bent his ear to listen to her song.

"Guard me, God, with your unending, unfailing love. Let me live my days walking in grace and truth before you. And my praises will fill the heavens forever, fulfilling my vow to make every day a love gift to you!" The light disappeared.

The last phrase stuck in her thoughts. *Fulfilling my vow to make every day a love gift to you.* "Father YHWH is one with me, even in the darkness." Such peace. Such joy. Such love. She closed her eyes, and rested in his embrace and vowed to make every day a love gift through her worship, even in the darkness.

***

Jerusha awoke to a jiggling lock and light from a torch shining in her eyes. She squinted and put her hands over her eyes. The door squeaked open, and a soldier waved the torch inside.

"Is this the cell of Jacob's family?" he asked.

"Yes." Jerusha tried to stand, and he helped her up.

Samuel rolled over and moaned, then slowly sat up.

"We brought fresh water and clean linen and herbs for your wounds." A young slave girl sat beside Samuel.

"Stephen, are you alright," Jerusha nudged him. "Stephen." She shook him harder. "Wake up." Puzzled, she looked at Samuel.

"He's alright. I heard him snoring." He smiled at the girl and turned his back toward her. The girl dabbed at his wounds with a wet linen, and he grimaced.

"I am sorry. I did not mean to hurt you." The girl seemed bashful but knew how to apply the medicinal herbs. "The blood sticks to the wound." She poured clean water on the dried parts and dabbed, then gently loosened the cloth. "Take off your cloak and tunic. I will not look. We have fresh clothing." She unwrapped a leather package, laid out fresh clothing, and turned away.

"What is your name?" Samuel removed his cloak and slipped the tunic over his head, then reached for the other garments.

"Rebecca." She held her radyid with both hands to cover her face. May I turn around now?"

Jerusha smiled at how much Samuel enjoyed the slave girl's attention.

"Why are you being so kind?" Jerusha looked at the soldier.

"Antonius sent us. Thanks to your father and Antonius, we are followers of the Way, too." He stepped over Stephen's feet and roused him. "Wake up."

Stephen moaned and sat up. "Who are you?"

"My name is Marcellus." He looked to be Antonius's age. He stepped to the corner and picked up the stinky bucket, replaced it with a clean one and took the smelly one outside the cell. Jerusha saw Yeshua's servant heart in his eyes.

Stephen rubbed his eyes and stared at the girl, who came over and sat behind him and dabbed at his wounds, her eyes on Samuel.

Ouch!" Stephen twitched. She poured water over his dried spots and continued dabbing, still watching Samuel. When Samuel winked, she dipped her chin and closed her eyes.

"I think you are blind or have your mind on something else." Stephen laughed.

Jerusha chuckled, too. Rebecca's dabbing had totally missed the wound.

"Oh, I am sorry." She grasped her face between her hands, as a red flush rose up her neck and colored her cheeks. She picked up the wet linen cloth and started dabbing again. This time she kept her eyes on the wound.

After Rebecca finished, she gathered the dirty garments and linens and rushed out, shooting a quick look over her shoulder at Samuel.

Marcellus laughed and picked up the smelly bucket. "I think she is enamored with you, Samuel. Much like Antonius is with Jerusha."

It was Jerusha's turn to blush.

"He has a wife," she countered.

"Yes, I know, and he would never betray their marriage covenant. That does not negate how he feels about you."

It felt like a weighted bag stirred in her stomach. A sick nausea swept over her body, and a conflict in her soul raged. She would not covet another woman's husband, even if she secretly loved Antonius. A man's shadow passed over the back wall. The soldier looked around his shoulder. Jerusha's heart raced. It was Antonius.

"I need to talk to Jerusha, alone," he said, and almost looked angry.

Chapter 24

Antonius grabbed her arm and pulled her away from the cell and into the darkened walkway. He smelled of pine.

"We will not be far," he told the soldier. "Give them a more spacious cell, a cleaner one. If you cannot find a clean one, then clean it, but make sure they have a larger cell. This filth is disgusting. Bring some fleece covers and three pallets, too." He turned to Jerusha.

"Now about you. Why were you at the barracks again?" His nearness caused Jerusha's body to quiver. "I would have thought you learned your lesson the last time you came here. If it had not been for Effah and me, you would have been raped or killed."

"I did not come alone. I brought my sons with me like you said to do."

"For what reason?"

"Joshua. I was looking for Joshua. You are the one who opened the door to his fascination with Roman soldiers."

"Do not change the subject. That ploy will not work with me." He rubbed the scar on his forehead. "Why would Joshua come here? I told him to stay away."

I do not know that he did." She felt like a reprimanded child. "Only that he took a warning to Paul's sister. Effah came to the villa. He said some Jews plotted to kill Paul."

"Yes, yes, I know about that. What does that got to do with Joshua and why you came here?"

"Well, if you would stop interrupting, you would find out." She was getting a better understanding of her son's annoyance with interruptions. A taste of her own medicine.

"Effah asked me to send Joshua to Paul's sister and have her son come to the barracks and tell Paul. When Joshua did not return until dark, I got worried that he went with her son and was ready to check on him, when Samuel and Stephen showed up at the villa. They told me after he delivered the message, he wanted to go with Paul's nephew, but they talked him into going with them to Father's tomb. On the way home, Joshua slipped away. We assumed he went to the barracks."

"Jacob's dead?"

"Yes. When we laid him in the tomb, we found a secret room. My sons found the scepter in it."

"Jacob told me of this plan."

"You knew? And did not tell me?"

"I promised Jacob."

"I do not understand. Why did he not want me to know?" She dropped her hands at her sides.

"He wanted you to trust Father YHWH's scepter of righteousness, not a physical scepter to gain your inheritance."

Jerusha looked at Antonius for a minute.

"Why did you return?" She hesitated, not sure if she really wanted to know, then added, "Is Sarah safe?"

"I sent Sarah and Brigid with Patrick to Perea. I am waiting word from Patrick of their arrival and safety." He lifted her chin. "I could not leave you." He locked eyes with her. "With your father lingering near death, it would not be right. I failed to keep him safe. I would not fail you. I promised him."

"Of course." She dropped her head. "It would not be right." Jerusha wanted a confession of his love, not a man doing his duty, as grateful as she was of his return.

"It is a good thing I came back when I did." His voice sounded angry and stern.

"And your wife?" Jerusha countered, "Is she still waiting?" Shadows flickered on his face.

"I have been thinking about that. I wonder if Brigid is lying. The more I thought back on that day, I became more certain of it. I held my wife's lifeless body in my arms. I started to take my own life, but your father stopped me." He looked disturbed. "When I am free of my promise to Jacob, I will question her further, maybe go back to the homeland."

"I see." She could not look at him. It might reveal her disappointment. "How soon before you leave again?"

"It is all in Father YHWH's hands. He knows all."

"Antonius, what will happen to us?" He cocked his head. She cleared her throat and tried to clarify she did not mean him and her. "That is, me and my sons?"

"I am afraid it might be awhile before you are released. I have written to Rome on your behalf. I signed it Regulus and sealed it with your grandfather's lion and butterfly signet ring, then, I sent a message to him along with his ring. Your father gave it to me after he hid the scepter in the tomb."

"But Rome believes my grandfather is dead."

"Then they will know he has been resurrected." Antonius laughed and took her hands. "One of my duties to your father these last years was to go to Rome, get access to your grandfather's records, and remove the accusation of treason. Whenever he is ready to return, he is a free man."

"Oh, Antonius, I love you," she stood on her tip toes, hugged his neck, and let her lips slide across his cheek. His arms wrapped her tight. She closed her eyes and savored his pine scent, her cheek resting against his.

"And I you." He lingered, then released her.

She got to her feet and straightened her cloak. "I am sorry for my-my-."

"No apology necessary." He grinned.

"Grandfather is free." She twirled around.

"Yes, but Rome is suspicious of all Yeshua followers. It will not be safe for him in Jerusalem. The corrupt Jewish leaders know him and will work with the sicarii and Rome to eliminate him and steal his property."

Jerusha dropped her shoulders. She longed for the old days before the persecution. Paul taught that "through many tribulations you enter the kingdom of God." She had all the tribulation she wanted.

"Well, then, we will leave Jerusalem."

"In Yeshua's timing. Jacob told me many times how much he loved those who dwelled here. He wanted all to be saved."

"Oh, I get so tired of this."

"Remember what James taught us."

"I know." She sighed. "When it seems as though you're facing nothing but difficulties, see it as an invaluable opportunity to experience the greatest joy that you can."

Antonius added. "For you know when your faith is tested it stirs up power within you to endure all things."

She looked at Antonius. Had his daughter really lied? Fear gripped her gut that his wife might be alive.

His slight smile annoyed her.

"Do not look at me like that," she snapped.

My Jerusha." He laid his hands on her shoulders.

"And do not call me your Jerusha. I am not your Jerusha!" She threw off his hands and spun around.

"Watch out, Jerusalem. Jacob's little lioness is on the prowl and ready to roar." He chuckled and walked away.

"Humph." She crossed her arms over her chest and glanced his way.

He looked back and winked. "Roar little lioness, roar." He chuckled. "I will find Joshua."

***

A short time later, Jerusha followed Marcellus, thankful he was a Yeshua follower. He carried a torch and urged Jerusha to hurry. Samuel and Stephen carried pallets and fleece covers and were guarded from behind by another Yeshua soldier. Moans and foul language spewed forth from each cell they walked past. She looked behind at her sons, their hands chained together, making it difficult to carry the pallets and covers. If only she would have listened to them, they would not be in this situation.

She wondered if Joshua was free or jailed in one of these cells. The torch lit up a cell, and she looked to see if the prisoner was Joshua.

"We must hurry, Jerusha, and get you settled before the changing of the guard. Your next guard will not be a Yeshua follower. I will pray protection over you. Sometimes, they try to use the women prisoners for their pleasure."

Jerusha sucked her breath in. She had forgotten about Sarah and what happened to her. A sick feeling in the pit of her stomach made her want to throw up. She clasped her shaking fingers. When would this nightmare end? She heard singing, cupped her ear, and listened.

"Those sound like Yeshua followers." Jerusha cringed as a little critter ran across her toes. She raised her cloak. The last thing she needed was for the vermin to catch a ride on her cloak. Of course, the thought of it running up her leg was not any better. She shivered and shuffled her feet. The soldier stopped. Paying attention more to her feet, she bumped him.

"I am putting you next to them. Their joy is contagious." He stopped and placed the torch in a holder. While he unlocked the cell, she got a glimpse of the singers' cell. It was smaller than the one he was unlocking for her; dirtier, too. Two young girls, a man, and a woman were cramped inside. The simple necessities at home became luxuries in prison. She felt guilty.

"Would you give my pallet and cover to them? My sons and I can share what is left. And could we get someone to clean their cell?"

Samuel and Stephen nodded their approval.

"Thank you." The woman looked tired. "My littlest is sick."

The guard opened their cell and handed the woman the pallet and cover. Jerusha grabbed his arm before he locked it.

"May I pray for her daughter?"

"The new guard will be changing in a short while. I must get you in your own cell before then."

Jerusha rushed inside the cell and knelt beside the girl. She laid her hand on her head. It felt like fire. The little one covered her mouth and coughed, then spit in a bucket. She lay on a cold limestone floor. Jerusha touched her forehead again.

"In Yeshua's name, be healed. I command this sickness to leave." She felt a warmth in her hand and a peace settled in her thoughts. She stood.

"Thank you," the woman's voice quivered.

Jerusha moved into the next cell and listened to the mother's quiet cry as the soldier locked both cells. He took the torch with him and total darkness fell. She felt her son take her arm and pull gently.

"I have a pallet ready." Stephen's voice sounded far away. She allowed him and Samuel to help her sit down. She took the fleece cover and curled on her side.

"My daughter is healed," the woman's voice rang out, "Yeshua is with us."

"Even in the darkness," Jerusha whispered and listened to their songs in the night and fell asleep.

Chapter 25

Jerusha awoke to the sound of keys in the lock and light in the cell. She sat up and squinted. Someone grabbed her arm and jerked her to her feet.

"I heard there was a new woman," a gruff voiced soldier held a torch close. "Quite a beauty, too. You are coming with me."

"No!" Stephen's deep voice shouted.

"You dog, you have no say over what I do." He waved the torch at Stephen, "Get back." He yanked Jerusha through the door, placed the torch in a holder, and locked the cell.

"Where are you taking me?" Jerusha demanded.

"Someplace to make you happy," the soldier said. He wore a thin tunic that smelled of body odor, his breath mixed with sour wine, and the stench of filthy teeth.

"I am not going anywhere with you," Jerusha crossed her arms over her chest.

Whack! Her head jerked around, when his fist met her jaw. She felt her lip and looked down at her hand. Blood.

"Brave man, hitting a woman," Samuel yelled.

"Shut up!" The soldier twisted her arm behind her back, smashed her face against the wall, and tried to raise her cloak and tunic.

She smelled his nauseating breath even from the back. "See what I do to women who fight me?" He slid her tunic up to her waist.

"Deliver us from evil," she heard as prayers ascended in the next cell. "Arise, Lord. Let your enemies be scattered." Jerusha's heart thudded. "Let all who hate you flee before you." She closed her eyes.

"Get away from her," Antonius grabbed the soldier, swung him around, and landed his fist square on his jaw, knocking him to the stone floor. "If I ever see or hear of you touching this woman again, you will be flayed by my whip. And I show no mercy."

"You will pay for this, Antonius." The drunk spit blood and staggered away.

Jerusha slumped to the floor, her face in her hands. Her whole body shook. Uncontrollable sobs burst from her mouth. Antonius slid his arms beneath her knees and lifted and carried her into the cell. She leaned her head into his chest and hung onto his tunic as he laid her on the pallet. He draped the fleece cover around her shoulders, knelt on one knee, and lifted her chin.

Jerusha sniffed and stared into his eyes.

"This will not happen again. I failed to protect your father." His voice trembled. He swallowed to get control. "I will not fail with you and your sons." He sat next to her on the pallet. "Even though you half brought this on yourself by your stiff-necked determination to have your own way." He put his arm around her shoulders, and caressed her arm. Numb, she stared motionless in the darkness. *He was right.* A total despair started to soak into her bones. After a while, she closed her eyes and rested her head on his chest.

"Antonius, what if I do not get out of here? What if I am summoned to Rome for trial? What if they crucify me like they did Grandfather?"

"Shhhh, my little butterfly. Rest. That will not happen."

"How can you be so sure?"

"I went to Gethsemane, poured out my concerns—surrendered my will to Father YHWH. In the quietness, he spoke—revealed his plan."

"It is good he showed you. Why not me? I am the one stuck in this filthy, dark, hell hole."

"Oh, Jerusha," he chuckled. "It is that fire, that fighting spirit, that endears you to my heart."

"Well?" She twisted and faced him, hands on her hips.

"Well, what?" He threw out his hands.

"What is his plan?" She lifted her chin.

"I think it would be better to keep that to myself." He grinned.

"Just exactly why would it be better?"

"That is for me to know and you to find out." He looked up. "Ask YHWH yourself."

"So, you refuse to tell me."

"For now, I think it would be better."

"Stop saying it would be better." She dropped her hands in her lap. "I see no reason it would, 'be better,' as you put it."

"In time, it will be revealed." Antonius stood. "Patience has never been your strong trait. Just know, you will be released from this 'hell hole' as you put it." He grinned.

Jerusha got up and paced.

"Antonius can be trusted." Samuel emerged from the corner and stretched.

"Ask Father YHWH like he told you."

"Yes, Mother, Samuel is correct. Trust Father YHWH to reveal it. Do not put your trust in man." Stephen encouraged, "You can hear his voice." He stretched out on the other pallet.

James's words floated into her mind. "*My fellow believers, when it seems as though you are facing nothing but difficulties see it as an invaluable opportunity to experience the greatest joy that you can! For you know that when your faith is tested it stirs up power within you to endure all things. And then as your endurance grows even stronger it will release perfection into every part of your being until there is nothing missing and nothing lacking.*" His words soaked into her anger and settled her thoughts. Antonius stood at the cell's barred door, his head bowed, mouth moving in silence. *Praying?*

He loves you, Jerusha. Her father's words echoed in her thoughts. She stood before Antonius and waited, his pine smell awakening a passion she had tried to shut down since hearing he had a wife. She desired to kiss him. She hesitated, then turned away.

"I am sorry I acted so rudely." She glanced over her shoulder. The shadows flickered on his face. "I have no right to demand you tell me what Father YHWH revealed. I will wait for him to tell me, as you have asked. Forgive me for my impatience." She felt his hands on her shoulders. She closed her eyes and breathed deep. His nearness sent tingles up her spine.

"I await the moment you hear." His breath warmed her hair.

What possibly could he be waiting for her to hear? That she did not need him? That Father YHWH's love is enough? He had a wife. She could not marry him. A gentle peace fell over her being like a warm cover, and quieted her questions.

"It will come to you, in time," Antonius whispered, "in his time."

She walked away, turned, and stared. *In his time, Father YHWH makes all thing beautiful.* Again her father's words came from the past. It almost felt like he stood with her in the cell. She pictured him sitting on his work bench carving. *"Never forget who you are. You are royalty from the tribe of Judah. You will dance before the king."* She smiled.

"I will not forget, Father," she spoke in the darkness.

"What, Mother?" Samuel asked, "What will you not forget?"

"I am, we are"—she waved her arms out—"royalty—through Yeshua's blood."

"Is this what Father YHWH revealed to Antonius?" Stephen wrinkled his brow.

Jerusha looked at Antonius and stared. His blue eyes glistened. Hers filled with tears also.

"No, Stephen," Jerusha kept her eyes on Antonius. "It is not time for me to know, yet. I, like Antonius, await that time."

"I do not mean to interrupt this somber moment, but has anyone found Joshua, yet?" Samuel asked.

"Not yet." Antonius opened the barred door, stepped outside, and closed it.

"Do you think he is in one of these cells?" Jerusha grabbed the bars and peered through.

"No. I checked." Antonius picked up the torch from its holder and turned.

"Where could he be? Jerusha's grip tightened.

"I do not know, but I will find him." Antonius said.

"He was not at the villa?" Her voice cracked.

"No. I told Moses about your arrest and that Joshua was missing. He is getting everyone to be on the lookout for him. We will find him."

"I hope he is not lying dead somewhere." Jerusha felt a tightness in her chest. She tried to breathe deep and relax. Only short breaths were possible. A sharp pain shot across her chest. She grimaced and gripped the bars, her body swaying back and forth.

"Jerusha, are you alright?" Antonius unlocked the door and swung it open.

Her legs felt weak. She closed her eyes and listened to ringing in her ears, then felt the cold sweat on her forehead. Antonius's voice seemed distant.

"I am alright," she answered. Her hands slipped from the bars. She felt Antonius swoop his arms under her legs. He caught her before she fell.

"I am alright," she said again and gripped her chest.

"Sure you are," Samuel said.

"I have seen this on the battlefield. Panic attack. She will recover." Antonius laid her on the pallet, then folded a fleece blanket and propped her head on it, then grabbed the other one and covered her, tucking in the edges. "Breathe, Jerusha. Deep breaths. You will be alright."

Jerusha opened her eyes. Three faces stared down, all three with crinkled brows. Antonius. Samuel. Stephen. She sucked in a gulp of air, expanding her chest, then let the air out slowly through her mouth.

"Again, Jerusha. Big breath, slowly let it out."

She breathed in again and let it out. Samuel dipped water and put it to her lips. It tasted good and soothed her dry throat. She sat up. The chest pain had stopped.

"Do not worry about Joshua. I will find him and bring him to see you."

"I hate for him to see me in here."

"He is considered a man now. He can take it."

"Antonius, is it night or day? Without light from the sun or moon, I cannot tell when a day has passed."

"It will be morning soon. The soldiers took Paul to Caesarea last night at the third hour. You have been in here for about seven or eight hours."

"We have been in here since nine o'clock last night?

He nodded.

"How long before we hear from Rome?"

It might take months. Maybe a year. I am asking the procurator for house arrest. I should hear soon."

The singing began again in the next cell. Jerusha thought of the mother and two daughters and what they must have endured. She sat up.

"Antonius, after what happened to me tonight, I cannot imagine what those girls and mother have been through. Can anything be done for them?"

"I have tried over the years to help followers of the Way. Some were freed. Others died of sickness and disease or worse. I will do my best to get them out." He walked out and locked the door. "It is almost time for the changing of the guard. I must go. I will return as soon as I can."

Chapter 26

Jerusha's stomach rumbled. How long had she been asleep? What else was there to do? When would Antonius be back? Had he found Joshua? She imagined what it would be like inside a chrysalis. How did that ugly caterpillar, alone in the darkness, change into a beautiful butterfly and find the strength to work its way out? A powerful mystery for sure. Somehow she was comforted by the fact that she was not alone, even though Samuel and Stephen sat in the corner scrunched together, shivering under one cover.

"I am hungry, Ima," the little girl in the next cell whined.

"Me, too," the other one moaned.

"Let us sing to Yeshua," their mother urged.

"I do not want to sing. I am hungry."

"It is written, man shall not live by bread alone, but by every word that comes from the mouth of YHWH. Let us enter his presence, that we may hear from him and live." The mother hummed a melody.

Jerusha recognized it as Tehillim 146, a poetic psalm by Haggai and Zechariah. The girls sang it in weak whispered tones.

"Hallelujah! Praise the Lord!"

"My innermost being will praise you, Lord!" Jerusha sang along, too. "I will spend my life praising you and singing high praises to you, my God, every day of my life!" She felt better already.

"We can never look to men for help; no matter who they are." Stephen's rich, deep voice vibrated with the women. *Not even Antonius.* "They can't save us, for even our great leaders fail and fall. They too are just mortals who will one day die."

"At death the spirits of all depart and their bodies return to dust. In the day of their death all their projects are over. But those who hope in the Lord will be happy and pleased!" Samuel added his voice.

"Our help comes from the God of Jacob! You keep all your promises." Antonius's voice rang out as he walked down the hall with a torch. "You are the Creator of heaven's glory, earth's grandeur, and ocean's greatness. The oppressed get justice with you." Light burst into the dark, as he placed the torch in place.

"The hungry are satisfied with you. Prisoners find their freedom with you." Jerusha got up and looked through the bars. Joy filled her being. "You open the eyes of the blind and you fully restore those bent over with shame."

"You love those who love and honor you." Samuel and Stephen came and stood beside her.

"You watch over strangers and immigrants and support the fatherless and widows." An older woman, gray-haired, followed Antonius with a basket.

"Lord, you reign forever! Zion's God will rule throughout time and eternity! Hallelujah! Praise the Lord!" Jerusha twirled around in delight.

"Look who I met at the gate. She brought you bread." Antonius towered over the frail woman.

"Do you remember me?" Her voice sounded weak.

Jerusha stared for a minute. "I do know you. You followed the bier at Father's funeral. Said my father gave you food."

"You do remember." The woman laughed. "You told me I would be welcome at your gate anytime. Instead, in your time of need, I am bringing you bread."

Antonius unlocked and opened the door. Jerusha took the
basket. It overflowed with fresh bread. Beneath the bread Jerusha saw
pomegranates.

"I got the pomegranates from your garden. Moses gave them to
me. He said he is coming soon to visit."

"May I share with those in the next cell?" Jerusha thought of the
hungry girls.

"Of course."

"Did Moses say how Miriam is doing?"

"No."

Jerusha waited for Antonius to unlock their cell. The two girls
jumped up and down.

"Father YHWH is a good father," the mother said as she wiped
tears from her face.

"It has been hard to watch my children starve." The girls' father
took bread and gave it to them, then a pomegranate. The girls
struggled to break the pomegranate's tough outer covering. Antonius
cut it in half. The girls bit into the red plump kernels. Red juice ran
down their faces. They wiped it away with pink-tinged fingers.

"Toda. Toda. We are so grateful." Pink teeth showed in their
smiles, too. It reminded Jerusha of her days with Father in the garden.
How she missed him. He would not be happy she was in jail.

"I will bring more when I can." The woman smiled a toothless
grin. "Take some for yourself and your wife," she added.

The father looked at Jerusha.

"May I? he asked, one hand on the bread.

"Of course." Jerusha knew he probably would save it for his wife
and daughters, like any good father would. That would be his choice.
She would do the same if in his position. *What am I thinking? I am
in his position.* She almost laughed. This whole prison thing seemed
surreal, like she would wake up anytime from a bad dream. While he
took from the basket, it began to droop in her arms.

"My apologies, Jerusha. Let me take that." Antonius waited for the
man to take all he wanted, then carried it into the other cell, where
Stephen and Samuel helped themselves.

"Did you find Joshua?" Jerusha tore and plopped a piece of bread in
her mouth.

"Not yet." Antonius's concerned look disturbed her.

"Is your son missing?" the widow asked.

"Yes, since yesterday." Jerusha thought it seemed like forever. It had only been one day.

"I saw him with Effah yesterday afternoon."

"You saw him? Alive?" Hope sprung up in Jerusha.

"They were going into Herod's palace," the old woman answered.

"Herod's palace, "Antonius perked up. "That is one place I have not looked."

"Herod's palace!" Jerusha cringed. "What was he doing there? And with Effah?"

"Do not worry. Effah would not let anything happen to him."

"I do not have your confidence. That man is a mystery to me." She crossed her arms.

Antonius reached for the torch.

"Mystery or not, I am convinced he would not hurt Joshua. If Joshua is with him at Herod's palace, I will find him." He raised the torch from the holder. Jerusha felt panic at being left in the dark again.

"Could you leave the torch? It is so dark in here without it." Jerusha's eyes filled with tears. She missed watching the sunrise and sunset. Even in the darkness of the new moon, the stars shined. If she could not see the shining constellations in her cell's darkness, then the torch's light would have to do. Yeshua said he was the light of the world, and anyone who embraced him would experience life-giving light and not walk in darkness. Singing his word brought life to her soul. A little natural light would be nice, too.

"Of course. I will leave it in the day and remove it at night. That way you will get a sense of the time of day. Besides, it will give me good reason to return." He grinned, "I have never enjoyed watching over a prisoner as much as I do you." He winked.

Jerusha blushed. She wondered why he had been emboldened in his display of affection. What did he know that she did not know?

"I am, we are"—she waved her hands toward her sons—"grateful for your help."

He locked the other cell, then hers. His eyes lingered on her.

"Hold on, little lioness, I will get you out of this place as soon as possible."

**

"Samuel is getting worse, Mother," Stephen knelt beside his brother.
"He is very hot. I think he may have what the girl had." Samuel
shivered beneath the cover. Jerusha knelt on his other side.

"Father YHWH, help him," Jerusha looked at the shadows
flickering on his face, dark circles beneath his eyes. His body stiffened,
then jerked uncontrollably. His eyes rolled back.

"What is happening?" Stephen jumped up.

"I do not know." Suddenly she thought of the witch. "It may be
connected to the curses sent from Kidron Valley. "Samuel. Samuel."
Her heart thumped so hard, it felt like it would burst. "He is not
responding."

"I am scared, Mother." Stephen knelt beside Samuel. "Blood
gurgled in his throat. I think he is choking."

"Quick, help me turn him over," Jerusha squatted on the other
side, tried lifting his upper body and push it over.

"Why doesn't he stop shaking." Stephen pulled him forward.
The blood rolled out the corner of his mouth. His body quaked for a
minute longer, then relaxed.

"Samuel, can you hear me?" Jerusha rolled him on his back,
propped his head on a folded fleece and wiped the blood off his face.
He moaned and stared, a blank look.

"He acts like he is not aware of us." Stephen patted Samuel's
cheek. "Do you know who I am?" He held Samuel's chin between
thumb and finger and turned it to face him.

"What happened?" Samuel scrunched his brow and pulled loose.

"You started jerking. Your eyes rolled back. You choked on your
blood until we rolled you over."

"My tongue hurts." Samuel stuck it out for Stephen and Jerusha to
see.

"Ugh! You bit it."

"I am tired of this." She placed her hands on her hips. "Father dies.
Joshua is missing. We are in jail. Miriam might lose her baby. Now
this. What is next. Lose our villa?"

"Father YHWH, deliver us from evil." Jerusha paced like a lion
trapped in a cave. "I count it all joy that the testing of my faith builds

endurance. I thank you that you are a good Father. Greater is he that is in me, than he that is in the world. Your lioness rises up. Give me wisdom."

My Son was manifested for this purpose, to destroy the works of the devil. In him, you have all authority in heaven and earth. Fight with it.

"Devil, I take authority over you in Yeshua's name. Stop tormenting my son." She wiggled her finger at the air. "Now! Leave him, now! she yelled. "He is royalty, son of the most, High God, Father YHWH."

A righteous anger burned in her bones. She was tired of the devil messing with her family. Was her faith tested to build this kind of fire? Maybe. Maybe not. All she knew was that she felt stronger, with more faith, to fight against evil, than she had all her life. She would not cave into this kind of intimidation. She wrestled not against flesh and blood. Her fight was against principalities and powers in heavenly places. Yeshua fought with "it is written." So would she.

"It is written—" She hesitated. *Help me, Holy Ghost.* "'No weapon formed against you will prosper, and every tongue that rises against you in judgment, you can refute.'" She paced back and forth, back and forth, a fire in her bones. "I refute and take authority over every word spoken against this family by the witch or anyone else, and put it under Yeshua's feet—and his blood. What the devil intended for evil, Father YHWH will turn for our good. It is written," She stopped and waited so thankful for her father's instruction in the prophets and Tehillim. She quieted her thoughts, then words from Psalm 91 came. "'He will rescue you from every hidden trap of the enemy, *praise be to Yeshua*, and he will protect you from every false accusation and any deadly curse." *Hallelujah.* "His massive arms are wrapped around you. You can run under his covering of majesty and hide. His arms of faithfulness are a shield keeping you from harm." The words flowed easily from memory thanks to her father's diligence and Holy Ghost, "'You will never worry about an attack of demonic forces at night nor have to fear a spirit of darkness coming against you. Don't fear a thing! Whether by night or by day, demonic danger will not trouble you, nor will the powers of evil launched against you . . . '"

She stopped pacing and looked at Samuel and Stephen. They stared, mouths opened.

"What came over you?" Samuel asked.

Exhilarated, Jerusha giggled. "I guess Father's lioness"—and another giggle erupted. She hardly could finish her sentence—"has come out of her cave"—she took a breath—"and roared." She heard the two little girls in the next cell laughing, grabbed her belly, and burst out laughing with them.

"Oh, my sides hurt." She bent over and held her gut. "Do you feel better, Samuel?"

"Who would not feel better after all that?" he responded. "Yes, I feel better."

"'A joyful, cheerful heart brings healing to both body and soul. But the one whose heart is crushed struggles with sickness and depression.'" Antonius stood on the outside of the bars and grinned. "I have good news. I found Joshua."

Chapter 27

Joshua stood beside Antonius, his sword strapped to his side, feet shoulder-width apart.

Joshua Caleb, where have you been?" Jerusha glared, "You ought to be glad I am behind these bars. I would—, I would—" Jerusha wanted to hug him, but felt he needed some kind of discipline for not obeying. He was not a man, yet, in her eyes, no matter what anyone else said.

"You would what, Mother?" Stephen chuckled.

"I would hug him until he cried for mercy." She smiled as a small giggle rose from her belly. Tonight she would rejoice and be glad, no matter what.

"Do not start that again," Samuel joked.

I have no idea what you are talking about. Do you, Joshua?" She giggled and shrugged.

"If you mean that belly laugh." Joshua grinned. "Yes, I do. I stood back in the shadows on purpose and watched. It was hilarious."

"Never mind that." Jerusha felt like a child. "Tell me where you have been? A widow said she saw you with Effah."

"It is a long story. Could we come in there and sit? I have a lot to tell you."

Antonius unlocked the door and swung it open.

"Welcome to our humble abode." Jerusha waved her arms out and laughed. It felt good to be able to be lighthearted. Her son was lost. Now he was found. "Sit." She motioned toward the pallet.

"Bread? Pomegranate? Water?" She offered what she had.

"I do not know how you can joke around." Joshua frowned.

"I am quite serious. I will be content and hospitable in times of plenty or in times of little. The joy of the Lord is my strength." She placed the bread and pomegranate in the middle and put one pallet on each side and one cover on each side. "Sit. And tell me, where have you been?"

After Stephen, Samuel, and I found the scepter . . ." He looked at Jerusha with raised brows. "You did know we found the scepter in the tomb?"

"Yes, I-I know. Go on, after you found the scepter, what?" She felt her impatience surfacing and took a deep breath.

"I slipped away from Samuel and Stephen and started walking to Paul's sister's house. I wanted to find out what happened when—"

"Too much curiosity for your own good," Jerusha piped in.

"Mother, you are interrupting."

"When what?" She motioned with her arms. "Go on. When what?"

Joshua rolled his eyes and looked at his brothers. Antonius laughed.

"When I saw Effah talking to the man I saw in Kidron Valley. You know, the one who followed you. He was standing in front of Herod's palace with Effah's Father and some other priests. I am not sure if the man was a priest or a zealot. Either way, he exchanged money with Effah's father—what's his name?"

"Caiaphas," she inserted. "I figured Effah's father was involved. But why is Effah warning us about his father's plans?"

"If you stop interrupting, I will tell you. I decided to get closer so I could hear what they were saying." Joshua looked at each of them—

Samuel, Stephen, Antonius, and Jerusha. He leaned in like he had a deep secret. "I overheard Effah's father ask him if he had gained your confidence yet."

"I told you he could not be trusted." Jerusha sat straight up.

"Effah told his father he was getting closer to you every day." Joshua puffed his chest out.

"And you trusted him." She glared at Antonius.

"Do not be so hard on Antonius. He had me fooled, too." Joshua looked from Jerusha to Antonius and back.

"And me." Stephen looked at Jerusha.

"And me." Samuel looked at Jerusha.

"Well, Antonius, it appears you have many advocates. Even Father was beginning to trust Effah." Jerusha cast her arms out palms up. "What is the matter with you men, anyway?"

"How were we to know he was lying? Wanted to impress you? Win your confidence?" Samuel asked.

"I still trust him." Antonius looked at Jerusha.

"How can you trust him after what you heard?" she spoke in exasperation.

"Because." He hesitated, never taking his eyes off Jerusha. "I know he loves Yeshua. He is in a hard spot with his father being a nonbeliever." Antonius's voice cracked. "I understand because it is hard being a soldier in an army of nonbelievers. I cannot imagine the conflict he endures with wanting to honor his father since he had been a high priest and yet, honor Yeshua., too, the great High Priest."

"How do you know he is not fooling you, too?" Jerusha kept her eyes on Antonius.

"Because I am the one who led him to Christ." He dropped his head. "I am the one responsible for his precarious situation."

"And how do you know it was genuine?" Jerusha's voice softened. She saw the pain in Antonius's eyes.

"Because I saw the transformation. He met with your father and me regularly before your father died—to learn of Yeshua's ways and teachings. Caiaphas thought he was spying on you for him, when all along he wanted to be near those who believed. It served two purposes. Helped us know what his father planned and gave him cover for being with us."

"Why did not my father tell me this?"

"Because he knew of what happened to you as a girl. He never told me
what it was, but he said he did not want to cause you any more conflict.
He trusted Father YHWH to reveal Effah's change to you in its time."

"Father believed YHWH makes all things beautiful in its time,"
Jerusha whispered. "I had no idea." Jerusha dropped her head and
fiddled with her fingers. "I do not know what to say." Tears welled up.
She rubbed her eyes and sniffed. "Father is gone. I miss him. In time,
we will see if what you say is true. Or if Effah is fooling us all. Father
YHWH makes the rain to fall on the just and the unjust. I will leave
Effah in his hands."

She felt like a child again and wanted to crawl up on Father's lap
and hug his neck. She closed her eyes. A beautiful picture unfolded.

She was enveloped by a light that sparkled and glistened. A young
woman with long black hair walked in a meadow. She knew somehow
it was her. She followed a path up a high mountain. The steep climb
was effortless, no trouble breathing, no tired muscles. She twirled
around in her white gown and enjoyed looking at the flowers, so many
kinds with every shade of color imaginable. Countless butterflies—
some yellow, some blue, some purple—fluttered from flower to flower.
She reached out to touch the varying shades of purple butterflies that
hovered around. She wondered where the path took her. As soon as
that thought came, she was transported to a brilliant throne room. A
dazzling emerald bow encircled the King. Multitudes sang praises to
him: Abraham and the forefathers, angels, strange creatures with four
faces with many eyes. She saw her father among them worshipping
the King. He did not see her. She began to sing with them and twirl
around in dance. When she did, the King's eyes fell on her, and he
motioned for her to come. She started to climb the steps and suddenly
was transported into the lap of Father YHWH. His face glowed.
Its brightness was almost more than she could look into. She felt
his smile and acceptance. A love blanket covered her being. "Now
listen, daughter, pay attention. Forget about your past!" His words
reverberated diamond-like sparkles into the atmosphere. Flashes of
her abuse as a child passed before her eyes, then disappeared. "Put
behind you every attachment to the familiar, even those who once
were close to you!" Her mother's beautiful face, her father's tender

embrace, dimmed in the glory of Father YHWH's presence. "Your many sons will one day be kings, just like their father." Knowing that Father YHWH had many sons—her sons, and countless more in every nation, beginning in Jerusalem—wiped away her doubts. She saw Effah's face in the multitude worshipping.

"Effah, too," Jerusha whispered as the picture faded.

"Mother." Joshua touched her face. "Your face is glowing. What have you seen?"

She sat for a while in silence. His presence quieted all in the room. She waited, not wanting to disrupt his holy presence.

"His throne." She felt a tingling in her hands, a warmth in her body, a peace in her soul and spirit. "Father YHWH took me to his throne."

"What did you see?" Joshua pursued his curiosity.

"Your grandfather. He did not see me. He was worshipping with the multitudes singing Holy, holy, holy. Worthy. Worthy. Worthy. Past, present, and future generations worshipped." She did not know how she knew that. She just knew. She saw all eternity in that split second in heaven. "Effah was there."

No one spoke for the longest time.

"I must tell you what happened next with Effah." Joshua touched her cheek.

"When I was watching the soldiers leaving the city with Paul, one of those men I saw with Effah snuck up behind me and jabbed at me with a knife. For some reason Effah was watching and intervened. He pushed me away just in time. Instead of the knife hitting my gut, it slit my arm." Joshua raised up his cloak sleeve and showed a white linen strip wrapped around his arm with a blood stain.

"Did the man attack Effah?" Stephen asked.

"No. He ran. Effah took me to Herod's palace. After he bandaged my arm, he went in another room to talk with his father. I snuck into the hall and listened at the door. His father was upset with him for saving me. I heard pottery breaking and furniture thrown over. Effah calmed him down, then told him that it would be another way to win Mother's confidence." He looked at Jerusha.

Her eyes dropped. She felt for Effah trying to appease an angry father, one who only cared about his own self. Effah had no father like hers, kind, loving, and protective. No wonder he was attracted to Father YHWH and His Son, Yeshua.

"Why so much hatred against this family?" Jerusha stared at the pomegranates in the basket. "We have done nothing to deserve this."

"Many priests and others hate followers of the Way, especially those that own property like Grandfather's. They covet it." Samuel spoke like a teacher. "It is quite an unusual combination. Corrupt priests, Romans, zealots. Enemies of one another, all bound together by their one common enemy—Yeshua."

Jerusha looked at Samuel, a wise prophet, then Stephen, a man of integrity and honor, and last of all at Joshua, a courageous warrior, all taught by the Lord. Their faces radiated a peace that, in these situations, could only come from him. *Thank you, Father YHWH.* She smiled, then sighed.

"Joshua, go back to the tomb and get the scepter. You may need it, especially if I do not get released soon.

"I already went back there. It is gone."

"Someone stole it?" Jerusha stared wide-eyed at Joshua.

"They must have been watching the tomb when Samuel, Stephen, and I went back there." He dipped his chin. "I am sorry, Mother. I should have taken it out of there when we had a chance."

"It does not matter. Our trust is in Father YHWH's scepter of righteousness. Father prepared me for this before he passed into the kingdom. I did not understand, then, what he meant.

She looked at Antonius.

"Will you be able to keep Joshua with you?"

"Most of the time. When I cannot I will be sure he is locked inside the villa."

"Do not go anywhere without Antonius. Do you understand?"

"You are treating me like a baby, like I cannot take care of myself." Jerusha tipped her head and pursed her lips together.

"Well, you may be right about that. It is hard to stop being a protective mother." She looked at Antonius.

He mouthed, *I'll watch him.*

"You might consider staying locked inside the villa." She chuckled. "Of course, any grown man would know that." She looked at Antonius. "When will you know about house arrest?"

"Maybe tomorrow morning." Antonius stood and helped Jerusha up. "It will not be long."

She looked into his eyes. If only he did not have a wife. *Father YHWH, what does he know that I do not know?*

"Thank you for everything you are doing. I do not know how I will ever repay you."

The corner of his mouth tipped up and broadened into a grin. "Oh, I can think of something." His eyes twinkled.

She scrunched her brow. A slow blush rose in her cheeks. Surely, he did not mean what she thought he meant.

"Cook me some porridge." He chuckled, then grabbed the torch and walked away. Joshua ran to keep up. The light disappeared, and she was left in darkness.

Chapter 28

J erusha awoke in the darkness.

How much longer until the new day? She blinked and listened. Moans came from the other cells, and it pained her as if the pain was her own. So much pain in this world, she thought sadly. Samuel and Stephen both slept, and so did the family in the next cell.

She thought of Effah's father and others like him in Jerusalem, and her heart hurt. Without accepting Yeshua as King, they walked in darkness every day and did not know it. Her present darkness lasted only until Antonius's torch came or she walked out of the cell into the sun light. She stared at the ceiling. No, she concluded. She walked in the light, even now in this present darkness.

I am in the darkness, too. She felt his presence, a peace that made no sense, and a contentment she had never known.

I understand now, Father YHWH. No matter how dark it looks, no matter how much evil surrounds me, you are one with me, shining your goodness and love in everything that happens.

Curses. Grumbling. Complaining came from the mouths of the other prisoners as the jailer shoved tiny morsels of bread into their cells. Jerusha smiled.

Give me this day my daily bread.

She was grateful for the light of his torch and the tiny morsels he threw into the cell.

"Thank you," she saw the emptiness in the jailer's eyes. "Yeshua loves you." He stopped and looked at her, his eyes softened.

"No one has ever told me thank you." His gruff voice cracked.

"Well, today is a new day. Yeshua wants you to know he loves you and gave his life on the cross for your sins."

"I have many." A tear rolled down his cheek. "Too many to be forgiven."

"No one is out of reach of his love." She reached through the cell to touch his hand.

"Just believe," she grinned. "It just takes faith the size of a mustard seed." Inwardly she laughed at how pleased her father would be that she quoted his words.

"I believe." He wiped the tear away. "Help my unbelief."

Another smile curved her lips.

"I, too, prayed that prayer, not long ago. Father YHWH heard and answered. I can assure you, he heard your prayer, too, and answered. Light has come into your darkness and wiped your sins away. The angels in heaven are rejoicing over your decision."

He hesitated a moment with his eyes closed.

"Hey, you, dog, jailer," a prisoner yelled, "Hurry up. I am tired of waiting down here."

"Do not listen to him. You are a beloved son of the King." Jerusha patted his hand.

His broad grin showed jagged teeth as he walked away. His eyes shined. Jerusha stood in wonder of Father YHWH's love. She looked up; her eyes closed, and she basked in it.

"Thank you," she whispered.

"Jerusha." Antonius stood outside the cell, his blond hair unkempt, his toga clasped at the shoulder, the golden emblem a striking contrast against the red linen. His chest looked broader than she imagined without the armor.

"Oh." She straightened her hair. "I did not know you were standing there. I think you are up to your old tricks again appearing out of nowhere."

Antonius burst out laughing. She stared, then started laughing, too, then stopped and looked at Samuel and Stephen gawking and shaking their heads, then burst into laughter again.

"Oh, my, that felt good, except my sides are sore from laughing yesterday." She bent over and rubbed her ribs. How is it she could laugh at being imprisoned? She realized the absurdity of it and smiled.

"I have brought you some visitors," he said, and he placed the torch in the holder and waved to someone standing in the shadows.

"Moses," Jerusha gasped. "How is Miriam?" She squinted into the light. "Is that her standing beside you?"

Miriam stepped out of the darkness, her face radiant as she came close to Jerusha's cell. "I have someone for you to meet."

Miriam opened her cloak and lifted a tiny bundle that hung inside the sling around her neck. It was the tiniest infant. "Abraham Jacob, meet Jerusha, the woman who decreed life in your darkest hour. We named him after your father." She uncovered his face, and revealed dark eyes that shined bright as Regulus.

"Oh, Miriam, he is magnificent." Jerusha reached through the bars and blinked back tears, touching his hand.

"He is a miracle. Father YHWH is good." Miriam grasped Jerusha's hand so that all three were touching. "How are you?" she asked, concerned.

Jerusha glanced at Antonius.

"I-I am wonderful. Father YHWH pours out his love in the darkest places. The jailer gave his life to Yeshua not too long before you came. You are here with this beautiful miracle. What more could a woman ask for?"

"How about her sons' deliverance from prison?" Samuel said, as he stood and came to stand beside them.

"Has the tribune made a decision about house arrest?" Jerusha clung to the bars and searched Antonius's eyes and drew little comfort from what she saw.

"The rumor in the barracks and among the priests is that the procurator was approached by the Sanhedrin, and a deal is being made with them. I have not heard from him, but will see him after I leave here this morning."

"Did you ask the release of the family in the next cell, too, that they be under house arrest in our villa?

"It may not be possible. They are Jews without Roman affiliation. It is because your grandfather is a Roman citizen that the tribune considers our request at all."

"Jerusha." Moses approached the cell. "Our villa is being watched."

"Where is Joshua?" She looked at Antonius. "Is he safe?"

"He stayed at the villa. The gates are locked. The servants help keep watch." Antonius unlocked her cell and swung open the door and let the others inside.

"Shalom." Stephen greeted each visitor with a kiss. Samuel watched and nodded, then greeted them as well. Jerusha hugged Miriam and looked at the miracle of new life in her arms. During her barren time, before getting her sons, Father quoted Yeshua's warning to the weeping women at his crucifixion. His words passed through her thoughts.

"Daughters of Jerusalem, do not weep for me. You should weep for yourselves and your children. For the day is coming when it will not be the women with children who are blessed but the childless. Then you will say, the barren women are the most fortunate! Those who have never given birth and never nursed a child—they are more fortunate than we are, for they will never see their children put to death! And the people will cry out for the mountains and hills to fall on top of them to hide them from all that is to come. For if this is what they do to the living branch, what will they do with the dead one?"

"What is it, Jerusha, that has you so serious?" Miriam touched her arm.

Jerusha blinked and looked up. She would not speak anything to Miriam that would rob her of the joy of this time. Father YHWH gave Abraham Jacob life. A strength inside rose in Jerusha to pray and stand for this child's purpose on earth to be fulfilled like she had prayed for her sons.

"Welcome to my abode." Jerusha sensed Father YHWH's presence as she spread out her arms to her surroundings, then made a place with the pallets and sheep skin covers to sit. Moses helped Miriam sit and took his place beside her. Her sons sat beside Antonius, one on each side. Jerusha sat on the other side of Miriam.

"There is trouble surrounding us, and it looks as though we have no way out. Let us sing King David's song when he was forced to flee from Absalom, his own son." She watched Miriam cover herself and help Abraham suckle at her breast. "First, let us pray." Jerusha bowed her head. "We come, Father YYWH, like a baby that suckles, as one who trusts in your provision. Deliver us from evil this day and give us our daily bread." Her heart then swelled with the melody to Psalm 3. She began to sing, her eyes on baby Abraham.

"Lord, I have so many enemies, so many who are against me. Listen to how they whisper their slander against me, saying: 'Look! He's hopeless! Even God can't save him from this!'" She swallowed and looked up at another voice who had joined them. Effah stood outside the bars in his Jewish garment, the blue corded tzitzits dangling at the corner of his cloak.

"But in the depths of my heart I truly know that you, Yahweh, have become my shield; You take me and surround me with yourself. Your glory covers me continually. You lift high my head when I bow low in shame. I have cried out to you, Yahweh, from your holy presence. You send me a Father's help." She pictured herself throwing her hands in the air before Father YHWH's throne, then bowing down. "I simply cry out to you: 'rise up and help me, Lord! Come and save me!' And you will slap them in the face, breaking the power of their words to harm me. My true hero comes to my rescue, for the Lord alone is my savior. What a feast of favor and bliss he gives his people." Jerusha's questioning eyes fell on Effah. She could not comprehend why he had come. She wanted to believe that he was a Yeshua follower. Everything about believing that went against what she suffered from his hands as a child. Could he be a changed man?

"Effah, my brother." Antonius jumped to his feet and greeted him with a kiss. "Shalom. What brings you here?"

"I came looking for you. The singing drew me into this part of the barracks. Not many prisoners sing the Tehillim.

"Do we need privacy or can you speak before all?" He waved his hand.

Effah's eyes lingered on Jerusha a moment, then scanned the others quickly.

"Have you spoken to the tribune, yet, concerning Jerusha's house arrest?" Effah walked away into the darkened hall, his voice growing softer as he conversed with Antonius, their words unintelligible. Jerusha shrugged.

"I think it is time we got back to the villa." Moses stood and helped Miriam up with Stephen's aid on her other side. "We pray Father YHWH brings you out of this place soon, maybe tomorrow."

"Tomorrow would be good. Maybe even tonight." Samuel walked beside Moses, who clasped hands with both sons, then followed Miriam outside the cell.

"I will be back tonight." Antonius shut and locked the door, then stared at Jerusha for a long moment, a troubling seriousness in his eyes. Jerusha waited for him to share what Effah had told him. Without saying a word, he turned and walked briskly away.

"Antonius," Jerusha yelled, "Antonius, what did Effah say?" Antonius?" She yelled to no avail. The only sound she heard was the clomp of his sandal getting softer and quieter the further away he got. "Antonious," she spoke in a soft tone and slumped to the cold floor. The torch flickered on the wall, and a tiny mouse scampered across the floor toward the bread.

"I will not share my bread with the likes of you." She crawled to the bread and lifted it high. He ran into the dark corner and slipped into a small crack in the stone wall.

"If only I could scrunch out of sight and get out of here so easily." She half smiled at Samuel and tried to put on a joyful front. She fought against her flesh taking control. Antonius's discussion with Effah and quick departure troubled her.

"Oh, well." she shrugged her shoulders. "If Father YHWH wants us out of here, he can send the angels like he did for Peter. Or the Spirit can snatch us out and take us wherever Father YHWH wants us, like he did for Philip. Until then, I will rejoice in His love and goodness." She preached more to herself than her sons.

"What about those who were not delivered?" Stephen took a bite of bread.

Jerusha thought for a long moment, then smiled.

"Father YHWH's ways are not our ways. They are better. If he chooses for us to partake of his sufferings, then so be it. I answer like Daniel. He is able to deliver. If he does not, I will serve him and only him all my life."

"What do you think Effah told Antonius?"

"I do not know. The way Antonius left all of a sudden without a word, makes me think it was not good."

Chapter 29

Jerusha paced back and forth. Her long cloak dragged on the dirty floor. When would Antonius be back? She watched a rat crawl up the side of the bucket of water and peer over the top before Samuel grabbed its tail and threw him against the wall. The filthy critter bounced up and ran through the hole the mouse had disappeared into. This entire scene made her laugh, and she scanned the tiny space and began to sing another psalm.

Patience had not been her strong trait. Even as she sang, a sense of impending doom ate at her stomach, and she cried out to him again. Father YHWH knew what lay ahead. It would be less unnerving if he told her. Her imagination played scenario after scenario in her mind. Death by crucifixion. Stoned. Locked in this dungeon of darkness for the rest of her life. She did not know what happened to her peace that passed understanding. It must have drained out her toes. Or the rat ran away with it. She chuckled under her breath again. Get serious, Jerusha!

Bring into captivity every thought unto the obedience of Christ. She inhaled and then exhaled loudly and let it out through her mouth. Father YHWH loved and understood. Even in her foolishness, he had spoken through Paul's teachings. *For though we walk in the flesh we do not war according to the flesh. For the weapons of our warfare are not of the flesh but had divine power to destroy strongholds.*

"In the name of Yeshua, I bring into captivity every thought unto the obedience to Christ." She prayed and continued to pace, then stopped and closed her eyes. A quiet rest came over her thoughts. She saw her sons' smiling faces laughing together under an olive tree in Father's garden. She breathed in a heavenly fragrance, covered her head, and sat on the pallet with her head bowed. No fear of rats. No concern about her future. No knotted stomach. A holy presence enveloped her being as she thought on the goodness of Father YHWH and kept her eyes focused on him. Other remembrances came into her thoughts. Miriam's baby. Eating pomegranates with Father in the garden. Dancing with the butterflies. Antonius's lopsided smile and twinkling blue eyes.

"Jerusha," Antonius called softly. "Jerusha," he called again.

His voice sounded far away. She kept her eyes closed and let the picture play in her mind—his last chuckle as he walked away. She missed his teasing.

"Antonius," she whispered. "If only you had no wife."

"Jerusha." He called her name with the same tenderness.

"Mother!" Samuel almost yelled. "Antonius is here!"

Her eyes flew open.

"He has been calling your name."

"Oh." She jumped up. "How long have you been standing there? Why did not you tell me you were there?"

He lifted the corner of his mouth in a half smile and had that same twinkle in his eyes. *Oh, no. He heard me.* A blush rose in her cheeks.

"He tried, Mother. You were too absorbed in your own thoughts." Samuel had his head propped up, his hands interlaced behind his head, and he sat on the pallet, grinning.

Antonius, dressed in full armor, held the torch in his right hand and placed it in the holder.

"You will be released to house arrest tonight. Effah will take us through the same tunnel we used with Sarah. The one that leads through the temple. He waits above." Keys jangled in the lock as he threw open the door.

"It will be good to see the moonlight." Stephen stood.

"And the stars," Samuel added.

"What about that family?" Jerusha pointed to the other cell.

"The Sanhedrin made a deal with the tribune that only you would be released. Your sons must stay along with the other family."

"I am not going without my sons." Jerusha crossed her arms over her chest. "Or without that family."

"You are not in any position to make demands, Jerusha. I do not like it any better than you. Get out of this hellish place while you can." He stood feet shoulder width apart, his words more a command than a request.

"You are a centurion. I know you, Antonius. You would not leave behind your soldiers. I am not leaving behind my sons, either." She backed against the wall.

"Mother, do as Antonius says. We will be alright," Samuel said.

"Yes. Do as Antonius says," Stephen added.

Antonius scowled and said nothing for a moment, then walked inside the cell and grabbed Jerusha's arm.

"You will come with me." He commanded with a sternness in his eyes.

"I will not." Jerusha jerked her arm away. "I am not a child to be told what to do."

"Then do not act like one." He grabbed her arm again.

"Nor am I one of your soldiers to be commanded around." She tried to jerk loose again. This time his grip tightened.

"Of that, I am quite aware, my queen," He let go and bowed, a twinkle in his eyes. "But you are Jacob's daughter, who I have vowed to protect. You will come with me." He swooped her up, her legs dangling free over his arm.

"Put me down." She kicked and squirmed against his armored chest.

"Samuel and Stephen, I am confident you will be freed as soon as I hear back from Rome, but that might take months." Antonius stepped over Jerusha's sleeping pallet and carried her, kicking and squirming, outside the cell, then dipped low and with one hand locked the cell and took the keys. "I will leave the torch until I return. I have not abandoned you."

"We believe you." Samuel stared through the bars at Jerusha as Antonius walked away.

"Yes, we believe you." Stephen's eyes filled with tears. "We love you, Mother."

"Love you." Samuel's voice cracked.

Jerusha stretched her neck and looked around Antonius's shoulder at her two sons.

"I love you, too." She swallowed, dropped her head on Antonius's armor, and stopped kicking, the tears running down her cheeks. Everyone seemed in agreement. She could not fight against all three loves of her life.

She lifted her head and took one last look at her sons peering through the bars.

"I am sorry," she mouthed the words. "I will be back." A claw gripped her insides. How would she ever forgive herself? How would they ever forgive her? One thing was certain. She would get them released from this dark, disgusting place, one way or another.

***

Antonius stopped. Effah hurried down the winding stairway, keeping next to the wall.

"Where have you been?" He looked at Antonius, then at Jerusha. "What's all this? Why are you carrying her?"

"She needed a little persuasion. Did not want to leave her sons." He grinned. "If you promise not to run, I will put you down."

"Put me down!" She wrestled and pushed against his armor.

"As you wish." He dropped her legs and held her tight at the waist. Her feet dangled a few inches above the stone floor. She looked up. His blues eyes lingered on her a while before he released his grip and let her slide to the floor. She fell against him, then stumbled. Effah caught her arm and steadied her balance.

Exasperated, she stared at Antonius and backed away. He raised his brows and stood like a statue, steady and unmovable, feet planted square with his shoulders. Jerusha wondered what he knew that he had not told her. His actions, of late, seemed different, more like the old Antonius. The one before Brigid came.

"Antonius, I need to talk with Jerusha alone," Effah said as he took her arm and tried to direct her to the alcove.

"If you want to talk to me, ask me, not him. I am not his possession that you need his permission." She glared at both men.

"I was only asking if he would leave us alone." Effah raised his shoulders and held his hands out.

"What if I do not want to be alone with you?" She crossed her arms over her chest.

"Do you?" Effah raised his brows.

Jerusha stood for a moment and contemplated. She eyed the row of cells where she had come from.

"Do not even think about it." Antonius dropped his chin and squinted, his thick lashes cropping his blue eyes.

She eyed Effah. "I will not be alone with you. If you have anything to say"—she turned her back and walked away, then swiveled around—"then say it. I want to get out of here."

"Oh, so now you want to get out of here." Antonius grinned.

She glared at him, then cocked her head and smiled.

"It is my idea now."

"Pardon again, your majesty," He chuckled.

Effah shuffled from one foot to the other, his head down.

"Well, Jerusha, your father is gone. I had no one to ask permission, as you put it."

He looked down, then mumbled. "Would you marry me?" He looked up.

Jerusha's eyes widened. "Are you serious?"

"It would solve your problem with the villa. My father would never take it away from us."

"Why are you asking me this now? Here? Of all places."

"Because the sooner I get your answer to my father, the sooner He will pay the tribune to free your sons. If not, your sons will be executed by crucifixion for conspiring to kill a Roman citizen."

"What!" Jerusha's heart pounded. "Did you know this?" She faced Antonius.

"I have heard the rumor." He spoke with a calm voice, not disturbed by the news at all.

"And you did not tell me? I suppose you thought it would, 'be better,' as you say, if I did not know." Jerusha's voice broke.

She gritted her teeth and clenched her fists and looked at Effah.

"I cannot marry you. I do not love you." The thought of being in a marriage bed with a man she did not love, Effah, sickened her. She looked at Antonius. He stayed so calm. What was he thinking?

"Well," she placed her hands on her hips. "Why do you not say something?" Her eyes were on Antonius.

"I cannot tell you what to do. This is your decision." His eyes never wavered; they stayed steady, peaceful.

"It is my fault my sons are in this horrible place. I cannot let them be crucified. She wrung her hands and paced. "But marry a man I do not love?" She stopped and stared at the floor. "Oh, I am so angry with myself." She stomped her foot.

Her mind raced. *Marry him. You can save the villa and your sons.* She scrunched her brows together. *There had to be another way.* Then she grasped her head. Her father's words spoken after Timon's death penetrated her thoughts. *His ways are not your ways. They are better.* Was marrying Effah his way? It most certainly was not her way.

She looked at Antonius. What did he know that made him so calm? Another way, perhaps? One she had not thought of? Why would he not speak up and tell her? He heard something from Father YHWH. What was it? He said Father YHWH would tell her in His time.

She closed her eyes, tipped her head back, and breathed deep, then let it out through her mouth. *Is this the time, Father YHWH, to know what Antonius knows?* She waited and listened for his voice. The prisoners cursed the jailer in the distance. Soldiers tromped their hob-nailed sandals in unison above.

"Help me," she whispered.

A quiet, soft voice spoke as clear as a song thrush in the morning. *There is a deception. You will be Antonius's wife.*

Chapter 30

Jerusha covered her mouth and looked at Antonius. Had she heard Father YHWH? Or were her own desires speaking? Antonius's wife? It could not be.

Antonius will be your husband. She shook her head.

It could not be.

Trust me.

He has a wife.

Deception.

There it was again and again. That still, small voice, so quiet, yet so clear. A miracle she heard him in this disgusting, distracting place, but she knew for certain it was Father YHWH's voice.

"Jerusha, will you marry me?" Effah prodded. "For the sake of your villa and your sons?" He drew near and reached for her hands.

"No." she turned away. "No. I will not marry you, Effah. I do not trust your father. And I do not love you. I do not know how Father YHWH will deliver my sons or me, but I will not bow to this manipulation and witchcraft worked by him and those around him. My Father YHWH is greater. I will trust him. If my sons are crucified, I will be crucified with them."

She approached Antonius. "I am grateful for your protection and all you have done for my family." A single tear rolled into his unshaven face. He knew what she was going to ask.

"Take me back to the cell. Neither my sons, nor myself will be bought by corrupt priests. We will pray and hope and believe."

"But Jerusha, my father does not know I am a Yeshua follower." Effah pleaded, then took her hand and pulled her into the alcove. "You and your family will be safe if you marry me." Jerusha looked at him. Shadows bounced on his face. His dark eyes were serious and kind. He meant well.

"At one time, when I was young, I would have married you. That was before I knew Yeshua as King. Now he reigns over my life. He would not want me to bow to another ruler, no matter the cost. Neither should you." She took his hands. "Today. Thank you for your offer of help. I hope, as Antonius has shared with me, that you have given your life to Yeshua. Then, if I am crucified, I will see you again in his kingdom. It is his will to rule on earth as it is in heaven. May that be so in all our lives." She reached out and wiped away the tears that streamed down his cheeks into his beard. "You are a good man, Effah, but I do not love you." She turned and looked at Antonius who stood by the stairs.

"Antonius, a prisoner escapes," a soldier yelled.

"Do not go anywhere without me!" Antonius commanded Jerusha. "For once, do as I say."

She nodded. "I will be safe with Effah." She smiled at the Jew.

Antonius fled down the dark passageway. In the distance, she heard cursing, keys jangling and thuds against the wall.

A slight movement in the darkness startled her. Effah moaned and slumped against her. She gasped and wrapped her arm around him. A bloody dagger flashed.

"It's the Sicarii; watch out, Jerusha." Effah staggered in front of her, his hand on his side. She stared at a man dressed in Jewish robes, his eyes narrowed slits that spewed evil. Hair stood up on her arms. He darted out of the alcove and ran up the stairs. Effah slumped at her feet and leaned against the wall and looked up the stairs.

"Father, why?" He spoke in a weak voice. His face showed the pain of betrayal.

Caiaphas stood at the top of the stairs robed in his priestly garments, stroking his long gray beard.

"You follow the Way. You are no son of mine." His father smirked and walked away.

"Effah," Jerusha gently eased him to the floor and pressed on the wound. The blood oozed through her fingers. "Antonius!" she yelled.

"I am here," He bent down and lifted Effah's head and shoulders and placed his hand on top of Jerusha's and applied pressure. More blood squirted out.

"Effah, my friend, I am sorry I was not here for you." His voice cracked.

"It is alright, Antonius." He struggled to breathe. "Be there for Jerusha." He half smiled. "She loves you. I saw it in her eyes." Blood trickled out the corner of his mouth. He gasped for air, closed his eyes, then opened them again and looked over at Jerusha. She felt helpless. Strange, after all these years, she loved him as a brother, wanted him to live. She wiped the sweat off his forehead.

"I am sorry for doubting you, Effah." She wept uncontrollably, her tears dropping on his face. "You only wanted to help."

He groaned and coughed. "I deserved it." He struggled to sit up and Antonius propped his arm beneath.

He gasped, his eyes on Jerusha. "Forgive me for what happened when we were children." I need your forgiveness before I die." His eyes clouded. "Yeshua forgave me. Forgive me. Tell me you forgive me."

"I forgive you." Jerusha saw the life drain from his eyes.

He stared wide-eyed. "I see the kingdom. It's beautiful." His chin dropped to his chest.

She stared at Antonius. "You knew all along. I am so sorry I did not believe you. It could have been so different. I was so hateful to him."

She placed her cheek on Effah's head, held him tight, and rocked back and forth.

"I am so sorry, Effah."

After a while, Antonius pulled her away from his body. She looked up. Marcellus stood over them.

"Give him a proper burial," Antonius ordered.

"There is room in Father's tomb." Jerusha sniffed and wiped her nose on her sleeve.

Marcellus lifted Effah's body and carried it up the stairs with little effort.

"You fought the good fight, Effah. See you in the kingdom." The legionnaire's voice cracked. Several tears coursed his cheeks.

Antonius held Jerusha and stroked her hair. She sobbed and sobbed, her face in her hands. After a while, she quieted, and he released her. She stepped back and looked down the hall where her sons were jailed, then at Antonius.

"How much more death and suffering? Will my sons be next? Or me? Or you?" She walked toward her sons' cell.

Antonius followed.

"What are you doing here?" Samuel asked as she approached. "We told you to go with Antonius."

"Effah is dead." She felt Antonius behind, his hands on her shoulders.

"What? How?" Stephen asked and stood up.

"Caiaphas's doing, by the hand of a sicarius. Had his own son killed." She felt numb. "I am leaving." Her voice quivered. "It is rumored you will be crucified." She stopped and composed herself. She could not break down in front of her sons. "Father YHWH, our Father, can be trusted. I must go through the door he opened and trust your deliverance to him." Antonius squeezed her shoulders.

She looked at both sons. Each blinked back tears.

"While at the villa, I will do everything I can to get your release." She took a deep breath. "Ultimately it is in Father YHWH's hands. Forgive me for putting you in this mess. If I had not insisted on coming here, but trusted Father YHWH to take care of Joshua, you would not be here."

"Forgive yourself," Samuel reached through the bars. "We have already forgiven you." She looked at Stephen. He nodded.

"That will not be so easy." Jerusha gripped the bars.

"You cannot fix this," Stephen said. "Only our Father can." He pointed up.

"We have been talking. We are at peace whatever happens." Samuel's voice sounded so at rest. "You be at peace, too."

Jerusha released the bars and stood back.

Your sons will be taught by YHWH and great will be their peace.

She closed her eyes and swallowed. *I am in the darkness, too.* A new insight arose inside. Her fight was not with flesh and blood. She would seek Father YHWH's wisdom and how to fight against this evil that worked through the corrupt religious leaders. Leaving her sons in this dark place tore at her soul. But she needed to be in Father's garden and ascend to Father's throne on their behalf. He alone had the answer.

"Take me home." She looked at Antonius. "Father YHWH is calling. He will show the way." She smiled and shook her head. "He waits only for my total surrender. And belief in his goodness." She stared at each son's face.

"You are men any mother would be proud to have as sons. I believe the oneness with Father YHWH will keep you. I love you."

She looked at Antonius. "Open the door so I can give them a hug before I leave."

The barred door swung open, and she rushed inside. She hugged each one and lingered as long as possible.

"You are not orphans. You are sons of a royal Father, who never will leave you or forsake you. You are royalty." She spoke, a new strength in her voice, as she backed out the door, her eyes darting from one to the other. "We will see each other again." Oh how she loved them.

She looked at Antonius.

"I am ready." She listened as he closed and locked the cell, her eyes on them.

Father YHWH loved them even more than she. Of that she was certain.

Chapter 31

Jerusha walked beside Antonius. Marcellus and the other soldiers surrounded them. She looked up at the clear sky and searched for Regulus. It twinkled against the dark back drop, brighter than all the other stars in the lion constellation. *Lion of Judah. You are my king. Ruler over all.* She stumbled and kept walking, then breathed deep of the fresh air and thought of her sons in that rat-infested place with unbearable stench. *Do not let my sons suffer in that place for long.* She felt guilty breathing clean, fresh air and seeing the light of moon and stars.

She glanced at Antonius, his helmet strapped under his chin, his armor in place, his sword in its scabbard. Somber, he stared ahead, his hob-nailed sandals clicking in unison with the other soldiers. She scrambled to keep pace with them as they climbed Mount Zion.

Short of breath, she slowed. "Can we rest?"

"Halt." Antonius put up his hand. He waited in silence while she struggled for air. A cool breeze blew across her sweaty brow. She smelled her own body odor and felt like gagging. She hoped Antonius could not smell it. He kept his centurion demeanor in front of his soldiers, never softening his firm set jaw, his eyes alert to the surroundings.

"Keep moving." He gave a signal the soldiers understood, took her arm, and started walking. She doubled her pace to keep up and leaned into the climb, her eyes on the ground, then she stopped and looked up the terraced steps. Almost there.

He and the other soldiers took one step to her two as they climbed. Step. Step. Up. Step Step. Up. She kept her head down and concentrated, being careful at each rise not to stumble. At the top, she raised her eyes and took a deep breath. Home at last. The thorny jujube tree flicked shadowy fingers across the grape-vined covered wall and villa gate.

"Halt," Antonius raised his hand again. "Take your guard positions." The soldiers hustled around the villa's outer wall, leaving her alone with Antonius.

"Someone has been watching." He stepped between her and the terraced steps, his back to her. "Joshua," he called, "open the gate."

"Mother." Joshua ran up the path. Keys jiggled in the lock, and the gate swung open. Jerusha hugged her little soldier. No matter how old he got, he would always be her little soldier.

"Oh, Joshua, it feels so good to be home."

"Phew!" He pinched his nose, "You smell."

Antonius chuckled.

She glared.

"Hannah," Jerusha slipped off her dusty sandals and ran up the path. "Prepare the mikvah bath." She stopped and looked at Antonius, who stood at the gate with Joshua.

"My little man, have you kept a sober and alert guard?" His eyes darted between her and Joshua. Joshua pursed his lips together.

"Someone is watching our villa."

"Very alert of you. All the more reason your mother needs a good son like you to keep watch. She is under house arrest and cannot leave without a Roman guard." Antonius stood up straight, his eyes on Jerusha. "It is just as well, with the villa being watched." He nodded at her.

She acknowledged with a slight nod, then turned and walked away.

***

Jerusha sunk her body into the heated bath and breathed in the fragrant Rose of Sharon oil in the waters. She leaned back and let the warm water soothe her sore muscles, her hair floating on top. It felt so good. She looked again at the stars above. She loved dipping in the rooftop mikvah at night. With no other rooftop as high as theirs, she felt safe from others' eyes. It was her time to be totally alone yet not, for the Lord her God was always with her. "Lord, thank You," she said, an overwhelming feeling of gratitude filling her. As she sponged away the filth, she felt like a whole new person and sensed that somehow a new and different life awaited. Father YHWH had a plan. She dropped the sponge in the water and dipped her hair under. When she arose and smoothed it from her face, she saw the back of Antonius, his helmet under his arm, looking out over the city. She grabbed the towel and slid slowly up and out, then hid behind a pomegranate bush. While she dried off, she noticed her garments hanging on a branch on the other side. Keeping her eyes on Antonius, she crept around the bush, scampered across the gap, grabbed her tunic, and slipped it over her head.

Whew! She put her arms in the cloak and walked down the steps, still keeping her eyes on Antonius until he turned and saw her.

"I wondered who wore the Rose of Sharon fragrance." He grinned, his blond hair blowing in the breeze as he walked the pomegranate-lined path toward her. "I took the side stairs. Thought I could see who watches the villa and where they go when they leave." He stopped before the mikvah. "Hmm. What do we have here?" He walked past the waters and found the towel on the bush. The corner of his mouth curled up and broaden into a smile. "I see I've missed something."

The blush rose in her cheeks.

"Like always, you appear out of nowhere."

She ran on down the stairs into the kitchen. Miriam and Chaya had a pot of smoked, green wheat porridge cooking over hot flames, the smell of fresh baked bread in the oven. Tomorrow she would take some of both to Samuel and Stephen. If they are going to be in that dark place, they can at least eat decent food. Maybe Antonius or Marcellus could take her. Jerusha dried her hair and braided it over her shoulder, then grabbed her blue and purple radiyd and wrapped it around her head, throwing the ends over her shoulders.

"Well, you smell better," Joshua said as he whittled at the bench by the fire.

"After I come in from seeing Boaz, I want some of that porridge," she said. She walked outside along the path to the herb garden, then veered off to the stable. She heard footsteps and stopped.

"Who is it?" She turned and saw a soldier at the gate. She had gotten used to seeing guards. The lamps smelled of burning olive oil, a wonderful smell. Much more pleasing than the pungent burning torch. Since being in that horrible place, she appreciated the simple things more, like stars and moon and a mikvah bath.

She unlatched the stable door and pulled it open. Oh, the smell of fresh hay. Boaz whinnied a shalom.

"I have missed you, too, my old friend," She rubbed his nose and fed him a handful of oats from a bucket. "Times are changing. Father's gone. Samuel and Stephen are in prison. The scepter is gone." She sighed, grabbed a brush, and stroked his back. "One day, Boaz, we will be leaving this place. We will ride like the wind across Judea, forge the Jordan River, and gallop up the mountains in Perea to our new home." She stopped brushing. "Grandfather does not know Father is gone into the kingdom. When I get free—if I get free—we will have to go to Perea and tell him. He will not be happy that the scepter is missing. Maybe we will find it before we have to tell him," She rambled on, knowing he understood not a word. It just felt better telling someone. "And it is hard to understand, but Father YHWH said I will be Antonius's wife. Can you believe it?"

"I believe it," Antonius said and stepped into the stable. He had removed his armor and wore the red undertunic.

Jerusha threw her head back. "Why? Oh, why, do you do that. It's as if you are a ghost. Appear. Disappear. Appear. Disappear. I think I know how the disciples felt when Yeshua appeared in their room. Then disappeared. Makes your heart skip a beat." She slapped at her chest.

Antonius roared in laughter. She laughed, too, and fell in the hay. He stopped laughing and stood at the stall leaning on his elbow. She placed a piece of straw in her mouth and chewed, then cocked her head and eyed him for the longest moment. He stared for a moment, then looked away. She tightened her radiyd and gripped her cloak together.

"You said you believe it. What do you believe, Antonius?"

"Boaz has a secret. That is what I believe." He grinned.

"Did you hear what I told him?"

"I think it would be better if I did not answer that. I have come to the stable to show you something." He walked past, pushed on the secret door, and shoved it open. Curious, she followed and ducked under the arched entrance. The lamplight bounced shadows on his face. He dug deep in a pile of fleece and found a wooden box, its latch locked. He pulled on a leather cord beneath his tunic until a gold key dangled at its end and unlocked the box. Jerusha moved closer.

"That box looks like the one Father gave me when I was a child." She felt the pomegranate reliefs around the edge. Tears formed. She missed Father's presence. Frankincense The smell of fresh wood shavings. Antonius let her savor the moment before opening the box.

"Father loved carving pomegranate reliefs. As a child, I put a hard shell around my heart because of Effah's abuse. I vowed no one would hurt me like that again. Father sensed it, but had no idea what had happened. He would cut open the pomegranate and talk to me about letting him inside the hard outer shell. Before we ate it, I would try to count the seeds. He would tell me that was how many thoughts Father YHWH had toward me. Too numerous to count, like the stars." She looked up at Antonius. "I miss him very much."

"He held out the box.

"Your father took great pleasure in watching his little lioness learn to roar." Antonius opened the box. "Take it out and look at it." He motioned with his head. Jerusha picked up a soft piece of leather and unrolled it.

She gasped, "You had it." and ran her fingers across the scepter's jewels. "Why did not you tell me this?" She placed the scepter back in the box. "And do not tell me you thought it would, 'be better,' for me." She placed her hands on her hips and stared at him.

"Your father told me when he died"—he closed the box—"to take the scepter from the tomb and hide it until needed. He asked me not tell you or anyone else in the family."

"Why?"

"He wanted you to put your trust in Father YHWH, not the scepter."

Jerusha cocked her head, smiled and nodded.

"I can see Father YHWH's wisdom in that decision."

"After your sons saw it in the tomb, I took it. Later, someone stole it from me." He motioned for her to sit on a bench in the cave. "It was only today I recovered it. The person, who stole it brought it back."

"Why would they do that?"

"Because it was the young witch. She saw me at the tomb and followed. When I went into Herod's palace to find Joshua, she snuck it from the pouch on my horse. She wants to talk to you."

"I do not want to talk to her."

"Effah's father paid her to release curses against your family. Her spells did not work. She hoped to get greater power from the scepter. When that did not work, she recognized Father YHWH's power is greater and wants to know why."

"This is the first night back in the villa." She held her head in her hands, then looked up. "Could you not tell me this tomorrow? I am not ready to deal with a witch."

"I'm leaving for Rome tonight. This scepter might help in your sons' release. I have to try."

"I thought you already sent word to Rome."

"With Caiaphas's plots, the messenger may not have gotten through. I must go myself." He took her hands. "Your sons may be crucified any day."

Jerusha's stomach felt like a rock dropped in it. She closed her eyes. "Father YHWH, help us."

"I have a plan." He moved onto the bench beside her. "Tomorrow, after I leave, I want you to go with Joshua and Moses to talk to the tribune Lysias. I have arranged for four soldiers to escort you with strict orders if anything happens to you, they will pay at the end of my whip. The tribune will listen. He admired your father. You are his daughter. He will listen to you. Ask for six months' delay. I hope to be back by that time."

"Antonius, if they are crucified, I will be with them. I will not allow them to suffer alone. You must make it back."

"Father YHWH promised you would be my wife."

"You *did* hear what I said to Boaz." She chuckled, then got serious and looked at him. "What about your wife?"

"That troubled me at first, too. I held my wife in my arms when she died. I saw her take her last breath. Brigid is lying. I do not know why I didn't see it, when she first told me."

"That may be so. Nevertheless, I die with my sons, if they are crucified."

"He hugged her shoulder. "Trust, little lioness, trust." He rose, took the leather covered scepter from the box, pulled Jerusha's chin up, and let his eyes linger on her face. She reached to cover her mole. He shook his head.

"No, my little butterfly. Do not cover the mark of your beauty."

Jerusha dropped her hand, her eyes filling with tears.

"I love you, Jerusha."

"And I you." She closed her eyes. When she opened them, he had gone through the doorway, his red tunic whipping in the wind. She rose and stared at his back.

"Come back, my love." She stroked Boaz, then laid her cheek against his silky nose and wept.

Chapter 32

Morning dew glistened on the leaves in the garden. Light filtered through the limbs onto Jerusha's face. Song thrushes sang and mourning doves cooed. Jerusha rounded the corner past Father's bench to the grape-covered wall and looked out. A fuchsia glow peeked through white puffy clouds and streaked across the horizon. It had not been but a few hours since Antonius left, and she looked in the distance for his return. Foolish she knew, but something she would do every morning until Father YHWH brought him back to her. She remembered the joyous occasion when Moses married Miriam in the courtyard. Laughter, singing, dancing. A mirthful feast. Were those days over? She hoped not.

Father YHWH promised Antonius to be her husband. How? She did not know. It only mattered that Father YHWH said it. Her wedding would be in this garden, Father's garden. He would be pleased. She turned around and listened to the birds' melodies and remembered Yeshua's encouragement.

Look at the birds of the air; they neither sow nor reap nor gather into barns, and yet your heavenly Father feeds them. Are you not of more value than they? Father YHWH knew things she did not know. She would trust him.

"We are here," Joshua called. "Where are you?" She forgot she had asked them to meet her.

"I am coming. Have a seat on the benches." She walked the path to Father's bench, where Miriam, Moses, and Hannah gathered with Joshua.

"This is the day that you have made. We will rejoice and be glad in it." She made her declaration to Father YHWH on the way. "Your joy is our strength."

She smiled at those sitting before her. "Antonius left last night for Rome with the scepter."

"He had the scepter? Why didn't he tell us?" Joshua squirmed on the bench.

"It is a long story I do not have time to tell right now. You and I have an assignment." She pointed to Joshua. "We are going to the tribune. It is rumored your brothers will be crucified any day."

"Crucified?" Joshua stood and grabbed his sword. "Not my brothers." He waved it in the air.

"Put that away. It is not the answer. We will ask for more time, hopefully six months, so Antonius has time to get back. I gathered us together to pray for favor with the tribune." Jerusha's eyes fell on Hannah. The beautiful young girl turned away and covered her face with her radiyd and whimpered. The others stared.

"What is the matter, Hannah?" Joshua bent over and tried to see her face.

"Leave us alone." Jerusha waved. Joshua looked puzzled and walked away. Moses and Miriam nodded, a knowing in their faces as they left the garden. Their new son slept in her arms.

"We will pray as you asked." He offered to take the baby from Miriam. She shook her head no.

Jerusha sat on the bench with Hannah, who held her face in her hands and wept. Looking above through the branches at the awakening sky, Jerusha wondered how to comfort a brokenhearted girl in love. She had seen it in Hannah and Stephen's eyes. Even though neither talked to her of marriage, most likely Stephen had talked with Father. Or Antonius. It was obvious to all that a wedding needed to be planned. That was before she decided to take things in her own hands. She listened to the grieving girl's hopeless cries, sickened by the pain she caused.

Father YHWH, what do I do?

Forgive yourself. I have forgiven you.

But I have caused so much pain for those I loved, all because I insisted on my own way.

You are forgiven. Forgive yourself.

I forgive myself. I only hope those I hurt can forgive me.

All of a sudden she understood how Effah felt before he died—why he needed her forgiveness.

Your sons forgave you.

She looked at Hannah, who had stopped crying and wiped her eyes with the back of her hand.

"Hannah, I know why you were crying. It is my fault. I am sorry. Will you forgive me?" Tears rolled down her cheeks.

"It is not your fault." Hannah looked at her with her big round eyes. "But if you think it is, I forgive you. I would not be alive, if it was not for you. I love you."

"Oh, Hannah, thank you. I needed that." Jerusha hugged her tight and watched a purple butterfly flittered above the pomegranate bush.

"Look. A sign." She pointed. "Father YHWH always sends me butterflies to let me know he is with us in the darkness." She wiped her own tears away, then stood and pulled Hannah's hands. "Would you like to go with Joshua and me to the barracks? After we talk to the tribune, we will take porridge to Samuel and Stephen."

"Could I?"

"I warn you. It is not a pleasant place."

"You forget. I lived in unpleasant places before coming to live with you. I can take it, if I can see Stephen." She blushed. "And of course, Samuel."

Jerusha smiled.

"I am not sure, yet, when we go. I do not want to rush ahead of YHWH's timing, although Antonius told me to go this morning. After we pray, if I feel a peace, we go today. If not, we wait. His timing is perfect. No more chasing after my own plans." An inner joy bubbled up, and she chuckled. Father YHWH had a plan. She would trust it.

***

Later that day, as Jerusha walked around the courtyard fountain, she heard Paul's nephew.

"I must talk to Jerusha."

She turned and walked the tiled path to the front gate. Ahead of her she saw Marcellus unlock the gate. Paul's nephew ran toward her.

"I need to talk to you, alone." He looked around untrustingly.

Jerusha motioned him to follow and rounded the corner and stood behind a large pomegranate bush.

"What is it?" she asked.

"I went to the tribune to plead your sons' case, to tell him that they were not a part of the conspiracy to kill Paul. He did not believe me. I do not understand it. He believed me when I told him about Paul." He wrung his hands. "I am afraid for your sons. It is rumored they will be crucified any day. And what will happen to you?"

"Do not worry about me. Ask your mother to gather the followers of the Way and pray for favor with the tribune. Joshua and I will ask for a six-month stay of execution, hopefully enough time for Antonius to get back from Rome."

"He went to Rome?"

"He was afraid the first messenger may not have gotten through. Pray for his safe return and favor with Emperor Nero. Be careful when you leave. Someone is watching our villa." Jerusha walked him to the gate and watched as he ran down the terraced steps. *Father YHWH, protect him.* She caught a glimpse of a man as he slipped behind an oxen-drawn cart and ducked down, then peeked above the bundles of goods piled inside—one of Caiaphas' s spy's, no doubt.

***

That night Jerusha paced the tiled path in Father's lamp-lit garden. She felt no release to go, yet. Wait, was all she heard every time she asked Father YHWH.

"Be patient, Jerusha," She talked to the hoot owls and crickets. Everyone else ate in the kitchen. What if she missed it? What if she waited and her sons were crucified because she thought she heard Father YHWH? She stopped, then closed her eyes, breathed in a deep breath, and tried to calm her thumping heart. *Fear not.* She leaned her head back and listened to the night sounds around her. One lone song thrush sang its melody in the olive branch overhead.

"If you can sing in darkness, then so can I." She hummed and swayed to an old melody, then broke into singing.

"I am the lion of Judah. Deep within my innermost being, dwells the Holy God of all Israel. I am the Lion of Judah." She dipped and swayed. "I am the lioness of Judah. Deep within my inner most being dwells the Holy God of all Israel." Raising her hands, she twirled and danced along the path before her King, her hair flying loose and free. "I am the Lion of Judah." Breathless, she stopped, then bowed face down on the cold tiles in honor of his majesty. She loved Him with all her heart. Live or die she would worship and dance before him. He was her royal Father. Yeshua, his son, was the King of Kings and Lord of Lords. A holy hush quieted even the song bird. The King had entered the garden. All creation seemed to pay attention. The crickets even stopped chirping. Jerusha sensed his nearness and looked up. It was him. He stood before her in radiant white clothing, his eyes like coals of fire.

Fear not. Your time is not yet. Neither is your sons. Go tomorrow to the tribune. His words reverberated in the air like tiny sparkling diamonds. She gazed, dumbfounded, unable to move. *A woman is at your gate. Let her in. She belongs to me.* As quickly as the vision appeared, it was gone. Jerusha felt a tingling all over her body. The song thrush began its song again. The crickets resumed their chirping.

"Mother, there is someone asking for you at the gate. Somehow she missed that Joshua had come into the garden. He talked softer than usual and must have sensed YHWH's presence, too. "I think she is the witch," he said. "Should the soldier let her in?"

Jerusha rose to her feet, and covered her head.

"Yes. Tell the soldier I will see her. Bring her to the garden." She turned and walked to Father's bench, then looked up and found Regulus. *Light in the darkness, shine in her heart tonight.* She sat on Father's bench and waited in the presence of the King.

A few minutes later she heard the garden gate open and clang shut. A young girl walked around the corner and stopped.

"He told me to follow this path. Are you Jerusha?" She kept her head down and fiddled with her fingers.

"I am her. Come and sit." She patted the bench.

The young girl walked hesitantly toward the bench. Her eyes had dark circles beneath. One had a bad bruise. Her cheeks were sunken in, and her hair was cut short and jagged. She looked like an orphan. Suddenly, Jerusha knew the girl had been abandoned, left to survive on her own, and assumed that she turned to witchcraft to earn money. His love flooded her being suddenly, for this lost girl, and for the first time she saw things differently than before.

"Your father abandoned you. What happened to your mother?"

"She died." Her eyes widened as she sat beside Jerusha. "How did you know that?"

"I only knew your father abandoned you. Father YHWH loves you. He's been waiting for this day."

"What do you mean?"

"He wants to be your Father."

"I know he has more power than the god I served. Every curse or spell I tried on you or your family failed."

"It is the power of his love that protects us."

"Why would he want me for his daughter? I have made money working against him."

"Are you ready to turn away from witchcraft?"

She nodded. "That is why I came here. I am tired of serving a god who only wants to kill, steal, and destroy. The girl looked defeated, as if she'd taken a long journey.

"He sent his son, Yeshua, to die on a cross for your sins, then resurrected him on the third day. He lives and reigns in his kingdom in heaven forever and ever. All who believe in him, Father YWHW cleanses their sins and welcomes them into his family as his child. Is that what you want?"

"Yes, yes, I believe." She sobbed, then bent over, gripped her belly and opening her mouth, she released a loud screeching scream. She slumped against Jerusha and cried softly.

Jerusha wrapped her arm around her shoulder. "I command every demon to be quiet and leave in Yeshua's name. His blood speaks against you. You no longer have authority to stay in this body. Go, and go without making a scene."

Breathe in and breathe out." She encouraged the young girl. "What is your name?"

"Adah," she spoke between whimpers.

"Adah." Jerusha laid her hand on her head. "Peace. Be still. You are royalty, Father YHHW's child. He will never leave you or forsake you. You belong to him."

"I cannot go back to my house." Adah sat up, fear in her eyes. "The priest will come again and want the witch I live with to do more spells and curses. She will beat me if I do not obey." She covered eyes.

"Is that why you have a bruised eye?" Jerusha fought to keep her anger under control.

Adah nodded her chin to her chest.

"Every time a curse or spell failed, she beat me," she whimpered.

"You stay with us."

She threw her arms around Jerusha. "You are too kind."

"Our royal Father is the kind one." Jerusha blinked back tears.

"Will you forgive me for working spells and sending curses against you and your family? I am so very sorry."

"Of course, you are forgiven. How could I do anything different than our Father YHWH has done for me? Let us get you something to eat and a place to sleep." Jerusha stood and walked toward the gate. Adah hurried past and opened it for her.

"Toda. Thank you." Jerusha waited, then walked beside her toward the villa. Another orphan in the house. Father would be pleased.

Chapter 33

Jerusha glared at Effah's father. He stood at her gate in the dusky light before the sun rose. Of course he came in darkness. He represented everything dark she had ever known. It made her sick at her stomach to look at one of the top religous figures in the city wearing his fancy robe and phylactery, the black box holding portions of the Torah, supposedly showing reverence to the law. What did he know of loving YHWH's law? He murdered his own son. The coward surrounded himself with temple guards.

"What do you want?" She stood beside Marcellus, who had summoned her.

"Your sons will die soon." The priest's voice sounded weak.

The parts of his body not hidden by his self-righteous robes appeared thin and frail, his face drawn and wrinkled. "I come to offer my help. If you will deed your villa to the priests, I can save your sons."

"You! Save my sons." She almost burst out laughing. "You are the last person I would trust for salvation. A man who despised his own son." She clenched her fists at her sides. "Get out of my sight." She pointed up the path.

"You will regret that you did not listen to my wisdom." He spoke slowly and deliberately, staring through narrowed slits. "I have authority to free or condemn."

"Yeshua was the only man who walked the face of the earth who had authority to free or condemn. I put my life in His hands." She surprised herself with her boldness to speak truth.

His jaw twitched. "Blasphemer! You shall die with your sons!" His faced turned red.

Jerusha smiled. "We will all die," she said, laughing. "Only you will die an old man, broken and bitter because you rejected Yeshua as your Messiah and King." Jerusha glanced at Marcellus, who cracked a half smile.

"Arrest her!" The priest spoke to the temple guard, then commanded Marcellus. "Open that gate."

Marcellus stepped in front of Jerusha and pulled his sword from its scabbard.

"I will not open the gate. Leave now." He directed the temple guards. "She is under Rome's jurisdiction. I have strict orders that nothing happens to her."

The priest glowered and turned. Jerusha watched the temple guards follow him down the terraced steps. The sun broke over the horizon, casting early morning shadows across their path, their dark cloaks whipping in the wind. It grieved her that he rejected Father YHWH's love. Severe judgment awaited him and those like him. Blind leading the blind.

"They will be back," Marcellus replaced his weapon.

"Get the soldier escort ready. We go this morning to see the tribune." She sighed and walked toward the villa. "I will get Joshua and Hannah. Moses and Miriam can stay here. It will be safer for the baby."

***

Neighbors in the upper city stared from their windows and rooftops as she walked the road leading to Antonia Fortress surrounded by Roman soldiers. Many hated her family. Some laughed and pointed.

Most of her neighbors in the upper city had not accepted Yeshua as their Messiah and King. She lifted her chin. Father taught her not to care what others thought. In the past it was one of her greatest weaknesses. She felt sorry they did not know the terrible judgment that awaited them.

"Do not pay attention to them," she said to Joshua and Hannah. "Keep your eyes on the road ahead."

A little further down the road they entered the open agora. Some shopkeepers shut their doors while women gathered their children, whispering and pointing at Jerusha. Others laughed. Father had kept his carpenter shop in the lower city. The people there loved him, especially the widows and the poor. Only a few in the upper city followed the Way. Most mocked. Father tried. He loved them. That was why he had not left Jerusalem. It cost him his life. It may cost her and her sons lives, too.

She looked at the donkey that carried the food and water for Samuel and Stephen. It plodded along in obedience behind Joshua, the rope held loosely in his hand. He patted his sword on his hip and strutted like he was a king. Jerusha smiled. He cared not what others thought.

Hannah kept her head down. She struggled with the fear of man, one of the deep wounds of her abuse. *Father YHWH, help her.* She and Stephen made a good pair. Her son, the giant with beautiful, bright eyes, walked in wisdom and spoke truth in love, lifting up and encouraging those around him, exactly what Hannah needed, if he lived long enough to marry. *His time is not yet,* Yeshua said. Jerusha imagined their wedding with her and Antonius in Father's garden.

The road curved and wound up the hill past the temple. People scattered as they approached. Many crippled and blind begged at its gates. Joshua dug in his girdle and threw a coin to one. Her son never passed the poor without giving them something. If he had bread, he gave bread. If he had coins, he shared his coins.

Jerusha remembered the time he gave a boy his favorite cloak she had made especially for him. "I have a royal Father. I do not need to worry about what to wear." Jerusha's heart swelled, thinking of her son's wisdom, and she patted his shoulder.

The climb became steeper the closer they got to Antonius Fortress. Jerusha felt Yeshua's strength in her legs as she scaled the steep steps to the gate. The donkey brayed. Joshua calmed him with soft words and kept a tight hold. Hannah stared at the massive barracks, then kept her head down and pushed ahead. At last, they stood before the immense gate.

"Antonius requests this prisoner see the tribune." Marcellus yelled at the guard in the tower above.

"Who is she?" the toothless guard spit.

"Jacob's daughter." Jerusha stepped forward.

"Who is this Jacob?" The burly soldier grunted.

"He rode with Rome in many battles, respected and honored by his authorities." Marcellus spoke with admiration in his eyes.

"Hmm. I do not know of him." He stared at Jerusha. "I remember seeing you with Antonius." He spit, again. "Who are the others?" He grinned, his eyes on Hannah.

Jerusha questioned her decision to bring her and leaned into Marcellus.

"Will our guards protect her, too?" she whispered.

Marcellus nodded and pointed to Joshua's donkey.

"The young man is her son. He and the girl bring fresh provisions to the woman's other sons.

'Seem harmless enough." The soldier motioned to someone below. The heavy metal gate started to rise. "I will send word to the tribune."

***

The tribune wore a red toga clasped at the shoulder, one end draped over his arm and sat at a marble table, parchments and maps strewn across its top and onto the mosaic floor. Jerusha walked beneath the arched entrance with Marcellus, who stopped and saluted. Jerusha nodded. The rhythmic beat of the other soldier's hob-nailed sandals behind stopped in unison. Jerusha glanced back at Joshua and Hannah, the soldiers at attention on all sides.

"Antonius informed me that you would be coming." The tribune leaned back against the gold-leafed chair. "I can see why he is so enamored with you. You are quite beautiful. What is it I can do for you?"

A slight blush rose up her neck and she could not discern his authenticity. It almost felt as if he mocked her with his words. She lifted her chin and tried to calm her thudding heart, knowing that her son's lives may depend on this conversation. She swallowed and hoped she controlled her emotions and her angry words if he made her mad. Father God, help me guard my heart, she prayed silently.

"It is rumored my sons will be crucified any day," she said, in a measured voice.

"Rumors travel fast in this godforsaken place," he scoffed.

He placed his elbows on the table, holding his chin in hand-clasped fingers.

"I am asking for a stay of execution, until Antonius gets back from Rome."

"You ask a lot."

"I ask for justice."

"I have great respect for your father, even greater for your grandfather, Regulus. What a shame he died a traitor—trumped-up charges by your Jewish leaders."

"My sons, myself—we are innocent, too."

"Paul's nephew told me you are not the ones involved in the conspiracy."

"It is a mistake we were arrested."

Are you saying I made a mistake?" He rose and leaned forward, both hands placed on the table in front, anger in his eyes. Jerusha straightened her back and shoulders and lifted her chin. She would not be intimidated.

"I am saying everything is not always as it appears." She stared unblinking and clenched her trembling fingers.

"You have courage like your father and grandfather. I believe you speak the truth." He sat and cracked a half smile.

Jerusha held her breath and kept her eyes on him. He placed his elbows back on the table, cupped his chin in interlaced fingers, and appeared to be in deep thought. Jerusha's heart beat so fast she thought he surely could see the thu-thump against her chest, so she pulled her cloak shut.

"In your father and grandfather's honor, I give you six months to hear from Rome. No more." He waved his hand in dismissal. "Go before I change my mind," then he bent down and picked up a parchment.

Jerusha breathed a sigh of relief, turned, and followed Marcellus outside into the courtyard. Naked men stood waist-deep in the bubbling waters of a nearby pool. She assumed naked. Their oiled upper bodies glistened under the sun and they laughed and teased as beautiful women, dressed in silk togas passed. She waited for Hannah.

"Do not look to your left. Keep your eyes on Marcellus ahead." She took her place on the other side to protect her innocent eyes and motioned their guards to move around the women. Joshua untied the donkey and hurried to catch up with Marcellus. Once past the pool area, Marcellus turned and walked around the fountain and toward another portion of the fortress. He opened a large cedar door and waited for all to pass, then swung it closed with a thud. He dipped an oil-soaked torch in a brazier and lit it, then carried it as he descended the dark stairway where Caiaphas had stood when Effah had been stabbed. She followed, then Hannah. Joshua tied the donkey to a hook, lifted the water and porridge off its back, and came behind Hannah.

"Stay close to the wall," she instructed Hannah. "Do not look over the edge." With the torch carried in front, she walked in darkness. "Be careful. Slow." She wound down the stairway step by step, keeping her eye on Hannah, then looking back at Joshua. "You be careful, too. The edges may crumble."

At the bottom she glanced at Effah's smeared blood and walked around it, thankful he was with Father YHWH. Halfway down the hall, she saw Samuel and Stephen holding their faces against the bars straining to see who was coming.

"It stinks in here," Hannah whispered.

"I brought some frankincense oil. We will anoint the place." Jerusha chuckled.

"Shalom, Father." A young girl came from the other direction with a torch.

"Rebekah, my daughter." Marcellus stopped and unlocked the cell. "Who are you here to serve?"

"This cell," she looked at him and winked like he knew she was coming.

"She is your daughter?" Jerusha's brows lifted.

"She is," he said, as he looked at the other solders, "a daughter of sorts." He winked at Jerusha. She understood he meant—a spiritual daughter.

"Mother, it is so good to see you." Samuel kissed her cheek.

"What have you heard about our release?" Stephen took her hands and looked into her eyes.

"Antonius went to Rome on your behalf. The tribune will give him six months to get back with an answer. If he does not make it by then, you will be crucified." Her voice cracked. "Yeshua said it is not your time, so we trust him that Antonius will get back before six months."

Stephen's eyes fell on Hannah. She smiled and handed him the wineskin filled with fresh spring water she had taken from Joshua, then sat and spooned porridge in a bowl. He sat and kept his eyes on her while he broke bread pieces and scooped bite after bite into his mouth.

Rebekah and Samuel moved to the corner. He lay on his stomach and let her dab salve on his old wound. Jerusha stood in the corner with Marcellus.

"Has she been coming to see Samuel?" she asked him.

"Only when I come with her. I bought and freed her. She chooses to stay and serve me. She has nowhere else to go."

It blessed Jerusha to see her sons with women who appeared to love them. She and Father had prayed daily for good wives for them. She took the frankincense oil from her girdle and dabbed a little on each son, the walls, and bars and prayed under her breath.

"Father YHWH, fill this place with your Holy presence and the fragrance of your love." Rebekah smiled. Jerusha leaned against the wall in the corner and watched. Joshua came and stood next to her.

"I wonder if Sarah made it to your grandfather's." His eyes clouded. "I miss her." A tear rolled down his cheek, then another.

Jerusha understood his longing. She missed Antonius, too. Blinking back her own tears, she quoted a portion of Tehillim 30.

"Weeping may endure for a night, but joy comes in the morning." She wiped his tears away, hugged his shoulder, and rested her head against him. "Tomorrow will be a new day."

Chapter 34
Fall, Tishrei, AD 57

Five months later, Jerusha stood atop her roof in the early morning light, as she had done every day since Antonius left, and scanned the horizon for the dust of a lone rider. A week earlier, she watched caravans of pilgrims traveling to the city for the Feast of Sukkot, making it difficult for a single rider to stand out from the crowd. An orange haze spread across the sky as the sun rose higher casting more light on the dark road. Her shoulders slumped and disappointment grabbed at her insides at the sight of an empty road winding up the mount. She sighed.

"Where are you, Antonius?" She feared for his life. He had hoped to get favor with Burrus, a prefect of the Praetorian Guard and advisor to Nero. She had heard rumors, though, that Agrippina, Nero's mother, a beautiful and ruthless woman, held sway over her son and had even urged Nero to poison Brittannicus, Emperor Claudius's son. What if Agrippina wanted Antonius for her own pleasure and insisted he stay in Rome? With every day that passed without his return, it became more difficult to control her thoughts and bring them into captivity to Yeshua's promise.

Sukkah booths lined the rooftops below, each family eating and sleeping beneath and peeking at the stars between the branches. She searched the sky. Regulus had disappeared with the sun's light. Laughter and singing rose in the wind as children awoke and waved their lulav branches in celebration. It grieved Jerusha that her sons slept in the dark prison cell.

She breathed the aroma of roasting lamb and listened to the crackle of dripping fat on hot coals.

"You must teach me the meaning of the feast," Adah talked to Chaya while helping prepare for their celebration on the far corner of the roof. The fire's smoke wound above their heads into the heavens, carrying the aroma of the lamb sacrificed at the alter the day before. More and more, these days, Jerusha saw Yeshua's glory in the feasts and how they all pointed to Him.

Jerusha turned and walked the pomegranate-lined path to the center of the roof, then ducked under the bough covered sukkah and smiled at Joshua's snoring. Miriam nursed baby Abraham, while Moses wove together their lulavs to wave on the way to the temple celebration.

"Can I make one for you?" He waved it over head. Jerusha nodded. "How about you, Hannah?"

Hannah sat alone in one corner, unresponsive. Moses shrugged and went back to his weaving. Jerusha sat and waited for her to look up. Hannah stared at the flames beneath the lamb on the other side of the roof for several more minutes.

"Are you thinking of Stephen?" Jerusha patted her leg.

Hannah looked up with sad, watery eyes and nodded, her chin dipping to her chest. Jerusha lifted her chin and stared into her eyes.

"This has been a rough test of your faith for one so young. But you will find Yeshua is true to His word. Stephen will be released." She heard footsteps and looked up. Marcellus and Rebekah walked toward the sukkah.

"Shalom," she rose, stepped outside the bough-covered booth and greeted each with a kiss. "Welcome to our sukkah."

"I will be at the gate. Can Rebekah stay with you until we leave for the temple?" Marcellus's eyes shined with a father's love.

"I do not know if I am going to the temple." Jerusha grimaced. "I think I cannot bear another day of watching the corrupt priests act so pious and self-righteous." She shuddered. "But of course, Rebekah can stay and go with the others."

"It may be better if you do not go. The crowded streets are perfect for the sicarii to hide an attack. Antonius would never forgive me if a dagger found its way into your side." He grimaced. "I would have a hard time forgiving myself."

"I understand what it means to forgive yourself." She chuckled. It felt good to be free of condemnation, although, every day Antonius delayed, it became increasingly more difficult to not slip back into self-hatred. "We will bring you and the other soldiers a plate of food." Her thought went to her sons. "Maybe we could take a plate to Samuel and Stephen?"

"The barracks is not a safe place during the feasts. It is crowded with more soldiers than usual. I will see that they get the food. No one from this villa goes." He meant his word to be final. She knew not to push it.

***

Jerusha stood outside the gate and watched Joshua and the others descend the terraced steps and merge with the crowd coming up the temple mount. The late afternoon sun cast shadows across their path, and each waved their lulavs and rejoiced. She sighed and wondered if her other sons heard the music and celebration inside their cells, or if they sat alone in quiet darkness. Every morning she had prayed for them, every night she had prayed for them, and every moment of every day she had prayed without ceasing.

"Samuel and Stephen ate well tonight." Marcellus seemed to know where her thoughts were. "I took them food myself to be sure they got it."

"Oh, Marcellus, you are a good man," She walked back inside the gate. The splash of the courtyard fountain soothed her thoughts.

"I am going to the stable to check on Boaz." She waited while he locked the gate, then walked up the path and stopped at Father's garden gate and watched a servant light the lamps. How she missed him. The garden seemed empty without the sounds of his saw and woodworking tools, and she missed the smell of acacia shavings. She decided not to go inside. She needed the comfort of Boaz's soft nuzzle.

Her steps echoed in the empty villa as she walked to the kitchen, then opened its heavy door. It shut with a thud. The fire popped and crackled. Its warmth felt good. She nibbled on lamb and bread, then lit a lamp and carried it outside through the herb garden to the stable. As usual, Boaz whinnied when she slid open the door. She nuzzled her face against his soft nose and remembered her last encounter with Antonius in this stable. She loved him. That she knew.

"I am worried, Boaz. Six months is almost up. If Antonius does not come, what will happen to us?" She grabbed the brush and stroked his back. "Yeshua said I would be his wife—that it is not my time—my sons' time, yet— to die. I think that is what he meant. What if Antonius is dead? What if that horrible woman in Rome closed in on him? What if? What if? What if?" She threw the brush in the hay, grabbed a handful of oats, and let him eat from her palm. She felt like a child again. She felt the same old frustration that came every time she tried to figure out His plans.

"Father YHWH, I cannot take this. Help me." She closed her eyes.

You ask too many questions. She smiled at the remembrance of Father's words.

His ways are not our ways. They are better.

"Alright. I understand." Jerusha rubbed her cheek against Boaz's nose. "He wants me to stop asking questions and trust He is working it out." She looked Boaz in the eyes.

"Good idea, don't you think?" Then she reached for the lamp, walked out, and slid the door closed.

***

As she walked up the stairs to the rooftop, she heard the tambourines, flutes, clapping, and singing at the temple. The sukkah rustled in the night breeze. The fire had burned down to orange coals, its smoke a tiny thread weaving up into the October air. She walked past the mikvah and wound along the pomegranate-lined path to the roof's edge and looked out over the banister at the light streaming from the four huge candelabras in the women's court. The crowd joined in the leaders' song, "Happy is every man on who guilt rests, he who having sin is now with pardon blessed." It grew in volume and intensity. She felt saddened by their ignorance. One day soon, the temple would be destroyed. What would the people do in a new era without sacrifices? Without faith in the true lamb of YHWH? There she went again, asking questions. She stopped, looked to heaven, and started to sway to the music. He held every answer to every question in His hands.

"This is the day You have made. I will rejoice and be glad in it." Supernatural joy bubbled up, and she began to dance, her hands lifted in praise to her King.

"You are my joy and delight. I will forever praise Your holy name." She sang a new song. "Holy, holy, holy are you Father YHWH, the one and only true God, my royal Father." Breathless, she stopped and looked at the lights that speckled the darkened city and spread over the countryside outside the walls. Her thoughts turned to what could happen to a Roman soldier traveling alone in these dangerous times. "Wherever Antonius is, keep him safe and bring him back," she whispered.

***

Jerusha opened her eyes and peered between the boughs for Regulus above in the fading starlight.

"Little prince, where are you," she whispered. Joshua and Moses both snored on the far side of the sukkot. Abraham suckled with Miriam. Chaya, Hannah, and Adah slept next to her, their breathing quiet and peaceful. She slipped out of the cover without waking them, rose, and walked to the rooftop edge, and as she did every morning, looked for Antonius.

A thick fog hung in the air and made it difficult to see. She lifted her radiyd over her hair and held her cloak tight against the damp mist and waited for the sun to rise. Within minutes, rays of light broke through the fog. In the far distance, something or someone moved. She strained to see and kept her eyes focused on whatever it was as it moved closer and closer. Maybe, just maybe, it was him. The fog drifted over the movement, and she lost sight of it, then it cleared. Someone traveled toward the city.

"Antonius, is that you?" she whispered, her hand above her eyes blocking the early morning rays that shone on her face.

"I am right here."

She jumped and turned.

"Antonius!" she gasped. "You scared me." She slapped her chest and bent over. "You would come back like a ghost. Sneak up on me without a sound in this creepy weather; you would think you would be more careful not to." She looked up, and he stood inches away, his eyes locked on her. Before another word escaped, he smothered her lips with his. At first she struggled against him, then surrendered and for a moment enjoyed the pleasure of his embrace, then remembered he may have a wife and pushed away.

"What are you doing?" She straightened her radiyd. "At this moment I am not your wife. As far as we know, you still have a wife somewhere out there." She waved her hand toward the mountain.

"No. He does not." Patrick stepped up behind Antonius.

"Patrick, Brigid," Antonius seemed surprised. "Sarah."

Jerusha looked past him to Brigid, who stood with Chaya and Miriam, their smiles indicating they saw Antonius's display of affection.

"It must run in the family"—she looked at Antonius—"sneaking up on people." She smiled.

Everyone laughed but Antonius, who only half smiled.

"I need to talk to you alone." His abrupt request and sober eyes alarmed Jerusha.

"Before you talk"—Brigid came forward—"I need to tell you both something." She looked down. "I lied about mother." She looked up at her father. "She is not alive. I told you that, Father"—tears brimmed in her eyes—"because I wanted you to come home." Her voice cracked. "Patrick helped me see how wrong that was and how much pain I caused you and Jerusha." Her gazed went from one to the other. "I am sorry. Will you forgive me, Father? Jerusha?" A tear escaped and rolled down her cheek.

Shocked, Jerusha's mouth dropped open. Antonius's was right. His wife had been dead all along. She looked at him and back to Brigid. He enveloped his daughter in an embrace and comforted Brigid as she buried her sobs in his chest, soaking his red tunic with her tears.

"You are forgiven, Brigid. In time, you and Patrick"—he looked at his faithful guard—"will know the deeps of Yeshua's love and come into his kingdom." He caressed her hair and whispered in her ear, "I love you, my daughter," then lifted her chin and looked deep into her eyes. "You are beautiful like your mother, who we will remember as a queen of our tribe. Never forget you are royalty. You will dance before Yeshua, my King, one day." He glanced at Jerusha.

Her eyes filled with tears. A picture formed in her thoughts. Father in the garden with his little girl. *Never forget who you are. You are from the tribe of Judah. You are royalty. You will dance one day before the King.* Tears rolled down her cheeks.

"Come." He motioned and she stepped close, then he pulled her into his embrace with Brigid. "The two loves of my life." Jerusha released her tears in his arms and looked up.

"I love you, Antonius," she mouthed the words and stared into his eyes.

"Sarah!" Joshua's yell startled Jerusha and interrupted her gaze. "You are back." He jumped up, grabbed his sword, and ran toward Chaya, who had her arm around Sarah.

"Slow down, Joshua. You will run us over. Or worse." Chaya put up her hand and stared at his weapon.

He made a quick turn and skidded to a stop before Antonius and drew his sword across his chest in a salute. Jerusha chuckled.

"You honor me, Joshua. For that I thank you. I believe Sarah is waiting." He motioned with his head.

"Yes, sir." He placed his sword in the scabbard, smiled at Sarah, and walked casually toward her.

Antonius's eyes rested on Jerusha. "We must talk." His sudden change of demeanor disturbed her. Why so sober?

Chapter 35

A fog drifted in the morning air. Jerusha sat on Father's bench in the garden and waited for Antonius to speak. His red tunic fluttered in the breeze as he stood with his back to her, rubbing his clean-shaven chin—such a contrast to the Hebrew men's beards. It took Jerusha a while to get used to seeing him that way. *Why had he shaved it? Was he going into battle?* Whenever he stayed in the barracks, the tribune allowed him to be unshaven. It seemed strange, since he had just returned. She cast off those questions. Father YHWH knew and could be trusted. Nothing would take away her joy of his safe return, although, she wondered what he found out in Rome.

Questions swirled again in her thoughts. She could not sit another moment. If he would not say something, she would.

"Antonius?" She stood. "Are you not happy about Brigid's confession? Why have you been so somber?" *Do you not want to marry me? What has you so disturbed?* A clammy fear swept her body. She clasped her hands. "What happened in Rome? Did Agrippina interfere? She must not have. You are here. When will my sons be released?" She stepped close. "I cannot wait to get them out of that dark place."

A sudden thought pushed its way into her mind. She had been so overwhelmed with the joyful possibility of becoming his wife that she had not allowed herself to consider it. Her heart sped up. She covered the thumping in her ears with her hands. A revulsion to hearing his news almost made her want to throw up, the nausea so intense, she gagged and coughed. Her insides screamed. *No! No! No!*

"I failed." The breezed carried and confirmed her worst fear. He turned. Tears coursed his face. "I have been ordered to carry out their execution tomorrow. They will be crucified at dawn"—his voice softened—"along with you."

Black spots faded in and out before her eyes. Her ears rang, and a weakness came in her knees. She slumped down and felt Antonius's arms beneath her legs as he scooped her up, his arm around her waist. She leaned her head against his shoulder.

"Jerusha, my love." He carried her to the bench. "Breathe." She opened her eyes and stared at his deep blue eyes as he sat her on the bench and steadied her against his body and rocked her back and forth in his arms.

"Let us leave this place tonight. I will get your sons out of the barracks. We could leave through the secret tunnel. Take Joshua and Brigid. Leave the villa to Moses and Miriam."

"They would not be able to stay here. It would put them in danger." A new strength energized her body. "I could not do that to them."

"Then we take them with us. Sarah, too. Go to your grandfather in Perea or, better, to my homeland."

Jerusha thought for a moment. "It is not my time, yet. Nor for my sons. Yeshua said not to fear. I understand better what he meant. It is not our time to die. If that is true, then there is no need to leave." She stood. "I will not bow to fear. Father YHWH has a plan. I will trust Him. If we perish, we perish."

"But Jerusha. The Romans took the scepter."

"You will not persuade me to change my mind."

"Then I perish with you." He stood up. "I will not be your executioner."

"No." She grabbed his hand. "Joshua looks up to you. He needs you to live. He might follow your lead and choose to die. Please, Antonius. Do not do this."

"You have your decision to make. I have mine. And Joshua will have his." He sat down, wrapping his arm around her. She lay her head on his chest. "I want you for my wife." His voice quivered. She looked up and drank in the love in his eyes.

"I am yours now and forever."

***

Jerusha awoke in the darkness of early dawn cuddled in the crook of Antonius's arm on top of the soft grass. She blinked and looked at the stars. Regulus shined brighter than ever. She breathed deep and listened to Antonius's breathing, then rose on her elbow and brushed the wavy blond locks away from his face. He opened his eyes.

"Is it dawn?" He traced his fingers through her black curls that hung down and wrapped his hand behind her head and pulled her in close and met her lips with his. She responded, then lay her head on his chest. His kiss, only their second, felt so natural.

"Mother. Antonius. We have been looking for you," Joshua yelled at the gate. "The soldiers brought Samuel and Stephen. They are at the front gate and want you. They wondered if Antonius was here."

Antonius helped her up. She covered her hair with her radiyd and straightened her cloak, brushing off the dry grass, then looked at Antonius.

"We are in Father YHWH's hands." Her heart raced. That old familiar knot in the pit of her stomach had returned. She wondered if she could stand the pain, then thought, *If Yeshua could do it, then she could—with Father YHWH's help.* Her inner declaration sounded stronger than she felt.

"You will not change your mind?" he asked, his eyes somber and questioning. "It is not too late. I might be able to buy us some time."

Everything within her wanted to run to the stable, jump on Boaz, and gallop away. She hesitated, then answered.

"I told you my decision last night." She could not leave her sons and the others to take the consequences of her actions. Besides, she would not get far before they caught her. "And you. What is your decision?" She hoped he would choose life. He glanced at Joshua. She saw the struggle in his eyes.

"I die with you." He took her arm and began the walk to the gate. "Joshua will have to choose for himself."

***

Puzzled, Marcellus unlocked the gate. The officer came through, marched up the path, grabbed Jerusha and tied her hands behind her back.

"Soldier, what are you doing with the woman?" Marcellus asked.

"She will be crucified with those two. Are you ready, Antonius?" He asked. The tribune said you are the one in charge of this order."

"I refuse. I choose crucifixion with her and her sons."

"Centurion?"

"Bind me. I will die with them."

"No." Joshua ran and hugged him as they jerked his hands behind and bound him. "What is happening? I thought you went to Rome to get their release!" Tears ran down his cheeks.

Antonius knelt on one knee, his hands behind him. "I failed. Burrus refused to let me see Nero and stole the scepter. I am sorry, Joshua. For now the villa belongs to you. It is your responsibility. Be strong." He stood and nodded. The soldier grabbed his arm and jerked him forward.

"This will be my pleasure." Jerusha recognized him as the depraved soldier, who tried to rape her. Rebekah wept and hung on Samuel. Hannah hung on Stephen. "Get away from the prisoners," he said as he shoved the girls, "unless you want the same as them."

Joshua grabbed his sword. "Do not do that." He held the sword steady in his face.

"Put your sword away." Antonius stared until Joshua glanced at him and dropped his arm, the sword dangling to the ground. Jerusha saw shame in his eyes.

"There is a time to fight and a time not to fight. You chose wisely, Joshua." Antonius spoke over his shoulder. Joshua replaced his sword in its scabbard. In his actions, Jerusha saw a boy who understood how to be a man. Sarah ran and threw her arms around him. He embraced her and looked over her shoulder with tear filled eyes. "I love you, Ima."

"Miriam and I will be there for him," Moses nodded at Jerusha.

"Where's Brigid?" Antonius's eyes searched the path toward the fountain.

Brigid stepped out from behind a pomegranate bush. "I am here." She walked toward him. "Father, I love you. Do not do this." She stopped and hugged him. "I have just found you." Her tears soaked into his red tunic. "Do not leave me an orphan again."

Antonius looked from her to Jerusha. Jerusha shook her head. "She needs you, Antonius. Live for her."

"I cannot carry out these orders, Brigid. If I do not, they will have me executed anyway; therefore, I choose to die now, with them. I hope you can understand."

"But I do not want to be an orphan again."

"Believe in Yeshua. Through him, you will have a better father than I." He looked at Patrick, who had come to stand beside Brigid. "Take her. You both need to embrace Yeshua's love for you."

Patrick pulled Brigid off. She fell against him, her hands over her face. Her whimper turned to a sob.

"Weeping may endure for a night, but joy comes in the morning." Antonius's voice cracked. "I love you, Brigid."

If you loved me, you would not do this," she said between hiccups.

"Enough," the toothless soldier said as he jerked Antonius up.

The cohort separated and opened a path. The soldier pushed Jerusha first, then Antonius, Samuel, and Stephen, single file through their opening. It astonished Jerusha that one hundred soldiers came to arrest her, like she was a hardened criminal.

She glanced back. Chaya's mouth moved in prayer, and she had her arm around Adah. Patrick held Brigid. Hannah and Rebekah cried in each other's arms. Joshua fell to his knees, his face in his hands, Sarah's hand on his shoulder. Jerusha heard his sobs for several minutes as she descended the terraced steps.

"Take care of him, Father YHWH."

The soldiers that surrounded them marched at a quick pace. Jerusha stumbled and fell face down. Her throat constricted as she held back tears. Joshua must not see her cry. She managed to get one knee up and under, then pushed herself up. *Though I walk through the valley of the shadow of death, I will fear no evil. Your rod and your staff they comfort me.* A peace flooded her body, and her heart slowed.

A tingling ran down her spine and into her hands. She glanced over her shoulder at her sons and Antonius. Their faces glowed, a calmness in their eyes. She smiled. They would all be together in His kingdom. She would see Father and Sarah and Timon. He would like Antonius. The people stood on rooftops and stared. Some were friends or Yeshua followers. Most were lost Hebrews, totally unaware of the destruction that awaited them. She glanced up at the temple as she walked past. Caiaphas, smug and self-righteous, stood high above and watched from a distance. Other priests laughed and pointed. One or two, probably Yeshua followers, had compassion in their eyes.

"Father YHWH forgive them," Her eyes filled with tears for them. She trudged up the steep incline to Antonia Fortress. At the top, the soldiers stopped and opened a way for them to walk through. She looked at the wooden cross bars lying on the ground and wondered how she would ever carry one.

"I will carry hers." Marcellus ran past, threw down his shield, and picked up a beam.

"You! Pick one up," the centurion yelled at Samuel. "You, too. And you." He pointed at Antonius and Stephen. Jerusha walked behind Marcellus as they wound their way down the slope.

He slipped a little on loose rocks, and she helped him balance the load. She looked over her shoulder at the others. Samuel struggled the most.

She closed her eyes and leaned her head back. "Strengthen him, Father YHWH."

Marcellus stayed steady. It made her sick to see the whip hit his back if he walked too slow. She cringed every time she heard the whip crack behind her and kept her eyes looking ahead. Only a short way to go. A few more yards, through the gate and up a little rocky hill. She felt thirsty. She could not imagine how the others felt. Jerusha looked up the road and saw a rider in the distance galloping toward Jerusalem, his dust swirls hanging in the air. From the red plume on his head, it looked like it might be a Roman soldier.

"Who is that coming?" the tribune asked as he galloped up from the fortress.

Marcellus, who had dropped the beam, shrugged and looked at Antonius, which drew the tribune's attention away from the rider to the centurion.

"Antonius, what on earth are you doing? I know you were enamored with the woman. But to die with her?" He leaned on the saddle horn of his black war horse, whose coat glistened under the hot sun. Antonius remained silent and dropped his cross bar, then looked at her. His eyes shined.

The thought of hanging naked before him and the world brought back the old shame. She dropped her head. What was it Paul taught? I am crucified with Christ, nevertheless I live. The life I now live I live in him. Or something like that. Yeshua had a royal Father and left his throne to make a way for her to have a royal Father. She surrendered to his ways. Somehow, they were better, even if she and the others died.

Jerusha watched Samuel, who fell to his knees beneath the load and looked up. She saw forgiveness in his eyes. "I love you," she mouthed. His parched lips formed the words, "I forgive you."

Stephen, her giant with a tender heart, dropped his beam beside Samuel and looked at her.

"See you in his kingdom, Mother."

She fell to her knees and wept. Her sons loved their royal Father YHWH. He had taught them his ways.

Chapter 36

"Remove your clothes," the soldier said. She covered her chest with her arms. Her thin undertunic whipped in the wind, and her radiyd flew into the air. She kept her eyes down. "Father YHWH, I am in your hands." He grabbed her tunic at the neck, and she closed her eyes, prepared for humiliation.

"Get your hands off my granddaughter!"

She looked up. "Grandfather, you came," She stared in awe and admired the white stallion he sat upon. The horse's height and strength in legs and chest bespoke a well-bred war horse. The substance of his armor outshined that of Tribune Lysias. His purple cloak, fastened at his shoulders with gold clasps, spoke of his higher tribunal rank. He winked at her, then became serious.

"Release these prisoners at once. They are under Rome's protection." The scar on his cheek twitched. He leaned in, his hands crossed over the saddle horn and glared at the soldier, who still had his hand on her tunic.

"You do not want me to get off this horse, soldier. It will not fare well for you."

Jerusha felt the release of her tunic.

"Move away from her," His blue eyes narrowed. "If you hurry and pick up her radiyd and return it along with her torn cloak," he ordered as he laid his hand on his whip, "I will not flog your despicable hide." He leaned back and watched. The soldier ran and grabbed her radiyd from the dust and threw it at her, along with the cloak. She caught them, slipped on what was left of her cloak, and covered her head with the radiyd, flipping its ends over her shoulder.

"Who are you?" The tribune rode over and reigned in next to her grandfather.

"I am Tribune Regulus."

Tribune Lysias stared at him for the longest moment. "I thought you were dead."

His astonished look tickled Jerusha and she covered her mouth.

"As you can see I am very much alive and have been with Tribune Burrus in Rome." He reached into a leather bag attached to the saddle. "This"—he pulled out a rolled parchment—"is a decree of freedom and protection for these prisoners." He handed it to Lysias.

Jerusha waited, breathless, while the tribune opened the seal.

"What is this lion and butterfly seal?"

Regulus lifted his hand and showed his signet ring. "By decree of Rome."

The tribune broke the seal and read the parchment.

"Get horses for these to ride back to my villa." Regulus grinned at Jerusha. "She rides with me." He removed his helmet and ran fingers through sweaty, silver locks. "Come Jerusha."

Samuel and Stephen and Antonius all stared with mouths wide open. She smiled in relief and held back the giggle rising in her gut. Grandfather came like he said he would—just at the right time. He extended his hand. She grabbed ahold. He lifted with strength of a young man and sat her sideways in front of him. He wrapped his arms around her waist and grabbed the reigns.

"Let's go home." Regulus looked around at the others, who now had a ride of their own, then galloped down the hill, reining in to a trot at the city gate. It all seemed like a dream. The stallion almost pranced through the city, his hooves clip-clopping in rhythm to her excited heart. She saw a priest run to Caiaphas and pointed in her direction. His scowl and look of disbelief caused her to laugh. Those who whispered and closed their shops earlier stared, their mouths open. The followers of the Way smiled and waved. His stallion maneuvered the terraced steps with no problem. She hung onto its mane.

"Ima, you are alive." Joshua swung wide the gate. "Who is that?" He pointed to Regulus.

"My grandfather." She held onto her tunic and cloak and slid to the ground. "Do not point. It is not polite."

"Shalom, sir," Joshua bowed. "Did you save my mother?"

Regulus laughed. "Father YHWH had more to do with it than I." He dismounted. "You must be Joshua. You were only one-year old when I last saw you. That is quite a weapon you have. Do you know how to use it?"

Jerusha smiled at how proud he was of his sword.

"I do. Antonius taught me." He nodded toward his teacher and father figure.

Regulus patted Antonius's back. "So you are the one Jerusha loves, and according to Jacob, takes good care of her sons." Antonius nodded and looked at Jerusha. Regulus's eyes glistened with tears. "I heard my son entered the kingdom a while back."

"Yes, Grandfather. Antonius sent word. Did you get his message?"

"I got it. That is why I am here." He swallowed and looked up at Moses and Miriam. "I see you have increased your family." Grandfather took a few steps and looked at the baby. "A boy?"

"Yes, sir. We named him Abraham Jacob after your son."

"A good name. Would you take my horse to the stable? Have him brushed down and fed." He gave him the reins, stood back, his hands on his hips, and stared at the villa entrance. Jerusha had forgotten what a giant of man he was. It felt strange hearing him called Regulus, his Roman cognomen. He always told her to call him Yogli in public, but Grandfather in private. No one could know he was alive until it was time. Now was the time, thanks to Antonius getting his treason charge expunged from his record.

"I remember, Grandfather, the day I rode into the city with Timon and baby Samuel and saw you on the cross. I could not understand how Father could let that happen."

She looked at Antonius, "Little did I know that Father had given orders to have Grandfather's body removed before he took his last breath. Everyone thought he had died. I found him in the secret tunnel."

"Oh, yes. I awoke to her pacing and declaring, 'you will not die, but live and declare the works of the Lord.' This little lioness roared that day and the enemy ran." He held his belly and laughed, then stopped, his eyes taking in his surroundings.

"The jujube tree has grown. Look at those pomegranate bushes. They look more like full trees. And who is this?" Adah peeked out behind the jujube tree.

'Grandfather, this is Adah." Jerusha took her by the hand and led her to Grandfather. "Not long ago, she came to know Yeshua's love and forgiveness, after she renounced witchcraft." Jerusha wrapped her arm around Adah's shoulder.

"Well, well, Adah. I expect you will be used in powerful ways in Yeshua's kingdom."

He moved out of the way as Moses led his horse around the wall. "Wait, Moses. Take the other horses too."

"I will help," Stephen dismounted and took the reins from Samuel and Antonius.

"Samuel. Stephen. How you have grown. Samuel you were only ten years old, Stephen only five, when last I saw you."

Rebekah and Hannah ran out to greet Samuel and Stephen. After hugging, they stepped back, a blush on their faces. "And who are these young ladies? Wives perhaps?" Regulus grinned. The girls smiled shyly.

"Not yet," Samuel smiled at Rebekah.

"Let me tend to your wounds, Samuel," She took his hand and pulled.

Stephen chuckled.

"What about you, Stephen?" Hannah fiddled with her fingers and kept her eyes down. "Do you want your wounds tended?" She looked up.

"Stephen, go with the girl." Grandfather gave him a little shove. Jerusha's giant of a son stumbled forward and followed Hannah down the tiled path, then looked back and showed his perfect white teeth.

"Grandfather," Jerusha hugged him tight. "I am so glad you are here. Like you always told me, 'YHWH's ways are not our ways.'" She looked up and touched his scarred cheek. "I believe Father was right. His ways *are* better. Let us prepare a feast and celebrate." She threw out her arms and twirled around up the path. "And dance." She giggled and ran ahead.

Chapter 37

That night, the lamplit courtyard smelled of roasted lamb, chicken, and fresh bread. Baskets of pomegranates, grapes, figs, and olives covered the table. A pot of porridge bubbled over a flaming fire pit. Jerusha dipped her fingers in the cool fountain waters and splashed her face, then pulled a clean radiyd over her head. Hannah sat at the gate and washed feet as visitors entered. James, Paul's sister and nephew, and many followers of the Way came to the joyous occasion.

Let us offer a tehillim of thanksgiving before we eat," Grandfather said as he smiled at Jerusha.

"How about Tehillim 100?" Samuel sat beside Rebekah on a bench. "I will lead it."

Grandfather nodded. Samuel looked at Rebekah, who lifted a flute to her lips and began to play. He stood. "Lift a great shout to the Lord! Go ahead and do it."

Joshua shouted. "Hallelujah!"

"Everyone, everywhere." Samuel looked around at their faces and a great shout erupted from the others. "As you serve him, be glad and worship him." Sarah and Rebekah stood and rattled tambourines to the melody. Jerusha twirled in dance.

"Sing your way into his presence with joy!" Stephen's white teeth gleamed as he lifted his voice in praise. "And realize what this really means—we have the privilege of worshipping the Lord our God. For He is our Creator, and we belong to him. We are the people of his pleasure."

Jerusha stopped dancing, breathless, and looked at Antonius, who stood by the fountain dressed in his royal garments from his homeland, looking so handsome. Ten years he waited for her love. He laughed and conversed with Moses.

The others formed a circle, hands on shoulders, and danced in their Hebrew garments with titzits, most with blue corded tassels on the corners. Step, dip, step behind to the right. Step, dip, step behind to the left. "You can pass through his open gates with the password of praise." Everyone sang.

Antonius stopped talking and watched. After a while, he tapped the shoulder of one of the circle dancers. The man broke the circle, opening the way for him to join. "Come right into his presence with thanksgiving. Come, bring your thank offering to him and affectionately bless his beautiful name!" The music kept flowing.

She put her hand over her mouth and giggled as Antonius tried to follow their footwork. "For the Lord is always good and ready to receive you. He is so loving it will amaze you—so kind that it will astound you!" Jerusha sang, moved behind Antonius, and tapped his shoulder.

"I am not the dancer you are, my little butterfly. Are you sure you want to dance next to me?" He spoke over his shoulder, a twinkle in his eyes and a mischievous grin.

"I believe I will risk it." She laughed.

He released one arm from the shoulder of the man next to him and waved a bow for her entrance. She placed her hand on each shoulder and dipped left, her eyes locked with his.

"And he is famous for his faithfulness toward all." She sang with Antonius. "Everyone knows our God can be trusted, for he keeps his promises to every generation!"

Brigid tapped her father's shoulder. "May I try?"

Jerusha saw a need in his daughter's eyes to be with her father. She nodded to him and bowed out of the circle, a longing in her heart for her own father. He so would have enjoyed this celebration. She slipped away from the crowd in awe of the moment.

Out of breath, she tried to slow her breathing and walked the familiar path to his bench beneath a canopy of olive trees. The music stopped. Amidst the laughter and quiet chatter in the distant courtyard, she heard the familiar garden sounds, a song thrush singing its night song and crickets chirping their praises to the Creator.

She knelt at the bench. "Father, I miss you terribly," she said and lay her face on her forearms. Tears welled up in her eyes. A slight whiff of frankincense hung in the air. "Father?" She lifted her head and looked around. She knew it was not possible for him to be in the garden. She sniffed and again recognized his familiar scent, arose, and walked among the pomegranate bushes. *Father said only a thin veil existed between here and the kingdom.*

Flashes of her times with him as a little girl passed through her memory. His fun way of telling stories from the Torah. His laughter as he removed smudges of sawdust off her face while he carpentered. Dancing with the butterflies in preparation for her dance before the king. Jerusha closed her eyes and swayed, then raised her hands and danced the same familiar steps she had danced before him.

"Father YHWH, tell my father this dance is for him." Her feet knew the way. She twirled, her hands lifted high, his laughing face in her thoughts. She stopped and stared above at Regulus. Its brilliance shined so bright she shielded her eyes as a dazzling city descended, its radiance like that of a jasper stone, clear as crystal, many layers of different jewels on it walls, its gates transparent pearls. A loud voice thundered like many waters.

"Behold, the wife of the Lamb."

She fell to her face. A tingling sensation coursed through her body. After a while, she rose to her knees. Colorful sparkles bounced in the atmosphere. She tried to touch the glittering jewels in the air and closed her fist. When she opened it, a crystal jasper stone lay in her palm. Stunned, she stared at it.

"What is the meaning of this?"

When she looked up, the sparkles had disappeared. She arose from her knees with the jewel enclosed in her palm. Someone placed their hands on her shoulders.

"My beautiful, little butterfly," Antonius whispered in her ear. "I love you."

She basked in his nearness, savoring the fragrant pine on his garment. Without turning, she answered, "I, too, love you."

"I could not wait one more day to make you my wife. Your grandfather gave permission to marry tonight. The ketubah is made and mohar paid. Do you accept?"

She sucked in her breath, opened her fist, and stared at the jewel. *The wife of the Lamb.* The moonlight glistened on the jewel.

"Antonius, with Father gone, I have no dowry to give, except this." She turned, her eyes on the jewel. "I offer it to you as my dowry, straight out of Father YHWH's treasury."

He looked at the jewel and closed her fist over it.

"Your love is the greatest gift of all."

Her eyes fell on her beloved Grandfather, who stood beside Antonius and winked. How she loved that man. Her eyes then moved from face to face; Samuel, her precious oldest son. Rebekah, an answer to his prayer. Stephen, her gentle giant in heart and build. Hannah, another answer to prayer. Joshua, her youngest, now a man, and Sarah, another orphan saved. Yeshua's love found in each one was more precious than the jewel she held in her hand. Her eyes filled with tears and she observed the other guests, who gathered near to witness the betrothal. *I see now, Father YHWH, our love for Yeshua, the Lamb, and his love for you in us, is what makes us the wife of the Lamb.*

"Stephen and I, too, asked permission to marry." Samuel's eyes beamed with Father YHWH's love. "Rebekah and Hannah accepted our Ketubah. Grandfather and Antonius witnessed it." She saw it in all their eyes. Yeshua's sacrificial love. She could not speak.

"Brigid stepped from the middle of those gathered. "My father talked to me of your marriage. I am happy to have you as my mother."

An overwhelming love for all flooded her being. She nodded at Brigid.

"Your approval blesses me."

She looked down at her worn garment and back at Antonius. He dressed like a king. She looked more like a beggar. She could at least dress in her old wedding dress that she had shared with Miriam. "May I have a few minutes to prepare?"

His grin spread wide. "I—we—will wait." He spread his hands to all those smiling behind her. "I waited ten years. You *would* need a few more minutes," he teased and took her hands. "You could not be more beautiful than you are right now, but go."

"I will hurry." She ran through the garden gate, the jewel still in her fist. The gate clanged. She glanced over her shoulder. "Do not change your mind. I will be back." She giggled like a little girl and ran as fast as possible to her room.

Once inside, she opened a chest and dug until she found her old wedding dress, but she never let go of the jewel. It was a chore raising the old tunic overhead with one hand. She dropped her old tunic and cloak and started to slip into the old wedding dress. She heard a tap on the door and opened it a bit.

"May I come in?" Chaya peeked in.

"Yes, of course." Jerusha held the garment to her chest.

"Aren't you going to wear that one?" Chaya pointed to the mittah. Jerusha's eyes widened. A white tunic and cloak with gold threads interwoven throughout glittered beneath the lamplight with colorful jewels around the neck and arms. Somehow, in the rush to get ready, Jerusha completely missed seeing it.

"Where did that come from?" She ran her hand over the silky material.

"Antonius gave me the materials and asked me to make it for you, years ago. He is from a royal family."

"Why did he not tell me? I almost got married tonight in this dirty old thing." She picked up the old garment with two fingers.

"He did not care what you wore. He only cared that you said yes. If you had not asked him to prepare, I would have spoken up. He had this planned for years."

Jerusha cried. She lowered her face in her hands and closed her eyes. The enormity of the moment overtook her.

"Help me, Chaya. They are waiting."

She slipped the tunic over her head and placed her arms in the cloak, then stood back and let Chaya wipe the tears away.

"What shall I do with this?" She opened her fist. The crystal jasper sparkled in the lamplight. "It came straight from the Father YHWH's throne."

"Oh, Jerusha, I lost a jewel. I think it will fit perfectly. She took the jasper stone and snapped it into the neck of her tunic.

Jerusha stood speechless for a moment in total astonishment of Father YHWH's perfect plan.

"Should I braid my hair up?" she finally asked.

"Leave it down on your shoulders and cover it with this." From behind her back, Chaya pulled out a white radiyd with gold trim and laid it over her black curls and wrapped it over the lower half of her face. Her green blue-rimmed eyes showed above the shimmering material.

"I am getting married." Jerusha blinked back tears.

"Come, they are waiting." Chaya opened the door. A shofar blasted.

"The groom comes." Grandfather's voice mixed in with her sons and the other men's voices. Music started playing.

Jerusha walked through the doorway and looked back in the room, hers and Timon's room.

"Later, Timon. See you in the kingdom."

Chaya's eyes welled up with tears.

"Timon would be happy for you." She kissed Jerusha's cheek.

As Jerusha entered the garden, she locked eyes with Antonius. He took her hand and led her to Father's bench beneath the olive tree canopy. Purple butterflies fluttered before them. The others circled round. Antonius took a golden cup engraved with pomegranates from Grandfather's hand and a pitcher of wine and filled the cup.

"Jerusha, as Yeshua entered into covenant with us through his blood, I enter into covenant with you this night. Yeshua said, 'This is my blood shed for you for the remission of sin. Take and drink.'" He held the cup up. "Drink from this cup, enter into covenant with Yeshua and me, flesh of my flesh, bone of my bone, one flesh."

Her hands trembled as she accepted the cup and drank, then Antonius, his eyes locked with hers, passed it on to the others. He took the bread from Samuel's hand and held it out. "Yeshua also said, 'This is my body given for you.' I promise, Jerusha, with the power of Yeshua who lives in me, to give my life for you in every way. Take and eat." He tore a piece and gave it to her. Tears coursed down her cheeks as she accepted and ate. Antonius passed the bread to the others, who also ate.

Grandfather directed Samuel and Rebekah, and Stephen and Hannah to come forward and stand next to Jerusha and Antonius. She grinned at her sons and their wives, then hugged each and gave a kiss on their cheeks.

"I am so happy for you."

"Are you happy for me as well?" Antonius teased.

She stared into his deep blue eyes. "My cup runs over." She blinked her thick lashes above the shimmering veil.

Grandfather placed one hand on Jerusha's head and one on Antonius's head. "I will give the Jewish blessing now over those of you who made this marriage covenant." She closed her eyes.

"May you increase to thousands upon thousands. May your offspring possess the gates of their enemies." Even though tough days lay ahead, tonight she rejoiced in Father YHWH's provision and Antonius's love. Tonight she believed in miracles. Jerusha opened her eyes and looked up. Antonius's deep blue pools met hers. She removed her veil and draped it over his shoulder and pronounced the Jewish declaration.

"The government shall be on your shoulder."

Antonius kept his eyes on her. She saw his passion and felt like they were the only ones in the garden, until she heard Grandfather's words.

"May you increase to thousands upon thousands." Grandfather had moved to Samuel and Rebekah, whose heads were bowed and eyes closed. "May your offspring possess the gates of their enemies. I bless your coming in and bless your going out. Samuel and Rebekah, open your eyes and look at me, he said. "Tomorrow when you leave Jerusalem, Father YHWH goes with you. He will never leave you or forsake you."

Jerusha's eyes widened. Neither Samuel, nor Grandfather, nor Antonius had told her about Samuel leaving. She crinkled her brow and looked up at Antonius, then at Samuel.

"You are leaving tomorrow? Where are you going? And why was I not told?"

"Now, now, little lioness, do not get upset." Grandfather looked at her. "Father YHWH called them to spread his kingdom to Antonius's homeland."

"Tomorrow? So soon?"

"Ima." Samuel came close. "It is because of you," he said, "that I have a desire to spread the kingdom to other tribes. You know as well as I, these are troublesome days. We must not delay. Patrick and Brigid will go with us and show the way to their tribe. We talked. They have given their lives to Yeshua."

"I-I-." She sniffed back tears, "I will miss you." She turned to Stephen. "I suppose you are going, too?"

He looked a little sheepish and shrugged. "We—that is, Hannah and I—leave for Rome with your grandfather. We will visit Paul before we leave from the port at Caesarea."

"Grandfather? You are leaving so soon? And you two approve of their decisions?" She glanced back and forth between Antonius and Grandfather.

"I am sorry we did not tell you before now." Her tall, tenderhearted Stephen spoke with tears in his eyes. "We were afraid it would steal your joy."

"Well, you were right about that." She struggled to get control of her anger, then flipped her arms out and let them flop at her sides. "I suppose there is no changing your minds?"

"They are more like their mother than you might want." Antonius smiled.

"Well, if you are going, then you will need Grandfather's blessing. Proceed." She stepped out of the way and watched Grandfather place his hands on Stephen and Hannah.

"May you increase to thousands upon thousands. May your offspring possess the gates of their enemies." She hardly heard his words. Father YHWH saved her sons for a reason. His ways were not her ways. *I know, Father, they are better.* Is that not what she prayed for him to do?

All your sons shall be taught by me and great will be their peace.

"What about me?" Joshua stepped up. "I want a blessing, too."

Grandfather laughed and extended his hand over his head.

"I bless your coming in and your going out. May Father YHWH establish the works of your hands. May He bring you a wise and beautiful wife." Grandfather glanced at Sarah. She blushed and hid behind Chaya. "Let us rejoice and be glad."

Jerusha watched as everyone congratulated her sons. Antonius talked with Brigid. She slipped away, walked to the back wall, and looked over the city. She had not anticipated her wedding day would be like this. As happy as she was about being Antonius's wife, she grieved over her sons' decisions. She glanced back through the olive trees at them and their wives, their smiles and laughter contagious to all. How could she not be happy for them? For years, she, herself, had wanted to leave Jerusalem. Maybe that is what troubled her. She wanted to leave with them. She sensed someone behind her and turned.

"Look out there, Jerusha." Grandfather put his hand on her shoulder. "Beyond the lights of the city, in the darkness beyond, there is a royal inheritance. Father YHWH reveals mighty power and marvels to his people by handing them nations as a gift."

"I want to leave this place." She glanced at Grandfather. "Jerusalem has changed. How much longer, Grandfather, will I be protected here?"

"Until Father YHWH says to go. It could be a few years before you leave. He still has some, here, that will turn to him before he brings judgment. Like your Father, you are called, for a season, to stay and bring them the good news of his kingdom." He wiped the tear that had escaped from her cheek. "Someone is waiting," He looked over his shoulder. Antonius sat on Father's bench, his elbows on his knees, his head in his hands. "Do not let your sons' departure steal the joy of union with your husband. He loves you and has waited ten long years for this night."

Jerusha walked the pomegranate-lined path. One purple butterfly came from its nighttime resting place, fluttered before her, and landed on the bench. Antonius looked up, then stood, tears in his eyes.

"Why do you weep?"

"I weep for joy that you are my wife. Your chuppah awaits. Shall we?" He led her to Father's room and opened the door. A small tinge of frankincense lingered. The whole room had been transformed. Its beauty was beyond words: a royal cover was on the mittah. In the middle of the room was a mosaic of a lion with a purple butterfly on its nose, and around the edges of the room were pomegranate reliefs in acacia wood.

"When did you do this?" she asked.

"I have been at work while you were in prison. I believed what Yeshua said, that you would be my wife and prepared us a place.

"Oh, Antonius, it is beautiful." She wrapped her arms around his neck, stared for a moment into his eyes, then yielded to his lips. She felt his passion as he lifted and carried her to the royal bed. "I love you, Jerusha, my wife." He pulled the silky cover back and gently laid her down. She watched as he disrobed and waited as he blew out the lamps.

She blinked in the darkness. "I love you, my husband."

"No talking." He drew her into his embrace. "And definitely no questions." He touched her lips with his finger. She yielded, her heart racing at his nearness. This time he could not see her blush in the dark. She was his wife.

Chapter 38

The sun shone through the window and warmed Jerusha's face.
She lay in the crook of Antonius's arm and admired his muscular
chest, then crept out from under the cover and tiptoed across the cold
tiles. After slipping her arm into her new cloak, she opened the door
and went outside. Her heart overflowed with joy. The cloak's jewels
sparkled in the sun's rays. She touched them, grateful for a loving
husband, and hurried down the steps into Father's garden. She twirled
and sang.

"This is the day the Lord has made. I will rejoice and be glad in
it." Dew glistened on the pomegranate's red blossoms in the early
morning chill. A song thrush darted to a nearby olive branch and
twittered its praise.

She hummed and skipped barefoot, then burst into song. "I am
the Lion of Judah. Deep within my innermost being dwells the holy
God of all Israel. I am the Lion of Judah." It felt so good to dance
and rejoice again with the beautiful butterflies fluttering along the

path. The Holy Ghost took over her feet. She leapt and bounced and twirled, her loose hair flying out and covering her face at times.

"Beautiful butterfly," Antonius called. Jerusha stopped, her hair flopped. She grabbed the loose strands away from her face and stared at her husband. His royal blue tunic with gold trim rippled in the wind, along with his golden hair. He held a wooden box.

"There you go again. Appearing out of nowhere." She teased and walked toward him, unashamed. "Why do you interrupt this little butterfly's dance?" She stopped and looked up at his blue eyes.

"I have a mattan gift," He opened the box. "I received instructions from Father YHWH." Jerusha looked inside.

"It is a scepter." Sparkles bounced on her face as the sun's rays hit the jasper stone set in the golden crown on a lion's head. A purple butterfly jewel glistened on the nose of a male lion. Etched in the crown were the words "Lion of Judah" in Hebrew. She picked it up and turned it over. On the other side was the same jewel but different words. "Lioness of Judah" was on a female lion's crown.

"You are one with him." Antonius grinned. "All aspects of who he is lives in you. A divine inheritance is yours, because you are one with Father YHWH. This represents his scepter of righteousness, his authority, that you carry through the blood of Yeshua and his holiness he clothes you in, especially when you are surrendered to his plan and will. He said to tell you, 'Mother of nations, rule.'"

Stunned, she crinkled her brow. "I am unworthy of such honor." She fell to her knees, her face in her hands. He lifted her to her feet and raised her chin. "Do not call unworthy what He calls worthy." His eyes lingered. "Your love, for him, endured, under great testing."

She saw behind him, Samuel with Rebekah, and Stephen with Hannah at the garden gate. Their belongings were packed in bags at their feet.

"They go to the nations." Antonius handed her the scepter. "They need your blessing."

She felt tears rising and choked them back. Joshua and Sarah walked up the path from the courtyard fountain, giggling, then stopped when they saw the couples, their expressions somber.

"Come, you two." Adah peeked around a bush. "And you, too, Adah." Antonius called. "Stand with the others at the gate." He walked with Jerusha up the path.

She stood before Samuel and Rebekah, their hands interlocked. Jerusha tipped her head sideways and looked at Samuel. "I remember the day we brought you home." Grandfather walked up beside her. She kept her eyes on her son. "Samuel, I love you. You brought great joy to one of the darkest times in my life." She looked at his wife. "And Rebekah, you brightened Samuel's life, an answer to his prayers for a wife." She grasped their interlocked hands. "I bless you and release you. Take the kingdom to the nations. May all that you put your hand to prosper. May you do the greater works Yeshua talked about as you fulfill everything he has written about you in your book of destiny. May he bless your coming in and your going out."

Infused with a new joy and strength, she moved to Stephen and Hannah. "Stephen, your eyes were so big and bright when you were a baby. Being a Gentile, you suffered rejection at times. You blessed me as I watched how you handled it with such a quiet gentleness and love." She looked at Hannah. "Finding you hiding in Father's garden that day gave me hope that I made the right decision coming back to Jerusalem. Another orphan saved." She grasped both of their hands. "I bless you and release you. Go to the nations. Spread the kingdom. May all that you put your hands to prosper. May you also do the greater works Yeshua talked about, as you fulfill everything he has written about you in your book of destiny. May he bless your coming in and bless your going out."

She looked at Joshua. "Smiley, my warrior son, what a blessing the day your nursemaid brought you to our house. Your enthusiasm and joy have always been contagious." She went to Sarah. "You remind me so much of the Sarah who is in the kingdom." She stopped in front of Adah. "And you, Adah, blessed me beyond words when you came to me with your revelation of Father YHWH's power, then renouncing witchcraft and embracing Yeshua." She placed her hand, one at a time, on each head and spoke the same blessing as the others, then stood back, Antonius on one side, Grandfather on the other.

"I am so blessed."

***

A short time later, Samuel and Rebekah, Stephen and Hannah, stood at the entrance gate ready to mount their horses. Brigid and Patrick sat on their mounts and waited. Grandfather, dressed in his Roman toga and cloak faced Jerusha, his reins in his hands ready to mount.

"I am no longer calling you little lioness. You are lioness of Judah. I foresee in the future days you will roar like you have never roared." He looked at Antonius, who stood behind her. "You are a mighty warrior in Father YHWH's army. You have trained Joshua well. I foresee the two of you fighting in the power of Father YHWH." He clasped his arm, then took Jerusha by the shoulders.

"I have a place prepared for you. When the time comes to leave, I will be back. A royal inheritance awaits. Stand strong in the power of His might. You will prevail."

She clung to Grandfather. "I love you."

"And I you." He pulled her away from him, then addressed Joshua.

"Mighty warrior, remember power comes with humility." He slapped his sword. "Fight with Father YHWH's word, and you will never lose." He mounted along with the others.

Jerusha watched and waved as they descended the terraced steps.

"Shalom, my brothers." Joshua choked back tears. Sarah comforted him with a hug.

"Until we meet again, Grandfather, until we meet again." Jerusha wiped the tears, turned, and walked inside Grandfather's villa—her villa now. Antonius hugged her shoulder.

"You may be lioness of Judah to Grandfather and Yeshua, but you will always be my little butterfly."

She looked up. A purple butterfly landed on her nose, then fluttered away. Her eyes locked with Antonius's.

"Your little butterfly loves you." She heard rolling thunder in the distance and looked into the darkening sky.

"Father YHWH is with us, even in the darkness."

Chapter 39
Spring, Nissan AD 63

Jerusha knelt at Father's bench, where she went every day in the early morning, like Yeshua had done, and talked to Father YHWH about her family. "Wherever my sons are, place a canopy of protection over their property, like you have this property, from the east to the west, north to the south boundaries, all the way to your throne and down to the core of the earth. Then place a boundary face down in the earth all the way to the outer boundaries. Set a sight and sound barrier that the enemy cannot hear or see what goes on where they dwell. For it is written, "'You give your people a peaceful habitation and a quiet resting place.'" She continued to encourage and strengthen herself with prayer from Tehillim 91.

"When I sit enthroned under the shadow of you, Father YHWH, I am hidden in the strength of YHWH Most High. You are the hope that holds me and the Stronghold to shelter me, the only God for me and my great confidence." Confidence. She smiled at that thought. At age forty-seven, she had grown in her faith so much since being an abused and fearful child serving Herod in his palace.

"You will rescue me from every hidden trap of the enemy, and you will protect me from false accusation and any deadly curse. Your massive arms are wrapped around me, protecting me. I can run under your covering of majesty and hide. Your arms of faithfulness are a shield keeping me from harm." She stopped and wiped a tear away. His faithfulness kept her these last years. And even though she had not heard from Samuel and Stephen, she trusted the same protection had kept them.

"I will never worry about an attack of demonic forces at night nor have to fear a spirit of darkness coming against me or my family. I will not fear a thing!"

She stood and twirled, hands lifted.

"Whether by night or by day, demonic danger will not trouble us, nor will the powers of evil launched against us. Even in a time of disaster, with thousands and thousands being killed, we will remain unscathed and unharmed. We will be a spectator as the wicked perish in judgment, for they will be paid back for what they have done!" She walked to the back wall and looked at the rising sun. Its rays broke through dark clouds, spreading an orange glow across the horizon and glistened against the city's walls.

"When I live my life within your shadow, Father YHWH Most High, my secret hiding place, my family, and I will always be shielded from harm." She watched the caravan of families coming for Pesach. Every year, for the last five years, for every feast, she looked for her sons to return.

"How then could evil prevail against us or disease infect us? You send angels with special orders to protect us wherever we go, defending from all harm." She saw a picture of angels surrounding her sons' lives as they walked the road of life and smiled.

"If my family walks into a trap, these angels will be there for them and keep them from stumbling. They even walk unharmed among the fiercest powers of darkness, trampling every one of them beneath their feet!" she decreed, letting her words ring over the city.

"For you have spoken, Father YHWH, to me and said, because I have delighted in you as my great lover, you will protect me and my family. You have set me in a high place, safe and secure, before your face. You will answer my cry for help every time I pray, and I find and feel your presence even in my time of pressure and trouble." She stopped. Oh how true. She remembered his tingling presence in the most, darkest hour, when she thought she would be crucified.

"You are my glorious hero and give me a feast." She tipped her head and thought about the wonderful feast he had given. A wedding feast. Joshua and Sarah's. Today, one day before Passover. What a joyous occasion. One she wanted to share with her other sons. She took a deep breath and exhaled. *Father YHWH, where are they?* She refused to fall into question after question—to let her thoughts run rampant, like she had done in the past.

"I will be satisfied with a full life and with all that you do for me. For I will enjoy the fullness of my salvation!"

She felt hands on her shoulders, turned, and saw Antonius dressed in his armor.

"You are back." She kissed his cheek.

"I am troubled." He stroked her hair from her forehead. "The zealots fighting against Rome has caused greater hostility toward followers of the Way and the Jews. More and more skirmishes break out every day. I just came from watching another one, where the zealots suffered a devastating loss." He rubbed his hands through his blond hair. "Nero is becoming ruthless. He had his wife, Octavia, put to death. The most disturbing news I heard is Tribune Burrus, the one who favors your grandfather, is now dead. Our protection may have died with him."

"Our protection comes from above." She grinned at her ability to trust Father YHWH. She glanced around his shoulder at Sarah, who walked into the garden. "No more talk of this. We have a wedding feast to plan. Where is Joshua?"

"Helping Moses at the carpenter shop. They sold many goods to the pilgrims coming for the Passover feast."

"Chaya and I will have the wedding feast ready by nightfall. Sarah will be ready when the shofar blasts." She kissed him again and hurried up the path to greet Sarah.

***

Sarah stood in Jerusha's room dressed in the wedding dress Antonius had made for Jerusha. Chaya made a few adjustments in length. Jerusha stood back and took a look. The lamplight glittered off the jewels and reflected sparkles on Sarah's face.

"Oh, Sarah, you are beautiful," she said and touched Sarah's hair with a dab of Rose of Sharon oil. A light rap at the door drew her attention away.

"Yes, Chaya, you may come in." Jerusha set the oil bottle on the table and turned as the door cracked open. Rebekah stood beneath the lintel, her belly round with child. Jerusha stood speechless and blinked back tears.

"I have never seen you speechless, Ima," Rebekah kissed her cheek. "May I call you Ima?"

Jerusha nodded. "Is Samuel with you?"

"If it is not alright for me to see the bride before Joshua, then you'd better send my mother out in the hall," Samuel hollered with his back turned in the doorway.

"Samuel!" Jerusha bumped his back and closed the door, then peeked back inside, "I will be back."

"Shalom, Ima," Samuel picked her up and swung her around. It is good to be back. I guess Father YHWH timed our visit perfectly. We had no idea Joshua was getting married."

Jerusha giggled like a girl. "I see he has blessed Rebekah's womb. What a wonderful blessing to have you here for the wedding. You will find Joshua with Antonius and Moses at Paul's sister's. If you hurry, you will be able to come up with them when the shofar blasts. I must get inside with Sarah." Jerusha giggled again. "I am so happy. A double blessing." She opened the door, stepped inside, then looked out again and grinned as she watched him descend the stairs.

She placed the veil over Sarah's head and wrapped it over her face, leaving just her eyes. Their sparkle beamed a deep love for her son.

"Look, Jerusha." Sarah pointed to a purple butterfly that came in the open window. Jerusha's heart warmed. From the royal-covered mittah, Sarah picked up the pendant Jerusha gave her when she left Herod's palace, the same one Father had given Jerusha. "May I wear this?" she asked.

"I have not seen this in a long time." Jerusha took it in her hand. Staring at the golden crown on the lion and the purple butterfly jewel, she quoted. "'Arise Lord, let your enemies be scattered.'"

"'Let all who hate you flee before you.'" Sarah quoted with her.

Jerusha slipped the pendant over Sarah's head. Yeshua's enemies had fled and would continue to flee. Of that Jerusha was confident. His word never returned void.

The shofar blasted.

Sarah's eyes widened. "How do I look?"

"Like a royal bride ready for her royal groom," Jerusha said and opened the door and watched Sarah walk down the stairs toward the courtyard and wait for the wedding procession. She peeked inside Father and Mother's room, now her room, made ready for her wedding night by Antonius. Joshua prepared Sarah's room in another part of the villa. How blessed she had been. "Father YHWH, you are a good father. May I never forget it," she whispered.

Rebekah waited at the top of the stairs. Jerusha took her arm and descended into the courtyard. The fountain bubbled. Song thrushes swooped before Sarah to the next olive tree. In the distance the wedding party sang; flutes and tambourines played. Their sound of laughter broke the silent darkness as they wound through the streets of Mount Zion. Jerusha thought of Stephen. *Father YHWH, where is he?* The thought that he was not alive passed through her mind. She shook her head and remembered her prayer declaration that morning. *Do not go there, Jerusha. Wherever he is, Father YHWH is protecting him.* She missed her gentle giant. She missed Grandfather, too. It had been five years.

Chaya opened the gate, and the wedding party came through with Joshua leading in dance. He wore Antonius's royal blue tunic and cloak with gold trim. He now stood nearly as tall and almost as thick in his shoulders and waist. Jerusha looked at the bench by the fountain. Joshua's sword and scabbard lay on it. It might be the only day since he received it from Antonius that he had not worn it. She chuckled. *So that is what it took to get him to lay it down.*

He took Sarah's hand and led her into Father's garden under the olive canopy. Jerusha followed at a distance. She heard a noise at the front gate. It could not be the feared Caiaphas. He was dead. She took a few steps back and glanced at the gate. Chaya swung it open. Jerusha picked up her cloak so she could run fast and scampered like a little girl.

"Stephen! Hannah!" She threw her arms around her son, her tears flowed unhindered. "Come, hurry. You are just in time. Joshua is getting married in the garden." She looked at Hannah's little round protrusion. I see Father YHWH has blessed your womb, too. Come." She waved. Hurry! I am so happy you are home."

Chaya grinned at Jerusha as they walked behind the couple. They turned the corner just in time to hear Antonius pronounce the wedding blessing.

"May you increase to thousands upon thousands. May your offspring possess the gates of their enemies."

***

Jerusha sat on a bench in the courtyard and watched. Joshua stared, lovestruck, into Sarah's eyes beneath a decorated canopy. Soon they would leave the party and go to the room he prepared. Samuel and Stephen talked and laughed between bites of lamb and bread. Adah watched Paul's nephew and giggled. The music started, and everyone formed a circle dance, Brigid and Antonius the first ones to join in. Overwhelmed with joy and gratitude, she slipped away to Father's garden to be with Father YHWH.

She swayed to the music and thought how much Father YHWH loved his children and prayed, "Your kingdom come. Your will be done on earth as it is in heaven." She twirled, hands lifted, along the path to the back wall and looked out over the city. Campfires scattered the mountainside of lost pilgrims, who thought this city and its temple were where they found holiness and love. How Yeshua loved them. Gave His life for them. If only they believed. His kingdom, a thin veil away.

She sighed. Sarah. Timon. Mother. Father. All the apostles except John are in his kingdom of heaven. Even James, Yeshua's brother, was dead by stoning after a fall from the temple pinnacle. She breathed deep of the night air. What a battle she fought to find the Way. Fear of man was her biggest stumbling block.

"Jerusha?" A familiar voice spoke behind her.

"Grandfather?" She ran along the path, turned the corner and saw him. "You are back."

"I have been looking for you. We must talk. Come, sit on your Father's bench."

She ran, threw her arms around his neck, and kissed his cheek, feeling like that little girl again who cherished every visit with him. He picked up a pomegranate, cut it open, and sat on the bench. She sat beside him, took one half, slurped the juice, and rejoiced inside that her family was back.

"What is it, Grandfather?" She peered up at his weathered face, his silver beard grown back. He wore his old Hebrew cloak with the tzitzits. He sat silent for a while. She remembered her times with him. His wisdom. His love. His protection.

"It is time, my little lioness, Yeshua's lioness of Judah." He looked deep in her eyes. "It is time to leave Jerusalem."

Epilogue

"Father YHWH, you are the One and Only Most High God, my Stronghold. Father of the fatherless. I lie awake each night thinking of you and reflecting on how you help me like a father." Her words pierced second heaven. Shafts of light burst through the darkness.

Evil minions cowered. "We failed to stop her." The watchers, alerted to the sounds, crept from their dens and sneered, their claw-like fingers covering their ears.

"Yeshua, you are the King of Kings and Lord of Lords, the Lion of Judah." She sang the new song and twirled in dance.

"Our master will not understand." The hooded creatures cringed and drew back into black caverns and shielded their eyes as the brightness grew in magnitude.

"Holy Ghost, you lead me into all truth." Vibrating sparkles burst out of heavenly Jerusalem through the second heaven's blackness into the earth's atmosphere in the garden.

"I will never worry about an attack of demonic forces at night or have to fear a spirit of darkness coming against me or my family. I will not fear a thing!" Heaven's trumpet sounded and reverberated through the dark kingdom, its vibrations shattering the castle's dragon reliefs on its walls.

"She fears nothing. After all the attacks, she rejoices. How can this be? Her dancing disgusts me." The guttural sounds of the black-hooded watchers startled the weak minions. Dark tunneled passageways of their great one, the serpent of old, shook and thundered.

"He heard." The evil hordes trembled and ran to their hiding places.

"You idiots!" The bejeweled serpent morphed and rose up on his back reptilian legs and stared with yellow globes. "She acts like a royal daughter. Not an orphan! He stretched his scaly neck into their hiding place and extended his forked tongue.

"Cowards!

"Father YHWH, your kingdom come. Your will be done. On earth as it is in heaven!

Set up a canopy of protection, Father YHWH, from the north to the south, from the east to the west boundaries. All the way to the throne and down to the core of the earth, and set one face down in the ground out to the boundary edges."

"She roars like a lioness. AHHHaaahhhh!" Their screams erupted.

Heavenly beams pulsed from the gates of the heavenly city. Flashes of light whizzed past the trembling evil creatures.

"The warring angels!"

"Stop them!" the serpent screamed. In a split second they swooshed to the battle and engaged. Shining swords clashed as the heavenly warriors locked shields around the lioness of Judah's property in Jerusalem and stretched high unto the heavenly throne, down to the core of the earth.

"Attack! Come up from below into her domain."

Click. Click. Click. A transparent shield covered the ground out to the boundaries.

"It's too late." The evil hordes bumped against the shield and retreated. "We are locked out. Cannot see or hear what is happening inside." Light flashed out of the brilliant canopy.

"Watch out!" The flashes hit the darkened creatures. The black hooded hordes screamed and fled.

"NO!" the serpent-like leader yelled. Cowards! Stop! The earth belongs to me!" Fiery flames exploded off his forked tongue and licked at their backsides as they retreated into their dark hiding places.

"Your kingdom come. Your will be done. On earth as it is in heaven." She twirled and danced in his protected garden.

Act III—The Son Speaks

I will reveal the eternal purpose of God. He has decreed over me, "You are my favored Son. And as your Father, I have crowned you as my King Eternal. Today I become your Father. Ask me to give you the nations, and I will do it. Your domain will stretch to the ends of the earth. And you will shepherd them with unlimited authority, crushing their rebellion as an iron rod smashes jars of clay!"

To my sons and daughters, who feel rejected, abandoned, or orphaned.

I am with you, even in the darkness. I will never leave you or forsake you. I have given you gifts and an inheritance that lasts for an eternity. You only have to ask, and you will receive. Nothing you have done or will ever do will separate you from my love. There is always a place for you on my lap. I am never too busy to listen and comfort. I have clothed you with my Son's cloak of righteousness. Do not be afraid to ask to come into my presence. I long for you to know me better. Again, I say, ask, and I will come in marvelous and unimaginable ways.

Your Loving Father,

Who created you to be you, before you became you, and has plans written especially for you, in your book of destiny.

To My Royal Father,

L ord, you know everything there is to know about me. You perceive every movement of my heart and soul, and you understand my every thought before it even enters my mind. You are so intimately aware of me, Lord. You read my heart like an open book, and you know all the words I am about to speak before I even start a sentence! You know every step I take before my journey even begins. You've gone into my future to prepare the way, and in kindness you follow behind me to spare me from the harm of my past. With your hand of love upon my life, you impart a blessing to me. This is just too wonderful, too deep, and incomprehensible! Your understanding of me brings me wonder and strength.... Wherever I go, your hand will guide me; Your strength will empower me. It is impossible to disappear from you or to ask the darkness to hide me, for your presence is everywhere, bringing light into my night. There is no such thing as darkness with you. The night, to you, is as bright as the day; there's no difference between the two. You formed my inner most being, shaping my delicate inside and my intricate outside, and wove them altogether in my mother's womb.

I thank God for making me so mysteriously complex! Everything you do is marvelously breathtaking. It simply amazes me to think about it! How thoroughly you know me, Lord! You even formed every bone in my body when you created me in the secret place, carefully, skillfully shaping me from nothing to something. You saw who You created me to be before I became me! Before I'd ever seen the light of day, the number of days You planned for me were already recorded in Your book. Every single moment you are thinking of me! How precious and wonderful to consider that you cherish me constantly in your every thought! O God, your desires toward me are more than the grains of the sand on every shore! (Ps. 139:1–18 TPT)

Your Royal Son and Daughter

Letter to Reader

Beloved Reader,

At seven years old I walked across the hardwood floor of my living room to my father, who sat in the lone wooden chair in the empty room. He picked me up and sat me on his lap. I hugged his neck and told him goodbye, then sat back and looked into his watery eyes and wondered what made him so sad. I was too young to understand divorce.

That incident along with sexual abuse by a neighbor one year earlier formed my opinion of myself for years to come. The enemy used these incidents among others to feed me lies that I willingly believed. I talked and lived like an orphan, until a man came into my life who helped me see through the eyes of my heavenly Father.

This man began to speak over my life the things my Heavenly Father saw in me. He introduced me to the One who created me, loved me, and had good plans for my life. Even though I had accepted

Jesus' love and forgiveness years earlier, I had no understanding of the Father's love and how He viewed me.

I am still on the journey of knowing and being one with the Father and seeing through His eyes. Every day is an adventure with Him.

I wrote this book with the purpose of revealing the Father to you. Each time I sat down to write, I asked Him what he wanted to say to you. My prayer is that you grow in your intimacy with the Father and walk in that greatness He had ordained for your life before you were born. It's a journey. Don't give up. Keep in touch. My email is lfergerson1950@hotmail.com. My phone is 620 255–6161. My website is www.lindafergerson.com.

I am hosting a Women of Destiny tour to Israel to give my readers a taste of Israel and an opportunity to be touched by a divine encounter with our Father. I am including in this book an ancient recipe from the chef of the restaurant we will be dining at in Jerusalem. Enjoy!

In the Father's love,

—Linda Fergerson

A Taste of Israel

First-Century Recipe

Porridge of the freekeh in the Bible referred to as "Geres Carmel," which is a smoked green wheat. In the Bible days it was harvested when it was still green. It was thrown to the fire; the straw and chaff would burn and the kernel remained. To extract the grain, they had a rubbing or threshing process, which gave the freekeh its name—in Arabic it means rubbing the hands together.

Carmel—Freekeh risotto

Serves 6

2 tbsp olive oil
2 onions, finely chopped
2 cups almond milk (
1 tsp salt
½ tsp pepper
1 tsp fresh thyme
½ cup diced mushrooms (¼ * ¼ inch)
2 cups smoked green wheat
2 cups vegetable stock

Pour the stock into a pot and bring it to a simmer over medium-high heat. Keep the heat at a simmer.

Heat a heavy-bottomed pot over medium heat. Add 2 tablespoons of olive oil and tip to coat bottom of pan. Add the onions and cook, stirring frequently with a wooden spoon, until onions have softened but not browned.

Add the fresh mushrooms and thyme, season with pepper, and stir fry until they give off their liquid and are tender. Add the cooked green wheat and cook, stirring constantly to coat it with the olive oil for about 5 minutes.

Ladle in about 1 cup of the stock and stir constantly, until the green wheat absorbs the stock. Continue to add the stock in half-cup increments, stirring constantly, and only adding more once the stock has been completely absorbed by the green wheat.

After about 7 minutes, ladle in about 1 cup of almond milk and add salt, stirring constantly. Add the remain of the almond milk and cook until the green wheat absorbs the liquid.

The Eucalyptus in Jerusalem
Chef Moshe

About the Author

Linda Fergerson, a gifted storyteller and dancer, has a passion to see the Father's sons and daughters enter into their royal destiny. Dancing in intimacy with Yeshua helped break many of the chains of worthlesness, anger, and rejection that accompanied the sexual abuse she experienced as a child from a neighbor boy.

For several years she held "A Night with the King" meetings for women in her basement. After the women partook of a meal at the King's table, they stepped into His royal presence and listened to His sweet voice as He whispered love songs in their ears.

Later, she ministered in Israel with Warring Dove International. She walked the shores of the Sea of Galilee, danced in Jerusalem, and had a divine encounter with Yeshua in Shiloh.

As vice president of Women's Aglow in her hometown in Dodge City, Kansas, she gained a desire to see Holy Spirit–led worship and prayer overtake the city.

She founded His Writers, a writers' group that prayed and interceded for editors, writers, and publishers to hear the Father's voice and bring forth the "child of promise" given to them that only they could birth.

Her greatest ministry is to her husband, Steve, and her three adopted sons, Samuel, Stephen, and Joshua.

She's available to speak. Some of the topics she speaks on are the following: Dancing with Yeshua, Intimacy with the King, and I Will Not Leave you Orphans.

Linda welcomes your comments or contacts for prayer or ministry at 620 255–6161, lfergerson1950@hotmail.com, or her website, lindafergerson.com.